SARAH

AN AUTISTIC AMONG

THE LYING NTs

SALLY RAMSEY

Sarah – An Autistic Among the Lying NTs

Copyright 2019 – Sally Ramsey

All rights reserved.

Printed in the United States of America

ISBN – 978-1-949802-04-7

Published by Black Pawn Press

FIRST EDITION

"To all the masked autistics trying to cope in this world. You know who you are."

Chapter One

My first memory is of playing on a porch. It wasn't like the porch of the house I moved to when I was four. That one was almost an extra room. It wasn't like the porch at my grandmother's house either, which was open and full of Grandma's plants. I know that small porch was from an earlier time. I just can't remember much else about it.

Mother remembered things about that time, but not about the porch, just about how strange I was. She was constantly telling me tales of a daughter who spent her nights not sleeping, but standing in her crib, staring silently into the darkness. Even when I got older, I still had my quiet periods, sometimes not talking for days. It wasn't that I couldn't talk. I just didn't feel like it. Mother worried about my silence. I liked making lots of noise too, composing little songs on the family upright piano, and singing duets with my older sister, Rachel. We Goldfarbs formed some sort of family band. Judith, my mother, had an almost operatic mezzo soprano voice. My father, Gabe, was a deep, stove pipe bass. Rachel was a soprano, higher than Mother, but not as high as I was. I was proud about hitting notes no one else in the family could hit, but I knew better than to say that to Rachel. Pointing out anything I thought of as being better than her, always caused her to figure out some kind of revenge. Bragging wasn't worth it. Our whole family played instruments too. Rachel and I both took piano. I liked making up my own music better. I schlepped to lessons and practiced the exercises the teachers gave me when someone leaned on me to do it. Compared to other kids' mothers, my mother didn't do that much. Mother played piano too, and Father played the violin. He'd told me that he'd made his money growing up playing for square dances. Mother looked down her nose at that kind of country music, so he didn't play it with her.

Even when I wasn't playing or singing it, there was usually music around me somewhere. I didn't sleep when I was supposed to take a nap, but Mother played old "78" fairy tale records for me when she made me lie still for a while. The stories from those records just flew into my head. I'd repeat them from memory and sing the songs that went with them for anyone who'd listen. Something like that happened when I stayed with my grandparents, too. Their records were all of Broadway musicals. I memorized the songs, and I could hear the background music in my head when I sang them myself.

When I was four, Mother started a choir with girls from Girl Scout troops. Most of the babysitters Mother got for me were Senior Scouts in the choir. Though I was younger than the other girls, it was easier to put me in the choir than to find someone to watch me. It worked. I sang with the choir, and when we went into the children's hospital wards or the veterans' hospital, I had solos. Rachel didn't, and she got mad about it.

Rachel and I both took ballet and liked putting on little shows. For some reason, I could go up on point even in soft ballet shoes, or even in just a pair of sneakers. I also liked gymnastics and loved standing on my head. There were times when I would stay upside down all day. I even wanted to eat that way.

I learned to read before I went to school, at least easy books like *The Cat in the Hat*. I could write holding a pencil with both hands and both feet, something Rachel made fun of and Mother told me not to do, at least not the feet part. She wanted me to stick to using my hand. I loved books and wanted a library card. The library was just at the end of the block. They'd give you a card at any age, but you had to be able to write or at least print your name. When I was four, I was proud to be able to do that. After that, I could have all the books to read that I wanted.

Mother's friends kept talking about the days I didn't talk and that I used weird words when I did. I also liked to bounce and flap my arms when I was excited thinking about something. Rachel and Mother hated that and kept trying to make me stop doing it. Rachel would go running to Mother yelling, "Sarah's flying again!"

I didn't use toys the way everyone thought I should, either. I built strange things and made up stories to go with them. I made a huge snake out of my Tinker Toys that went all the way through the house. Rachel and Mother couldn't understand why, but I saw my snake as doing things like greeting the man who came to fix the TV. He didn't get it either. While the repairman couldn't have cared less, other strangers to our family thought what I did was strange, and told Mother. Finally, they talked Mother into thinking there was something wrong with me. She took me to someone I later found out was a child psychologist. He gave me a bunch of tests which my father hated having to pay for. Then he just told Mother that I was smart. She put me in kindergarten early. I didn't fit in there.

People thought Rachel wasn't smart enough. Her reading was slow, and her math was bad. Her teacher told Mother that Rachel was a dull normal and wouldn't do much with her life. It was years before Mother said anything about that to my sister. She always treated her like the dumb one, even if she acted more normal than I did. For Mother, if I was smart enough, I was allowed to be a little bit strange.

Rachel could feel what was going on and it made her mean to me. Whenever I flapped my arms, Rachel would run to Mother and tattle. When Rachel's friends came to our house, she would lead them in teasing me by saying I had cooties. After a while, when they showed up, I'd hide in the attic or the pantry.

I spent a lot of time in the pantry. Mother kept old clothes in in a pile there that were too ripped to give away. It was called the rag bag, even though there was no bag. It was a safe place for me. I loved having my little nest in the soft fabric, and I could let stories run through my head there, without anyone bothering me.

School was a much better place than home. I missed much of it because I was sick a lot, but I loved kindergarten when I was there. I didn't care much about the other kids, but Mrs. Grossmith let me read books from the school library. I liked the stories and felt safe in her class. That all changed when I entered first grade.

There were two first grade classes, Miss Parker and Miss Emerson's. Miss Emerson's class was a combined first and second, with some of the smarter kids from first, but since I missed so much school when I was sick, the principal put me in Miss Parker's class. Mother had enough of being told Rachel was dumb. She wanted me with the smart kids. She complained, making the principal, Dr. Edith Vaughn, and Miss Parker both mad at her. Miss Parker took it out on me every chance she got, making me stand in the corner for nothing and keeping me after school. I hated her.

The only good thing about Miss Parker's class was my best friend, Arlene Rosenbaum. Arlene lived only a block from me, right across the street from the library. Her family was on the first floor of a three-family house that they owned. They didn't rent like we did. Every day, Arlene and I would walk the eight blocks to school together. The Rosenbaums had a dog, Debbie, who was small. She barked at everyone who came to the house. She could be scary so instead of knocking or ringing the bell, I would stand at the foot of the stairs leading to the back door and call Arlene's name. After all the times Mother told me to "breathe from the diaphragm" in the choir, everyone could hear me, even with Debbie barking. Arlene would come out and we'd walk to school together.

Mother didn't like Arlene. She said that whenever I was with Arlene, we got into trouble. Sometimes that was true. We were braver together than we were apart. We joined the boys in a football game on the library lawn. We walked a long way from our neighborhood. We even talked to the bikers who were on the street sometimes and asked for rides on the back of their motorcycles. Mother didn't know any of that. She didn't keep track of me. What Mother did see was Arlene and me climbing the little house that covered up the garbage cans in our back yard. Whether it was because she was afraid that I'd fall, or just because I was so close to what she called filth, I don't know, but she got very mad. I was grounded, and Arlene wasn't allowed to play with me anymore.

Mother did mention another reason. She said that Arlene was dirty. That wasn't true. Arlene's skin was a little darker than mine. Just about everyone's was. She was always cleaner than I was. Her nails didn't have dirt under them like mine did. She brushed her teeth more and washed her hair a lot more. Mother had never quite gotten the hang of washing her own long hair and had to go to see Mr. Richard to get it done. She never taught Rachel and me to wash ours. Rachel picked up tips from her friends, but I wasn't any good at it.

Arlene and I stayed friends anyway. It got harder though. Miss Parker's class was crowded, and we all took some kind of test that another lady gave us. I guess the test said I was smart because I was moved with a few other kids to Miss Emerson's class.

It was a much nicer place to be. Miss Emerson was just as strict, maybe stricter than Miss Parker, but more quietly. She gave me a little book that I took home to show to Mother. Mother thought I should be reading something with bigger words, but the book was still harder than the one I was reading in Miss Parker's class. Without Mother seeing us, Arlene and I still walked to school and back together, and I played at Arlene's house whenever I could get away with it. Debbie and I even made friends, and she liked to rub her tummy against my leg.

Soon it got even easier to see Arlene. My mother and father didn't grow up the same way. My father grew up on a farm owned by his family, the Goldfarbs, and he liked working with his hands. He had a business putting glass in things. As a member of some club he called a union, he got a lot of papers with job lists on them. He spent a lot of time getting and doing as many of those jobs as he could. When he was finished with the paper, Rachel and I were allowed to draw on the back side of it. My father owned a truck for work. It was yucky because there was a lot of the putty that he used to seal windows on the inside. Putty was even on the seats. Mother hated it.

Mother's family loved books. Her father, Pacey Levi, was a chemical engineer and her mother was a social worker. Her younger brother Nahum was a chemistry professor. Mother bragged a lot that she had a master's in chemistry but had left the lab to edit textbooks. Her family was somewhat snobby. They had offered to send my father to college, but I heard that he told them that the world was his school. From what else I heard, the rabbi who had married my parents didn't think they should get married. They did anyway. While my father was gone every day, Mother did her editing work, what she called freelance, in a little area off the living room behind a bamboo curtain. While she was supposed to be very good at it, she wasn't that hard a worker and didn't finish things on time. That made people not want her to work for them anymore. She had to look for something else to do to earn money. She got a job as a teacher, but she didn't have certificates, like my teachers at school, so they didn't pay her as much.

When Mother started teaching, Rachel and I were on our own even more than we had been before. I was six, but I could let myself into the house with a key I kept around my neck. Arlene's parents, the Rosenbaums, found out that I was at home alone, and wanted me to stay at their house as much as I could. The parents of one of Rachel's friends also wanted her to be at their house, instead at home by herself.

Mother spent less time at home, but still wasn't making much money, and she and my father fought. My father got up early, making his breakfast and getting into his truck before Mother was awake. I got up early too and found Mother asleep on the couch instead of in the bed she shared with my father. Mother explained that she felt better sleeping on the couch when she had a headache, which seemed to happen a lot. That made no sense to me. I liked my own bed all the times I was sick.

Without Mother or Father around, I was sent to my grandparents a lot. My mother's and father's parents were different. The Goldfarb grandparents were like the opposite of the nursery rhyme about Jack Spratt. Grandma Goldfarb was short and thin. She worried all the time and never stopped moving. She shoveled coal into the coal furnace in the basement, washed walls, and was always trying to make me eat, but her cooking tasted terrible. She was always telling me, "eat *mein kind*, eat." The more she said it, the less I wanted to eat anything. I was okay with tomato soup from a can, and I liked the little crackers that went with it, but I wanted to throw up anything else she made.

Grandpa Goldfarb loved Grandma Goldfarb's cooking. He was about the same distance around as he was tall. That confused me. When I asked Grandma Goldfarb why she just didn't feed him less, she told me that if she didn't give him the food, he'd just get it himself. I wasn't sure that was true. Grandpa Goldfarb spent almost all of his time in a chair. I'd bounce on his belly sometimes, which made him smile. It made gurgling noises that sounded to me as if his tummy was full of orange juice. He never said it wasn't, but I never saw him drink any.

There were two things I liked when I visited Grandma and Grandpa Goldfarb. One was that they had a piano, even though neither of them played. I could make up songs and play them, and they didn't mind. The other fun thing was the typewriter, which belonged to Uncle Manny, my father's brother.

Uncle Manny wasn't like my father. He went to college. He'd studied about how to write plays. That's how Mother and Father met. Mother was tutoring Uncle Manny and he introduced them. Uncle Manny still lived with his parents, and so did his Aunt Golda. He was always trying to sell his plays, but to make a living Uncle Manny worked as a glazer like my father. When he was home, he was always writing. He liked putting me on his lap so my fingers could reach the typewriter keys. Manny never tried to push food or anything else on me, and he was my favorite person in the Goldfarb house.

Mother's mother, Grandma Levi, was almost as small as Grandma Goldfarb, but she didn't move as fast, and didn't lift anything heavy. There was no coal furnace at her house, but Grandma Levi would never have been able to shovel coal if there was. Mother told me there was something wrong with Grandma Levi's heart. I knew that Grandma always had a bottle of tiny pills in her pocket to take when she had trouble breathing. Her heart was why Grandma Levi didn't work as a social worker anymore. I usually didn't worry about that too much. I took a lot of medicine when I was sick, and it usually made me better.

Even when she needed her pills, Grandma Levi got a lot more done than Grandma Goldfarb did. She had a garden. I loved playing there, especially around the bottom of a lilac tree. I liked digging in the dirt, even if it gave me dirty fingernails. I liked finding earthworms too. Grandma said they were good for the soil. She also said I had a green thumb. I thought that was strange because it was the same color as my other fingers. Grandma told me she meant I was good at growing things, and I was. All the seeds I planted grew, and I had a little garden of my own under the lilac.

Grandma Levi let me work in her garden too. She taught me how to pull weeds and how to tell which plants to leave alone. She also told me which plants could make me sick. I loved making fans from big rhubarb leaves, but Grandma always made me wash my hands after I played with them.

I think Grandma was an ecologist before the word was even invented. She would never kill a spider. She just shooed them outside, so they could eat the bugs that hurt the garden. She saved the pits from the prunes she and Grandpa ate every morning for breakfast and fed them to the squirrels. She also fed fat cut off the edges of meat to the birds to keep them warm in the winter. Grandma Levi was a good cook. She cooked the vegetables we grew in the garden. She wanted to teach me to cook, too. Mother didn't like making meals much, except sometimes really fancy ones. That didn't make my father very happy. Rachel didn't like cooking either, but I did. I beat batter when Grandma's arms were tired. I could tell by smell when something was done, and even Grandma couldn't do that. She said I had a special nose like Grandpa. I was also very good at holding or tasting hot things without getting burned. I got that from Grandpa too.

Grandma and Grandpa Levi kept a schedule, like my school did. That made me feel good because I always knew what was going to happen. Grandpa Levi came home from his job at the chemical company at six o'clock every weeknight, so Grandma always had dinner ready just when he got there. She was strict about when I had to go to bed and when I was allowed to wake her up in the morning. Grandpa Levi always got up early to squeeze orange juice from a machine with a crank. Grandma told me Cousin Jacob had put it on the wall. I never met him. She always slept until eight, at least when I was around, and I wasn't allowed to go in her room until then. I had a box where all my books and toys were kept and I was supposed to play with them until Grandma woke up. I liked knowing what the rules were, something that didn't happen a lot at home. Mother would yell at me for things she hadn't even told me were wrong until I did them --- like climbing on the garbage house. That was never a problem when I was with Grandpa and Grandma Levi. I always knew where I stood.

The fighting between Mother and Father got bad when my father told Mother that he and Grandpa Goldfarb had bought a house. If the house had been in the city, Mother might not have cared as much, except for my father not asking her first. However, the house was in the country, like where my father grew up. Mother loved what she called culture. She liked ballet, concerts, and museums, and took Rachel and me along with her whether we wanted to go or not. She also liked nice restaurants. She was afraid that there wouldn't be any of those near the new house. Mother kept getting a driver's license by mail, but she didn't drive. She couldn't ride a bike, either. With no buses in the country, she'd only be able to go where she could walk, or where my father took her.

Rachel was upset about the new house because she was allergic to pollen. That's why Grandma Levi didn't teach her how to work in the garden the way she taught me. Rachel thought a house in the country, where there were all kinds of plants, sounded scary. My father didn't seem to care what Mother or Rachel said. He made us all get in the station wagon and he drove to the house. I was kind of excited to be where so many things were growing.

There were farms all around the house. I thought everything looked pretty. The fields were full of wild flowers, including tall golden ones, which stuffed up Rachel's nose. There was a stream too and I caught a toad to take home. Rachel didn't want to go near him. The best thing about being at the house was that one of the neighbors had a big collie. Rachel was a little scared around dogs, and Mother didn't like to be around them either. After getting to know Arlene's dog Debbie, I wasn't afraid. The collie and I made friends right away.

Sleeping in the house was hard, even for me. The next-door neighbors kept chickens, and they stank. The smell was the final straw for Mother and Rachel. They both said they'd never come back.

When we got back to the city, my father and mother hardly talked to each other. When my father was home, Mother always slept on the couch. He wasn't home much. He spent a lot of overnights with Grandma and Grandpa Goldfarb, and some at his new house. I heard Mother whispering on the phone about suspecting my father was having an affair with some woman Mother called a Kallikak. Kallikak was the name of a country family in the Sunday funnies. I had no idea what an affair was, but I knew Mother was mad at my father. One day, Mother sat Rachel and me down on the floor near the piano and told us that she might leave our father someday. She asked if we were with her. After the experience in the country, Rachel sided with Mother. I wasn't sure what Mother meant, but with the way they were both looking at me, I agreed too.

Chapter Two

It was years before Mother went anywhere. She said she had a plan she wanted to put into effect first, and she did. The first step of that plan was going back to school to get her teaching certification. That meant she'd be paid more. It also meant even more time away from Rachel and me. I spent some of it with Grandma Levi, and I didn't mind. Rachel, who was four years older than me, was left on her own.

I started second grade in public school, which meant first grade, *Aleph,* at Hebrew School at the temple. I'd already gone to some classes there, learning a little Hebrew. I liked the idea of learning more. Rachel went too, but she didn't like going. For her, regular school was hard enough. She talked me into not liking Hebrew School much either. Nevertheless, Mother, as part of her culture thing, made us go. Along with Hebrew school, we also had music lessons and scouts. I didn't have much time to play on my own or invent my toys and games. I didn't like that.

What was worse was Arlene was not in the same second-grade class I was. With all the stuff I had to do after school, I hardly ever saw her. I tried to make another friend. Lauren Kane was in Mrs. Kessel's second-grade class with me. We were also in the same class at Hebrew school, and we had the same piano teacher. Lauren and her little sister Kara had very long hair, which I thought was interesting. Mine was cut short to keep it from tangling, but it got dirty and tangled anyway. Lauren and Kara had a brother, and their parents were both psychiatrists.

Lauren enjoyed getting the better of people, especially grown-ups, and dragged me along with her. One of the people she got the better of was Mrs. Gershon, our Hebrew school teacher. Lauren worked out a plan where we would say the Hebrew words to be excused, and meet up in the ladies' room. Then we'd keep our feet up on the toilet seats so they couldn't be seen, and stayed out of class as long as we liked. The plan worked fine at Hebrew school, so we tried it on Mrs. Kessel.

Mrs. Kessel was too smart. She caught us, and made us stay after school. Mrs. Kessel told us that before that day she would have said we were the nicest girls in the class, but now she was ashamed of us. Lauren didn't care, but I was afraid Mother would find out.

Whenever she thought I'd done something bad, Mother would punish me by hitting my bottom with her hand, or with a paddle or wooden spoon if one was handy. It was even worse when she yelled. That was the scariest thing of all.

I kept my secret about Mrs. Kessel until the night I had a sleepover birthday party. I invited Lauren, but she acted more like Rachel's friend than mine. Lauren told Rachel about what happened with Mrs. Kessel. From then on, whenever Rachel wanted me to do something for her, she just threatened to tell Mother.

For six months, Rachel forced me to take her turn setting the table and washing dishes. I also had to make both our beds and clean up Rachel's side of our room. Mother knew something was going on and that I was being blackmailed. Other than telling me she might find my terrible secret silly if I just told her, she let Rachel go on with what she was doing.

I still wanted to think of Lauren as my friend. I was just very mad at Rachel. Lauren and I still played together at her house. I watched Lauren's mother sit beside her when she practiced the piano, something Mother never did for me. Because of that, even though our teacher said I had more talent, Lauren got better pieces to play. When we had a recital, she got to play when the bigger kids did. I was first, which was the worst spot.

I was the one who always thought up the pretend games that Lauren and I played. I wanted to make us invisible, and I mixed some soap and shampoo to make a magic potion. I knew we couldn't be invisible with clothes on, so we took them off. I pretended I couldn't see Lauren at all. Mrs. Kane caught us. She was mad and made me put on my clothes and go home.

Most of the time, Rachel and I took buses when we went to the temple for Hebrew School on Monday and Wednesday afternoons. Sometimes, when he was around, and if the weather was bad, my father would pick us up and take us home. One afternoon, Lauren and her older brother Roger needed a ride home and asked if my father would take them. Roger and Rachel were sitting next to each other in the third seat of the station wagon. Roger kissed Rachel, who pushed him away. My father was too busy driving to see what happened, but Lauren and I did. Lauren made me swear that I would never tell what happened. I didn't want to, but I swore. Even though Rachel was still blackmailing me, I thought what Roger did was wrong.

It bothered me for a few days until I finally spilled the secret to Mother, who was mad. She yelled that Roger was spoiled and was taking advantage of Rachel. Mother called the Kanes and yelled at them too.

After that, Lauren wouldn't talk to me anymore. She wouldn't even look at me. By that time, we were in third grade, but I was still in a different class than Arlene. That left me with no friends in my class at regular school or in Hebrew school. I saw Arlene when I could, but with as much stuff as Mother piled on me, that wasn't often. Rachel was also still blackmailing me.

Rachel and I never had much money. We had ticket books for bus fare and went home for lunch, so we didn't need lunch money. If we needed anything for school or scouts, we got that, and no more from Mother. Grandma and Grandpa Goldfarb gave Rachel a quarter and me a dime every week. I saved up my dimes. Sometimes Uncle Manny would give Rachel and me some money. If he did, I saved whatever he gave me, too. Rachel didn't save anything, but one day she wanted to go to the movies with her friends. Children's tickets were only thirty-five cents, but Rachel didn't have thirty-five cents. I told her I'd give her the money, but she couldn't make me do anything for her anymore. Rachel didn't want to say okay, but she did. I finally felt like I could breathe again. After that, I started lending money to Rachel and even to

Mother sometimes, but I acted the way I learned banks did. I always asked for a little more back.

Then I found something I wanted to spend money on --- comic books. There were two kinds, Marvel and D.C. I didn't like Marvel. Their heroes were always sad. I liked stories where the heroes always did the right thing, and the endings were happy. Soon things started happening that made me want those happy stories even more.

Mother finally did what she'd told Rachel and me she was going to do, back when she sat us down on the floor with her. She left my father and took us with her. She found an apartment where the three of us could live. That meant I had to change schools. Rachel would have changed anyway. She was going to high school, although they almost didn't let her in because her grades were so low. My new school was right next door. Mother had gotten a job as a laboratory assistant at Rachel's high school. She still wasn't making much money. Sometimes Grandpa and Grandma Levi had to loan her some. The supermarket was a long walk from our apartment, but we could manage with a folding cart. We could walk to the post office and some restaurants too, so Mother still didn't need to drive.

After we had moved, Mother decided she had to get a divorce. She said the way she had to do that would be to stay in Georgia during the summer when she wasn't working. Rachel went to stay with her friends, and I stayed with Grandma and Grandpa Levi, who had also moved. Grandpa had been fired from his job at a chemical plant after forty years working there. It happened just before he would get the money they were supposed to pay him when he retired. They cheated him, but there was nothing he could do about it. He and Grandma had to sell their house and live in a one-bedroom apartment. There was no garden and no room for me to sleep in, either. I had a cot in the living room, but I didn't mind. I liked staying with them and I still cooked with Grandma.

Grandma Levi kept me busy. She gave me scraps of cloth to make doll clothes, but she wouldn't let me sew anything that would look sloppy. Every edge had to be finished, so what I sewed looked like real clothes for people, only smaller. She also taught me to darn, like weaving little pieces of cloth with a needle and thread, to fix holes in socks and things.

Grandma kept teaching me in the kitchen. Her beef had no red inside and was somewhat hard to chew, but I loved the chicken. It was easy to chew and juicy. I liked baked apples. They were sweet and smelled spicy. The vegetables were from the supermarket. They weren't as good as the ones we grew in the garden, but they were okay.

Grandma also baked, but she didn't have an electric mixer, and beating batter by hand tired her out. I was happy to do it for her, especially since she let me lick the bowl. When Grandma finished teaching me, I could make brownies that were smooth in the pan with no hard edges. I was proud to show them to Grandpa. They tasted good, too.

Both Grandma and Grandpa spoke many languages. Grandpa had come from Russia. He said he was in a revolution in 1905, that didn't work. He was sent to a very cold place called Siberia. His family gave money to Russians to get him out; then he came to the United States. He knew Russian, Hebrew, and Yiddish, and of course, English. When he wrote for himself, it was in Yiddish.

Grandma had come from the part of Austria that became part of Poland. Her family had sent her to the United States. A guy who was supposed to marry one of her older sisters fell in love with her instead. When she came, she spoke German and Yiddish, but only a little English. Grandpa had helped her learn English, and they fell in love with each other. They told me that before I was even born, Grandma's English was better than Grandpa's. She used to tease him about saying the "a" in my name wrong. I was already learning some Hebrew and could make the sounds like clearing your throat, which aren't in English. Grandma thought that there should not be any sound that I couldn't do, at least in the languages she knew. So, she drilled me on things like "ts" sounds until I could say them the way she wanted me to.

Even with all the stuff that Grandma taught me, she thought I was still bouncing around the apartment too much. I watched Jack LaLanne's exercise show on the big heavy television. I made the motions with him but thought they were too easy. I went on walks with Grandpa to buy groceries. That still wasn't enough exercise to help me sit still. I still jumped around the living room, but I tried hard not to flap my arms, because Grandma and Grandpa didn't like it. I also walked around the hall of the apartment building and met some of the people who lived there.

Most of them just said hello, if they said anything, but not Mrs. Ludlow who lived across the hall. I don't know why, but Grandma and Grandpa didn't like Mrs. Ludlow. I did. She lived there by herself, but she was happy that way. What I liked was her shell collection. Her apartment was full of them in glass cases and tucked away in drawers. I went over to see Mrs. Ludlow every chance I got. She told me stories about where the shells had come from and how she found them. Mrs. Ludlow even gave me some shells for my own. I hid them in my suitcase so Grandma wouldn't get mad.

Grandma and Grandpa never talked about why Mother was gone so long, at least not where I could hear, or in English. I heard Mother's and Father's names sometimes when they spoke in Yiddish, but I could only understand a few words. I was glad when Mother came back. I didn't miss her that much, but it meant I got to go home. I'd made a new friend named Ellen, and I wanted to see her. I wanted to try to see Arlene, too.

Chapter Three

When Mother came back from Georgia, she was snobbier than ever. She talked a lot about how dumb people were there. She said they gave her tea by the cup instead of in a pot, at a Chinese restaurant. She thought that was all wrong. She told Rachel and me that in Georgia they wanted to serve grits with every meal. I'd never tasted them, but Mother seemed to think they were awful. She also told us that she was glad that she wasn't married to my father anymore.

It was strange, though. She talked to Rachel and me about the divorce, but we weren't supposed to tell anyone outside the family. She told us to tell anyone else that our father was dead. I was confused. I had been told repeatedly that lying was bad, and I believed it. I learned it in regular school and in Hebrew School. But now Mother wouldn't let me tell the truth. When I argued with Mother, she warned me that if I said anything about the divorce, she could lose her job. She also told me that if my father came to visit, or anyone saw me with him, I was to say he was my uncle. I hated to lie, but I didn't want Mother to lose her job, so I did what she said.

Even when Mother was married to my father, she liked other men. She even liked some of her older boy students. She invited them home and knit sweaters for them, something she never did for my father, Rachel, or me. After one of those students had gone off to college, Mother treated a trip to visit him as if it was like the dates they showed on TV. She bought new clothes and new shoes. She also got very upset if guys, even younger ones, were more interested in Rachel than they were in her.

Mother liked Bernie Stein, a teacher at the high school. After the divorce, she acted as if he was her boyfriend, but he didn't act that way. He introduced Mother, Rachel, and me, to his real girlfriend, Marsha. He ended up marrying Marsha. Bernie seemed to like fat women. Mother was fat, but Marsha was much fatter. She couldn't sit anywhere but our strongest chair. Maybe that's why Mother thought she had a better chance than Marsha did with Bernie. However, when he and Marsha got engaged, Mother looked for other men to be her boyfriends.

Mother was so proud of being smart, she joined a club called Mensa that only very smart people were supposed to be able to join. She didn't join just because the other people in Mensa were smart; there were a lot more men than women. I guess she thought that gave her a better chance of catching one. She went to meetings and stuff a lot. She brought men home, or stayed out all night and left Rachel and me alone. Sometimes she wouldn't even tell us that she was going to be gone. That was scary for me. One night, Rachel had decided to stay with a friend, and I was by myself, not knowing if Mother was coming home or not. Rachel didn't like the way Mother was acting. She said it meant that Mother only cared about herself, and not us.

Things between Mother and Rachel got very bad when Rachel was sixteen. She was failing everything but art in high school, but she passed the Mensa test anyway. She and Mother started going to meetings together. From what I could figure out, they both wanted a thirty-year-old man named Joe Flick to be their boyfriend. Mother was sure that Joe would like her better, but he liked Rachel.

Mother was mad that Joe chose Rachel. She and Rachel hardly talked to each other. Rachel decided to be with boys much closer to her age. She stayed out all night a lot, like Mother. One time, after Rachel was out all night, she found out that the only way Mother knew she was gone was that the chain was on the door the next morning, and her key wasn't enough to get her in. Rachel decided that Mother didn't love her or care about her at all. She dropped out of school and moved in with a boyfriend. Later she moved again, farther away. She got a job in a place called Wall Street and an apartment in the part of New York City called the East Village. I visited her there once. Her apartment was old, and the bathtub was in the kitchen.

I think Mother did care about Rachel, sort of. One early morning, I heard her crying and saying Rachel's name.

Mother had always complained a lot when she was sick, but she was doing it more and more. Almost every week she asked me to call the school and tell them Mrs. Goldfarb was ill and would not be in. Mother had switched to teaching at a junior high school in another neighborhood that wasn't as nice as ours. When she did make it to her job, she made fun of her students, telling me how stupid they were. I was in sixth grade, and Mother taught ninth. She had me mark their papers anyway, and I wasn't supposed to even try to be nice. I put a big red "F" at the top of many papers. To Mother, being good in school and at taking tests, was everything. She wanted me to think about things that way too. The principal at the junior high school didn't like the way Mother was teaching, and gave her a bad grade as a teacher. At the end of the school year, Mother was fired. She always blamed the principal for that. She never thought she was a bad teacher.

Because of what the principal said, Mother couldn't get another job teaching. She decided to go back to editing, but there were no publishers where we lived. She had to work in New York City. Since she couldn't drive, she had to take a bus and two subways in the morning and come back the same way at night. That left me alone even more than I had been before. I was already doing the shopping and most of the cooking. Now I had to do all the other housework too. Mother made it even harder because she just kept saving things. There were piles of stuff and boxes everywhere except my room, the kitchen, and the bathroom. When I tried to clean, I could hardly run the carpet sweeper or the vacuum cleaner. I did the best job I could, using what Grandma Levi taught me, but things were always a mess.

Because of her heart, Grandma Levi always thought she'd die before Grandpa Levi. It didn't happen that way. Grandpa Levi got cancer. Grandma Levi was very upset and very weak. I had my arm around her at the service by Grandpa's grave, because she couldn't stand up by herself. Before Grandpa died, I heard that Grandma Levi had said some things about Mother being unfit and was thinking that she and Grandpa Levi should take care of me, instead of Mother. Instead, after Grandpa Levi died, I had to take care of Grandma Levi. I took buses to get to her apartment. Sometimes I had to stop along the way to pick up special salt-free bread or something else she needed. I was a mother to my mother and to my Grandma, but no one was taking care of me.

My hair was very long. Part of the reason was that I thought long hair was the only thing pretty about me. There wasn't any money to get it cut, but I didn't know how to keep the tangles out of it or wash it. Mother had never taught me, and Grandma couldn't. My hair was a mess. I was a mess. My friend Ellen, who also reminded me to brush my teeth, helped me with my hair sometimes. It took her more than an hour to get the knots out. Ellen helped me be cleaner and look better, but still not as good as the other girls at school. Mother didn't want to spend any money on clothes for me either, so I wore the things that Rachel had left behind. They were old and weren't what the other girls bought at the store. I didn't have anyone at school who liked me except Ellen. I still tried to see Arlene, but I usually didn't get a chance.

Even though I tried to take care of her, Grandma Levi had to go to the hospital. She was in a big room called a ward, with lots of other sick, old people. She wouldn't let anyone but me feed her, so I took a bus to the hospital after school every day to do it. I hated what I saw in the ward. All the people were so sick and sad that it made me feel sick to look at them.

Until then, because I got sick so much, I wanted to be a doctor. Rachel and I had played hospital, with me as the doctor and her as the nurse. Rachel had wanted to be a nurse, but after my parents were divorced, she realized there was no money for nursing school and her grades were too low to get a scholarship. She told me her dream was hopeless. Even though I was out of school so much, my grades were good, so I hadn't given up on my plan. That changed after I was with Grandma at the hospital. I didn't want to be a doctor anymore. I didn't want to be around sick people. I didn't know what I wanted to be anymore.

After Grandma got out of the hospital, the whole Levi family decided that even with my help, she couldn't live alone. They decided that she would go to live with Mother's brother, Nahum, in Massachusetts. That left me with only Ellen and Arlene to like me, and soon I wouldn't have either one of them, either.

Arlene's parents said that it was time they moved up in the world. They sold their house and bought one out of the city. It wasn't like my father's house in the country. It was much closer, with many nice houses around it, but it was still far away. I could visit, but it meant a long ride on a bus I would have to catch from Port Authority terminal in New York City. That made visits to Arlene not just hard, but cost a lot of money. We talked on the phone, but we hardly ever saw each other.

Mother had gotten tired of how long it took her to get to work and how hard it was to bring men home to New Jersey. She decided to move to Manhattan. Then she could take a short subway ride to the publisher where she worked. I didn't have a choice. Mother looked for apartments on her lunch hours and after work. She told me she found one that would work. She said it was rent controlled so she could afford it. We moved to New York.

The apartment was in an old building that had once been very fancy but wasn't anymore. The floors were wood, like our old floors in New Jersey, but even dirtier. The dining room had a fireplace, but we didn't know if it was safe to use. There were some good things about our new apartment. I wouldn't have to drag a shopping cart full of groceries up three flights of stairs, after walking to a market that was very close. There was an elevator, which usually worked. There was a delicatessen downstairs too. It was summer when we moved. Mother gave me money to buy cold cuts and salads there, when she said it was too hot to cook in the apartment.

There were some scary things too. There were rats sometimes and a lot of roaches all the time. With all of Mother's boxes, they hid and it was impossible to kill them. I got big bites all over me that blistered. Mother had a window air conditioner in her room, but the rest of the apartment, including my tiny room, was hot. I was always itchy and sweaty. I wanted school to start again.

Mother had told me that in New York, I'd be able to go to the Bronx High School of Science. She said it was one of the best high schools in the country and good for smart kids. It turned out that would have to wait. When we'd moved, Mother didn't know you could only get into special New York Schools from a New York junior high school. I had to go to the nearest one. There were many Puerto Rican kids in the school. Most of their families didn't have much money either, so the school gave everyone free lunches, unless you wanted dessert. You had to pay for that.

Coming to junior high as a senior in ninth grade, I was too late to be in the smart kids' track, even though my grades were good enough. The principal was nice and did the best she could to put me in the best classes she could manage. That still made me the smartest kid in most of my classes. Many of the other kids didn't like that at all. One class, which the other smart kids were in, was Core, a mix of English and Social Studies. My homeroom teacher, Mrs. Yost, taught core. I never had a problem with Social Studies because it was mostly just memorizing dates and events, but I liked the English part of the class more. Because I liked writing so much, I was as good or better than any of the other kids. Without telling the class my name, Mrs. Yost picked my work to read in class. It was nice to know I did so well, without anyone thinking I was teacher's pet.

Not all the classes were that good. Because Spanish was supposed to be an easy class for the kids in the slower track who already spoke it, I was put in French class. I was good at it, but Spanish would have been a whole lot more useful. At least I might have known what other kids were saying behind my back. The good thing about being in French was that one of the other kids in the class told me about *Star Trek*. I got to watch it and love it, almost from the first episode.

I was also put into sewing class, something that was easy for me because of Grandma Levi. After I had to sing in front of the whole class, the music teacher offered me a place in Glee Club, which I could have been in instead of sewing. Glee Club would have been more fun, but I didn't know the rules. I didn't know I could switch, so I stayed in sewing. That turned out to be a good thing. I was able to make clothes like the new ones in the stores.

Sciences were taught in four sections. The first one was chemistry. I was good at all of them, but that wasn't such a great thing. The chemistry teacher, Mr. Painter, didn't keep who got the best marks a secret, the way Mrs. Yost did. He told the class how much better I did on tests than they did.

Mr. Painter graded on a curve, something I'd never had a teacher do before. That meant that when I knew all the answers and the rest of the class didn't, it made their grades lower. They gave me a nickname, "Curve Breaker." It meant I was the enemy. They hit me on the back of the head in the big elevators that took a bunch of kids upstairs at once, because the school building was so tall. The other kids always looked at me as if they were mad at me, and they'd try to steal my stuff.

I wouldn't have thought it would help me that the weather got very cold, but it did. Because I took a regular city bus to school, I always got there early. So did many of the other kids who took city buses. Most of the time we had to line up outside until the doors were opened. However, when it was cold enough, raining, or snowing hard, we were allowed to wait in the auditorium until it was time for homeroom.

One freezing day, I was in a seat next to Jeanie. She was in the eighth grade, so she wasn't in any of my classes and didn't know who I was. When we started talking, we found out we both loved *Star Trek*. Jeanie asked me who my favorite character was, and I told her, "Mr. Spock."

We would never have been friends if I'd said, "Captain Kirk." Neither one of us liked him very much. Jeanie liked me because I picked Mr. Spock. She invited me to join her *Star Trek* club, which met after school in the apartment where she lived with her mother, Mara.

Jeanie and I had a lot in common. Our mothers were both divorced and looking for boyfriends. They were both gone all day too, but doing very different jobs. While Mother spent the day at the publisher where she worked, and many nights at Mensa activities, Mara was a singer. She had gone to a fancy music school called Juilliard. Sometimes she was even on Broadway, but she wasn't a star. She was in the chorus. She was also one of those women who do the "oohs" and "ahs" behind big shot singers. When I met Jeanie, Mara was in a Broadway show called *Brigadoon*. She had to be on stage almost every night. Jeanie loved that her mother got to perform, and wanted to be like her. Jeanie played the guitar and sang too. She also took three ballet classes a week. When she found out that I had taken some ballet and could do the positions and go on pointe, we did some of the exercises together. Jeanie told me what I was doing wrong, and we even made up some dances together.

Jeanie and I, and the other girls in the *Star Trek* club, liked not having adults around. We each put dibs on a *Star Trek* character and invented a girlfriend for them. We made up our own stories, playing the girlfriends and playing all the other *Star Trek* parts too. Jeanie had already claimed Mr. Spock, and Kirk and Scotty were taken too. I ended up with Dr. McCoy. I tried my best to get a crush on him as fast as I could. Sometimes, I acted the parts of Kirk, Spock, and Scotty. I found out I was good at doing a Scottish accent. I loved losing myself in another world, one where people liked me or at least liked whomever I was playing.

Mother had found herself two new boyfriends. One was Bill, whom I liked. The other was Sam. He made me feel like there were roaches on my skin. I hated it when Sam moved into our apartment, sleeping in Mother's bed. He smoked all the time, and I couldn't stand the way it made everything in the apartment smell. His clothes were in the laundry I had to take to the laundromat every week. I had a hard time getting the greasy rings in his shirt collars clean. Most of the time I couldn't do it at all. He was always standing or sitting too close to me. It was as if he was everywhere I wanted to be, except my room, and Mother wouldn't even let me have a lock on that. To get away, I imagined myself in the *Star Trek* world, but when I was home, I wrote my *Star Trek* stories down, instead of acting them out.

Every week, after *Star Trek* was on, I would write a story of my own. I used my own character, Talinda, the characters my friends made up, and all the people on the show. I wrote about alien worlds and dangerous things, but I always made everything come out all right. I was kind of hard on Captain Kirk. I made him get hurt or sick a lot.

I took my stories to school to share with the other Trekkies, but one day I was caught by Mrs. Yost, and she took my story away. I thought I was in trouble, but Mrs. Yost decided to read my story to the rest of the class. The other kids had seen Mrs. Yost take it, so they knew who wrote it, even though she never said my name. Mrs. Yost couldn't finish the story before the bell rang. Captain Kirk was left passed out from an alien poison dart. I expected to be teased or worse by the other kids, especially the ones who hated me from Mr. Painter's class. I couldn't believe it when the other kids gathered around me, wanting to know what happened to the captain. I told them, and they were nice to me. It felt good. My writing gave me a way to talk to them. I decided to write a lot more and make a world for Talinda. It was called Craydon.

The first thing I came up with was the clothes Talinda wore when she wasn't in a Star Fleet uniform. At first, I made a paper doll of Talinda. She had long dark hair with no tangles and bright green eyes that slanted a little. Then I made paper uniforms, paper magnetic boots to keep her from falling when the ship was knocking around, and pretty gowns that were what was worn on Craydon. The dresses were down to her ankles and gathered on elastic at the neck, leaving her arms bare.

The paper dolls were great, but when I bought fabric to make the clothes in sewing class, I found out about fabric remnants. They're pieces of a roll of cloth too short to be sold at the normal price per yard. I'm so short that all I needed to make Talinda gowns was a remnant, little pieces of elastic, and thread. By forgetting about buying snacks or comics, I got enough money together to make the Craydonese dresses. I sewed them at home and wore them around the apartment, and even when I did the grocery shopping and the other errands Mother gave me to do. The guys in the stores in my neighborhood were used to seeing me in my old ratty clothes. When I wore my Talinda gowns, they told me I looked pretty. That felt wonderful. As Talinda, I could be pretty. I tried to be Talinda as much as I could, at home and with my club.

When my fourteenth birthday was coming, two things happened. Mother told me my father threatened to withhold the little bit in child support he paid her, unless he could see me. Because Mother always needed money, she told him he could, but everything she said to me about him before he came, was bad. Because of the fun, I had dancing with Jeanie, I asked my father to take me to the ballet. My father had never been to the ballet; that was one of Mother's culture things. He agreed to give me what I wanted for my birthday. My father didn't understand what the dancers were doing, and he was bored. I was embarrassed. When he took me to dinner after the ballet, I was even more embarrassed that he couldn't pronounce the French words on the menu. That was something I didn't have any trouble doing and neither did Mother. Because of what happened on my birthday, and because of what Mother had been saying, I didn't want to see my father anymore. I didn't.

Back then, fourteen was the youngest age anyone could take the test to get into Mensa. Since Mother and Rachel passed it, and I was supposed to be the smart sister, I had to. Three weeks after my birthday, I took an IQ test. I was nervous while I waited for the results, but they let me in and said my IQ was 175. I was relieved. I didn't care about my score. I was afraid of what Mother would have said if I hadn't made it in.

There were some good things about Mensa. I didn't want to do what Mother was doing, but I liked boys, and there were a lot more of those than there were girls. At my first meeting, I had a circle of six of them around me. I couldn't believe it! The boys offered to lend me their science fiction books, and I was invited to parties. It was exciting to have that many boys like me, but I was always afraid they'd find somebody pretty and go away. I thought I'd at least have them as friends until that happened. I had three safe places to be: with the Mensa boys, with my *Star Trek* club, and in my mind, on Craydon.

As ninth grade went on, Mother talked more and more about high school. She said all the time that I was too smart to go to a regular one. I had to get into the Bronx High School of Science.

Many of the Mensa boys went there, so I liked the idea of going there too. I'd missed a lot of stuff, not being in the smart classes in New York all along, so I studied as hard as I could. I stayed after school to go to a special tutorial class taught by the vice principal, Mr. Goldman. Most of the students thought Mr. Goldman was scary. He was the one you were sent to if you got a cut slip or were in some other kind of trouble. Nothing like that had ever happened to me. I thought Mr. Goldman was nice and went to every class he taught. That meant less time with Jeanie and my *Star Trek* friends, but it worked. I got in.

I was a little bit nervous one day near the end of the school year when I was called out of my music class to go down to Mr. Goldman's office. The other students were whispering that Curve Breaker was in trouble, but when I got to his office, Mr. Goldman was smiling. He told me that I had been chosen to make a speech at the end of the term, on academic achievement, and assigned a teacher to help me write it. I was afraid it would be another reason for the other kids to pick on me, but I was glad that Mr. Goldman was proud of me. I had never met the typing teacher, Mrs. Maas, who was supposed to help me with my speech. Mrs. Maas had her own ideas about what I should say. She wanted the theme to be excellence, and about how important it was supposed to be. I couldn't see the point in what Mrs. Maas was saying. The last thing the other kids wanted was a lecture from me. If anything, it would get me smacked more in the elevator. I decided to write my speech the way I wanted to. Mrs. Maas might be mad, but I knew she wouldn't hurt me.

I had been working on my speech for a week when Mother told me I wouldn't be at graduation. She wanted to attend a Mensa Annual Gathering, which would be in Montreal that year. She also wanted to see the World's Fair that would be there at the same time. She was going to make me go with her.

Mother was always complaining that she had no money, and I had no idea where she was going to get some for a trip to Montreal, but I didn't dare bring that up. I did remind her about my speech, but she didn't care. Sam had to stay in New York to work, and she didn't want to go alone. She'd made up her mind and there was nothing I could do about it.

The next day, I was afraid I was going to cry when I went to see Mr. Goldman. He told me he was disappointed that I wouldn't be around for graduation, but he said my speech would be at the awards assembly when I would still be in the city. I was grateful that I'd be around to give it, but I was also afraid of what the other kids might do to me after the assembly, when I'd still have to be in school with them.

Mother spoiled the Awards Assembly day too. Just before I left in the morning, she told me I was getting the general science medal. Having to give a speech had already made my stomach hurt, but after a year as The Curve Breaker, I didn't know what the other kids would do about that.

In a way, things got even worse. I gave my speech. Then I got the science medal and a certificate of merit in math. Math has always been a bad subject for me. But I had a crush on Mr. Morris who taught Algebra. He was tall, with a nice beard and a nice smile. I did my best for him. However, getting any award for math was still a surprise. Then I got the English medal. From what Mrs. Yost said when she made the announcement, writing stories on my own had something to do with winning it. Then Mr. Goldman got up from his seat on stage and waved at me to sit in it. When he sat down in it again, I knew he was joking, but that didn't help me from being scared about what the other kids would do when the assembly was over.

I stayed away from the elevators. I took the stairs to class as fast as I could, without breaking the rules against running. I got some nasty looks, but no one hit me. For the first time, I was glad that I would be going to Montreal.

To save money, Mother and I were flying standby. We had to be ready to get on the plane when they called us. My period started just when they did. It was the wrong time for it to come and I didn't have anything with me. Mother carried a tiny cardboard tube with an emergency pad and a couple of safety pins, in her purse. I used it as fast as I could. Mother was afraid we'd miss the plane and kept telling me to hurry up --- as if I wasn't trying. We just made it onto the plane.

I had cramps, and I was very nervous I would leak, but the flight went okay. Getting through customs went okay too. Mother was mad that we had to stop at a store in the Montreal airport to pick up sanitary napkins. Everything was expensive there, but they had what I needed.

Mother had booked rooms in one of the cheaper hotels in Montreal, in an area where most of the people only spoke French. I found out then that Mother's French was not nearly as good as she had bragged it was. With my one year of ninth grade French, I was doing a lot of the talking. I wasn't that good, but I was able to figure out whose room was whose and understand easy instructions. I didn't like being stuck with being a translator, and Mother was upset that I'd found her out.

The next morning, Mother said that because she already had tickets, we would be going to breakfast at a much larger hotel, the one where the annual gathering would be held. We had come from the airport by cab, with a driver who spoke English. This time we would be taking the Metro, where instructions were in both English and French. That helped. After the rough, noisy rides on the New York subways, the quiet cars of the Montreal Metro, which ran on tires, were amazing to both Mother and me. After growing up hearing about how great America was, I began to wonder if it was as easy for people to lie about our country, as it had been for Mother to ask me to lie for her. That made me feel very nervous and unsure.

By the time Mother and I reached the Mensa breakfast, I was desperate for tea. That usually helped my cramps. The trip just made them worse. There were no young people to talk to at the table where Mother and I were seated. As far as I could tell, there was no one my age in the room. I just drank my tea while Mother talked to the adults at our table. I made sure a teacup covered most of my face when a photographer came around taking pictures.

After the breakfast, there was a meeting of a special interest group for some reforms in Mensa. I knew Mother was a member. She'd held meetings at our apartment, and I'd helped run off newsletters on an old mimeograph machine. My cramps got better while I was sitting there and when Mother said she wanted to go to the fair, that was all right with me.

I remembered from a trip to a World's Fair in New York when I was little, that routes on subway trains were marked with colored lines to follow. It was the same on the Montreal Metro. Mother and I got where we were going with no trouble.

The fair in New York had been a lot of fun. There were all kinds of booths and things. I had ridden on Disney's "It's a Small World" ride before it was moved to Disneyland. I ate my first taco there. There was also someone selling oysters with pearls, and mine had an extra one, shaped like a teardrop. There were pavilions and booths in Montreal too, but nothing that was as much fun as in New York. The best part of the trip was the quiet cars on the Metro.

Mother and I went to more meals with Mensa, but there still wasn't anyone my age there at all. If Mother was looking for men, none of them seemed interested in her. I had heard everything they were talking about before, and I was bored.

To cut down on the cost of food when we weren't at the Mensa gathering, Mother and I went to a little store near our motel.

They didn't speak English, and I had to do the talking again. Mother liked cheese. She couldn't remember the word in French, but I did. We also bought some oranges and a knife to cut them with. There weren't many knives for sale, and the one we bought looked a lot like the switchblades the bad guys have on TV, except that the blade didn't pop out. Mother said it was a gravity knife, and that one like it had been taken away from one of her students, before she went back to being an editor. In the U.S., switchblades were illegal, but gravity knives weren't. She assumed that since one was sold at a store, they weren't a problem in Canada either.

When it was finally time to go back to New York, the man at customs looked at the knife for a long time before he let us go through with it. Mother had eaten all the cheese, but she'd decided that we could take the leftover oranges back to New York with us. They were even more of a problem than the knife. The Customs man kept looking for a mark on them. He told us that if they said "Sunkist," it would be all right because they would have been from the U.S., but they didn't say anything, so we had to leave them behind.

My sanitary napkins were in a paper bag inside my suitcase. When the Customs inspector asked what was in the bag, Mother told him it had "personal items." After the knife and the oranges, that wasn't enough information, so he looked for himself. I wanted to die, but he didn't say anything. He just put them back in my suitcase.

There was nothing about the trip that I felt was worth missing my graduation for, but when we picked up the mail when we got back, there was a little package addressed to me. It had a General Excellence medal that I was not at graduation to get. I wasn't sure if I would have wanted to face the other kids after getting it, but I was done with junior high school anyway and getting the award in front of them might have been nice. I'll never know. Now that I was away from the other kids, I liked my medals, and I wanted something I could pin them on.

Chapter Four

I got a chance to buy something to put my medals on, that summer. Uncle Nahum and his family had rented a cottage on Cape Cod, and I was invited to stay with them for two months. The cabin was a little rough for Grandma Levi, who would be spending the time with a cousin instead of coming with us. To me, a cabin in the woods near a beach was almost as good as going to another planet, especially since I would be away not only from Mother but also from Sam. I was also excited that Nahum's family would be bringing a dog.

Though he was four years younger than Mother, Nahum was a professor with lots of awards. He didn't think much of the life Mother was living. When they thought I was asleep, sometimes I heard whispers between Nahum and his wife Bebe, about Grandma Levi having asked that I be given as much time away from Mother as possible. That's how I found out that I was at the cabin with Nahum's family. Not because they liked me, but because they considered my mother a bad influence. I didn't know whether to be mad or grateful. I knew that Arlene's, Ellen's, and Jeanie's mothers all paid more attention to them than Mother did to me. Their mothers were stricter about knowing where they were and what they were doing, too. They all had chores, but none of them had to take charge of everything, the way I did. None of them ever had to spend a night alone, either. I still didn't like the way that Nahum and Bebe talked about Mother, even if I thought they might be right.

I could tell the difference between my life and the one my cousins lived when we had to go to the laundromat. I was used to doing that every week and could have done it with my eyes closed. Nahum had started to make a speech about the kids not knowing what they were doing, and it hurt my feelings until he hurried to explain that he didn't mean me, but his kids, who had never been to a laundromat before. I also found out that despite my cousins getting to go to a good school, I was better at schoolwork than they were. Like the kids in junior high school, they resented me for that. When I managed to beat Uncle Nahum at Scrabble, he seemed mad, too.

One thing I liked about the summer was the trips. They weren't like traveling with Mother. No one was trying to make themselves look smart by seeing or knowing things other people didn't. Going to the beach was just going to the beach. I learned how to body surf and didn't even mind getting sunburned. The trip I liked most was to a military surplus store. I had saved some money from babysitting for the two kids in the apartment two floors up from Mother's place. I hadn't spent any of it that summer because I didn't know what I would need or when. The surplus store gave me a chance to buy the thing I'd dreamed about, a light blue military style jacket that I thought would look right with my school medals pinned to it, and a hat that matched. I'd left my medals in New York, but I wore the jacket and the hat all the time. I felt strong and safe, like when I was wearing my Talinda gowns. Even if my cousins and my uncle didn't like me much, I hated to see the summer end. I was looking forward to starting school, but not to going home to Mother and Sam. The thought of being in the same apartment with Sam made me nauseous.

After being in a cabin for two months, where no one used cigarettes, the smell of tobacco smoke on everything in the apartment when I got home, was awful. There was also dirt and dust everywhere. Mother hadn't even tried to clean while I was gone and neither had Sam.

I couldn't breathe, especially at night. I practiced the dance moves Jeanie had taught me until I was so tired that I could fall asleep around the time I'd soon be getting up for school. I needed all the time out of the apartment I could get. Long days at school would be more than okay.

I viewed my time at Bronx Science as a new start, and I wanted a new look that the other students might like. I was lucky to get some nice clothes. They were hand-me-downs, but they were new. A co-worker of Mother's had a daughter, who luckily was my size, but older. She had broken up with her fiancé and called off her wedding. The girl could no longer stand to look at clothes she'd bought for her trousseau, so they were passed on to Mother for me. They weren't high school style, but they were beautiful, and I appreciated them. I'd noticed from TV, that scarves were in that year. I didn't have any, but I did have scraps of fabric left over from making my clothes. I tried to make those odds and ends look like scarves.

Getting to the Bronx from where I lived in Manhattan required a five-block walk to one of two subways. The trip took one or two trains, depending on whether I could catch an express or a local, and then another walk of a few blocks at the other end. The total commute was about forty-five minutes long, meaning that I would always be getting up before Mother and Sam in the morning, in order to make it to school on time. I didn't even want to think about being late.

My first day at Bronx Science was both less and more than I'd hoped for. The other students in my homeroom weren't mean, but they weren't that friendly either. Many were already in cliques with other kids from fast tracks. They had all passed the test together. The rules at Science were even stricter than they were in junior high school. Every class a student had was listed on a program card. We had to carry our program cards all the time. If students were caught where they didn't belong, they'd be sent to the Vice Principal. There was also a dress code, which I heard was a less strict version of what the school used to have. Girls were never allowed to wear pants, even during cold weather when there were icy sidewalks. Kilts and skirts anywhere but to the knee were also against the rules. So was wearing your blouse untucked, unless it was meant to be an out blouse. That would be judged by having a special pattern on the hem. If you wore something you weren't supposed to, at least if you were a girl, you were sent home to change. I'd grown up with a dress code, so I didn't think it was too bad, except that my legs would be cold in the winter, and if I fell, there would be nothing to protect my knees.

We had assigned seats in the lunchroom. That was great. I didn't have to worry about tables full of cliques; I could just sit in the spot printed on my instruction sheet. Right away, I met two people I liked, who seemed to like me back. They were both super-sophomores, students who had come to Science after eighth grade instead of ninth. They were also both boys, Les and Mark. Les was skinny, with glasses over brown eyes and blond waves above a high forehead. He spoke with a Bronx accent, something I heard a lot at Science. Mark was short and blond with blue eyes. His face was handsome but round. I could see there was no food shortage at his house. They both were happy to tell me about the ins and outs of the cafeteria. It was not only cheaper but sometimes healthier to bring your lunch and buy milk for just the four cents it cost. They also told me about a student protest about the lousy taste of the meals, in which for a day, all the students paid for everything in pennies. Grinning, Les quickly added that under Federal law, pennies were legal tender and could not be refused.

Another student at the table was Anita. She had come after ninth grade like I did. She was tall but pudgy, not what the other kids would consider pretty. She wanted to make friends. She and I recognized each other as being outside the cliques. That was kind of a bond.

Sophomores at Science had very full schedules. We had no study periods. That didn't bother me at all, as I'd never had an empty spot in my school day. We were required to take English, Social Studies, Math, a foreign language, a science, and mechanical drawing. The school day started at eight in the morning, had less than an hour for lunch, and ended in the middle of the afternoon. Most of the students chose biology as their sophomore science, but to me, it made more sense to take chemistry first, since chemistry was a part of biology, but not necessarily the other way around. My chemistry class put me with some juniors, something that was a little intimidating.

Partly because of my commute, and partly because of the curriculum, my days started very early. I woke up at five twenty in the morning. I used the only alarm clock in the house but usually woke up before it went off. I made my own breakfast. That was nothing new. I was the first person in the kitchen in the morning, and I'd see the roaches run away when I turned on the light. Both Mother and Sam would leave dirty dishes in the sink overnight. That made things worse, but I got used to it. In the morning I washed whatever dishes they'd left, same as I'd done with the dinner dishes the night before. There wasn't enough storage space for all the food Mother liked to keep around. She loved cans of foreign foods and the small table in the kitchen was always covered with them. That left me with very little space to cook, but I did the best I could. Since at breakfast I didn't have to worry about pleasing anyone but myself, I could have some fun. I plumped up raisins in slow cooking oatmeal and spiced the combination with cinnamon.

Once I finished breakfast, I walked to a subway station to catch a train. There was not usually a local that went all the way to the Bronx at the time I needed. I took a train that went part way, and then changed trains at a station in Harlem. Back then, Harlem, especially the area over the station where I changed trains, was not a safe place to be. But below ground, there were transit cops and crowds. Not too many attacks happened.

I spent my time on the train in two ways. My favorite way was to read. Most of what I read were series of books, like the Lensmen and Skylark series by E.E. Doc Smith. Those books were written when scientists still believed there was ether in space, so some of the science was wrong, but I decided to ignore the errors and liked the books anyway. Sometimes I did the reading required for my classes as well, but I usually did that at home, and if I read it on the subway, I was reading ahead.

The second thing I did was to sleep, but not the kind of sleeping that would keep me from knowing what was going on around me. There was too much chance of having my purse or books stolen, to let myself sleep the way I did in bed. Instead, I did what I called skimming. My eyes were closed, but I could hear and feel everything going on around me. I thought of it as time stretching. The minutes seemed to pass very slowly, like in a dream. Time stretching helped me catch up on rest I wasn't getting at night, and let me stay awake at school.

On the way back from school, I was more likely to be able to catch a local, which made whatever I decided to do on the train easier. When I got home, I would sometimes try to catch a little nap on the couch in the living room, before starting my homework, and working on it until it was time to make dinner.

How complicated supper would be depended on whether Sam would be around or not, as well as what food was in the house to cook. If I was cooking for just Mother and myself, a piece of meat wrapped in foil and cooked in boiling water with vegetables would do the trick. Mother sometimes also had cheese snacks and bowls of cereal for herself.

If Sam would be at dinner, I had to serve an appetizer, then meat, vegetables, and a starch. For him, there had to be a dessert as well. When they were together, Mother and Sam liked wine with supper. I never wanted anything like that. Sam often added a glass of scotch, which he drank while smoking a cigarette.

Once I cleared away dinner and cleaned up, I could go back to my homework, many times it took me until eleven at night to finish. I usually worked with the TV on, something many other students' parents didn't allow. Mother didn't care. She said that it didn't matter as long as my grades stayed up. I used the background noise to shut out whatever Mother and Sam might be doing in the apartment. I suspected Mother wouldn't have cared even if my grades had fallen. She wasn't interested in most of what I did. Her attention was almost always focused on Sam or of course, herself.

After a while, Mother found that she had a use for me, other than cleaning and cooking. She had been assigned the production of an introductory chemistry textbook and had no idea how to find someone to write it. I suggested Mr. Painter. When he wasn't available, I told her to try Mr. Wulff, who had been my physics teacher. Mr. Wulff wrote the main part of the book, but there was more to do. Mother's publisher wanted her to write blurbs and puzzles for the margins of the pages.

She was stuck. She was sure she was a very good editor, but she'd never written anything except scientific papers. She asked me for help. I became Mother's ghostwriter. Normally someone would have been paid for that. She couldn't get me paid because her bosses thought she was doing the work herself. She did buy me a pair of leather boots that had been marked down to half price at a Broadway boutique. Even on sale, I had never had anything nearly so expensive or pretty. I cleaned them with saddle soap every time they got white lines on them from the salt on the sidewalk. They reminded me a little bit of the boots Talinda wore in my stories.

Jeanie and I were still friends. Jeanie had stayed behind in junior high school when I graduated. I couldn't go to *Star Trek* club meetings anymore, but I kept writing stories, even if it meant losing even more sleep than I already was. About every third weekend, I crashed, sleeping for about fourteen hours. I spent as many weekends as I could, when I was awake, with Jeanie. We played our improvisational games, doing all the parts.

Jeanie also had a lovely singing voice, although not as good as her mother's. She played the guitar and wrote songs. I wanted to have a guitar too and began saving for one out of my babysitting money and the gifts Grandma Levi still sent for my birthday and Hanukkah. When I managed to put together forty dollars, Jeanie and I went to a pawnshop, where I bought a used guitar that Jeanie said had a good sound.

I worked very hard to learn how to play it. There was no way I could afford a guitar teacher. Jeanie showed me chord changes, but I wanted more, especially since I could read music. I found a way, on educational TV. There were lessons in classical guitar every week. All I had to do was send in money for the books and make sure I was watching when the lessons were on. I got lucky. The people upstairs needed me to babysit a lot, so I earned enough money for the books. I learned to put my left hand in a different position from what Jeanie used for the folk songs she sang. I practiced every day until my fingers built up the calluses that I needed to hold the strings down. Once I'd worked my way the through the first book, I started adding in folk chords and singing folk songs like Jeanie did. I also wrote songs of my own. Jeanie and I played together. Jeanie thought she had the better voice, and she took the lead. Between making our music and playing *Star Trek*, being with Jeanie was the most important thing in my life. I couldn't imagine being separated from her and hoped that Jeanie would be able to get into Science and we'd be in the same school again.

One thing I didn't want to think about was sex. I knew it happened. There were always little bits about it on TV shows and movies. I'd learned about periods when I was ten and Rachel had suggested to Mother that I read a little pamphlet put out by the company that made sanitary napkins. I hadn't had a sex education course, so what was in the pamphlet was all I knew, and all I wanted to know. Mother and Sam slept in the same bed, but I didn't want to know what they did there. Other than on the cheek, I'd never kissed a boy, and one had never kissed me. I wasn't in a hurry to try. However, one night I saw something I wish I hadn't seen.

When I was going to bed, I noticed that my alarm clock was missing. I thought Mother had borrowed it as she sometimes did. I needed it, so I went to get it back. Mother's bedroom door wasn't locked, and when I pushed it open to ask for my clock, I saw Sam on top of Mother. I pulled the door closed again and just stood in the hallway trying to breathe. After a few minutes, Mother came out. She explained that Sam thought I might be upset, and asked if I wanted to talk about what I saw.

What Mother said, confirmed what I had been thinking for a long time. Mother didn't care about me, only about what Sam said. Mother went on to say that she and Sam had been making love. She was smiling. I just wanted to shut out the words, and get rid of the image stuck in my brain. Mother handed me my clock, and I went back to my room and just lay there.

I didn't feel much better the next morning. I went through the day just by routine. During the rest of the week, I tried to have as little to do with Mother and Sam as I could, eating just a little bit of supper and leaving the table while they were still shoveling down what I'd cooked.

Anita didn't know what was wrong, but she decided that I needed cheering up. She suggested that the two of us might go to a movie, *To Sir with Love*. I had just enough money for a ticket, and the idea of going anywhere but home sounded wonderful. I almost never saw a movie before it was on television, and most of the time not even then. I had no idea who the star, Sidney Poitier, was or what the plot would be, but I thought Sidney was handsome and I lost myself in the story --- until things came crashing down on me again. One of Sir's students confessed, with tears running down her face that she had walked in on her mom when she was having sex with a man, just as I did. For the first time since it happened, I started to cry. I cried without making any noise, through the rest of the movie, until the final song, which cheered me up a little. After that, I felt like my insides had been washed by my tears. I would never forget what I saw, but I knew I wasn't alone. Things like what happened to me happened to other people. Knowing that helped.

That year, Jeanie got interested in Jewish things. Her mother was officially Christian and celebrated Christmas, but Jeanie's father was Jewish. The way I was taught, by Jewish law that meant that Jeanie wasn't. Judaism was passed on from your mother. That didn't bother Jeanie. Zionist youth organizations were big then, at least in New York, and Jeanie loved the clothes and stuff, like the blue shirts, neckerchiefs, and hats like the one Gilligan wore on his island.

I'd had enough of religion and the rules that went with it, in Hebrew School, but I went along with what Jeanie wanted. When the Six Day War broke out, Jeanie wanted me to cut school for the first time in my life, to collect money for the United Jewish Appeal. Many members of Jewish youth groups did it. After that, she talked her friend Dierdre, who was Irish, into marching in the Israeli Independence Day Parade. I went along with that for Jeanie, too. The three of us marched together. Jeanie and I both read *Exodus* at the same time, and then *Mila 18*, the story of the revolt in a Jewish ghetto in Poland. After that came *The Source*, a huge book by James Michener, which took Jeanie a month to get through, but I finished it in a week. We also sang and played Jewish folk songs on our guitars, although I had to teach Jeanie how to pronounce the words. Jeanie was convinced that when she was old enough, she would go to Israel. I wasn't that excited about the idea, but I tried to be, and it was years away. I didn't have to worry much about it.

What I was worried about, was Jeanie's exams for entrance into special high schools the next year. Jeanie wanted to try out for two, Music and Art, and Bronx Science. Of course, I wanted Jeanie at Science, but I helped her practice for both. I listened to her sing her audition song, repeatedly, and made up sample math problems and English questions.

When the day came for Jeanie's exam for Science, I went with her and another girl, so they wouldn't get lost in the subway or on the walk to the school. It was a cold day, and the school was closed except for testing. I stayed outside, trying to keep warm by walking around until the test was over. Jeanie told me that she hadn't had time to finish. That worried me. When I took my test, I finished before time was called. Jeanie's friend said that she had been able to finish just fine, which scared me even more. When the test results came out, Jeanie had failed the entrance exam to Science, but she had made it into Music and Art.

It turned out the tests hadn't mattered. Mara married her boyfriend, Arthur. The two of them announced that they would be buying a house in Nyack, New York, and moving there. Arthur, who was Jewish, was willing to adopt Jeanie if her father gave consent, and Jeanie would be moving to Nyack with her mother and him.

I didn't know what I would do. I'd completely lost touch with Ellen when Mother and I moved to New York. A few times I made a bus trip to see Arlene, but there were months in between the times I saw her. I wondered if Jeanie would be at the other end of a long bus trip too. I decided to save all the money I could for bus fare to see Jeanie. One good thing was that I got an invitation to spend part of the summer in a cabin in the Hamptons on Long Island with Jeanie, Mara, and Arthur.

Arthur had bought one of the vans that were very popular with hippies back then. Jeanie and I used it as a getaway from the cabin, going in there to play *Star Trek* games, which Mara and Arthur didn't know anything about. We played our own characters and acted out all the other parts with just the two of us. I also wrote more *Star Trek* stories, and stories from other shows where Jeanie and I thought the men were cute. Jeanie tried to write too. She had many ideas and told her stories out loud, but she wasn't good at putting them on paper. That was the one talent that I had that Jeanie didn't. The summer, the games, the writing, and my time with Jeanie went way too fast. I went back to the city for my junior year at Science. Jeanie started her sophomore year at an ordinary high school in Nyack.

Chapter Five

Junior year meant a lunch table without Les, Mark, or Anita. There were some boys, but I didn't think any of them were cute. I didn't feel like being friends with them, and they didn't pay much attention to me. Two girls named Estelle and Gloria were also there, and they were fun to talk to. I kept being friends with Anita and saw Les, whose table was not far away, but I lost track of Mark. Elliott, who I knew from Young Mensa, was in my biology class. We saw each at picnics and meetings. Even for a Sciencite, I was good at biology. So was Elliott. I was the smart kid in the front of the room, and he was the smart kid in the back, but that was pretty much the only way I thought about him. I also met Sharon, who took the subway with me, a lot.

The thing I liked most was creative writing. I signed up for creative writing English, which meant that I had to learn all the regular English required in New York for the Regents exams, plus study all about writing. I'd also have to write stories and poetry to prove what I'd learned. The class was taught by Mr. Ross, a professional writer, who was married to a much more famous writer. Her novel had been made into a movie. Mr. Ross paid attention to all his students, really getting to know what we were like --- or at least what our writing was like. He was not an easy grader and gave a lot of criticism to help his students improve.

I was more used to having my writing praised than criticized so at first, his comments hurt my feelings. After my first big story, they became a challenge. He gave me a B+, which to me, was low. Ross' explanation for marking me down was that the intervention of an outside character constituted *deus ex machina*, a god from a machine. He insisted that was not a good plot device. I was surprised because I'd seen writing like that on TV a lot, but I listened. After that, I let my protagonists solve their problems on their own.

After a while, my favorite thing about the class wasn't the chance to improve my writing; it was Nathan. He was tall and thin with dark curly hair and eyes that smiled from behind his glasses. He sat across the room, where I couldn't see him without turning my head, but I couldn't help staring at him. Sometimes I was amazed that I could remember what Mr. Ross taught because I was staring at Nathan so much. Nathan paid a little attention to me. We walked to lunch together, even though we sat at different tables. I could see Nathan from where I sat in the lunchroom too, and kept staring a lot. Both Gloria and Estelle noticed how much time I spent looking at him.

One of the more interesting characters in the Science lunchroom was "Mary the Witch." I never heard her called anything else. No one ever used her last name. She was Wiccan. She didn't have a black hat or a broom; she only believed in doing good magic, and she very was interested in sex. Les was very interested in her, but she didn't have a thing for him. He kept trying to get her attention anyway. To distract him, Mary attempted to put Les together with me. She wanted us to kiss, and not on the cheek.

I had no idea what to do. It would be my first kiss on the lips from anyone. From what I saw on TV, it should have been important, maybe earthshaking. I liked Les and sometimes thought I might be interested in him that way, but when our lips touched, I didn't like it. I was very disappointed and wasn't sure if I'd ever want to try again. Les was nice as a friend, but I didn't want him to be anything else. The only boy I thought about wanting as a boyfriend was Nathan.

The most beautiful girl in Mr. Ross' class, and in the school, was Lana. Her face was perfect, and she moved very gracefully because she'd studied ballet for many years. As fascinated as I was with Nathan, he was with Lana. From across the room, becoming more and more discouraged, I watched their relationship develop. Lana had started walking with us after class, even though she had a different lunch period. Once I saw Nathan bring Lana a flower. I was upset, and I couldn't think about anything but him. In English, Hebrew, and Craydonian, I prayed for a chance to spend time with him.

Nathan mentioned in class that he was very interested in Gilbert and Sullivan. I knew about the operettas because of all my mother's culture stuff. After Nathan had mentioned them, I tried to learn everything about them I could. I found a way to bring them up when I talked to him, and he seemed to like that. Finally, it looked like I would get what I'd wished for. Nathan and Lana drifted apart. Like Mary the Witch had, Lana played matchmaker for me. After school, the three of us danced down the sidewalk cross-handed and singing, "We're off to see the Wizard," like in the *Wizard of Oz* movie. Not long after that, on our usual walk from class to lunch, Nathan asked me to go to the Gilbert and Sullivan Society with him.

I was so excited I could feel the joy shining from me like sunlight. Even the boys at the lunch table noticed and asked me why I was so happy. I didn't want to break the spell by telling them, but when Estelle wondered, I whispered in her ear that Nathan had asked me out. She hugged me. The same thing happened with Gloria. Nathan came to the table to get my phone number and wrote it on the inside cover of his paperback copy of Hamlet. I never forgot that moment.

Unlike most of us who commuted to Science every day, Nathan lived with his parents in an apartment a few blocks away from the school building, and on my way to the subway. Before our official date, he invited me up to his room. I had no idea how to act, or what would happen. First, Nathan's mother sent him out for ice cream, a short walk to a nearby drug store. She used the time he was gone to question me about my family and myself. I don't remember what we said. I know I answered her questions, but I just remember my stomach trying to jump out of my mouth while we were talking.

In a few minutes, which seemed to me like hours, Nathan came back. He invited me into his room. I didn't know what to do there either, but I thought that being there was dangerous. Anything having to do with sex seemed to cause so much trouble for both my sister and mother, that I was afraid of doing anything with a boy, especially in his bedroom. I was the good girl. I wasn't like Mother and Rachel. Then there was the kiss with Les. Yuck! I liked boys, but I wasn't ready to do anything like that about it again. Things seemed to be alright anyway. Nathan had left the door to his room open. He didn't try to touch me and I relaxed a little. He had a collection of records of every Gilbert and Sullivan operetta written, except Thespis, the lost one. He asked me what I wanted him to play, and I picked Ruddigore, the ghost story. Because not many people know about that one, Nathan was very pleased that I did, and put an LP on the turntable. The music was loud, and Nathan's mother came by and closed the door. I believed that good girls did not stay in boy's bedrooms with the door closed, so I opened it again.

After a couple of songs, Nathan lifted the phonograph needle. He explained that he wanted to show me what he was good at. I was nervous but curious. Then he took a clarinet out of its case and started to play. I thought he was good, very good. I was also glad that was all he wanted to show me. After Nathan had finished playing, we both agreed that we had homework to do and I walked the rest of the way to the subway to take the train home. The ride went by in a dreamy blur.

The timing didn't work out for Nathan to pick me up for our date. We agreed to meet near where both of our trains had stops, at the corner of Fifty-ninth Street and Avenue of the Americas. I got there first. I stood in a crowd of people, hardly seeing any of them, just looking for Nathan. Finally, I heard his voice behind me saying, "Hey Lady!"

No one had ever called me 'Lady' before, and I loved it. After that, it became my favorite thing to be called. Nathan and I walked the rest of the way to Steinway Hall, where the society would be meeting. Nathan was obviously a favorite of the mostly older members, and they smiled when he introduced me to them. Nathan had never brought a date to a meeting before. I felt special and welcome.

The meeting had lots of singing, mostly from guest performers from a light opera company. Sometimes, the audience was also allowed to sing along. Since I memorized the music to impress Nathan, I loved singing Gilbert and Sullivan with him.

After the meeting, Nathan and I went to get a snack with a group of the younger members. One of the things we talked about was picking colleges. Nathan had no doubts in his mind. His older brother Matt had gone to Cornell, majoring in biology. Nathan loved his brother, and he planned to go to Cornell too. I hadn't thought that much about college yet, but I had been thinking about a writing program at a small school outside Chicago. Nathan smiled and joked about switching schools and going there too. That made me feel all warm and floaty.

Our group sang all the way to the subway station, and Nathan and I sang a duet, even after we were inside. He took me home on the train and to the door of my apartment. I could tell that he was going to kiss me. I had to stand on tiptoe for my lips to touch his and I did. It was nothing like kissing Les. I loved kissing Nathan. After he left, I slid down the inside of the door, as I'd seen girls do on TV, after a goodnight kiss. If I'd thought I was in love before, I was sure of it then.

After that, every move I made was to see Nathan. Now when I looked at him across the room, he sometimes looked back. Our short walks after class were the best part of my day. The halls glowed when he was in them.

Besides the clarinet and saxophone, Nathan played an ocarina. He brought it to school and sometimes played while he walked through the halls, taking long steps that matched the music. The sound of it called to me. Whenever I heard the music, I'd follow it, even if it took me out of my way to class. Whenever I was alone, I could close my eyes, see Nathan, and hear his music. He was always in my head.

Chapter Six

The world back then was a mess. The Vietnam War was on, and students were protesting in the streets. African-Americans were still fighting for their rights, too. On April fourth, Martin Luther King Jr. was shot. His death made me very sad. One good thing that Mother had done, was serving as a freedom rider with Dr. King. She taught Rachel and me about racial equality --- even though she still thought she was smarter than everyone else. It turned out not to matter. I came home from school the way I always did, the day after the assassination. My apartment building had a front door that had to be unlocked either by pressing a buzzer from upstairs or by the key of someone who lived there. I was using my key when two African-American boys came up behind me. One held a club, and the other put a knife to my throat. I couldn't believe what was happening. It was as if I was outside my body and watching a TV show. One of the boys told me to keep unlocking the door and go inside.

I always stopped to get the mail out of the locked boxes in front of the elevator, on the way to my apartment. With my mind running on automatic, I asked if I could do that. With another tenant coming down the steps toward us, the boys told me to go ahead. The other tenant hardly even looked at us. Maybe he didn't see the knife. Perhaps he didn't want to see it, but he kept on going. After that, there was no one there but the boys and me.

The boy with the knife lowered it and began kissing me. It didn't feel like a kiss, just someone pressing on my mouth. I didn't do anything back, and he told me to open my mouth and tried to kiss me again. Then he said, "What we're going to do now …," and started lifting the hem of my dress. I remember it was one I liked, pink with a paisley print.

When he went under my dress, I was pretty sure what he wanted to do. I couldn't let him. It was still like I was watching from somewhere else. I remembered a self-defense demonstration I saw during a Mensa picnic at the beach. I ran through the instructions in my mind: a kick to the shins; slide your foot down the leg and stomp on the instep; raise your knee to the groin. And I was supposed to scream as loud as I could. I followed the list. The boy with the knife, the one who had kissed me, doubled over as I screamed loud enough to be heard a long way away. The boy with knife yelled, "Let's go!" and limped away with the other boy. I didn't know what else to do, so I went upstairs and called Mother at work. She wasn't at her desk, but the department secretary, Alix, could hear my voice shaking and went to get her. Mother didn't like having her work interrupted and wanted to know why I was calling and bothering her.

I was crying by then. I asked her to call the police or something and told her what happened.

She said she'd call Sam and see what he thought.

After hanging up with Mother, I made myself a cup of tea, almost spilling the hot water. I don't know how long it took, but the police came to hear my story. When they asked me if I could describe the boys, I couldn't. I've never been good with faces. I don't remember them the way other people do. Unless I've known someone for a long time, I always have to focus on something special about them. Like weird hair or a mark on the cheek to recognize them, especially if they aren't where I expect them to be. I can draw a person's face fine, but I have to be looking at it, or a picture of it. With the boys, I couldn't remember their faces at all. The police were nice, anyway. They wrote down what I could tell them, and left the apartment.

I was angry, but not at the boys who attacked me. I understood how mad they must have been about what happened to Dr. King. I could see why they might want to take it out on someone, even if it was someone like me who believed that everyone should have the same rights. They didn't know that. I was mad at Mother because the first thing she wanted to do was call Sam. I stayed mad. Mother came home at her usual time. I did what I always did; I made dinner and did my homework until it was time to go to bed. I don't remember if I slept.

Not knowing what else to do, I went to school the next day. My friends noticed that I was quiet, quieter than usual, and wanted to know what was wrong. I only told the story at the lunch table. The boys there laughed and teased me about taking down muggers. I didn't think it was funny. Anyone could see the scratches on my neck from the knife, but I didn't say anything to any more boys, not even Nathan, just girls. The girls took me more seriously, especially

Anita. She offered to take the subway home with me after school and walk me home. I was grateful and agreed. When we were walking to the apartment building, I noticed a police car sitting across the street. I thought I'd be safe with them there. I knew that Anita had at least as big a stack of work to do as I did, and she wasn't as quick at getting through hers. I waved at the police and sent Anita home. Still, I was breathing hard by the time I was behind the door and made sure the safety lock of the apartment was working.

I worked out a way to deal with what happened, the way I always did with things that scared me, I used a character. The one I used on *Star Trek* wouldn't work. I'd never had Talinda fight. Talinda was a healer, the doctor I would never be. My new character, Illyanina, was based on an old TV spy show I'd liked. That show was one of the first things I wrote a long story about. Illyanina wore a black turtleneck and black pants and had a knife in her boot. In the days after the attack, those were the clothes I put on as soon as I came home from school. I had a real knife, too. It was one Mother used on Mensa hikes. I put on the outfit almost every day, except for the ones when I wanted to wear a Talinda gown. I even made up a song to go with my new character. Being Illyanina made me feel safer.

Most months I kept on going to the Gilbert and Sullivan Society with Nathan. Besides walking with me in school, when the weather got warmer he sometimes bought me something from the Good Humor truck that parked outside the school building. He never asked to see me on weekends or holidays. I felt closer to him on those days by playing the Gilbert and Sullivan records Mother owned, and singing along.

I did see the Mensa boys on weekends. I was usually with two boys; Stephen, who was a year older than me, but three years ahead in school and already in college, and Harris. We were the elected officers of Young Mensa. We held meetings in Central Park, which was only a few blocks from Mother's apartment. Sometimes we just hung around inside. Elliott, from my biology class, sometimes joined our group. I liked going places with the Mensa boys. Sam got nasty about that and told me that I'd know I'd grown up when I preferred one boy to three. I would have, if the one boy were Nathan, but he wasn't around.

With summer coming, Mother thought I should go to camp. She didn't want me to go to just any camp, but a Zionist youth camp where she thought I might learn more self-defense skills. It scared me that Mother thought I might need them. It was months since Dr. King had been killed. I wondered if Mother was trying to get rid of Illyanina, or just get me out of the apartment so she could be alone with Sam. But Mother's idea worked with Jeanie still being into everything Jewish, so I agreed. Whatever I could tell Jeanie when I came back, would make her happy. It might even give us something else to play games about.

The first part of camp was on a farm in New Jersey. It was supposed to be the only kibbutz in the United States. Almost everyone there knew each other. They were part of a youth group during the school year. That left me on the outside of a couple of big cliques. One of the rules was that we had to turn in whatever money and treats we had, to be shared by everyone. I didn't expect that, but I followed instructions. After a week, I found out that although sharing was supposed to be equal, like in the book *Animal Farm*, which I'd read in ninth grade, some people were more equal than others. The cliques ruled and gave out little bits of things to newcomers.

I made friends with some of the other new girls. I also had some things I could do for the group. There were certain hours when we were supposed to do work like weeding the corn field and cleaning the chicken house, which the counselors taught us we were supposed to be glad to do. There was also singing, dancing, and drama. I brought my guitar and was able to join in the singing. I also auditioned for and won a good role in a drama production. The casting was done by counselors, not clique members. I also learned the dances. Even the clique members liked my singing and acting. Almost everything we had to do was called by its Hebrew name, and soon there was almost as much Hebrew coming out of my mouth as English.

When my age group was finished with our time on the farm, we went to the main camp. There was still a strict schedule, but it wasn't as hard as working on the farm. Mother had been wrong about self-defense classes. There weren't any. The training they gave us was like an introduction to the Israeli army. We learned how to vault walls. We used ropes to go over the tops of the trees and made tents out of ponchos and stones.

I was also able to keep going with drama, singing, and dancing. I was cast in several productions, including a musical. In one of the plays, I was a soldier who gave a long monologue about being stitched by a machine gun through the middle, to a barbed wire fence. The blue military jacket I'd bought when I was staying with Nahum's family became part of my costume, with smears of red paint across it. The counselors promised me that the paint would wash out, but it didn't. I was very upset about that, but they acted as if it was nothing.

I joined the choir at camp too. It was a serious group that met for at least an hour every night, singing songs mostly in Hebrew. I was told that the choirmaster, Yankele, was a popular composer in Israel. He was fun to work with. We all worked hard, and being in the choir was my favorite thing at camp.

One night the counselors came into the cabin where I bunked with seven other girls. They told us to get up, get dressed, and get our packs ready. After that, we were assigned to groups and told to get into vans. The clique campers seemed to know, but the counselors explained to the new kids that what we were doing was a celebration of World Youth Day. It didn't seem like much of a celebration to me. Besides the clothes and sleeping bags in our packs, we were given enough food for one meal. Then we were dropped off somewhere in the Catskills. Once we got there, we had to find a place to camp for the night and a way to earn the rest of our food and make it back to camp. The leader of each group had a map.

I was scared at being dropped in a strange place in the middle of the night, but the other members of my group didn't seem to be. They saw it as a chance to prove how tough they were. After a long walk, we found a spot where we could put down our sleeping bags for the night. I wouldn't have thought I could be comfortable in a sleeping bag on solid rock, but I was so tired, I fell asleep right away.

Jeff, the leader of our group, woke me at sunrise. I was the only one who had put a poncho in my pack, and he needed it to help set up our one meal, breakfast. There were small boxes of cereal, which we ate dry, oranges, cheese, and bread with apple butter. Once our group ate, we started hiking toward what Jeff decided was the nearest resort. Most of the resorts had older Jewish people staying at them. Our plan was to put on a show; singing and dancing. We hoped that when we passed a hat, we'd get enough money for food and a bus ride back to camp.

It turned out that food wasn't a problem. At the first resort we found, the vacationers were happy to give plenty of it to a bunch of teenagers who sang in Hebrew, jumped, and kicked in folk dances. We passed a hat around too, but there wasn't much money. My group returned to the road to hike the five miles to their next resort. By the time we arrived, we were tired, and it was harder to sing our songs and dance, but we had no choice. It was worth it. We earned enough money to pay for bus fare, with even a little left over to buy candy and snacks.

The money in the organization was kept in common. It was only divvied up to purchase bus tickets, and whatever was available at the small store near the bus station. I was still in heaven. It was the first time I'd had more than a couple of bites of chocolate all summer. The one time Mother had sent me some, I was pressured to give it to the treasurer, who was part of the main clique. Out of the whole package, I got one small piece. There was a catch this time too. Since the money had been divided, I could eat whatever I had coming to me, but once we made it back to camp, I would have to give up whatever was left and most likely never see any of it again. I wasn't going to let that happen. I'd worked hard for whatever I had. I ate it all before we made it back to camp.

When camp was close to ending, all the campers held a meeting to decide who would get the blue shirts that would show that someone had officially been accepted into the organization. Since I'd always felt on the outside, I was surprised that I would be getting one, but they voted for me to. I think it was because I worked so hard on singing and plays. Whatever the reason was that they let me in, I was now officially a member of the club.

After a couple of months of using so much Hebrew, I had a hard time speaking straight English again. When I went back to school, the Hebrew kept getting mixed up in my mind with French. That made French harder.

Chapter Seven

Since I was now a member of the organization, I was expected to go to meetings, which were on Friday nights in the Bronx. That was a real problem for me because the TV network had switched *Star Trek* to Friday nights. It was one of the worst things that could have happened. My friendship with Jeanie had been built around *Star Trek*. A lot of my writing came from the show. Even Craydon was connected to the *Star Trek* universe. Jeanie was so excited about my new shirt and everything I'd done over the summer that I wanted to stay with the group, too.

No one had video recorders back then, but there were audio tapes. I'm not sure why, but Mother agreed to record *Star Trek* on a cassette recorder that I had, to help me study. Mother and Sam talked while she was recording, and I could hear their voices on the tape. I could also hear them laughing, but the tapes were a lot better than nothing. I took the subway to the Bronx and back home on Friday nights. Sometimes I ran all the way from the subway station to catch the last five minutes of the show.

The best thing about starting my senior year of high school was being able to see Nathan again. We had both applied for AP Biology and Drama English. That turned out to be a problem. We both wanted to be in the school play, which was put on by one of the Drama English sections, but the class was scheduled against A.P. Biology lab. We had to make a choice between science and drama. Nathan and I both chose the same way and ended up in the same section of AP Biology, but different sections of Drama English. I was in the homeroom of the drama teacher, but Nathan wasn't. I wished that he was.

AP Biology was a very popular class. Even with four sections, there weren't enough seats for all the students. For the first couple of weeks, Nathan had a seat at a desk, but since I was small, I sat on the windowsill. The class was hard. We used the same textbook as the students at City College. Some kids dropped the class, leaving open chairs. I couldn't believe how lucky I was when I ended up next to Nathan. The margins of my notebook were filled with notes we wrote to each other, and I couldn't remember being happier in my life. What made it even better was that Nathan and I were lab partners too.

The labs were as crowded as the classrooms, with very little room at the tables and benches where we did the required dissections. That was fine with me. I was squeezed in close to Nathan. On what I remember as one of the best days of my entire life, I took the whole nervous system out of a frog while sitting on his lap. I was surprised that the team of teachers, both of whom all the students called "Mr. G," allowed it. I was good in that class. I removed the nervous system all in one piece, and my grades were high. That might have been why they let Nathan and me get away with lap sitting.

Outside of school, Nathan and I, with Jim, a member of a light opera company, did a play at The Gilbert and Sullivan Society. Nathan and I also learned music together. He never did anything but touch my hand sometimes, but I didn't care. I couldn't imagine loving anyone as much, let alone more. I planned my day around seeing Nathan. I lived, ate, and breathed for him. The other boys around me could never be more than friends. I thought about Nathan and me as being together forever. He didn't.

One day, everything in my world fell apart. Nathan and I were leaning over a stereomicroscope in the AP Bio lab, and he told me that he didn't want me to be his girlfriend. He was fine with being friends and lab partners, but that was all we would ever be. I could barely breathe. We were in the middle of a room full of other kids, and both "Mr. Gs" were there. I couldn't scream, I couldn't cry, I couldn't do anything. Almost no one noticed anything unusual was going on between Nathan and me. When one boy from the workstation next to us asked, both Nathan and I told him that nothing was happening. Our acting skills must have been convincing because he believed us.

I was due at a meeting of the Hebrew Culture club after class, but I couldn't face going there. I couldn't face going anywhere except home. I made it to the subway and caught a nearly empty local train. With no one to see me, the tears I had been holding back, wouldn't stop. I cried all the way home. I cried until I fell asleep from exhaustion at three the next morning. I don't even know if Mother and Sam were there that night. I don't remember anything except crying.

When I woke up, I didn't have any more tears, but I didn't know what I was doing, either. I was like a robot following my programming. In my homeroom, I drew my legs up under me. Since it was the same room the drama classes met in, it had auditorium seating. There was no desk to keep me from sitting that way. The walls seemed to waver like something out of a dream. Somehow, I managed to smile as if it would erase what had happened the day before, but inside, my heart was screaming. When a girl in one of my classes said that I looked happy, that I seemed to be a happy person, I just nodded. I was actually thinking about jumping off the roof. It was a bright and sunny day. I've always thought that if it had been dark and cloudy, I would have jumped. As it was, I couldn't see any future for me anymore, and I didn't care.

There was no way I could avoid Nathan. He still sat next to me in class. He also asked me why I looked happy. He seemed upset that I could look that way after he'd broken up with me. When I told him that I had to do something to dry out the upholstery, he laughed. He couldn't believe that I had soaked the living room couch with my tears.

The school year went on, and I did the best I could to get through it. I had to work extra hard in French class because of Hebrew messing me up whenever I tried to think in anything but English. My escapes to the world of Craydon came more and more often. I created a language for the planet, complete with its own alphabet and grammar. I made a calendar with Craydonian holidays, which I celebrated. I started to pray more to Partentheles, the god of Craydon. I didn't expect any help from him; it was just that the God I had prayed to for most of my life seemed to have deserted me.

I spent a lot of time with the Mensa boys. None of them were happy either. All of them wanted some girl they couldn't have. I began dating Stephen. I thought the fact that he was a junior in college, even if he was only a year older than me, was kind of a status symbol. He took me to the school play put on by the drama section that was mostly kids from my homeroom. Nathan was there too, and when he walked down the aisle with another girl from our biology class, I couldn't keep my eyes off him. Stephen noticed. He was upset and asked me how much he was being used. I knew that Stephen had started dating me because a girl named Michelle, who was in my French class, had told him she didn't want to be his girlfriend. I convinced myself that we were both doing the same thing, so I told him that I wasn't using him. It was a lie, but I didn't think of it that way, then. During intermission, Stephen offered me his class ring, but even if he would have rather been with Michelle, I knew I still loved Nathan, so I didn't take it. My lie couldn't go that far.

Even if I wouldn't take his ring, around the other Mensa boys, Stephen acted like he owned me. I liked the attention, but I didn't want to be tied to him that way. I was the second-choice date for four different boys. Stephen wanted Michelle, but couldn't have her. For Les, it was first Claudia, then Andrea, For Harris it was Georgia, and for Elliott, it was Lauren. Lauren, along with a girl named Sue, were new in Young Mensa and not part of the leadership yet. We all kept each other company, but no one was very content. Les had joined our group when he became best friends with Elliott after they had been assigned seats next to each other in physics class. I was in another section of the class, which met a period earlier. They found out that they were both friends with me when I forgot a book in the room. I came back to get it, and they both said hello to me at the same time. They looked at each other and said, "You know Sarah?" Once they knew, they coordinated their schedules, sometimes both dating me in the same week.

Choosing what college to go to for my friends and me got serious. Except for Jeanie, who still had another year of high school. Like most of the kids at Science, I'd scored high enough on an exam to win a Regents scholarship. At the time, students could go to the city colleges in New York, without paying tuition. If I lived with Mother and Sam, my scholarship would have covered books and fees, and I could have gone to school debt free. Then something happened to make that impossible for me.

Although Sam being around and touching me gave me the creeps, I'd learned to put up with it. I stayed away from him as much as I could, and when I wasn't writing or doing my homework, I tried to keep myself busy with other things. One of the things I did was paint. I knew I wasn't an artist like Rachel, but painting was fun anyway. A store in the neighborhood sold acrylic paints, but they were expensive, and I usually couldn't afford them. Watercolors were cheap, so I used them instead. I usually painted in the living room where there was more space than in my tiny bedroom. I had finished a painting of the jungle on Craydon and left my paintbrush in a cup of water on an end table near the couch, while I sat there to write a story to go with the painting. I'd stopped wearing my Illyanina outfit after my summer at camp. I was wearing my school clothes, but not my boots. I didn't have a knife.

Sam came in wearing boxer shorts and stood near me. He smelled like scotch. I tried to ignore him, but then he was on top of me, trapping me in the corner of the couch. His hands were pulling at my panties. I screamed for him to get off me, but he didn't. He was almost a foot taller than me and weighed at least twice as much. He just pushed me further into the couch. I had to get him off me. I reached for the only weapon I could, my thin wooden paintbrush. I jammed the pointed handle into his thigh, and he yelled loud and backed away.

Mother was just getting home from work. She ran into the room and started yelling, asking what happened. I tried to tell her. Then Sam took her aside and told her his side of the story.

I expected Mother to call the police, or at least throw Sam out of the apartment for what he did. It didn't happen. She bandaged Sam's leg and screamed at me for coming on to him. She told me that Sam said I had been giving out all the signals that I wanted him to have sex with me.

I was confused. I couldn't imagine that being true. The last thing I wanted was Sam anywhere near me. I hated how he looked, all fat, and I couldn't stand the smell of sweat, scotch, and cigarettes. But Mother believed him instead of me. Sam would be staying. I couldn't stand the thought of being there with him and Mother anymore. That meant that getting a free ride at City College would be impossible for me. I didn't want to be anywhere near the city.

I felt like I needed to grow eyes in the back of my head. I could never relax. I was always afraid that Sam would find another opening to come after me. I hadn't told anyone at Science except for Les and Elliott, what Sam had done. I was afraid that no one would believe me. Les and Elliott joked about me being deadly, first because of what happened with the boys after Dr. King was killed, and then stabbing Sam, but they stayed around Mother's apartment much more, even when no date or meeting was planned. While they were there, Sam stayed away from me, and I could breathe. I hated to think of managing without them, but Elliott would be going to MIT and Les to a political science program in Michigan. No matter where I decided to go, our little group would still be together at most school breaks and during the summer. I still dreamed of getting back together with Nathan somehow, but that was impossible. Nathan's brother had studied biology at Cornell and Nathan had decided to be like his brother and go there too.

I still liked the idea of going to Illinois for the writing program, but Mother didn't. She had seen a feature on *Sixty Minutes* about Barnum, a little school in Ohio, whose president was very good at raising money. I'd never heard of the place, but to keep Mother from nagging me about it, I applied. It was out of state, which meant I couldn't use my Regents scholarship, but I could qualify for a different one. With student loans, I could manage to go. The good part was that it was far enough away so I wouldn't be home except on school breaks.

The workers at the post office went on strike and acceptance letters from colleges were not going out, but I got a phone call from the admissions office at Barnum. They told me that they wanted to make sure I knew I had been accepted. They said they would be proud to have a student of my caliber and that the school would do everything they could to make it possible for me to come. I accepted their offer.

The economy of the country was very bad. Even my babysitting had tapered off. I'd been earning money during the school year by tutoring, but that would end when summer came. Despite its promises, the scholarship and loans from Barnum wouldn't cover everything. I needed to find a summer job. It wasn't easy. I applied for one selling books door to door. It was commission only and meant I'd be walking through the streets of New York all day, but it was a job. It also meant I'd be away from Mother's apartment. They gave me a script to learn. I and the other girls I worked with were fielded to different neighborhoods every day, usually where the people were middle or upper middle class. I found that for me, selling books to richer people was impossible. I walked around, climbing stairs to cold-water flats, where the parents had almost no money, but were anxious to spend what they had on their kids. My supervisor decided that I had found my niche, and sent me out to the poorest neighborhoods. I liked the people there, and they liked me enough to buy what I was selling. By the end of the summer, I had a good tan and some cash to take to Barnum with me.

I was looking forward to getting away from Sam and from doing all the housekeeping for Mother, but not to leaving my friends and my responsibilities in Young Mensa. I hated to say goodbye to Jeanie who had another year to go before she would graduate from high school. The thought of never seeing Nathan again, even if it was just at school, still hurt too.

I was worried about Stephen. He would be staying in the city. Though he was the smartest of the Mensa boys, he was also the most easily hurt. Though he knew I didn't feel the same, and in spite of wishing he was with Michelle, he convinced himself he was in love with me. Because of Nathan, I knew how that felt. I asked Sue to take my position in the group and take care of Stephen. She liked him, so she said okay. We all agreed that we'd stay friends. We'd write letters, and we would meet up for holiday breaks and in the summer. I hoped we could all keep our promises.

Chapter Eight

I arrived at Barnum two weeks ahead of the start of the regular school year, for Freshman Institute. More than an orientation, it was an evaluation of our skills before classes were chosen. Small groups of students were assigned to professors who would get to know them personally. I was assigned to a theology professor, Mr. Tate. All of the students had been told to address professors as Mr. or Miss, rather than professor or doctor, the theory being that it would be less intimidating to continue the form of address we had used in high school. I didn't care one way or another. It wasn't professors I found intimidating, it was the other students.

Somehow, they all seemed to know how to make friends right away, something I couldn't manage. Most of them had none of the geekiness I was used to and comfortable with from my friends at Science and in Young Mensa. Some of the boys started right away to ask girls out on dates, but none of them asked me. All I had to get me through my first days at college was being a good student.

That helped. One of the things that Freshman Institute was designed to reveal was writing skills, or the lack of them. Students who were not up to par would be directed to remedial instruction before taking regular classes. Three papers and a short story were assigned to us within the space of a week. My papers all earned "A's," and my short story was read to the group as an example of excellent descriptive writing, like in junior high school. That earned me points with Mr. Tate, our professor, but none with the other kids in my group.

The next thing we had to do was make a short movie. Because of my experience with writing and drama, I co-wrote the script, acted in, and directed the movie. That got me into trouble. While we were writing, Kristie my writing partner, and I lost track of time. That hardly ever happened to me. I have a clock built into my brain. When we looked up it was past eleven. We were locked out. Kristie and I sat on the curb across from the dorms, trying to figure out what to do. She decided to stay with a boy she'd gotten to know. That was just what the rules for girls were supposed to prevent, but she believed that doing it would be the best thing for her.

I didn't have that choice. I decided to go bang on the front door of my dorm and explain what happened. My housemother was sympathetic. She couldn't promise that I would get no penalty, but she told me that she would talk to Mr. Tate, and if my story about writing the movie were true, I would probably be let off on my first offense.

The theme of the movie that Kristie and I wrote was loneliness, something I had no trouble understanding. Other than needing to reshoot because the protagonist had worn two different pairs of pants during what was supposed to be the same scene, filming of the movie went pretty well. The students who saw it understood what we were trying to say. I liked the way the movie came out, but not everything else that was happening at Barnum.

Kathy, the other girl, assigned to my room, wanted to be a theater major. She came from a city not far from Barnum and started the school year with friends she'd had in high school. We didn't fight, but we weren't friends either. Kathy had her own circle and I wasn't part of it. Because I was into science, Kathy was surprised that I was interested in drama, but she mentioned that auditions for plays were open to all students. She told me she'd let me know when she would be going to them because I wanted to try out too. The worst thing that could happen would be that I wouldn't get a role, and doing theater would be a way to be part of something I knew how to do.

My first audition didn't go well. I had to kiss someone I'd never met before, and I had a hard time doing it. I almost couldn't do it at all. I didn't even make callbacks. I told myself that I had more than enough to do without being in the play, anyway.

One good thing happened. I finally managed to make one friend, Alyne. We had a class together, a small colloquium on evolution. I wasn't sure why Alyne was in it. She didn't want to major in biology. In fact, Alyne had no idea what she wanted her major to be. She was an artist, and like me, she collected comic books. Alyne was into Marvel, while I was still sticking with DC. As Alyne shared her back issues, I began to have more appreciation for the character flaws integrated into the Marvel stories. Alyne was also a Trekkie. She didn't write stories like I did, but she appreciated Craydon. When I celebrated the holidays on the Craydonian calendar, Alyne was happy to celebrate them with me.

Alyne wasn't healthy. She'd been an insulin dependent diabetic since the age of eleven and had spent a lot of time in the hospital. She knew a lot about depression and teenagers who were depressed. Alyne realized something wasn't right for me at home, even if she didn't know what. Having problems was something that brought us together.

Part of Barnum's mandatory curriculum, in addition to Freshman Institute and the colloquia, was a course for all the freshmen, called Century. It was a mishmash of subjects, with a lot of the faculty from different departments coming in to teach. One of the requirements was to keep a journal, something that was easy for me. I kept two, one for Century, and one for myself.

Alyne encouraged me to go to another audition. That play, Tartuffe, by Moliere, was directed by a different professor than the first one was. He insisted on being called Keith, instead of a Mr. anything. The audition went very differently from the first one. I was sitting in the back of the auditorium and heard Keith talking to someone else from the drama department about a scene for a character named Doreen. I wanted that part. So did almost every other girl at the audition. I heard Keith say that he wanted the scene to be almost balletic.

I ran back to my dorm room and got the ballet slippers I'd used when I'd practiced dancing with Jeanie. When I auditioned, I slowed down my movements, so they looked more graceful. The positions of my arms and fingers were what they would have been if I was dancing a ballet. When I bowed, my head almost touched my knee. Keith liked what I did, and I made callbacks.

Going to callbacks was complicated. I had a biology exam the next morning, a problem that the theater majors didn't have. I went anyway, taking my books with me and sitting in the auditorium with them all around me. I studied the best I could, while the other actors were on stage. The auditions went late, and it was almost time for lockdown. The senior girls were allowed to have keys to the dorm and Pat, who had the dorm room next to mine and was trying out for a different role, agreed to let me in if I cleared it with the housemother. I was nervous, but I called the dorm from the theater. It turned out my housemother had done auditions herself when she was a student, and she said I could stay and finish.

Both Pat and I were cast. I got the role of Doreen and Pat got the role she'd wanted, Elmire. Tartuffe would be played by Howard Carson; a junior who everyone thought was the second-best actor in the school. Another role would be played by a boy known as Thibault. Howard was very sweet, and Pat had a crush on him right away. I might have had one too, but I knew I owed Pat, so I tried to have one Thibault instead.

I used my Century journal to write about current events, and how I perceived them. I used my second one as a diary, and I put thing in it that I wouldn't share with anyone. One of those things was being touched. Since Sam did what he did to me, I didn't touch other people, and they didn't touch me. That was one of the reasons

I had so much trouble with my first audition. Sometimes I missed being able to touch someone. One day I wrote in my personal journal that I had touched Thibault and liked it. I made a mistake. I left both of my journals on my desk. There was no place in my dorm room to lock anything up, but I should have put my diary in a drawer or something. A few days after I wrote about touching Thibault, I came back to the room, with Alyne, and found Kathy reading it. Kathy looked up and said, "This isn't your Century journal, is it?"

I could only say, "No it isn't." My voice came out in a croak.

Kathy put my diary down and left the room in a hurry. I lay on my bed with my knees drawn up to my chest and hugged my pillow. It didn't help. I didn't even cry. I felt as if someone had taken all my clothes and left me paralyzed. Alyne sat on the edge of the bed, not sure what had happened, just knowing that I was very upset. A half hour went by. "Sarah," Alyne whispered, "I have a class, but I don't want to leave you like this."

I appreciated Alyne's sympathy, but I didn't want to get her in trouble. There was no way she could help me. What Kathy did couldn't be fixed. I told Alyne to go to class, and I lay there, through the afternoon and dinner. Finally, I did what I'd done before when I needed to hide from something. I became a character. I went to rehearsal for Tartuffe as Doreen.

From that day, I spent as much time inside the character of Doreen as I could. If anyone asked me why, I explained that I was just using what I had been taught about method acting in high school. I tried to believe that myself. In truth, I was more comfortable wearing my character's skin than my own. Alyne was not fooled, but she played along. A lot of the time, she called me Doreen.

Being Doreen was not without its problems either. The biggest one was the hard time I had doing anything with a boy, even when I wanted to. The script called for Doreen to have large breasts, which provided a temptation to Tartuffe. I was barely an "A" cup and wasn't getting any bigger. The costume mistress decided I needed a special bra called a push-up. I'd never heard of one before. Even with it, I'd still need padding and makeup to look busty. I was okay with the bra, especially since another girl took me to get it. The padding was okay too. The makeup scared me since it was supposed to be done by John McDonald. He was also the best actor in the school. Finally, everyone could see what a hard time I was having with that; John's girlfriend Jane took over. She drew on my chest and made it look like I had what I didn't.

I'd always had an easy time memorizing things. The iambic pentameter of the lines of the play just flowed into my brain. By the time the deadline was reached for all of the actors to go off book, I not only knew my own lines, but everyone one else's too. I thought I was being helpful when I supplied them to the other actors when they forgot them, but some of them got mad at me. So did the stage manager.

When the play opened, the audience seemed to like me a lot, and I got a good review in the school paper. For a week afterward, wherever I went on campus, other students approached me and complimented me on my performance. Having people say they liked me was wonderful. I was a science major, but being in the theater made me happy. The play stopped running a little before classes ended.

The schedule at Burnam was not typical for colleges back then. There was a break lasting from just before Thanksgiving through New Years. I would have rather stayed on campus, away from Sam and Mother, but it was not allowed. I had to go back to New York.

I immediately had to take over the cooking again, including Thanksgiving dinner. I enjoyed making it. I didn't enjoy the people at the table. Sam was there, and he had invited his sister Irene. I had made roasted chestnuts. Grandma Levi had never made them, so I followed the instructions in a cookbook. I did exactly what the recipe said. My turkey was beautiful, and everyone liked it. They loved my stuffing and the vegetables too, but Irene spent the entire meal complaining that the chestnuts were underdone. They seemed fine to me, tender and sweet. However, they were missing the charring on the shells you see when you buy them from a street vendor. I wasn't sure if Irene was right or not. If having to feed Sam hadn't been enough, Irene completely ruined my day. To make matters worse, Mother's guests all wanted to spend the rest of the day watching football. I didn't like watching football on TV, so while they were in front of the set in the living room, I was in the kitchen cleaning up. After I had finished, I went to my room to write about Craydon.

When it was closer to Christmas, my Mensa friends, who had gone off to other schools, came back to New York. So did Nathan. I desperately wanted to see him. We'd written a few letters to each other. Nathan just wrote them like a friend. I wrote them hoping that I could somehow get close to him again. We had been telling each other about what we were doing in the theater. I told him about Tartuffe and he told me about working with the Savoyards, the Gilbert and Sullivan group at Cornell. With every bit of courage I had, I called him and asked him if he wanted to come over and talk more about what we'd done on the stage. I was surprised that he said yes. He was free for three hours on December twenty-fourth. Since we both came from Jewish families, the fact that it was Christmas Eve was not a big deal to either one of us. We agreed that Nathan would arrive at two in the afternoon and stay until five. I scrubbed, polished, and vacuumed the entire apartment, hiding Mother's collection of junk as well as I could. I put together a tray of hors d'oeuves, Ritz crackers with cream cheese, and wore the best dress I had. My hair had grown below my waist, and I made sure there wasn't a knot or tangle in it.

Nathan didn't show up at two. At three, I began to cry. When it was almost four, Nathan called, saying he had been standing in line for tickets to something, but if I still wanted him to, he could come for a little while. I wanted him to come. He showed up at four and said something about how much trouble I went to with the hors d'oeuvres, which he didn't eat. While I wanted him there more than anything else in the world, I was embarrassed. After crying for an hour, my face was swollen, and my eyes were red. It was nothing like the way I'd dreamed his visit would be.

We talked about acting. I told Nathan all about Tartuffe, saying my lines and acting them out. He didn't say much about what he did, but he told me about another actor who he thought was great. He imitated him, doing a funny voice, and bending his knees as I'd seen light opera actors do at the Gilbert and Sullivan Society. The time went too fast for me, even though to make up for being late, Nathan gave me an extra fifteen minutes. At five fifteen he was gone, and I felt drained and deserted.

I was glad to go back to Barnum. I was looking forward to my next biology class, which was more advanced. I was also looking forward to being in a new play. Neither of those things happened. After trying out for a role in *A Funny Thing Happened on the Way to the Forum,* I didn't even make callbacks. The girls chosen were beautiful, or at least pretty, and I wasn't. I joined the costume crew, which at least gave me a chance to be at the theater. In fact, I was there for more hours than I had been as an actor, coming in before the rehearsals and the play, to prepare the costumes, and staying behind afterward, to repair them.

The first biology class I had taken had been an introductory one. Though I'd received full college credit for the AP Bio class I'd taken at Science, it had been focused on molecular biology. My advisor, Dr. Barns, who'd also taught my colloquium, was interested more in what he called organismal biology and made me take the introductory course in that. Even with my time in the theater, I'd earned an easy "A." My next course, invertebrate biology, would also be with him. It involved the capture and dissection of a number of specimens. To me, that sounded interesting. It wasn't as great as I thought it would be. One of the first things that I discovered was the equipment at Barnum was not as good as what I'd used at Science. The lenses on the microscopes weren't as powerful. At Science, I'd used oil immersion scopes for strong magnification, and there were none at Barnum. There were no stereo microscopes either. The scalpels were more like Exacto knives. I ended up using a dissection kit I'd brought from home. My partner was another girl, so I wasn't interested in sitting on her lap. There was no reason to look forward to being in class.

I was also having trouble with calculus. I liked the professor, Mr. Concord, who was mostly a computer science expert. He was handsome and fun. He seemed to like me too, but the way he taught didn't work for me. I had been used to detailed instructions and explanations in math, and Mr. Concord didn't give me any. He wrote the symbols on the board and expected me to understand them. I didn't. I didn't even understand what calculus was about. It just seemed like a secret language that I would have to learn because I couldn't take upper-level science courses without it. I was very used to working hard at school assignments, but I wasn't used to not getting them right. I put in hours on problems that Mr.

Concord said should have taken a few minutes and didn't always make it all the way through my exams.

The one good thing that was going on was that I was getting to know more people who were interested in the same kinds of geeky stuff that I was. There was one boy, Tim, who was part of a group that played bridge with Liz. She was a sophomore girl on my floor in the dorm. He wore a cape, a leather pouch with jingling bells on his belt, and boots that seemed too large for anyone's feet. He reminded me of a character from Lord of the Rings. When he joined Liz and me in the dining hall one day, I discovered that Tim shared my love of science fiction and fantasy. Gazing at Tim, I felt like I had when I was staring across the room at Nathan.

I had played many card games. I'd liked the hours of poker using buttons for chips that I'd played with Arlene, most of all. I'd never tried bridge because Sam liked playing it. He went to a gaming parlor in our neighborhood in New York, to be in tournaments. I'd wanted nothing to do with anything that would give him an excuse to be close to me, so I stayed away from it. I decided to learn, to be close to Tim. Liz was always trying to get new players, so she lent me a book by Edmund Hoyle. It was long and complicated, teaching about counting points and cards. I'd never done that before, but I did my best to memorize Hoyle's instructions. Tim needed a player to make four, so he invited me to be his partner in a game at the student union.

When we started, Tim thought I was bidding too high, but we won the hand, and we won the game. From then on, I was part of Tim's group, playing bridge and hearts. It helped to be able to count cards, for both, but for bridge I needed the most points, and for hearts, I needed the least. Sometimes, after cards were dealt, our foursome would vote on whether to play bridge or hearts. I liked those times a lot, and I liked Tim more, too. He also seemed to like talking to me, about Tolkien and *Star Trek*. Like Alyne and me, he was also a comic book collector.

Unfortunately for me, Tim had a girlfriend. Her name was Thelma. I didn't like her, but I would have liked to take her place, at least in some ways. I was sure she and Tim were having sex. I didn't know if I could do that, even if I had the chance. Falling for Tim was kind of like falling for a celebrity. Being with him was a wish I had almost no chance of getting, no matter how much I dreamed. There was more than that keeping me from liking Thelma. She was a math major, but couldn't explain anything to me when I asked for help with my calculus. Something about her just didn't seem right. I just couldn't figure out what. During bridge games, meals, and just talking, I spent as much time as I could with Tim. What time I could get, was like a gift to me.

A Funny Thing Happened on the Way to the Forum finished its run and Spring was coming. The snow and ice that had covered the Barnum campus all winter melted and students started taking walks into the woods.

Barnum was surrounded by maple trees. Years before I got there, students at the school had helped to make maple syrup. When they stopped doing it, the remnants of the syrup making operation had been left behind. There was a quarter-mile long path leading from the football field through the woods, to a falling down building known as Sugar Shack. What was left of the structure still contained the rotting wooden skeleton of a vat that had been used to boil down sap. A small, but very pretty stream, known as Sugar Creek, ran next to the remains of the shack.

The way it was coming apart, the place could have been depressing, but it wasn't. The stream sounded merry, the woods were beautiful, and there were wild flowers everywhere. I had been there with Alyne, who was looking for subjects to paint for an art class. I fell asleep by the stream, with a hat from the military surplus store, over my eyes, and Alyne sketched me. That sketch became a painting. Most people who saw it thought it was a fallen soldier, and that it was beautiful but sad. No one knew it was me, and I was not about to tell them. Neither was Alyne.

Liz was an art major like Alyne. She and I also walked to Sugar Camp. She was looking for things to shoot for her photography class. Thelma was visiting her parents that weekend, so Tim came with us. Both Tim and I still liked climbing trees, something I'd loved to do in the yard of Grandpa and Grandma Levi's old house, and when I was running around the neighborhood with Arlene. While Liz was wandering around, Tim and I climbed. I had no trouble because I was wearing sneakers, but in his huge boots, Tim did. He fell out of the tree and cut his head.

I'd left my favorite military jacket, the one that still had paint on it from playing a wounded soldier, at the base of the tree. Tim grabbed it to stop bleeding, which he was doing a lot. I didn't mind that he was using my jacket. I would be keeping a part of Tim. I was sure that the real bloodstains wouldn't wash out any better than the painted ones had.

The dispensary at Burnam only had one doctor, who didn't work on weekends. In emergencies, a nurse was called in, but Tim didn't regard his head as an emergency and wasn't looking forward to the idea of a lecture on the dangers of tree climbing. I suggested that Tim might go back to my room with me, where I had some first aid supplies, including sting-free Bactine. The bleeding had mostly stopped. I told Tim I could clean the cut and then he could decide if he needed stitches or something. Liz urged him to go with me

Many of my stories had the same fantasy in them. I called it, "Nurse him back to health." It involved a heroine, who was a stand in for me, finding a fallen hero and taking care of him. I felt as if I was walking in a dream as I, Tim, and Liz took the path back to campus. I carefully sponged all the blood out of his hair with cotton balls. Tim didn't know it, but I kept some of them. I imagined them as holding some kind of magic. Once I'd cleared away all the blood, the cut looked small. Tim said he was fine, thanked me, and went to his own room. After he left, I still felt like I was floating. I hid the cotton balls in a back corner of a high shelf in my closet before I went to the dining hall for supper.

Tim never mentioned his accident again, and it didn't keep him from going back to Sugar Creek. The next time, he took his own pictures --- of Thelma naked. He couldn't take those kinds of pictures to a drug store to be developed, so he was going to do it himself. I liked using chemicals and equipment, and I'd helped Liz in the darkroom that belonged to the art department, so I offered to help Tim, too. I wasn't crazy about the idea of developing any kind of photographs of Thelma, but I liked the idea of a couple of hours alone in the dark with Tim. Thelma was thin and had long hair like I did. With her glasses off, she made a good model. Tim said she looked like a wood nymph and liked the photos we developed, a lot. He thanked me for my help and told me he would have liked to take pictures of me too, but I just wasn't pretty enough.

I felt like there was a fist clenching my heart. It was no news to me that I wasn't pretty, but some boys still liked me. Tim didn't even think it was worth taking my picture. He sure wasn't going to like me as a girl. I had no idea what to say, so I said nothing. It was like what happened with Nathan. I used my acting skills to keep my tears inside until I could cry alone.

I felt like I was moving through quicksand for the rest of the year. I still hung around with the bridge group, but most of the time I had little hope of getting any closer to Tim. Being around Tim did get me some attention I could have done without. Tim's roommate, usually referred to as Big Josh, because there was also a Little Josh who was part of the bridge group, was the campus radical. I had barely noticed Big Josh, or anyone else in the room when Tim was there, but he noticed me. One reason was that both Joshes were some of the few Jewish students at Barnum, besides me. I had usually liked Jewish boys better, or so I thought. Almost every boy

I'd known in New York was Jewish, so it wasn't ever an issue. It made no difference to me that Tim was Episcopalian. Since I'd come to Barnum, I thought very little about religion, except when I did my Craydon rituals.

I'd brought my guitar to school with me, mostly playing it in my room when I needed music. There was a place, not part of the music or drama departments, where students could play. It was a tiny coffee house called the Dell, in the basement of a dining hall. Some students were invited to perform, but when there was no one booked, any student could sing and play. Alyne went to the Dell because she was dating one of the boys who managed it, and she dragged me along. Big Josh was there, giving one of his usual political rants. He was talking about the oppression of labor, though I don't know if he'd ever actually done any. I couldn't picture him weeding a cornfield or shoveling out a chicken coop as I had. He was wishing for someone who knew the words and chords to a protest anthem called "Union Maid." It was a song that had been popular with my Zionist youth group. I mentioned that I knew the words and music, but didn't have my guitar with me and didn't like to play anyone else's.

That was the opening Big Josh wanted. He offered to walk me back to my room to get it. I couldn't think of a way to say no, and Alyne was too busy with her boyfriend to help. Big Josh did as he promised. He walked me back to my dorm and even carried my guitar to the Dell. The people at the Dell liked the way I sang the song and invited me back to sing again. Unfortunately, Big Josh got a crush on me. Whenever I was with Tim's group of friends, Big Josh found an excuse to be there too. I was a little bit flattered, but also annoyed. I didn't find big Josh attractive in the least, and I wished he would just go away. I spoke to him as little as possible. Since he was more interested in politics than card games or science fiction, that wasn't hard.

One improvement in my life was a new calculus class. My new professor, Mr. Merrick, had made it very clear from the first day of class exactly what he wanted and expected from his students. He even outlined what it would take to earn an "A," something I found out later, was not unusual in upper-level classes. His explanations were great, with easy to follow instructions. I was very relieved. Even though mathematics was not on the top of my list of favorite subjects, I wasn't accustomed to struggling with school work. If my love life couldn't be on the right track, at least my academic life was.

At the end of the school year, I went back to New York. Even though I missed my New York friends, I would have liked to stay at school and away from Sam. I couldn't. One of the stipulations to getting my student aid package, was that I had to earn at least several hundred dollars over the summer. That meant getting a job. That was another problem. The economy was still bad, and there weren't many summer jobs for students. Mother came up with a solution. Her publishing house needed someone to write a glossary for a junior high school textbook. I was old enough then, to write without being a ghost. As a student I worked cheap, though I still was paid more than I would have earned in most student jobs. I would be working from the apartment, something I hated to do with Sam around, but he would be away all day and many evenings too. He was not only working but also trying to earn a graduate degree in psychology. He had a bachelors, but he wasn't using it. I couldn't think of anyone worse to help people with their problems, but at least his job and his classes kept him out of the apartment and away from me.

It was long before the days of computer search engines, not that it mattered. I had no access to even the simplest computer or even a word processor. My job consisted of going through the text and finding every word in bold print. I put them on index cards with a typewriter, then typed the definitions. The cards would be alphabetized to produce a glossary. The work was both tedious and creative. There were times when I felt stuck. One of the words in bold print was "time." Who could define time? The definitions had to be simple, not the kind you'd find in a dictionary. I began to look at the job as writing mini-stories and came up with explanations that the publisher liked.

I didn't spend all my time in front of my typewriter. The Mensa boys were home for the summer too. Les was working in the neighborhood at a funeral parlor, a job his father had arranged for him. It wasn't his choice of a dream occupation, but he was glad to have any job. On his lunch hour, he would often walk the few blocks to Mother's apartment, where I would make lunch for both of us. He told me his co-workers were teasing him, saying that he was visiting me for nooners, but there was nothing romantic about the visits, and absolutely nothing sexual, just some nice time with a friend.

There were Young Mensa events, too. There were regular trips to Jones' Beach, and we spent a lot of time in Central Park. Harris had come up with a fantasy that he described to us. He wasn't into dreaming up other planets like I was, but he did invent then imaginary country of Prosnia. My entire little group became citizens.

Like the comic book Bizarro world, in Prosnia, nothing was quite the way it was supposed to be. When we rowed a boat on Central Park Lake, we were asserting the inferiority of the Prosnian Navy. For Prosnian time, Harris had rewired an electric clock to run backward. The Brosnian flag had three vertical colored stripes, but they were so close to the edge near the pole, that from a distance it looked like a white flag. It was supposed to. Brosnia was always surrendering. While it was fun to play at these things among ourselves, we decided to share the joke.

At the time, Adult Mensa held regular get-togethers at the Newsom Club downtown. The drinking age in New York had been dropped to eighteen with the justification that if someone was old enough to die fighting in Vietnam, they were old enough to drink alcohol. The Newsom club was a safe place for any Mensa member over eighteen to drink. Harris planted a notice in the monthly Mensa Newsletter that Young Mensa had arranged a visit from the

Prosnian Ambassador. My friends and I expected that to be taken as a joke, but we arranged the details.

Stephen, who spoke fluent Russian and always sounded like he had a little accent, became the Prosnian Ambassador. I was the Secretary of Social Affairs, casting against type. Les, Harris, and Elliott were Prosnian officials. A menu was planned that featured the cheapest native Prosnian dishes our group could manage. They were made as disgusting as possible to keep people from eating too much of them.

We dyed cocktail hot dogs green and called it dormant goog. The Prosnian slogan became, "Don't wake up the goog!" Goog tasted fine, but I had to close my eyes to put one in my mouth. We called orange onion dip bempf. We sprinkled white bread with different colors of food coloring to make it look moldy, and called it Natal Dough. We carefully laid all the food out on a table and identified the dishes with index cards I'd lettered using calligraphy. My friends and I were sure that once those at the gathering had a good look at the food, they'd realize that they'd been fooled. However, members who prided themselves on their high IQ's were still standing around and whispering that the ambassador should be arriving soon.

One of the bigger, more imposing, adult members, Del Lambro, had agreed to announce the playing of the Prosnian National Anthem and introduce the ambassador. Harris had intended to use a Brandenburg concerto as the anthem. I'd borrowed a reel-to-reel tape recorder from Sam to play it at the appropriate time. I should have known better. The recorder didn't work. Harris told Del to announce that the anthem had been played at thirty kilohertz, way above the range of human hearing. Stephen went before the audience and began a speech that sounded impressive but was just nonsense sentences strung together. The adults finally realized that they had been hoaxed, and most of them immediately began insisting that they had known all along. Our little group knew better. From then on, "Don't wake up the goog!" became our secret signal to each other.

Harris had even pushed Prosnia a step further. Even after the Newsom Club, Harris wrote Prosnian music, featuring choruses of "goog, goog, goog," and "bempf, bempf, bempf," sung in counterpoint in a weird rhythm of five against nine. During a late-night trip to the Staten Island Ferry, the three boys and I sang loud and clapped our hands. The ferry ride only cost a nickel, and the terminal was like a big metal cave. A group of people nearby joined us singing "Up on Cripple Creek." They were also clapping and stomping their feet. The metal walls began to ring. Usually, New Yorkers ignore almost anything, but the other people in the terminal were smiling, and some even clapped along.

That summer had seemed magical to me. Although the smell of tobacco in the apartment stuffed up my nose every night, Sam had been too busy to bother me. I felt like I'd been part of something wonderful. I'd even earned the money I needed. I went back to Barnum feeling good.

Chapter Nine

When I came back to school, the new freshmen were already there, and had been, from the start of Freshman Institute. We had new roommates, and some of us even had the ones we'd requested. My new roommate Amy and I had asked for each other. Amy's former roommate had graduated, and mine wanted to room with another member of the theater department. Amy and I got along, and Amy had a TV, which almost none of the other students did. Amy also had family not far away, who sent regular care packages. My contribution to our partnership was my expertise in writing. I could help her with papers.

We arranged the room the way we wanted it. That meant moving furniture and renting a small refrigerator for drinks and snacks. We also hung curtains I'd made, across the room, not to separate us from each other, but so the beds would not be visible from an open door. Amy had a boyfriend, and while I didn't like to think about it, I knew they were having sex.

Amy's boyfriend Craig was older than most of the students. He had started school after returning from Vietnam. He was also unusually handsome. Most of the girls on the floor considered Amy very lucky to be his choice. He played guitar, although not as well as I did. He had the chords, but not the ear to immediately match them to a song. We played together sometimes, and it worked all right. Craig also had a car and would sometimes take me to places where I needed to go.

With incoming first-year students, there were new girls on our floor, Debbie, and Melissa. Liz had met them and liked them, so when I went with Liz to the dining hall, I ate with them. I liked them too. Unlike what I'd experienced, some of the new freshmen had managed to form strong bonds in Freshman Institute. Debbie already had a boyfriend, James. He was friends with Reid, who liked Melissa. Tim had a new freshman roommate, Peter, who didn't have any more social skills than I did, but also became a member of the group. For the first time in my life, I was a member of a clique. The other members were Liz, Tim, Thelma, Reid, Melissa, Debbie, James, and Peter. Mr. Concord, he became friendly with all of us because of Tim's closeness to him.

I still would have liked to become closer to Tim, but when I wasn't in the middle of a daydream, I knew it wasn't going to happen.

Like me, Peter wrote stories. He was a Christian with very strong beliefs. His stories were often based on biblical mythology, something we enjoyed discussing with each other. Peter, Debbie, and I were also all in the same physics class. Debbie was a talented math major. She'd had calculus in high school, and so had Peter. Unlike most of the students at Barnum back then, Peter owned a calculator. I would borrow it when we did physics problems together, curling up on a brown fuzzy rug he'd brought to cover the cold linoleum floor in the room he shared with Tim.

Besides going to my classes, I kept trying out for plays. Finally, I got the role of a demon in *The Tragical History of the Life and*

Death of Dr. Faustus. It wasn't a big part. I pantomimed and grunted instead of speaking lines. The demons were also supposed to double as stagehands. Even with a small role, it was fun to be doing a play again. Rehearsals were scheduled to pick up again the week before winter break ended. The cast and crew had to return to Barnum a week early.

When I got back to New York, the first thing I did was look for a job. Gimbels was hiring for the Christmas season. Most of the applicants wanted to work anywhere but the toy department, but I actually wanted to be assigned there. I liked the candy cane striped smocks we wore, I loved the toys, and I preferred being busy. It made the day go much faster. That year, the store was also paying in cash, which made my life simpler. I didn't have to find time to go to the bank or pay a percentage of my paycheck at a check-cashing store.

I also met up again with the Young Mensa boys. There were some new relationships. Stephen was dating Sue; the girl I'd asked to take care of him. Elliott was with Sue's friend Lauren. Les didn't have a girlfriend. Harris had taken off for a year in Germany and didn't even call any of us. We had holiday parties. No one cared much about Christmas because we were all Jewish, but Lauren threw a big party on New Year's Eve. We all stayed over in sleeping bags on the basement floor of her parents' house.

I knew it would be better not to get in touch with Nathan, especially after what had happened during the Christmas break the year before. I had more than enough to keep me busy and happy.

Yet somehow, I found myself dialing his number. I loved just hearing his voice until I realized what he was telling me. He bragged that he was a stud and told me that he was having sex with a girl named Molly, who had originally been having it with his older brother but had moved on to him. With every word, I felt as if a knife had been plunged into my heart and twisted. I wouldn't have thought anything could be, but hearing what Nathan said now was worse than what I felt the day he broke up with me in the AP Bio lab. When I hung up the phone, I couldn't think. I couldn't even stand up. I sat on the floor of the kitchen, rocking and shaking, for forty-five minutes.

Mother had almost never given me advice about my love life, and when she did, it had never helped. However, I was falling apart, so I went to her. I begged her to tell me how I could forget about Nathan. I was surprised at how sympathetic she was. She explained that at one point in her life, she had fallen in love with a Christian boy, and he had fallen in love with her, but Grandpa Levi forbade the relationship. Mother did what her father had told her to do and stopped seeing the boy she loved. She told me that she'd never forgotten him and that I would never forget Nathan either. She said that I would just have to pile other things on top of the memory until it didn't hurt as much.

I had no choice. The dorms were closed when I returned to school for rehearsals, and I was put up in a house off campus with a bunch of other theater people, almost all sharing the floor at night. A couple of the people in the house were brothers, Toby, and his brother Saint John, which sounded to me like Cinjin. Cinjin had just returned from a stint in the Peace Corps and said he wanted to be a musician. He played the guitar and sang, and the theater majors in the house liked him and gathered around him while he sang and played. No one was paying attention to Toby, who also played the guitar. Toby propped himself up against a wall, playing softly but well, while everyone but me was watching his brother. I understood how left out Toby felt and decided to talk to him. I found out that he was good at a lot more than playing the guitar. He was very mechanical and handy and was one of the set builders for the play. Toby and I played together, and before the week was over, I felt like I was half of a couple. We began having make out sessions. We never got close to real sex, but I went further with him than I'd ever gone with any other boy.

Rehearsals took a lot of my time, but Toby and I still went to the Dell, where he introduced me to Dan. He was also a musician, as well as Toby's best friend. One thing I found out about Toby was that besides playing the guitar, he played the best jazz piano I'd ever heard. He was a much better performer than Cinjin. Besides playing piano at the Dell, he also played on the piano in the lounge of my dorm. Many other girls would listen with me. I didn't like having them around at all. Toby could tell I was jealous, and he didn't like it. The closer to him I wanted to get, the more he pushed me away. Walking back from the cast party after the final performance of Faustus, he told me that he wanted a relationship that would include hanging out together and plenty of making out, but he also wanted to be free to date other girls. I felt embarrassed and ashamed.

As I saw less of Toby, I found out just what other girl he wanted to see. It was someone I knew slightly because she was involved with the drama department. She had also been one of the demons in Faustus. Even if I hadn't met Betty Jean Merveaux personally, I'd heard about her. There were stories around campus that Betty Jean only had sex with her friends, but she didn't have an enemy in the world. The rumors were that Betty's roommate was the same way and that their room was where boys went when they wanted a girl to go to bed with. I had never paid much attention to that kind of gossip, or any gossip, until it involved a boy I liked. I guessed that what Betty Jean was offering was what Toby wanted, but I wasn't ready to give it to Toby myself. Eventually, I was okay with letting Toby go. I satisfied myself with concentrating on my courses, spending the rest of my time with my friends, and playing at the Dell when Toby wasn't around.

One night, there was a boy there I thought I'd never seen before, but it was hard to tell in the dim lighting. I would never be sure if my reaction was due to being on the rebound from Toby, but for some reason, Jonathan and I had some kind of thing going on between us. We ended up sitting together, and I put my hands on the table, with my fingers spread out, near his. I'd never done anything like that before. He put his fingers on the table the same way, touching mine. For the first time in my life, I had picked up a boy! We talked until the Dell closed for the night and agreed to meet in the dining hall for breakfast.

The next morning, I was trying to eat with my eyes on the door. I was afraid that I might not recognize Jonathan if he walked in. Besides the lack of light in the Dell, since I've never been good at faces, and I couldn't remember exactly what he looked like. It didn't matter. He didn't show up. I was a little bit relieved, but things with Jonathan didn't end there.

He hunted me down later, which wasn't a hard thing to do on Barnum's small campus. He apologized and said he wanted to spend time together. By that point, I'd had a good look at him in the daylight. I was sure I'd made a mistake having anything to do with him. Since I'd been the one to pick him up, I had no idea how to tell him to go away.

If I'd had been too clingy with Toby, Jonathan was even more like that with me. I found out that I was not the only one on the rebound. A girl named Nancy, who had coincidentally been dating Toby's friend Dan, had as Jonathan put it, "ripped off my virginity," before returning to Dan. Jonathan talked a lot about feeling betrayed. More than that, I found out that he had been thinking about suicide because of Nancy. It reminded me of how I felt after Nathan broke up with me.

I didn't know what to do. As the second-choice date for four Mensa boys, I'd listened to all their problems. It had been a routine. If the problems weren't too big, they would take me to dinner. If they were feeling really down, they'd add in a long movie and talk more during intermission. I kept all their secrets, from what girl they wanted, to seizures, to one's father killing himself. I never told anyone else, or even wrote any of it down. I just tried to listen and be as comforting as I could.

I tried to be comforting to Jonathan too, but he was turning me off, more than any boy ever had before. He was a heavy smoker of both tobacco and marijuana. Toby had smoked too, but nothing like Jonathan, I found out that in his case, the saying, "Kissing a smoker is like licking an ash tray," was true. If anything, it was worse. Sometimes after a make out session, I felt nauseous. Everything I did to pull away made Jonathan try to hold on tighter. He began picking me up in his arms and carrying me around the dorm. Some of the other girls found that romantic. I didn't. I just wanted him to give me some peace.

I finally lost it with him when I was working on a project with my lab partner, Pam. We had to build a small mass spectrometer, and there was a time limit. I spent every available moment in the lab. Jonathan got more and more jealous of the time I spent working on the project and even toward Pam. I could understand Jonathan wanting more time with me; I remembered that from trying for every second with Nathan. However, Jonathan's jealousy of my lab partner was ridiculous. I knew some girls were interested in other girls, but I was not one of them. Pam and I were at a critical point in putting the equipment together when Jonathan walked into the lab and carried me out.

I was furious. I made Jonathan put me down and told him that I wanted nothing more to do with him. Jonathan wouldn't accept my decision. He came by the dorm to see me and asked a girl who knew both of us, to speak for him. However, there was no way I could accept what he did. I did everything I could to avoid him, until the end of the school year.

While I was busy keeping as far away from Jonathan as I could, something hit me hard, too. Tim proposed to Thelma. I knew Tim wasn't interested in me. He had made his opinion of my looks way too clear. Nevertheless, I still had fantasies about him sometimes. After Tim put his ring on Thelma's finger, I never had a fantasy about him again. He'd made her a promise, and I would not even think about interfering with it. That was when Peter started to attract my attention. He had always been there as Tim's roommate, and I had always enjoyed doing schoolwork with him, but suddenly things were different.

To give Tim and Thelma some privacy, Peter had a habit of spending his evenings in Denny Center, the building that held the student union, a dining hall, and some common areas where students could get together and talk. It also had a piano, which Peter played sometimes. I began meeting him there at nine o'clock every night. We talked, and sometimes just spent the time not saying anything. Slowly I knew I was falling in love with Peter. It was different than it had been with Nathan, but my feelings were more intense than they had been for anyone since him. When the school year ended, I hoped I'd maintain my connection with Peter through writing, which he liked to do as much as I did.

To keep up my financial aid, the first thing I had to do during summer break was to get a job. I found one at a local five and ten, a short walking distance from Mother's apartment. The job required working on Saturdays, which cut down on the time I had available for weekend activities with the Mensa group, but it also kept me out of the apartment and away from Sam.

Sam had announced that he was planning to write a dissertation to get his PhD. on pornography. It gave him the perfect excuse to leave dirty books everywhere around the apartment, including a stack in the bathroom. I couldn't help being curious. I started reading, especially when I had nothing else to do, sitting on the toilet. I didn't even know the meaning of some of the words, and I thought by the standards of my creative writing teacher and my professors, the stories were very badly written. Still, they were interesting. I felt things I'd never felt before when reading a book.

Every night, at nine o'clock, I wrote to Peter. My letters were long, and I wrote them on special stationery I'd bought. I told him some of the things I might have said if I were talking to him at the Denny Center, about fantasy worlds and making up adventures. I didn't mention anything about Sam's books, or tell him about what I did with the Mensa boys. In my head, the Mensa boys were New York and Peter was Ohio. They were separate worlds.

The New York world flipped one Sunday. Elliott and I had a casual day in Central Park. We walked, sat on the rocks by the lake, and took a ride on the carousel. When we returned to the apartment, we sat on the cramped space on the floor of my room. Suddenly our lips were meeting. Way more than with Sam's books, I felt things I couldn't recognize. I wanted my body to touch Elliot's in ways I never had with a boy before, not even Toby. As we pressed together, my desperation grew. Nothing was real to me except rubbing against him. It was like climbing a hill, the higher I climbed, the more I felt, and the more she wanted to get to the top for I had no idea what. The answer came to me in the explosion of sensation that swept through me, releasing the tension from every muscle I hadn't even known I'd clenched.

From what I could tell, Elliott had something like that happen to him too. He rested, breathing hard, his back partially propped against the edge of my bunk beds. He had an expression on his face I'd never seen before. I couldn't interpret it, but to me, he seemed more confused, than happy. I told him that he looked like he'd lost his best friend, and asked him what the matter was.

He turned to me with the same strange smile and said, "I think I just found her, but Sarah, you can't just go crazy like that. If I had been someone else, another boy, I could have taken advantage. Things could have gone too far."

I realized that if he had pushed things further, as the new feelings overwhelmed me, I might not have tried to stop him.

From that time, I thought of Peter and Elliott as the two halves of my life. In the evening, I poured out my creative energy to Peter in answer to letters I received from him, full of plots, drawings, and maps. When I wasn't working, I went on dates with Elliott. Those times had the feeling of real dates instead of confession sessions. We went to concerts, movies, and out to dinner. I was losing my inhibitions in other ways. At one Sha-na-na concert in Central Park, until Elliott grabbed my elbow to pull me down, I was standing up on my seat shouting for a fourth encore. We also had more sessions in my room.

There were still things I wouldn't do. Like many of my friends in New York and Ohio, Elliott smoked marijuana, but not nearly as much as Jonathan. He didn't smoke tobacco, and to me, his kisses tasted fine, but I still didn't want to smoke anything myself.

Elliott decided that he wanted to go to a Jefferson Airplane concert at the old Yankee Stadium in the Bronx. He and I brought a blanket and sat on the grass instead of in the bleachers, just as many people did. Vendors were walking up and down the rows selling pipes and papers. No one seemed to be afraid they'd be caught by the police. Elliott wanted to smoke a joint but not alone, and I didn't want to join him. He knew I never smoked, but he was still a little mad at me for not trying.

The concert started, and Jefferson Airplane played a few songs, but it began to rain. The band stopped playing because they were afraid of getting shocked by their equipment. The audience didn't like that at all. After a few minutes, Grace Slick suggested that if the girls took their tops off, it might stop raining. I didn't do that, and neither did any other girl I could see, including Grace

Slick. Finally, the rain stopped, and the band began to play again. With or without marijuana, the crowd became very happy and friendly.

When the concert ended, most of the people there packed themselves into an elevated train for the trip back to Manhattan. There was barely room in the train to move or breathe, but the riders didn't care. Someone lit up a joint and passed it around. Elliott finally got a puff, along with a contact high. I didn't take any for myself. Somehow, the roach, the last tiny piece of the joint, was lost. When Elliott and I got off the train, I discovered that the roach was wedged under one of the straps of my sandals. I didn't think that was funny, but Elliott did.

I kept up what I was doing with Elliott and Peter all summer. I dated Elliott. Other kids called what he and I did together, "everything but." However, I put my love into my letters to Peter. I was sure that if I hadn't learned ways to compensate for the lack of the "but," Elliott would not have been spending nearly as much time with me as he did. As far as I could figure out, whatever I saw in his face wasn't love, at least not like I had felt for Nathan. I believed I was coming to feel that kind of love for Peter. It seemed strange to me when I realized that though I enjoyed what parts of sex I was willing to do, at least with Elliott, I didn't feel as attached to him as I did to Peter. When the summer ended, I was more anxious to see Peter, than I was reluctant to leave Elliott.

Chapter Ten

I arrived at Barnum before Peter did, but I knew he'd have the same room as he had the year before. It was empty and unlocked, and I went in to sit on the bare mattress on the bed to wait for him. When Peter arrived, he just looked at me. There was no chance of a kiss or even a hug. Peter resisted being touched by anyone. At the time, I didn't even know that something like that had a name. Now I'd probably call it, "tactile defensiveness." Whatever it was, Peter had it. Instead of a hello, he handed me several rolled-up sheets of paper.

I could see that Peter had given me a story. It was different from any of the stories he'd given me to read previously. It was about a mythological creature, a merman, but there was no religious content. Instead, Peter had the sea creature coming to land and becoming close with a woman there. The merman was always marked by the sea. The cuffs of his pants were always damp. He and the woman he loved both knew that he would someday return to the ocean, following the song of the waves and the foam, but both their hearts still shattered when he did. I was crying when I finished reading what Peter wrote. I hoped that the mention of love, even in a story, meant that our relationship was growing.

Academically, it was a difficult year for me. I'd realized that the biology taught at Barnum would never be the molecular biology I'd loved in high school, and that had come so naturally to me. I had one course in it, and it wasn't even to the level of what I'd had been taught at Science. Instead, Dr. Barnes' students spent a lot of their time sitting on the ground studying the behavior of guinea hens and other animals. That was not what I'd wanted to do. I liked laboratories, with benches, hoods, and analytical equipment. I officially switched my major to chemistry, leaning toward physical chemistry. I would have become a physics major like Peter was, but I knew my math wasn't up to it, so I settled on what I could handle.

I had an easy time with inorganic chemistry and biochemistry. I didn't like organic chemistry, but it wasn't the direction I wanted to go so I put up with it. Qualitative chemistry was a challenge. Much of the analytical equipment was fairly primitive. Back then, there were no computerized interpretations of readouts. We identified unknowns mainly by wet chemistry. The process was long, frustrating, and sometimes dangerous. We used many things that could burn or poison us, didn't have goggles or gloves, and even sucked things up with our mouths. I wasn't nearly as good at the course as some of the students who lived for chemistry. Using concentrated sulfuric acid scared me to death, and I often picked the longest, most round about analyses to avoid using it. That meant I spent long hours in the lab. I would get to the dining hall at the last possible minute, running as fast as I could. My face was stained yellow, and the cuffs of my lab coat were shredded from what acids I did have to use. All that lab time also meant that I had almost none for the theater. As much as I wanted to, I couldn't be in two places at once. I did appreciate having free access to just about any chemical, including cyanide. There were still some times when I thought about using it to put an end to everything.

One nice thing was that since I wasn't in his classes anymore, I got to be friends with Mr. Concord. Our whole clique had kept on having pick up football games with him. When it was cold, we played badminton in the gym. He never flirted with me or touched me in a way that meant anything, but he did touch me sometimes, and some people started talking. I heard some of the gossip. I was even a little proud that the other students would think a professor might be interested in me, even if he'd never done anything to make me think that he was. My stomach did somersaults when the resident assistant told me that Mrs. Concord had called and wanted me to go see her. I was terrified. I wondered if Mrs. Concord had heard the whispers and believed them. I asked Pat, one of the girls in my physics class, who babysat for the Concord's daughter and knew where their house was, to walk me over. I shook all the way.

Mr. and Mrs. Concord were both there, and they seemed glad to see me. Mr. Concord explained that after being paid singers in the choir of a synagogue in Cleveland for years, he and his wife Meg had decided to convert, but they still didn't know a lot about Jewish customs. Meg went on to add that Mr. Concord's father had died and they weren't sure what to tell their daughter. With me being one of the few Jews on campus, they were looking for someone to ask.

My stomach settled down, and I told them what I'd been told when my grandfather died. It was simple enough for a kid to understand. Meg Concord thanked me, and as I was about to leave, asked me if ever did any babysitting. Meg added that Pat was a good sitter, but they didn't want a *shiksa* taking care of their daughter anymore. She went on to say that in any case, Pat was spending more time sitting for the daughter of one of the physics professors, Mr. Roth.

I winced at a word that wasn't very nice being used about my friend, but from the casual way Meg said it, I realized she didn't know she was putting Pat down. Pat had also told me she liked sitting for the Roths because the professor picked her up and dropped her off in his Porsche. Pat wouldn't be losing anything if I took the job. I told the Concords they could use me as a sitter, as long as it didn't conflict with my lab work.

Babysitting was one more thing in my schedule, but it was a nice source of spending money, of which I had very little. Elizabeth Concord was easy to take care of, much more so than the kids I'd sat for in New York. I also liked being around Mr. Concord, but I wasn't going to admit that to anyone.

The end of my qualitative chemistry course was dramatic. The majority of the students had voted for a practical exam instead of a written one. I'd voted the other way, but I was forced to go along with the results. For the test, we were given twenty-four hours to determine the identity of a compound. For a lot of us, that meant staying up all night, mostly on our feet. It was almost sunrise the next morning when I turned in my results, then went to bed. I woke up screaming, with terrible cramps in both my calves. Amy panicked. She was convinced that I'd somehow managed to poison myself in the laboratory. It took me longer to calm Amy down than it did to rub my cramps out.

A few weeks after all the students had returned from the break between quarters, Debbie was sitting at a table for meals with the rest of our regular group, but she wasn't eating. She said she was getting over the flu. Not long after that, Peter said he wanted to try alcohol, something he'd never done before. He thought if he did, he might be able to stand being touched. Tim was old enough to buy it for him, and gave Peter a fifth of vodka, before leaving with Thelma, for a weekend with her parents. Melissa was gone that weekend too, so James, Debbie, Reid, Peter and I, all gathered in the room James shared with Reid, to drink.

Debbie and I both had laboratory work to do the next morning, so we stuck to one drink each. I could have easily done without that. The boys seemed eager to drink every drop. At one point, it seemed to be working. Peter stood in the center of a circle of all of us, with everyone taking turns touching him. He was able to handle it. However, a little later, when I tried to stroke his thigh, as I had done to Elliott, he asked me not to. Still, he was happy with what he'd accomplished --- until he started to get sick. He threw up in one of the common bathrooms in the dorm, and then was feeling sick enough to allow me to put a wet towel on his neck. He slumped on one of the beds while I held a wastebasket. After he finished heaving, he lay down with me sitting at his head, listening to him say things he would never have told me without the vodka. He talked about the great loves he'd seen at Barnum: Tim and Thelma, Reid and Melissa, and Debbie and James. He told me he hoped to have one for himself one day, but he didn't say it would be me. The words stopped when he fell asleep. Reid and James had fallen asleep too, leaving Debbie and me awake to talk to each other.

When it was just the two of us, Debbie told me something that was awful to hear. She said that those days when she couldn't eat, she'd lied about why. What Peter had said about Tim and Thelma being a great love, wasn't true, at least on Thelma's part. Thelma had cheated with James, and Debbie had walked in on them. It had almost broken James and Debbie up as a couple, and Debbie still had moments when she wasn't sure about James, but she blamed Thelma. Debbie told me about Thelma flirting with both James and Reid, from the time they'd met her at Barnum. In fact, the boys had admitted to Debbie that they had a bet as to whom would actually have sex with Thelma first.

I'd always thought that I didn't like Thelma because she was Tim's girlfriend and I was jealous. When I found what she did, I thought maybe I'd realized somehow, that she just couldn't be trusted. Now that I knew, I struggled with what to do with that knowledge. Debbie, James, Reid, and Melissa had agreed to keep the truth from both Peter, whom they thought was too innocent to hear it, and Tim, for whom it could cause nothing but pain. I wondered if I could go along with that decision. Tim was going to marry Thelma. Shouldn't someone say something? In the end I realized the wisdom of my friends. It would be unlikely that Tim would believe me if I told him anyway. All bringing it up would accomplish would be to make him hate me, and tear our group apart. Like the secrets I'd kept for the Mensa boys, I decided to keep what Debbie told me to myself.

The end of the school year was approaching and with it, Tim and Thelma's wedding, which was supposed to take place in Tim's hometown in Massachusetts. Given what I knew, I kept wondering if it should even happen, but the planning went on. Alyne and Liz came to stay with me in New York for a little while before all three of us went to Massachusetts for the wedding. Liz was the only one who drove. Alyne didn't because she had problems with her eyes from her diabetes. Going to high school in New York City, I never had drivers' education. I wouldn't have had a car to practice in anyway. Liz and Tim had both graduated, and Liz' parents had bought her a car as a graduation present. She'd barely had the car a week. She hadn't had a license much longer, but she was sure she could drive us.

It was a nice sunny day when we started our trip. Liz' car was small, and having the shortest legs, I was in the back seat. The drive to Massachusetts was going fine, except that Liz misjudged the time it would take, and missed our exit when we were almost there. The normal thing to do would have been to get off at the next exit and come back. Since Liz didn't know the area and we were almost out of time to make the wedding, Liz used the shoulder to back up. She was lucky, and there were no police around to see her. We arrived just before the ceremony started.

The wedding was in the backyard of Tim's parents' home. Many of the people from town were there. I only knew the people I came with, plus one other student from Barnum, Lily. Lily was a close friend of Thelma's but at one point had her eye on Tim as well. Tim matched her up with George, a best friend he'd had since elementary school. During the school year, Lily had made a trip to Massachusetts to meet George, complete with her suitcase. They became a couple, but had a fight at the wedding. I heard that George had told Lily that he thought they should break up. They stood in the middle of all the guests. Tears were pouring down Lily's face, and George was trying to calm her down.

At that moment, I found out that Thelma wasn't the only member of the newly married couple who didn't behave herself. During the confusion, I realized that Tim's hand was on my behind. My first reaction was that he had picked a hell of a time to finally show some interest in something other than my mind. I was ashamed to realize that I enjoyed it. I didn't want to go, but I knew that it be a good idea to leave as soon as possible.

When Liz took Alyne and me back on the road to New York, it was getting dark. The temperature dropped as the sun went down and moisture began to gather on the inside of Liz' windshield. Her driving skills were so new that she had no idea about turning on the defroster. Alyne and I were just as clueless. Liz didn't think that she'd have the problem when the car had been sitting out in the cold for a while, so we looked for somewhere to stop. Liz pulled into the parking lot of a bar. Chilly as it was, we wanted to order tea. The bartender started laughing at us and announced that the place was a gin mill. Liz was old enough to order alcohol but was smart enough to know it was the last thing she needed.

We settled on club soda and peanuts and sat down to wait. I couldn't help blurting out where Tim put his hand. Liz and Alyne both told me to forget about it. Tim and Thelma were married, and that was pretty much the end of the story. I knew I could never forget, but it wouldn't make any difference.

Elliott had taken a job at school that summer and wasn't in New York. Les was in the city, and he and I went out together, just as friends. Les had managed to learn to drive and buy himself a car, but not a very good one. It needed oil about once a week to keep the engine from overheating. Still, he decided to give me driving lessons. I wasn't a good student, and we both thought that if we were going to stay friends, it would be better if I stayed in the passenger seat.

There weren't many jobs I could get that summer. I hated making phone calls, especially to strangers, but I took a job as a telemarketer anyway. I was in a room full of other telemarketers. We were supposed to be selling chalets in the Poconos. I had gotten very good at keeping things to myself, but another thing I hated, ever since Judith had made Rachel and me swear that our father was dead, was straight out lying. It turned out that was the other part of the job.

We were all given scripts. We told whoever answered the phone that their number had been given to us by a friend. The truth was that the numbers came from pages torn from the phone book. The scripts told us how to talk the people on the other end of the line into letting a salesman into their homes to close the deal in person. Those appointments were referred to as "sits." Our supervisors told stories about the miracles the salesmen could do at sits to make people buy a chalet shell. Then there were all sorts of add-ons to make the shell into a real house. Every add-on cost more money and we were told there was small print in the contracts detailing all of that. That made it legal, but they were still fooling people. To legally sell the chalets, those of us making the calls would also be required, after a few weeks, to take a state exam to sell real estate. That meant memorizing a book, which was like what I did to get a permit to try to learn to drive.

I decided that the only way I could manage my job would be to become a character, something our supervisors encouraged. I called myself Doreen because I'd liked playing her in Tartuffe so much. I lowered the pitch of my voice as I'd done on stage.

The boy who sat next to me, Ronny Price, was working in character as well. He was better than I was. He changed his character to fit the last names of the people called. If the customer sounded Greek, he would be Nick Sakis, if Jewish, Ari Goldman, and if Irish, Tim Kelley. He could do them all, better than most of the theater majors I knew. I was fascinated by Ronnie but disturbed by how easily people could be fooled. Ronnie and I were sort of friends. We went to lunch together, with separate checks. Ronnie usually topped the tote board for sits, making him a star in the room, but one day he was gone, as were a few others. The supervisors told those of us who were left that the others were gone because they had failed their real estate exams. He advised us to study.

I studied the real estate book, but it didn't take me very long to learn it. I was more interested in reading my comic books. While doing that, I found something that looked exciting. At the New York Comic Con, DC Comics would be giving evaluations of portfolios of young writers who wanted to become part of their Junior Bullpen and actually to write comics. After I read that, I could barely think about anything else.

Instead of the giant affairs comic book conventions are now, back in the early seventies, they were small, with just some people from the industry, fans, and vendors. There were panels in a ballroom, some informal autograph sessions, and a costume competition. There was also a sales floor where comics and comic book bags and magazines were sold out of boxes. Anyone could buy a ticket cheap and just go. It was held at a midtown hotel, an easy subway trip from Mother's apartment. I was even more excited when Alyne said she wanted to come to New York and go to the Comic Con with me. The number of sits I'd been getting was barely enough to keep me from being fired. With Ronnie gone, I decided to quit. The job made me feel nervous and dirty, and I wanted to work on putting together stories for DC. Mother didn't like that at all, but I convinced her that going to Comic Con might lead to a job.

I spent the time until Comic Con started writing. My stories were short, only about half a page, but covering what would fill a comic book. I wrote not only about the super heroes I loved but also about other characters, hoping to show the professional writers from DC how much I could do.

Alyne would only be coming for the last two days of the con, so at the beginning, I went by myself. I thought the con was a very friendly place to be, with almost everyone interested in the same things I was. I found a group of people to walk around with, in particular, Ben, a boy who was only fourteen at the time, but a wonderful artist. I thought he was more talented than either Liz or Alyne. As I'd come to be evaluated as a writer, Ben had come to be evaluated as an artist. Ben and I sat in sessions together with Ben constantly drawing characters, especially the Shadow, and me making notes about comic book history and story ideas. Ben had more nerve than I did. He walked up to any of the comic book artists he saw and showed them his work. Thirty years later, I found out that he'd grown up to draw comic book covers. I was willing to wait for the time that DC had told us to come to see them, but when it happened, they didn't say anything about my work. They just told me to hand over my portfolio, and they'd mail it back with the comments.

I was disappointed, but until Alyne got there, I kept on making the rounds with Ben and some of the other fans. Alyne had stopped by Mother's apartment to drop off her luggage. Then she came to the con with a letter from Peter, which had been in the mail. I couldn't wait to see the stories and drawings inside. I thought Peter would enjoy the con and wished he could be there.

With Alyne's diabetes, she needed regular meals, preferably with a lot of protein in them. We decided to go to a local steak house. It wasn't supposed to be that great, but it was cheap. Alyne made the mistake of hanging her purse on the back of her chair. Before she knew it, the purse and all her money was gone. The restaurant staff searched for it, but it was obvious someone had stolen it.

Alyne and I ran out to the street where a cop was directing traffic, but he refused to take a report. The only fortunate thing was that Alyne's insulin had been in her suitcase and not in her purse. From my own money, I gave Alyne cash to get through the rest of her trip. The two of us went back to the con. Some of the fun had gone out of it, but we did manage to get some great autographs. Back then, instead of the high prices, tokens, and the long lines at cons today, the autographs were free and the wait only about five minutes. Before the con was over, we both had signatures and drawings from comic book artists we loved on our programs.

After Alyne had gone home, and while I was waiting to hear something from DC, I looked for a job to last the rest of the summer. There were even fewer jobs than there had been in June. With almost nothing in the *New York Times*, I looked at the classifieds in the *Village Voice*. There was an ad for exotic dancers.

I heard from Rachel sometimes. Mother did too, especially when Rachel was broke. One of the things we both knew Rachel had done to make money was that kind of dancing, but neither of us understood how it was done. I realized later that almost any mother on the planet would have told her daughter not to answer that ad or any ad from the *Village Voice*, but Mother didn't. She thought dancing was glamorous; Rachel had told us that the money was good.

I went to see the woman who had placed the ad, an agent called Sugar. Rachel's agent was called Angel, so one named Sugar didn't seem too strange to me. I thought the address Sugar gave me was on the upper edge of Harlem, but Sugar insisted it was actually in Washington Heights, which was supposed to be a safer area.

Sugar lived in an old brownstone, which she and her daughter, a high school student named Pi, were fixing up. They had been painting the molding gold, which would have been called gaudy in my neighborhood, but seemed to suit Sugar.

I wasn't the only person applying for work. Sugar was seeing women and girls, as long as they were over eighteen, for jobs as both barmaids and dancers. She was telling one woman how to tape her breasts so they would look higher in a tiny barmaid's outfit. Sugar told her she would be more likely to be hired and she'd get better tips that way. There was another girl about my age, Amy, who long hair like mine but blonde. Amy was already dancing for

Sugar and had come for another assignment. Sugar was hesitant to give her one, because the owner of the last bar where Amy had danced had told Sugar that Amy wasn't very sexy.

Sugar asked me to dance for her before she sent either of us anywhere. I did what I thought was go-go stuff like I'd seen done in a cage on a TV dance show. Shaking her head, Sugar told me it was about the worst thing she'd ever seen for an exotic dancer, and asked me what my dance background was. I mentioned modern dance, which I'd taken with the theater majors at Barnum, and folk dancing and ballet. Sugar told me I should slow things down as I would in ballet. That reminded me of my audition for Doreen. Sugar also told Amy and me to dance like we were fucking.

Amy and I looked at each other. We had to tell Sugar that we were both still virgins and we didn't know how. Sugar asked if we had at least ever ground with a guy. She explained that when she was growing up, she and her friends would grind with guys against a wall. If some color rubbed off on their clothes, that spot was theirs."

Remembering what I'd done on the floor of my bedroom with Elliott, I told Sugar that I'd done some grinding. Sugar put the music back on. She told me to try again and told Amy to watch. I imitated the rotation of my hips against Elliott's jeans. I also did the contract and release of all my abdominal muscles that I'd learned in modern dance. Sugar liked what I did and decided she could send me out on dancing jobs, and if Amy could imitate me, she'd send her out again too.

Sugar showed us a few more steps, explained about her commission, and then offered to rent me a costume until I could make some of my own. She also explained about the makeup she wanted me to wear, including heavy black eyeliner. I'd never gone near that before, not even for the stage, but I was willing to try it. Sugar finished by explaining how to attach false eyelashes and pasties with surgical adhesive. She said I had to come back to see her before going out on a job, so she could check that my makeup, costume, and the clothes I was wearing over it were right.

When I told Les what I was going to do, I was surprised at his reaction. He and they boys talked a lot about sexy girls, and I thought he'd approve. He did approve of exotic dancing, but not for me. He made a deal with me. I'd be coming home on the subway after two in the morning when the bars closed. In exchange for being introduced to some of the other dancers, Les would come out in the middle of the night and pick me up in his car instead. I hadn't been crazy about riding the subway that late at night, although I'd done it before. I made the deal with him.

Sugar decided to ease me into things by making me a barmaid --- a topless barmaid. I knew even less about mixing drinks than I did about sex, but I went along with what she wanted me to do. I had pasties that Mother had gotten for me in a store downtown, and if I wanted to, I could use my long hair to cover my breasts. I made a few mistakes, but I found that as customers got drunker, the tips got bigger. The job also meant that besides wearing almost nothing, I had to spend an eight-hour shift on my feet in four-inch heels. I was jealous of the girl who was dancing. She was on and off in twenty-minute sets and sat and did needlepoint in between. Drinks were marked up when a dancer was on stage, and I had to remember to charge twice as much for them. I watched the other girl's moves and was sure I could do as well or better. At the end my shift, Les came to get me. I introduced him to the dancer, but he couldn't get a date with her.

To give us more of an idea of the world we were dancing in, Sugar took Amy, me, and some of her other girls on a tour of bars to watch the other dancers. Sugar was proud of being able to predict and call out the dancers' moves before they made them, and she advised all of us, to show more variety and creativity.

One of the more interesting members of Sugar's stable of dancers was Miss Candy Sweetness. Candy had not started life as a woman, and physiologically still wasn't one, a fact disguised by her costumes and by silicone injections in her breasts. Since I was very small breasted, Sugar had wanted me to talk to Candy about the possibility of getting the injections myself. Candy was very honest, and even let me feel her breasts, but I didn't want the injections. There had already been stories in the paper questioning their safety, and not long after that, they were banned. I thought that if I wanted to dance as a career, the injections might have made sense. The bustier dancers made better tips. But if I was going to be a writer, a chemist or both, the risk wasn't worth it. I couldn't afford it anyway. I did learn some great dance moves from Candy, and we liked each other.

I found most of the employees and customers of the bars I worked in nice. I ran into trouble at one place, a bar in Brooklyn called Black Keys. The bar was famous for only taking the better dancers, and not those with white skin. Despite Sugar's recommendation, I was required to audition for the owner before I was allowed to dance. I later found out that I was the first white dancer who had been allowed to dance there. I took it as a compliment. The dancing was supposed to follow the standard schedule for sets, of twenty minutes on, twenty minutes off.

At the other bars where I'd danced, I danced either on the actual bar or on a stage that I could get on and off by myself. It wasn't like that at the Black Keys. The stage was elevated, with a retractable staircase controlled by the manager, Johnny Disco. Johnny could leave a girl up on stage to dance as long as he wanted to, and he did, trying to force the dancers to do more than dance. He didn't ask for sex, at least not from me, but he wanted to put his fingers on the small part of me that my costume covered. He tried it once. I was scared and surprised, and he managed to succeed. Later, he tried again, and I said no. He stuck me on stage for forty-five minutes, more than twice the length of a set, and wouldn't open the stairs. Suddenly Sugar showed up, with her boyfriend, Spice. Spice was tall with big muscles. After a look at him and the glare on Sugar's face, Johnny unlocked the staircase and let me down.

At the end of my shift, I was in the dancers' dressing room in the basement getting dressed, when I heard a pounding on the door. It was the owner. I never knew if Sugar had said anything or not, but he was afraid Johnny Disco was inside, trying to do something to me. Sugar must have known about Johnny, from other dancers. I think Spice scared him away from me. By the time I was dressed, Sugar and Spice were gone. Les had been sick that night and couldn't pick me up. I was nervous, but I took the subway back to Manhattan.

The next time I was at the Black Keys, Johnny Disco was gone. I met with the owner at the end of my shift, so he could pay me in cash, the way all the dancers were paid. It was fifty dollars a night, a six-hour shift, twenty minutes on, twenty minutes off. In all, that came to almost seventeen dollars per hour of active dancing. That summer, the minimum wage was a dollar and sixty-five cents an hour. The money for dancing seemed incredible. The owner asked me what I was studying in college, and when I told him it was chemistry, he told me to come and see him when I had a degree; that he would have something for me to do for him besides dancing. Nice as he'd been to me, I still figured that he wanted something to do with making drugs. I decided I'd never go back after I graduated.

When it was almost Fall, Sugar planned what she called a "Disco Sip, as presented by Sugar and Spice." She had tickets printed up by a printer whose store was around a hundred and forty-fifth street in Harlem. She gave me cab fare to pick them up and bring them back to her. I got a warning from the cab driver that it was not a good place to go, especially for a white girl, but I picked up Sugar's order without a problem, and the cab driver waited and took me back.

Sugar had planned to use all of her dancers, with Candy Sweetness as the star. She thought it would be funny to have me dance in slow, more balletic type moves around Candy while she did her act. On the day of the sip, I put my nicest outfit over my costume and made myself up the way Sugar taught me. Mother said I looked as nice as she'd always wanted me to look. I thought it was strange that Mother thought stage makeup was my best look, but then it was Mother. I just said, "Thank you."

Sugar's ticket sales were very successful. The Disco Sip was packed with people holding drinks and waiting for the dancers to dance. When I did my number with Candy, there was a lot of applause. I wasn't sure if the audience actually liked me, or was making fun of me, but Sugar was happy, so it was all right. I kept my sipping limited to Coca-Cola and went home feeling good about myself. After that summer, I was more confident in my ability to look good to men. I'd seen how they looked at me. I didn't care as much anymore what Tim or anyone else had told me before.

A couple of days later, Les asked if I wanted to go on a road trip to see Elliott. I thought that would be great. He and I packed the trunk of his car with several cans of oil for the engine, and started on the drive to Massachusetts. At the first stop we made, when the oil temperature was going into the red part of the gauge, Les realized that he had forgotten a funnel. I used *origami* to make a paper cup out of the special stationery I always had with me for writing to Peter. We cut the bottom off it and used it to put more oil in the engine. We had to do that twice more along the way. That left me with only one sheet left of my paper, but I doubted I'd have much time to write, or even want to, since I'd be with both Les and Elliott.

When we got to Cambridge, we went to the campus building where Elliott was working. Les told me to stay out of sight while he talked to Elliott so that he could spring me as a surprise. Les started talking to Elliott, while I waited around a corner where I could still hear them. Les asked Elliott how he had been doing and Elliott told him he had been depressed, but mostly horny. He joked with Les about trying out being gay. An image of Elliott acting like Candy Sweetness flashed into my head. I walked into sight, my hips moving as if I was about to dance. I told Elliott, "That kind of talk has to stop."

Elliott's mouth dropped wide open, but all that came out was my name. He took me in his arms and gave me the hardest kiss I could ever remember getting. The two of us held on to each other until Les joined us in going to the little summer apartment Elliott shared with another student. We picked up some sandwiches along the way.

While we ate, Les kept looking back and forth between Elliott and me, as if he was trying to figure out what would happen next. We all talked until late. Elliott's roommate was away, so there was an empty bed in the one bedroom. Elliott suggested Les could take it and Elliott could share with me.

Les was confused at the idea that Elliott would even want him in the room. I was too. Les told us to take the room and that he would sleep on the floor in the hall outside it, in a sleeping bag.

Elliott and I started the night in one bed fooling around as we usually did. Neither one of us knew where it was going, and we were both nervous. Finally, Elliott told me that he was very tired and needed to sleep, and suggested I take the other bed. I was surprised, but I didn't know whether to be disappointed or relieved. I wasn't on the pill, and Elliott didn't say anything about having condoms.

Elliott woke me in the middle of the night. I didn't understand when he told me he'd believed that he could cope with something himself, but decided that he couldn't. Then explained that he thought his retinas were detaching again. He was afraid that when we were making out, something shook loose.

I was still confused and asked him what he was talking about.

He explained it happened before, during the school year. He'd had surgery, and they had to use a catheter so he could urinate. It was very uncomfortable, and he hated it. He didn't want to have to go through it again."

I tried to look at him in the dark room. After all the secrets I'd kept for him and the other boys, I was upset he hadn't let me know what happened at the time.

He confessed that he had been seeing a girl at school. She'd helped him through recovering from surgery, and they had started having sex.

Elliott said that Les knew about the surgery, but he hadn't even told Les about the girl. She broke up with Elliott because she was on the rebound from another guy who decided he wanted her back.

I didn't know what to say to him. I knew how it must have hurt when the girl went back to her boyfriend. Then Elliott told me he was very glad to see me, but he didn't feel right about doing anything with me because of the other girl. He was so scared I could feel him shake. I climbed into bed with him and told him that I understood. I stayed there all night, just holding him.

Les was grinning when Elliott and I came out of the room the next morning, but he stopped when he saw our faces. Elliott explained what he thought was happening to his eyes. He called his ophthalmologist's office and got an emergency appointment. Les drove all of us over, and he and I waited while Elliott saw the doctor. When Elliott came out of the examination room, he looked embarrassed. He said things were fine. I hugged him, but there was nothing sexy about it.

Les confessed on the drive back to New York that he really thought Elliott and I were going to have sex.

I confided that for a while I thought so too, but maybe it was better we didn't. I didn't want to explain anymore, and Les didn't press me. At a gas station, where we picked up more oil for the return trip, Les also bought a funnel. At least I could use my last sheet of stationery to write on. For a while, I buried myself in writing to Peter. Our correspondence seemed like the one thing I could still count on.

In the last week before the next term would begin at Barnum, DC mailed my portfolio back to me with the comment, "You sure can write, but your stories are too violent." I knew they were right, at least for what their stories were like then. I had put all my anger against Mother and Sam into my stories, and it showed. With nothing ahead of me but chemistry, I went back to school.

Chapter Eleven

Senior year for chemistry majors at Barnum was hard, and I didn't do anything to make it easy for myself. I decided to take Nuclear Chemistry, which was a seminar available only by permission, in the same quarter with Nuclear Physics and Advanced Inorganic Chemistry. Peter was also in Nuclear Physics, and I would have loved to have him as a lab partner, but the assignments were alphabetical, and I missed by one. He didn't seem to be in any hurry to be partners anyway. Of the three courses, Nuclear Physics was the least amount of work.

In Advanced Inorganic, Professor Morse took a very practical approach, advising us that no matter how elegant we might think a process would be if, in the real world, you couldn't afford it, you couldn't do it. He gave an assignment, due at the end of the quarter, to find out what the fifty top chemicals in the world were, how they were produced and what they cost. There was no internet, so what might have taken a couple of seconds to google now, took hours in the library, if we could find the information at all. In addition, with no word processors, there was no cutting, pasting, and editing. Everything was copied by hand and then typed on manual typewriters.

Nuclear Chemistry, a seminar taught by Bertrand Bosch, also had a quarter-long project, a list of problems using matrixes to calculate things like atomic radii, the way Heisenberg would have done it. Since math was not my favorite thing, I'd never used matrixes, but Dr. Bosch gave his students, all four of us, instructions we could follow.

I was still earning money babysitting for the Concords and was spending a lot of my time at their place. I was beginning to have fantasies creeping into my mind in which Mr. Concord's wife was absent. From my experience with my parents, I hated the thought of married people cheating on each other. I did my best to put the fantasies out of my head and concentrate on my babysitting job, which had grown. Elizabeth had a friend, Susie, the daughter of two psychology professors, Nan and Brock Duggan, who had moved into the other half of the duplex the Concords occupied. Elizabeth and Susie fought a lot. When I took them to the park, Susie would want to go home after about half an hour, while Elizabeth would want to stay. I had to learn to be a referee, something I'd never done before, even with the Mensa boys. I did the best that I could, and both sets of parents seemed happy with the job I was doing. I took on as much as I could handle, maybe more.

I'd picked up another interest. I took folk and square dancing in high school and did folk dancing with my youth group, so I took the Folk and Square course at Barnum too. I thought that it would be fun and earn me an easy credit. There was a square dance at Barnum, but I had a babysitting job that night, and by the time I arrived, Peter had another partner. I was surprised the touching didn't bother him, but to hold someone's hand dancing, seemed to be fine. I wished he was holding mine. Since I knew all the steps, and because of my time with Sugar, I was confident as a dancer. I just walked into a set to join a boy who didn't have a partner. His name was Clint.

Clint was happy to have a partner who knew what she was doing, and by the end of the evening, he asked me to partner with him the following week. He would be going to a session of the Fancy Flashes, the folk dancers at Kent State University. I wasn't sure what to say. Elliott was still in my life, but the closeness between us was less, because of what happened with the other girl. Peter still couldn't do anything physical with me, and we seemed farther apart than we had been the year before. I also needed something to keep me from thinking about Mr. Concord, so I accepted Clint's invitation.

During the week, Clint showed up at my dorm with another suggestion. He was doing a radio show at the Barnum student station, and he wanted me to join him in the radio shack to get acquainted. That was fine with me. I loved being around electronic equipment.

What Clint had in mind was more electric than electronic. He wanted a make out session. I was okay with that, too. While Clint's choice of records spun on the turntable, we were kissing. By the time we had our dancing date, I thought we were a couple on and off the dance floor.

Clint had a car, an old one, even by student standards. He told me that he had spent a summer pulling transmissions at a car repair shop, had bought his car for fifty-four dollars, and fixed it up.

The engine and everything else worked, except for the heater. I wondered if Clint had left it broken for a reason. The drive to Kent State was cold, and it gave us an excuse to cuddle up.

Clint had danced with the Fancy Flashes before, and they said hello to him as a friend. I was welcomed as his partner, and they liked how I danced. I enjoyed going to Kent State, and I wanted to go again.

Clint had been working on forming a folk dancing club at Barnum, which I joined. My signature move with Clint was "Swing Like Thunder," in which couples form a circle with their arms around each other's shoulders. The boys put their weight toward the center, as they go around in a circle, with the centrifugal force allowing the girls to be off the ground, their legs flying out away from the circle. It reminded me of a Flying *Hora* I'd seen in my youth group. There were only three girls on campus who could manage to let their legs leave the ground at all, and I was the only one whose legs could fly straight out. Clint was proud of the move and wanted us to do it whenever we had a chance.

Between the folk dancing group at Barnum and the trips to Kent, Clint and I spent a lot of time together. I found the make out sessions exciting too, but Clint seemed to want more from me.

I'd never been to a prom or any kind of a formal school dance. The prom at Science had been canceled when they only sold two tickets, but I wouldn't have been invited anyway. It wasn't the sort of date I could have with the Mensa boys. None of them could dance at all. They might not have always fit a geeky stereotype, but when it came to trying to move their feet, they did.

Barnum only had one big dance a year. It was called the Bowery and was mostly for the stars of the school social scene, like cheerleaders and athletes. Up to the time I started dating Clint, I'd never even thought about going, but now that I was with a boy who actually liked to dance, I loved the idea. I believed that Clint had agreed to take me. There was no way I could afford to buy the sort of dress the other girls would wear, so I made one. I bought pink satin and pearl buttons and designed a full-skirted pattern. The dress made me feel like a fairy tale princess, and I couldn't wait to wear it.

The weekend of the dance, Clint disappeared. He wasn't in his room, and his car was gone. He'd left a note on the door of my dorm room, quoting lyrics from Neil Young about being a woman's country man. Amy thought it was romantic, but I didn't understand. How could he just go off and leave me the weekend of the dance? I hoped he'd be back in time and kept watching the road into campus, but there was never any sign of his car. When he returned to Barnum after the dance was over, he didn't apologize. He acted as if nothing strange had happened. I was afraid to ask him about it. I left the dress in my closet to use as a Halloween costume.

In November, there was a presidential election, and Barnum students were given a few days to go home and vote. Usually, I stayed at school during short breaks, but I had enough babysitting money to catch a student standby flight to New York. Elliott went home to New York too, and we saw each other and had a good time. It made me feel better about what happened with Clint. I wasn't even sure I wanted to see him anymore.

When I went back to campus, I saw Clint in the dining hall, and we hugged, but there was no feeling in it. Then he used song lyrics again and told me, "He'd lost that loving feeling." It was the easiest break up I could have imagined. After what had happened with the Bowery and seeing Elliott, I didn't feel attached to Clint either. I did miss the dancing, but with my workload, I didn't have much time to worry about it.

The end of the quarter was coming fast, and I figured out that the only way I'd be able to finish my projects for Morse and Bosch would be almost to give up sleeping. I set goals for myself every night, and when I met them, I would sleep an hour or two before grabbing breakfast in the morning. I'd kept that up for about two weeks when I was trying to wake up in the shower and couldn't get myself to do it. It felt like I was standing in a dream, and giant crabs and Bobby Darrin, who had a TV show then, were in the stall with me.

I dragged myself to the dining hall where Peter was at breakfast. He took one look at me and told me I'd have to start sleeping because I was going to start hallucinating. I told him that it had already started happening, but I was almost done, and I'd be able to turn in all my work and start sleeping again. He seemed relieved at that news, and for a moment, I thought I might be getting closer to him again.

It turned out to be just the opposite. Every day, I felt Peter drifting further away. We still met for some evenings at Denny center, but our talks were strained. We no longer shared tables at meals and he seemed to walk away whenever he saw me coming.

As Peter retreated, I just wanted to be around him more. Other than the night when Peter had been drunk, he'd only touched me twice; once was when he'd thought I was in was going to get hit by a car and he pulled me out of the way. The other time, he'd lifted me up so I could see a *Star Trek* game Tim had designed, play out on a big plotter in the computer lab run by Mr. Concord. It didn't matter to me. Our letters, sharing stories and ideas had made me want Peter more than I had wanted any boy since Nathan.

When I could no longer stand having him trying to avoid me, I went to his room and confronted him. With tears flowing down my face, I told him I loved him and asked if he had any feelings for me at all. He told me that what he felt for me was pity.

I was stunned. Of all the things I had imagined I might hear, that was not one of them. I left Peter's room and closed the door behind me.

I felt heartbroken, but also free. Without ever holding hands, Peter had been a constant tug in the back of my mind whenever I'd been with Elliott, Clint, or any other boy. Now, even in my fantasies, that tug was gone. I wasn't sure I wanted any part of any boy again. I was going to concentrate on making myself happy and stop looking for some boy to do it.

My freedom was reinforced with more pain when I returned to New York on my last break for the year. Elliott was there, and we went out a few times together. On the last one, he took me to Central Park, and we both sat on a bench by the carousel. He told me he had been doing a lot of thinking. Senior year was when guys started planning their lives ahead, including marriage. He had concluded that even though he loved me, he didn't love me that way and never would. He wanted to marry someone with whom he could sit and gaze into her eyes. I just didn't fit his vision.

I went home and cried. I wasn't sure if I was crying because I'd never marry Elliott, or for the insult that I wasn't good enough to marry, after all the years we'd been seeing each other. Sam, who was unfortunately still around, said what I thought was the stupidest thing I'd ever heard. He suggested that Elliott saying that he couldn't marry me meant that at least he was thinking about it. Big deal!

There was nothing for me to do but go back to school to finish the year, and my degree. Having managed to get through what I thought was the hardest academic quarter of my life; I decided to add something else into the mix. I was on track with my grades to receive departmental honors, but I had to do a project. For years, I'd been playing with the membranes that were inside the shells of hard-boiled eggs. They fascinated me.

Osmosis was a big deal at the time, so I decided to see if my favorite membranes could do it. My professors, especially Bertrand Bosch, whom I had again that quarter for physical chemistry, thought the project was a very strange idea. My advisor Dr. Doss, who had made a lot of money from a gasoline formula patent, thought it was weird too, but signed off on it.

I was given a small workspace space in the physical chemistry lab. My first and most difficult job was obtaining my membranes. That required carefully boiling eggs and stripping out the membranes by hand. I cooked my eggs in distilled water, which was much cleaner than what came out of the tap. They were edible, but since they came out of a lab, my friends refused to go near them. I ate a few myself. I hated wasting the rest but had to throw them away.

I designed a simple and cheap apparatus to test my theory. I only needed plain glass pipettes, sewing thread, salt solutions, and more distilled water, all of which Barnum had plenty. If my theory were correct, I would be able to get a solution to rise in a glass tube made out of a pipette. I'd learned how to shape glass, in Advanced Chemistry in high school, so that was easy for me.

I set up my experiment and went away to wait. When I returned to the lab, I could see right away that my crazy guess was right. I had discovered an osmotic membrane. I was actually bouncing when I went to grab Dr. Bosch by the hand and bring him into the lab as a witness.

Dr. Bosch was always a gentleman. In fact, he was known for it on campus. I would never have expected to hear a curse word from him, but when he saw the water in the tube, he just grinned and exclaimed, "I'll be damned!"

The news spread through the school. I was surprised when Mr. Concord stopped me in the hall and asked if I was selling shares. I hadn't even thought of anything like that and didn't seriously consider it then. I'd just wanted to run my experiment.

One thing I did have to plan was what I would do when I graduated. A couple of chemical companies were on campus recruiting, but when I told them I wouldn't work on any projects involving weapons, they weren't interested in me. The Vietnam War was still going on, and weapons were where most of the positions for chemists were. Oil companies were offering very well paying jobs for chemists --- in Saudi Arabia. Unfortunately, I had two strikes against me that would make getting that kind of an offer impossible; I was female, and I was Jewish.

That left graduate school. It was sort of like figuring out a choice for college. I was thinking about two different directions, but neither of them was writing. The University of Virginia was offering MBA's for graduates in chemistry. The logic was that a background in both science and business could lead to executive positions in science-based companies.

The other direction I could go would be to go for an upper-level degree in some branch of chemistry itself. I was thinking about physical chemistry, the hardest one. I'd never had a single business course, but I took the business exam. It was mostly math, and compared to what had been required for my major, seemed very easy to me. There wasn't even any calculus. I scored in the eighty-fifth percentile.

I took the Graduate Record Exam and the graduate exam specific to chemistry as well. I found the chemistry exam very hard, and so did the other Barnum students in the room. Some of the questions were about stuff so unfamiliar, that we just laughed. It was better than crying. I got through it the best that I could. After that, I just had to wait for my results.

I sent out a bunch of applications, far more than the three Bronx Science had let me send out for college. One was to the University of Virginia for their business program. The rest were for graduate degrees in chemistry. I had to get recommendations. Dr. Bosch seemed the happiest about writing one. I quickly found out that I had been accepted everywhere I'd applied, but I would need a full scholarship and a stipend to live on. All the chemistry schools were offering what I needed.

Mr. Concord was leaving Barnum at the end of the year. He'd finished the PhD. he'd been working on during the time he was teaching. While I was around the Concords to babysit, I'd heard them adding to the list of things they would do when he had his PhD; it was a long list. Now he had one, and he was thinking of taking a position at the University of Virginia. He asked me if I would be going there, telling me that my presence would be a factor in the Concord's decision. I was sure Mr. Concord was talking about having a reliable Jewish babysitter. Still, it started the fantasies rolling in my head again.

The offer I got from the University of Virginia was for only a half scholarship. Even if I had steady income sitting for Elizabeth, that wouldn't be enough. I had to pick one of the chemistry schools. I sent off an acceptance to Iowa State University, mostly because they had a nuclear power plant and I thought it would be interesting to work there. After I did, I began receiving calls from a professor at the University of Utah, trying to talk me into being a student there. I also received a letter from the University of Virginia saying they'd found the other half of the money. It was too late. I'd given my promise to Iowa, and I didn't go back on my word.

With the year almost over, I was interested mostly in finishing my work and going on to graduate school. Without a boyfriend, I felt free. I convinced myself that I liked it that way. I was still babysitting regularly for the Concords, but it was obvious that Meg was pregnant, and with the chance of ending up at the University of Virginia gone, my fantasies toward the Mr. Concord, except as a friend, were gone.

To finish my work most easily, I spent a lot of time in the Math Physics Library. It was in the basement of the science building and down the hall from Mr. Concord's tiny office, and was the only place on campus with a calculator that could handle complicated functions. A few of the students hung out there every day. Except for me, they were all physics majors. One of the occasional drop-ins, Joe, was a senior who'd been my teaching assistant in my last physics class. Another one was my friend Pat. There was also Peter's current roommate, John. The same person picked on all of us.

There was a holography lab in a room off the library. The room had been assigned to Mick Chester, who acted like he was also entitled to the control of the Math Physics Library. He was always objecting when we stayed after hours or used a corn popper. He didn't like our choice of radio station, either. I put up with him because he was married to a girl I'd known and liked since freshman year, but I thought he was a real pain.

Like most of Northeast Ohio, Barnum was sometimes in danger of flooding. I'd been through one heavy one. I even had my foot right next to Barnum's president's foot, bracing a hose that was being used to pump water from a basement laboratory. Another heavy storm was coming, but no flooding had been predicted. The prediction was wrong.

That afternoon, both Pat and I had fought with Mick. Pat hadn't been able to come up with the right words to answer him, but I'd gotten my licks in. Mick was very mad and slammed the door of his lab. After that, I went back to my room to get some reading done.

Half an hour later, Pat came to see me, in tears. She told me that as soon as I was gone, Mick had come back to the library and screamed at her. He took a Polaroid photograph of the corn popper and threatened that all the students would banned from the Math Physics Library by the next day when he took his picture to the head of the department. I felt sorry for Pat and wanted to kill Mick. I gave Pat a little wine that had been stowed in the top of my closet since I and the few other Jewish students on campus had used it for a Passover celebration. Pat and I walked back to the science building together. The storm had come in full blast, and we could see water leaking into the basement. We were afraid it would ruin the equipment, a lot of which was on laboratory floors.

The labs that were threatened were locked, by that time the faculty was gone, and there was no one in the building with keys. I remembered that Peter's roommate John had some for a project he was doing. Going to John and Peter's room made me nauseous, but Peter wasn't there. Pat and I got John, and the three of us went back to the science building.

The water was getting deeper, and we went from room to room making sure equipment was unplugged and out of reach. Then we began mopping. Some other students joined the three of us, but our group was small. Many other low-lying places on campus were also flooding, and students, faculty, and staff were trying to cope with all of them. It was very late when Pat and I had a chance to get the water out of the holography lab. Even if it was Mick was using the equipment, we hated to see the work destroyed. The chairman of the physics department was there. He thanked us for what we did and for getting the other students in to help. As casually as I could, I asked him what he would think of a picture of a corn popper in the Math Physics Library. He just gave me a strange look and said he wouldn't care.

After that night, our group in the library didn't see much of Mick. We did see Irv, a new face. Irv was not the sort of advanced student who usually ended up there. He was a freshman, one of the ones who had been assigned to remedial writing classes after Freshman Institute. He had bad anxiety about taking tests and the low grades that went with it. Normally, he wouldn't have gotten into Barnum, but his father had been a student. His dad was a professional fundraiser, who also had a seat on Barnum's Board of Directors, so Irv was admitted. Irv was not the kind of boy I would have usually paid any attention to. He was the same height as I was, with nothing cute about his face. He did have one quality that I found intriguing. He could build things. He could visualize something in three-D and make it happen. He got the attention of our whole group, by constructing a pendulum-operated device that automatically drew beautiful designs. His talent made him welcome. I helped him as much as I could, with his writing and some of his other classes.

Barnum was a dry town. No alcohol was served, and you couldn't buy any either. The nearest liquor store was five miles away in the next town. My freshman year, students were not allowed alcohol in their rooms, or anywhere not specifically designated and supervised. Those rules had been relaxed a bit, but the rules were still that all that could be served at official student gatherings was weak stuff called three-two beer. A dance had been planned where there would be kegs of it. It was my last chance to go to a dance at Barnum that didn't involve folk and square. Most of the group from the Math Physics Library decided to go, including Irv. I decided to try it too.

The music was loud and bouncy. A woman with a fiddle was at the center of things. The more the students wanted to dance, the faster she played. The beer was served in huge paper cups. It didn't seem to have much of an effect, so most of the students drank a lot.

Because he'd been sick as a kid, with the bone disease that made him short, Irv didn't have much experience dancing. Despite that, after his second beer, he looked at me, and said, "You know what, let's dance." While he was flopping around, I could feel something about our relationship changing. When the dance ended, we decided to go for a walk. We ended up on swings in the town playground. As we swung, Irv told me that he was a pilot and had earned his pilot's license even before he'd qualified for a driver's license. The idea of going up with him in a small plane sounded exciting.

Our swing in the dark was interrupted by Joe. He was very drunk and very upset. He asked if we had seen his wife. He said that she'd been pissed off at him at the dance and said she was going back to their trailer, but she wasn't there. Irv and I agreed to help look for her. We walked all over town before finally going back to the Math Physics Library. Joe was there and miserable, saying he would stay there because it was the one place his wife knew to come. Irv and I stayed with him until he went back to his trailer to check again to see if she'd come home. Then we said goodnight, but we both knew we wouldn't look at each other the same way we had before.

Irv had a car, a Karmann Ghia. No other student had a car like it. I loved riding in it and took regular drives with Irv into the next town, to go to the Dairy Queen. Irv did his own maintenance, and I chipped in for parts. Irv decided he was going to teach me to drive, something no one had tried since Les gave up.

The area around Barnum was very hilly. The Ghia was the most difficult car I could have tried to learn in. It had a manual transmission, meaning I had to keep it from slipping down a hill, just to start it. I'd never tried to drive anything but an automatic before, and the manual was almost impossible for me. Neither one of us wanted to give up, but we began spending more time taking long walks and using bicycles. We messed around a little, but Irv didn't know what he was doing and was nervous. I felt like I was playing teacher, but what we did together never came close to what I'd done with Elliott or Clint.

Even without making out much, Irv and I were very close and spent all our free time together. Irv's father planned to come to campus for a Board meeting to review Barnum's finances. He would be piloting a small plane and promised that Irv could borrow it to take me up to do "touch and goes," practice landings and take offs. When he arrived, I was surprised by what he looked like. He was tall, making it obvious that Irv's lack of height was not genetic. He was also handsome and charismatic; two things Irv was not. I couldn't help wondering what else was in the gene pool.

Irv's father kept his word, and Irv and I went flying. The sky seemed so much more real in a small plane than it ever had on a commercial flight, putting space fantasies into my head. After flying with Irv, I was more interested in him than ever, but it was almost time for graduation. I would be returning to New York for a little while, then attending both Alyne's and Liz's weddings. After that I would travel to Iowa in July to start graduate school. For the summer, Irv would be going back to Wisconsin where his parents lived, before starting his sophomore year at Barnum in September. Irv and I didn't even think about breaking up. He invited me to Wisconsin for the two weeks before I would need to be in Iowa. When we left Barnum, it gave us both something to look forward to.

Irv's family couldn't have been nicer. Before I flew to Wisconsin, Irv's mother called to formally invite me to their home. His family was all, including Irv's younger sister, as tall as I'd suspected. The house rules would not allow Irv and me to share a bedroom, let alone a bed. That seemed like a relief to Irv, but we found our moments for make out sessions, especially on a beach on the shore of Lake Michigan. We even took a trip to a brewery. I'd had only had a sip or two of full strength beer up to that point, and hadn't liked the taste at all. I was surprised that I liked what flowed directly from the production line, and the two of us drank beer together. The beer reminded me of the better parts of the night at the dance where we'd become a couple.

There was one thing I found disturbing. Irv's family, especially his sister, kept bringing up the possibility that Irv and I might get married someday. Irv flatly refused to allow for the possibility, saying he loved me as a girlfriend but couldn't see me as a wife. My stomach clenched as I flashed back to my conversation with Elliott at the carousel in Central Park. Somehow, I was good enough to play around with, but not good enough to marry. I tried my best to push the thought from my mind, but it was always there, coming back at odd times.

After two weeks, I flew straight to Iowa. All the things I wanted to have with me at graduate school, including my books and my bicycle, had been shipped there from New York. I had only the little pack I'd taken to Wisconsin.

Chapter Twelve

I had a room, at least temporarily, in a graduate dormitory. I also had a new roommate, Linda. She was very nice to me, and had a car, which was handy. Linda also had something to which I didn't pay much attention, but many of the other residents of the dormitory did.

The huge tower in which Linda and I had our room, had recently been converted from all male to coed. Linda and I occupied one of only two rooms assigned to females. That would have been enough to attract our neighbors, but there was more. Linda had a big bust, so much so that she had to make all her clothes because nothing off the rack would fit her. That situation was one of the things that had made Linda decide to go into home economics. It was also how she learned to sew. She started work on a project of making clothes for the disabled, using Velcro fasteners, which were new at the time. The dorm was not air conditioned, and the July weather was super-hot and humid. Linda sat in the doorway of our room, trying to catch a breeze while she sewed.

The guys in the dorm would do a double take when they went by, first noticing that there was a female in the doorway, and then noticing her measurements. They started to gather around our room like fans waiting for a celebrity. Linda wasn't surprised or overwhelmed by what happened. She was used to being noticed. One guy, Tom, caught a little of her interest, but the rest kept hanging around offering to help Linda and me with whatever we needed.

When my bike arrived, there was a guy to help me put it together. Another one helped me get my trunk to my room. One guy even masqueraded as my boyfriend when I had to return a defective record player I'd bought. He made a great authority figure, and customer service did whatever he asked of them.

Linda and I were invited to almost everything, including a hearts game on the lawn of the dormitory. After playing so much with Tim and Liz at Barnum, I'd become very good at the game. We weren't playing for money, but I was memorizing every card and taking every round until a new player arrived. His name was Tim, and something about his looks, his long haircut, and the fact that he was a computer major, made me think of the other Tim. I found out quickly that they weren't much alike. This Tim, like almost all the other guys, paid attention to Linda, but it seemed to me like I'd known him all my life. I'd never felt that with a guy before, not even Nathan or Elliott. Tim was older than most of the other students, a man rather than a boy. From the time he joined the game, he was winning. I wasn't upset; I was impressed.

For me, the summer was limited to studying for placement tests, orientation, and one class, chemical pedagogy, as preparation for my job as a teaching assistant. I was also searching for another place to live. A snafu in the paperwork had left me with a place in the dorm only for the summer. Most of my fellow chemistry students were male, like they'd been at Barnum. I didn't pay much attention to that. Even if Irv and I were hundreds of miles apart, and would continue to be, I considered myself attached. One of the other students, from China, tried to date me by arranging to meet at a square dance, even though I told him I was taken. He also let me know there was a vacant apartment in the building where he lived.

I had to duck a pass from him at the square dance, but I was glad to find a furnished apartment. The building with the apartment was talked down by some of the other students, especially those from richer families. They referred to it as an Anderson slum. I didn't see it that way. I could afford it on my stipend, with enough left over for a very lean but manageable budget. The apartment needed a lot of work. It took me two hours just to scrape the built-up grease out of the oven and broiler. The kitchen sink was low and old fashioned, like one in a New York apartment, but without the roaches. The bathroom had a tub, but no shower, and the old linoleum in both the kitchen and bathroom needed a good scrubbing. There was thick new shag carpeting in my small bedroom, which I looked at as an extra seating area. I plugged my radio/cassette player into the speakers for the turntable I'd bought, and could play whatever I wanted, including my *Star Trek* audio tapes.

Grandma Levi had died when I was a sophomore at Science and the last thing she'd left me, that I knew about, was a thousand-dollar bond that had matured that summer. Mother had held onto almost everything I'd been given over the years, including bonds from relatives, but she couldn't do anything with them because they were in my name. The bond from Grandma Levi had paid for my move to Iowa and had even left me with enough to buy small black and white television, the first TV set I'd ever owned myself.

My world was complete. My apartment was mine alone. I didn't have to worry about all Mothers' junk or Sam's smoke. There were no roommate's boyfriends. For the first time in my life, I was in control. I liked it. I liked it a lot. I hadn't heard from Irv in weeks, other than to let me know that his family would be moving to Texas, where his father had a new job. When I was in Wisconsin with them, they'd talked about it, so the move didn't come as a surprise. I realized that I missed him a lot less than I'd expected to. What he'd said about marriage was still stuck somewhere in the back of my mind, and it hurt. One of the first things I did after settling into my new place was throw a party for Linda and the other friends I'd made at the graduate dorm.

My apartment was packed. There were even people I didn't know, who had come with their friends for beer, making it run out sooner than I'd intended. Even when it did run out, most of my guests seemed happy. One of them was the new Tim. All through the party, we kept looking at each other and even sat together. I hadn't planned on it, but I was flirting with him, and I knew it.

It was very late when everyone but Tim left. He'd volunteered to help me clean up. That only took a few minutes, but we didn't want to say good-bye, so we took a walk. Even in the sweaty Iowa August, it was cool at that time of the early morning. We didn't say much while we walked; trying to figure out what was going on between us. We met a dog, the only other being out. He was very friendly, and when we started walking back to my apartment, the dog followed us. I suggested we could try feeding him a little leftover pot roast I had in my refrigerator. When we returned, to the "slum" where I lived, the dog was very grateful for the meal. Tim and I named him, "Pot Roast." After the dog had been fed, Tim went back to the graduate dorm. We hadn't even held hands or kissed, but we both knew things had changed.

I had noticed that occasionally if all conditions were right, I was able to get a snowy but watchable version of *Star Trek* reruns on my television. One thing Tim and I had discovered about each other was we were both fans. When I ran into Tim on campus, I asked him whether he would like to come up to my apartment and try to watch the show. He said that he would. I was making sure everything was picked up first, and I had no idea where the thought came from, but I imagined I might even marry Tim. When he came, the two of us sat on the bed, the only place we could both see the TV, while I tried to get a signal. All I got was a blizzard of snow. I didn't want Tim to leave, so I suggested that we listen to one of my *Star Trek* audio tapes. We were both big enough Trekkies to know exactly what had been happening on the screen.

Tim agreed, and I slipped a cassette into the player I'd wired into my stereo. The sounds of a voyage of the U.S.S. Enterprise filled the room. Tim and I continued to sit on the bed, our backs against the wall and our eyes closed, picturing the action. Tim took my hand and held it. As the tape ended, he kissed me, and I lay back on the bed under him. He wasn't pushing anything. The kiss was gentle, but I kissed him back. After a minute, he smiled at me and said, "Hello."

I didn't know what to do, except to kiss him again. We had our hands all over each other. I was as uninhibited as I could remember myself being, except with that first time I made out with Elliott. Tim didn't try to get past the "everything but" stage, but his fingers made me feel very satisfied. I had trouble doing the same for him, and he confessed that he'd been playing with himself too much. I'd heard many confessions from boys over the years, but never one like that. I was surprised, but it didn't bother me. I just wanted to do better for him the next time.

When Tim was dressed again, Linda called. She had been curious about the vibes she'd detected between Tim and me at the party, and wanted to pump me about what happened after everyone left. Tim was right there, and I could only give Linda yes or no answers, and giggle. It didn't take Linda long to catch on. "He's there, isn't he?" she asked.

I gave her a short, 'Uh huh."

"Call me after he leaves," Linda demanded before hanging up.

I think Tim had figured it out. He asked me how Linda was. I told him that she was fine. Tim told me that he had to get ready for a rehearsal for a madrigal group, and left. I called Linda back, but I didn't know what to tell her. I had no idea where things were going with Tim, but I had a feeling that it might be somewhere I'd never been before. I wasn't sure where that would be, but I had a pretty good idea. Linda reminded me that Tim was twenty-seven, six years older than I was, and had been a student for a long time. It didn't matter to me. For the first time, I didn't have to answer to anyone. I could make my own choices, and I intended to do it. Again, the thought danced across my brain, that I might even marry Tim.

The next time Tim came to my apartment, I made it clear that I wanted things to go further. I also confessed that it would be my first time. That was unusual for a twenty-one-year-old woman in the seventies. Tim confided that it was not too much different for him. He had only gone all the way twice before in his life. He had been engaged to another girl, Meredith, but she had broken it off and moved on when she received her masters, and he didn't. He described her as very beautiful, a practicing Catholic, and a daddy's girl, who hadn't wanted to be fully intimate with him. I understood the implication. Beautiful was something I had never been and never would be. However, I was more than willing to give Tim what Meredith wouldn't. I wanted to give it to him.

Neither one of us had anything for birth control. I'd always been regular in my cycles. I'd also not lost any of my knowledge of biology. I was sure that I wouldn't get pregnant at that part of my cycle, but at the moment, I didn't care. When it came to actually having Tim inside me, I thought he'd never fit, but he did. Neither one of us knew what we were doing, but we fumbled around together. I wasn't sure if I enjoyed it or not. I'd expected it to hurt a little and it did. My bleeding was clear evidence for Tim that I had never done it before. I took a bath to try to feel better, with Tim anxiously wanting to make sure I did. He also assured me that if I did get pregnant, I was to come to him and we'd deal with it together.

From then on there was no doubt or secret that the two of us were a couple. Within a week, I'd given Tim a key to my apartment and redone my budget to allow for cooking meals for the two. It made living on my small stipend even a little tighter, but I didn't mind. I was a teaching assistant, but Tim was a research assistant and made even less money than I did.

One thing I would never have believed would happen was that I started going to church. There was no synagogue around. Tim went to church, and so did some of my friends from the dorm. Tim and I usually couldn't go together. The professor who led his madrigal group was the church organist. Some of the singers in the choir knew Tim and had suggested that he join them. That meant he had to be at church an hour before I did, but I watched him from the pews, and he knew we were there together.

Church was a challenge to me. I'd only been in one once in my life, and then just to look around. The only thing I recognized was the Lord's Prayer, which I had been forced to say in school, until the Supreme Court made forcing kids to say it, illegal. The hymns were all strange. As I sang out of a hymnal, I was glad I could sight read music. Singing in church was about the only singing I did. I'd been afraid my guitar would break if I shipped it, so I left it behind in New York, hoping I could get it sometime, preferably when Sam wasn't around. Sometimes I'd sing a little around the apartment, but it didn't feel right singing when I couldn't play.

I also found the prayers in church strange. What I'd grown up with, mostly in Hebrew, had been much the same every week. By the time I was seven, I'd memorized all the regular parts of the service. I didn't have to think about the prayers, I just said or sang them. Most of the time I didn't care about what they meant. Church was different. The songs changed every week. The prayers were about the events going on in the world. I felt like people meant them. There seemed to be more worship going on in one service at church as there was in a year at the synagogue. I was drawn in.

What I didn't like about church, was the attitude about money. It was almost never mentioned in services at the synagogue. Members paid dues. Donating money wasn't thought of as part of worship, just something needed to keep the lights on and the staff paid. When I was in Hebrew school, I was taught that handling money on the Sabbath at all, was a sin.

In the church, offerings were part of the service, something I couldn't understand, or do anything about. As small as my stipend was, the dollar I figured I should put in the collection plate was significant to my budget. It was lunch.

I did find one other way to help the church. Tim had been cast in a performance of *Amal and the Night Visitors*. The church wanted people to make costumes. I made his. I thought it was very weird to see my very Jewish name listed in the acknowledgments in a church program.

Tim sang at other places than church. One of them was a madrigal dinner. He was able to get me a ticket for that. There was also a concert, featuring *The Planets*, by Holst. It had been sold out before Tim and I started seeing each other. The night of the performance, I buttoned him into his tuxedo and waited in the room he still had in the dorm, until he came back.

One of the things I did while I was waiting was to look at Tim's collection of magazines, mostly Playboys. Even though he claimed he read them mostly for the articles, he'd told me about what else he did with them, that first time in my bed. After my experience with Sam and his dirty books, I felt a little spooked, but I found the magazines much more worth reading than Sam's cheap paperbacks. Since Tim and I were having real sex, I could understand some of the things the magazines said. I even found the jokes and cartoons funny, something I would never have thought would happen. Still, I thought it was better to have the real thing than to read about it in the magazines. I could also feel how reading about it could make someone want it.

After our first time, Tim decided to make sure that there was no more danger that I'd get pregnant. Planned Parenthood gave him strips of packaged of condoms. They were near their expiration date, so they were given to students for free. The condoms weren't always fun, and sometimes broke the mood, so I decided I'd better do my part too. Planned Parenthood arranged a free doctor's appointment for me. He was a Doctor of Osteopathic Medicine, not an M.D. He was gentle and made my examination easy, and it was legal for him to prescribe birth control pills. He also drew my blood for testing for venereal diseases. He wasn't very good at that, but I didn't realize it. I'd never had my blood drawn before, except as a finger stick. When my arm had a purple bruise from my wrist to my elbow, I had no idea it wasn't normal. I thought it worth it, not because I was afraid that I might be infected; I didn't think Tim could give me anything; but because the test was required to qualify for the pills.

Soon after I began taking birth control pills, I started getting migraine headaches. I wasn't surprised to get them because Mother had them. I didn't understand that they might have anything to do with the hormones in the pills. At most, the headaches happened one or two days a month. Other than being resentful that I was Mother's daughter, while I was sitting on the floor of the bathroom leaning over the toilet, I didn't worry much about them.

Tim and I made love a lot. We were pretty much living together, even though he hadn't officially given up his dorm room. My bed was too small for two to sleep in comfortably, so we bought a foam pad and slept in a double sleeping bag on the floor.

We divided expenses as best we could, with me picking up the grocery bill but Tim paying for things like going to the movies. It soon became obvious that I had money at the end of the month while Tim often had month at the end of the money. Part of that was due to my stipend being larger, but we both could tell that even though Tim was better at math, I was much better with money. We decided I'd be in charge of whatever financial decisions involved both of us.

A lot of the time, I couldn't believe I was with Tim the way I was. I'd never expected to have any kind of a boyfriend at graduate school, let alone a live-in one. There was also the problem that I hadn't actually broken up with Irv. He still could hardly write, so there were no letters back and forth between us. There weren't any phone calls either, and since Irv's family had moved to Texas, I wasn't sure where he was.

One day, I had a Cat Stevens record playing in the apartment while I was washing dishes. Tim was in the bedroom reading. I listened to the song and started to cry. It was "Moon Shadow." It had been on the radio in the Math Physics Library a lot when Irv and I were there. Irv and I had also listened to it in his Karmann Ghia. I realized that I was in two relationships, and since Irv didn't know about Tim, I was cheating on him. That was something I'd always thought was wrong. It was even against the Ten Commandments. Tim wandered into the room and saw me crying. He asked me why I was upset.

I explained, but I didn't think that I'd have to do anything about Irv so soon. A couple of days later I got a call from him. Mother and I still talked sometimes, and she had given Irv my number. Irv told me that he would be driving from Texas to Ohio and was going to stop in Iowa to see me. I panicked. I had no idea what I would do or say, but I knew I couldn't just tell Irv about Tim on the phone. I told him to come.

I also told Tim that Irv was coming. He didn't tell me what to do; he just told me he'd use his room in the dorm while Irv was around. When Irv arrived, he was excited to see me, but he could tell there was a problem. I told him about Tim and said that I loved both of them. Irv stayed the night, but we just lay beside each other. He told me he was mad at himself for leaving me alone so long and that he should have known better. In the morning, he said that I was going to have to choose between him and Tim. Until that moment, I wasn't sure what I would say, but the words just came out. I told him I wished I could be with both of them, but I was choosing Tim.

Irv had intended to stay another day, but after that, he decided to leave. After he did, I realized that I had very few regrets about my decision. Even though I was only two years older than Irv, the difference in our ages seemed to make more difference than the six years between Tim and me. Tim and I were both independent and on our own. We were supporting ourselves and making our own decisions. I saw Tim and myself as adults. Irv was still a boy, under his parents' control. They were picking up all his expenses, telling him where to live and where to go. I didn't want a boy; I wanted a man, one with whom I could picture a future. That wasn't Irv.

After Irv was gone, Tim knocked on the door of my apartment. He told me he'd been checking the parking lot for Irv's car and saw it was gone. I told him I'd chosen him. I didn't even feel like crying. It was a relief. However, Irv didn't just let me go. On Sunday morning, a special delivery letter came from him, saying he wanted me back. When I read the letter, it didn't even look like a college student had written it. I remembered that his writing skills had needed improvement, but what he wrote looked more as it had been written by a young child. I was even more convinced that I needed someone who had grown up. Any doubts about my decision were gone.

To Mother, I'd never made a secret of the fact that I was pretty much living with Tim. With her relationship with Sam, I felt there was no way she could criticize me. Tim's parents, Monty and Alice Scott, were different. They knew that Tim had a girlfriend, but Tim hadn't told them we were together in the way we were. With them, he acted as if we were more as he'd been with Meredith, except not engaged. They did have my phone number and would call me, looking for Tim. For Christmas break, they offered to pay for both Tim and me to visit them in Glendale, a city near Los Angeles.

I was nervous about going to see them. I'd paid my way to visit Irv, and if anything went wrong, I could have left. However, the weather in Iowa was freezing while California was warm. Tim wanted to go, and I didn't want to spend the holidays alone, so I went with him.

The Scotts were nice to me, but insisted, as Irv's parents had, that Tim and I sleep in different rooms. They gave me the guest room and put Tim in a sleeping bag on the floor of the living room. Neither Tim nor I had much money, but we took advantage of what we had, to see the tourist spots of Southern California. Tim had already seen most of them, but I hadn't. Tim and I went with his parents to Hollywood and Graumman's Chinese Theater. After living in New York, the tourist attractions in L.A. didn't impress me much. For a city that wanted to make money from tourists, it did very little to help them. All the restaurants near the theater had big signs saying that restrooms were for patrons only. I was also confused by my reaction to the temperature. At the same temperature in Iowa, New York, or Ohio, I would have been warm, but somehow what little dampness there was in California, penetrated my body, and I was cold. My winter coat was too heavy, so I ended up spending some of what little money I had, on a sweater.

I'd wanted to see Disneyland since I was a little girl and had watched the *Mickey Mouse Club* on television. I also saw it on *The Wonderful World of Color*, even though I'd never had a color television to watch it. I thought it would be great to see it for real. Tim's parents went to Disneyland with us too, which was lucky because it was expensive and they picked up the tab. While we were in the park, they went different places than Tim and I did. They claimed there was no way they could go on the scarier rides, but wanted Tim and me to have a good time on them. I did, but every minute I kept expecting to see Mouseketeers singing and dancing their way through the park, as they had on TV. There weren't any. There were a few costumed characters, like Goofy, but I wasn't interested in them. I enjoyed the rides, but no more than the ones on Coney Island in New York, and the lines were much longer in Disneyland. I was beginning to realize just how much I'd believed what I saw on TV. I was ashamed about how I'd been fooled.

One thing that was new and wonderful to me was Christmas. I helped decorate the Scotts' tree, finding out for the first time about things like bubble lights. I thought they were amazing. I also helped Monty wrap a present for Alice. Usually, he had his presents wrapped for him at the store, but he'd bought that one at the last minute and didn't have time. On Christmas morning, I hadn't expected to get anything, but when the presents from under the tree were handed out, there was one for me, a little teacup. Alice collected them and thought I should have one. That felt weird but good.

Celebrating Christmas was not the only thing different from the way I'd grown up. I'd seen alcohol used mostly for ceremonial purposes on Friday nights and Passover. My father didn't drink it at all. Mother liked a glass of wine sometimes, especially if it fit in with her snob appeal. Sam had his scotch, but I had never seen him down more than a glass except when he had a toothache. I'd considered drinking too much, as a student thing, something to stop as an adult. Monty and Alice Scott, especially Alice, had alcohol all the time. They drank it with every meal, including mimosas or Bloody Marys at breakfast. I didn't like it that much, and usually said, "No thank you." Tim would have a glass to join his parents but never came close to being drunk. Alice seemed to use celebrations as an excuse to drink enough to make her say things that should have been private.

I was embarrassed when she said that Monty had an affair with a secretary at work. It was over, but he had been fired. Alice was working, but they'd had to move to a cheaper apartment. Monty had found a new job recently, and the Scotts were going through marriage counseling.

After a few of glasses of wine, Alice also accidentally called me Meredith, and then got down on her knees and pretended to crawl to apologize. I'd never seen an adult behave that way. What Alice did was more upsetting than being called the wrong name.

Alice also confessed that she and Monty had known Tim and I were living together. I'd accidentally given it away when Alice had called my apartment looking for Tim; I'd had told her Tim wasn't home. I blushed when she told me about my mistake, but couldn't help wondering why if the Scotts knew, they didn't just say so. I couldn't understand how their minds worked.

The final part of our visit, Alice and Monty decided it would be a great idea to go to Las Vegas. I knew how to play twenty-one, which is called blackjack, and how to count cards from bridge and hearts, so the idea of real gambling was exciting. I practiced with Monty and Tim and I won. Los Angeles and Las Vegas were both warm, but the mountains in between weren't. The drive took a long time because Monty had to stop so he and Tim could put chains on the tires to get through the mountain pass. Then they had to take them off when we were out of the snow. By the time we arrived, I was anxious to try my luck at a blackjack table. I'd put aside ten dollars for gambling, but in five minutes it was all gone. I was disappointed and wandered around the casino while Alice played her favorite slot machines. I had a couple of quarters in my wallet, so I decided to pick a machine of my own and give it a shot. On my second quarter, the machine rolled to triple bars. Bells went off, and quarters clunked into the metal pan. I scooped them into a paper cup. It was only twenty-five dollars, but I had more than doubled my gambling money, and I was thrilled. I avoided blowing what I'd won for the rest of our time in Las Vegas. When Tim and I went back to Iowa, two days later, I was sure that anytime I had a chance to go to Las Vegas again, I wanted to do it.

When Tim had the chance to move out of his dorm room, he did, but to him, my apartment wasn't much better. He had grown up in more upscale conditions than I had, and wasn't impressed with the old sink and showerless bathroom. He started talking about future plans, speculating aloud that by the next summer we would be living in married student housing. When I pointed out that we'd need to be married to live there, he said nothing. I saw that as a tease and not a funny one. No conversation I'd ever had with a guy on the subject of marriage had worked out in anything resembling a positive way. I was upset that Tim would mention it and then just leave me hanging. Finally, I'd had enough. When we were lying side by side in the sleeping bag on the floor, I just asked

Tim if we were going to get married or not. Tim grudgingly asked me to marry him, but the next morning when we woke up, he asked again spontaneously.

There was no ring. Tim still had the one Meredith had returned when they'd broken up, but I didn't want to wear another woman's jewelry. Tim had no money to buy me one of my own, but I was okay with knowing I was engaged. Tim and I planned to get married at the end of the term, but things were not going well academically for either of us.

After getting a four point in Chemical Pedagogy, I had officially chosen physical chemistry as my major but was having a hard time again with the math. This time it was differential equations. I didn't fail it, but to bring my grade point up, I repeated the class. I also discovered that most of the other grad students in chemistry had much more of a passion for it than I did. They had chosen chemistry. I'd just fallen into it. I was surprised that I enjoyed teaching. I'd been assigned as a laboratory assistant, by the professor in charge of Freshman Chemistry. He had met Dr. Bosch when the professor had visited Iowa. He'd liked him and been very impressed that he'd recommended me. He told me something that I didn't know. Dr. Bosch was famous and had an equation named after him. That explained why graduate schools had been so anxious to accept me on his recommendation, but it didn't help me with what was happening that semester.

Tim's problem was different. I write anything I have to, with no difficulty, but he couldn't get the words to flow. He was behind with finishing his thesis and wasn't catching up. He was in real trouble, and he knew it.

Meredith came back to Iowa to visit and it scared me to death. After getting her masters, she had moved to Minnesota but wasn't happy there. She convinced herself that she missed Tim and came back to try to make up with him. She met him in the little office he was assigned to as a research assistant. I might never have known if I hadn't run into Pat, Tim's office mate, who told me that Meredith had been there.

I was shaking, and thought I might throw up. I'd never seen Meredith, but I knew she was pretty. She was into computers as Tim was, and she was a Christian, which despite going to church, I still wasn't. After what Elliott and Irv had said about marrying me, I was afraid Tim would drop me too. Meredith would take back her ring, and I'd be alone.

When Tim came to the apartment, he didn't say anything about Meredith showing up. I could barely get the words out of my mouth, I was shaking so much, but I asked him about her. Tim admitted that she'd been there and had tried to get back together with him. He told me that he'd said no. He and I had made each other a promise, and he wasn't going back on it.

I was overwhelmed. When he had a choice, Tim had chosen me, as I had chosen him instead of Irv. It was the first time I knew I was at the top of anyone's list, and I was going to do whatever it took to stay there.

We planned our wedding. It was going to be small, very small. We had originally pictured using the huge sanctuary of the church, but we realized our tiny group would be lost in it, and chose the chapel instead. Most of the guests would be my friends and family. Les was coming. Elliott would be bringing his fiancée. I'd never met her, but Elliott and I had continued to exchange occasional letters, and he had described Dee as perfect in every way he could see. Alyne would be my matron of honor. Rachel was coming, with her current boyfriend. Mother would be arriving and even pitching in a little on expenses. Unfortunately, Sam would be coming too. I didn't invite him, but Mother did.

Tim would have his parents there, with Morty serving as his best man. His grandparents were also coming. His office mate Pat was the only friend of his that would be there. Counting the minister and the organist, there would be seventeen people at the ceremony.

With as little money as we had, I spent thirty dollars on materials to make my wedding dress. I sold some of my textbooks to buy a wedding ring for Tim. I would be wearing one Grandma Levi had left me. The chapel and the minister were free, although Tim planned to give the minister something. Besides that, Tim only had to come up with the fee for the organist.

Tim and I had chosen to be married by the senior pastor, Lester, who had a Jewish daughter-in-law and was sympathetic to me. The church required pre-marital counseling, which Lester would be giving to us. The counseling involved sex, which made me very nervous, but Lester never said anything about Tim and me living together, he just told us about what he believed worked in a marriage. Before the church would let us get married there, Lester gave us his final advice. We should not expect to change the other person. If we couldn't accept each other as we were, we shouldn't get married. We both agreed to what he said.

When a larger apartment became available in my building, we took it. There were two beds we could push together to make a king, and a real living room. Tim still looked at it like a slum, but I loved it. I could imagine our future taking place there, but it wasn't going to happen.

Disaster struck not long before our wedding. Tim was out of chances to finish his thesis. He was being dropped from the master's program. At the end of the term, there would be no more classes and no more stipend. He cried when he told me what had happened and that he would have to go wherever he could find a job. I suggested that it might be a sign that neither of us belonged in graduate school. I decided that wherever he had to go, I would go with him.

After some very nervous weeks, Tim lined up a job in Minnesota, to start soon after we were married. We had never planned a honeymoon. We had no money to take one, but now there would be a quick trip to Saint Paul to scout out a place to live before we moved there.

Our wedding ceremony was short, but not without glitches. Lester had been called out of town, and another minister performed it. Mother was not happy that I wanted Elliott and Les to walk me down the aisle, although the fill-in minister insisted that they say they were doing it in the name of the family. The words the new minister used for the ceremony were not the choice I would have made, and upset Mother. Tim's grandfather, who had dementia, had times in and out of awareness. He woke up during the ceremony and shouted out, asking if the groom was Tim. I was afraid I was going to faint, or wished I would, but we made it through our vows.

From the church steps, I threw Dee the tiny bouquet that had been stuck onto the Jewish Bible Mother had insisted I had to carry. Then everyone at the wedding, except for the minister and the organist, went to a steak house for what was the closest thing we'd have to a reception. All fifteen of us gathered around a table. As best man, Jim's father made a toast. Elliott also stood up, after looking at Les, and with a hostile stare at Sam, and made part of his toast a threat to Tim that if I were mistreated, Tim would have to answer to him. The presents weren't big, but we had some. Tim and I opened them and cut a little cake.

Since Tim and I had no plans to go anywhere until our trip to Saint Paul in a few days, we invited Les, Elliott, Dee, Alyne, Rachel, and her new boyfriend to our apartment in the evening after the wedding. The atmosphere was much looser than at the restaurant. We told jokes and did a water sharing ceremony taken from Robert Heinlein's *A Stranger in a Strange Land*. The pressure was off, and Tim and I made love that night for the first time as husband and wife.

Tim and I did get lucky about a few things. One was that along with my guitar, Mother had brought along several hundred dollars' worths of savings bonds that I had received from relatives on various birthdays and graduations, and she had hidden away. I had no idea that the bonds existed, and they would be a start, if a small one, for our married life. There was also some money in wedding presents, including a gift from Sam. I wondered if he somehow thought it let him off the hook for the way he'd treated me, but I was glad to have the money. The bank had also just issued low limit credit cards to the students, making travel, especially the rental of a car, easier.

Tim made the drive to Saint Paul. In June, the city was a comfortable temperature and easy to move around in. Using a local rental guide, we targeted an area within a bus ride of the publishing house where Tim would be working on computers. We found an apartment there. Though still small to Tim, it was beautiful to me. The kitchen was up to date and featured the first dishwasher I'd ever had. There was even a timer on the oven to turn it on and off. The living room and bedroom were both a good size and the bathroom had a real shower. There was even a bus stop out front, with a bus that would take Tim to work without a transfer. A supermarket was close enough so we could get there on our bikes.

One serious drawback was that the apartment was unfurnished, and neither Tim nor I owned any furniture. The building manager was able to direct us to a furniture rental agency that featured specials that would fit within our budget. I hoped we could save up for our own things later. I was still in charge of the money, so I put down a deposit.

We went back to Iowa just long enough to load what stuff we had into a small one-way U-Haul, and Tim drove it to our new apartment. It was a Friday, and Tim would be starting work on Monday. I now saw myself as a wife, the kind I'd seen on TV while growing up, like on *Leave it to Beaver*. I didn't have any shirtwaist dresses and pearls, but I could spend my days cooking, cleaning, and making sure all Tim's shirts were ironed, while he was working.

When Tim got his first paycheck, with all the deductions that hadn't been applicable to a research assistant, it was clear that my ideas about staying home, wouldn't work. If we were going to be able to afford a car, and eventually buy furniture of our own, I would have to find a job. Employment opportunities for chemists were not much better than they had been when I graduated from Barnum. I took a job operating an industrial sewing machine at a luggage factory. The high-speed sewing of leather was nothing like the sewing I used to make my clothes. I was terrible at it, and before they could officially fire me, I took the civil service exam. I did well at that, as I was with most tests, and ended up at the top of the listings. After an interview, I lined up a job as a file clerk at the State Retirement System.

I was in charge of 149,000 files, and I was good at keeping them in order. I was too good at it. I usually finished my work too quickly and wanted to spend the extra time reading something, anything. I figured that it was part of my job to read the informational booklets about the agency itself. I did, and I was called on the carpet for it by my supervisor, who told me I wasn't allowed to read anything, while on the job. Her decision was reversed by the director, but only for when I had nothing else to do, which had been the case anyway. I got myself into more trouble when I thought I was following the rules and just asking to do what was fair.

I didn't drink coffee. Mother loved it, and so did Tim. I liked the smell, but not the taste. If I drank anything hot, it was tea. A large urn was used to make coffee for the majority of the workers in the office, who did drink it. Responsibility for loading and starting it was assigned by passing a decorated rock called a coffee rock from employee to employee, in turn. With more than thirty employees in the office, I didn't get the rock too often.

I made coffee for Tim every morning. I would have gone along an occasional day making it at work, even if I didn't drink coffee myself, but my boss, Deborah, decided that she thought the other employees were too busy to make coffee so that the stone would remain in the file room. I protested. From my reading, I had memorized all the regulations relating to my job. Aside from the fact that I got nothing out of making coffee, cooking or food preparation of any kind was specifically excluded from the duties of the employees of the agency. It was against the rules for Deborah to demand that I, or anyone, make coffee in the first place. I handed the rock back to Deborah and quoted the rule to her. Deborah didn't deny that I was right, but wrote me up for a lack of diplomacy, something I had no idea was required of a file clerk. That wasn't in my official job description either. I not only filed faster and found lost files better when compared to my co-workers; I began to think this job might not be the best one for me, either. When the civil service exam for the next level up came around, I took it and scored at the top.

Something was going on in the office besides deciding who would make coffee. A union had begun organizing, and a vote would be taken as to whether the workers at the retirement system would be part of it. A union sounded good to me. They would enforce the rules. I never was given the details of exactly what being a member might mean, but I was told a union would stand up for me. I took that to mean that I wouldn't be written up when I did my actual job well and hadn't done anything wrong. Along with most of the other workers, I voted for the union.

I thought Tim and I should put as much money in the bank as we could. Health insurance had gone into effect for both of us, and I wanted to be a mother. I was sure that I could do a much better job than Mother did of protecting and loving a child. Tim wanted a child too, and after a few months, we decided that I should go off the pill. Neither one of us assumed I'd get pregnant right away. Most of what I'd read, said that after coming off the hormones, it could take a year or sometimes more to conceive.

My hormones hadn't read the articles. Within a month, I began to get nauseous. When I didn't get my period, I arranged for a pregnancy test. When the results were called to me at the office, one of the other clerks heard the conversation, and the news spread quickly. Though normally I didn't want people in my private business, I wasn't upset. In any case, I knew that it couldn't be a secret very long. I realized that in a few months I wouldn't be able just to climb the ladders to get to the files on the upper shelves. I waited for a job to open up at the new level I'd qualified for, so I could sit behind a desk.

When I'd applied for the exam, the rules said that qualification for jobs was strictly on the basis of score, which should have given the next available position to me. Unfortunately, one thing I had not been told about voting for a union was that those rules would change. Getting a job wasn't just based on test scores anymore; it was also based on seniority. I was beaten out by another girl in the office who had scored lower but had worked two months longer than I had. I would need to put in for next level jobs elsewhere in the civil service system.

I tried for the other jobs, but most of them didn't want me. There was one that I could have had, but it would have meant being on the phone all day. I hated phone calls with strangers; I had all my life. I didn't know why, but I was very afraid of them. Tim knew it, and usually, if a phone call needed to be made for something at home, he'd make it. It was an even exchange. I took care of the budget making and bill paying that Tim couldn't stand, and he took care of phone conversations.

The time of the year came for a computer-generated form to be put in every file. I spent as much time as I could climbing ladders, while I could still do it safely. I also suggested an improvement in a form, which would speed up the filing system. For that, I won a Governor's Award, which included a certificate and a little bit of cash. In my personnel record, it was more important than a lack of diplomacy. I managed to stay in the file room and do my work until I was starting my eighth month, when I applied for the maximum leave of absence, six months.

During the time we were in Saint Paul, Tim and I had kept going to church together. Tim joined the choir, and I joined with him, but I never stopped being Jewish.

Tim was a bass, and I was a first soprano, which put me in the first row of the choir loft. Members of the choir were the first to figure out I was pregnant, being the people I talked to the most. There was no one at the church I would have called a friend, but my friendliest acquaintance was Wendy, the minister's wife. Wendy was also a first soprano, the best in the choir. She sat next to me and figured out the strategy to keep it from being obvious that I didn't take communion. Wendy suggested that when the choir went to the altar, I could hide behind a pillar and rejoin the choir without being noticed when they recessed back to the loft. I didn't see anything wrong with that. My situation was strange. I was welcome for my high notes but didn't believe church teachings. That was something that would go on for many years.

At church was where I fainted for the first time. I was about four months pregnant, just enough to show, because I was thin, and the choir noticed the change. Pregnancy also added a little resonance to my voice. Normally the adult choir only sang one service, with a youth choir singing an earlier one, but it was Easter, and we sang two. It was a very full program, almost a cantata. I did fine the first time. I thought I was fine the second time too, until the last page of the last song. My ears began to buzz, and my vision grayed. I was told later that I turned even whiter than usual. I was stubborn enough to finish the last note but then sank into my seat in the loft. Wendy knew that something was wrong and offered to take me downstairs, but I wanted to stay where I was. I wasn't sure I could move anywhere anyway. When the congregation and the choir were dismissed after the benediction, I was feeling much better, but I was worried about the baby. On the first appointment that I could get with my obstetrician, I was surprised that he found the whole thing funny. He just told me that all the blood had pooled in my legs and to try not to sing any more double services until the baby was born. I was still worried, but after fainting, my pregnancy seemed to go a lot more smoothly.

I did have one real friend in Saint Paul, Jane. She had been on my floor in the dorm at Barnum. We had known each other slightly. We talked in the dorm lounge sometimes. Now we were in the same city. Jane was in Saint Paul because she had found a job there, no easier for a sociology major than a chemistry major. We ran into each other accidentally, and we were both glad to see a familiar face. Jane came to dinner with Tim and me. Jane and I also went shopping together.

Tim also had people he knew in the city. One of the scared them heck out of me and was one of the reasons I'd wanted to get pregnant as fast as I did. It was Meredith, Tim's former fiancée. Tim only saw Meredith at meetings of a computer society, but Meredith was single, and I was afraid Meredith would make another try to get Tim back. Pregnant with Tim's child, I felt more secure.

Tim's other friends in Saint Paul were George and Jo Markey. George and Tim had been friends when Tim took his first job working with computers, after high school. Jim knew Jo too. We all played bridge and soon Jo and I started competing, not just at the bridge table, but also in the kitchen. It began when Tim and I were invited to the Markey's apartment. I thought I should bring some kind of hostess gift to Tim's old friends so I baked cinnamon bread. Jo took it as a challenge. She came up with fancy cookies the next time we got together. It got to the point where who won the game didn't matter, just who made the best food. I would have rather have just played friendly games, as I had at Barnum, but I also worked on my skills with an oven.

I went through several months of morning sickness and migraines triggered by the same hormones that had been in my birth control tablets. Our visits with the Markeys began to taper off until they stopped. I missed being able to play bridge, but I didn't miss my endless contest with Jo.

My pregnancy brought another complication into our lives. The apartment building where we lived didn't allow children. We had to find one that did, that we could also afford when I stopped working. My bonds paid for the down payment on a car so we could look all over the city. We finally decided on a building on the same bus route as our old apartment, but in a more commercial area.

The building was right next to a shopping center. That made it cheaper, but better for me. It meant I could walk to a supermarket and a fabric store. I could buy enough remnants to make clothes for the baby and even decorations for our new nursery. The halls of the building were long and dingy. The walk from our apartment to the mailboxes was at least five minutes long. There was one thing that I looked at as a real luxury, an indoor heated swimming pool. I thought it might help when my back and legs hurt from being pregnant.

Tim and I moved in. Jane kept visiting me, and I also made a new friend in the building. Sue and Gary Jensen weren't from Minnesota either. They came from Georgia and were serious Baptists. Sue had made a point of telling me that she and Gary had held out and not had sex until they were married. Remembering my first time with Tim, I wasn't sure that would have made for a great wedding night or even a honeymoon. Sue was so proud of what they'd done I didn't say anything.

Aside from understanding each other because we'd both had only one real lover, Sue and I were scheduled to deliver within two weeks of each other, with me due first. We looked at childbirth very differently. Sue had plans to do things like most mothers did, and took anything her doctor could give her for pain. Her breasts were much bigger than mine, but she didn't like the idea of nursing.

I didn't want to be anything like Mother. I decided that I would sacrifice anything to do what was best for my child. To me, that meant natural childbirth and breast-feeding, which I read would provide the best nutrition.

Tim was willing to go to Lamaze classes with me. They were free under my health insurance. He did his best to act as my coach. I practiced sleeping between contractions and was sure I'd be fine.

When Tim and I went to the hospital, it wasn't because I had contractions. Tim was up at two A.M. to do maintenance on a computer system, and I'd gotten up to make breakfast for him. When I noticed my panties were wet, I thought I'd just peed a little bit. After I changed twice, I realized that my water had broken. Tim never got his maintenance done. I was examined, and the nurse said I was right about my water breaking. I still didn't have any contractions, but it was the day before my due date, and I was told that if labor didn't begin by itself, the doctor would induce, to prevent infection. I was put in a room by myself and told to try to sleep. Tim didn't want to, but he obeyed when the nurses told him to go home and wait for a phone call.

I didn't sleep. I lay in bed watching the clock and waiting for something to happen. At five o'clock in the morning it did, with contractions making it obvious that I was in labor. The nurses told me to walk the hall to speed up my labor and gave me access to a phone to call Tim. The walking did its job and then some. I leaned against a wall and slid down to squat when the pain hit. The nurses were sympathetic and asked if I wanted to reconsider having a natural birth. I was not changing my mind. I wouldn't do anything that might hurt the baby. I wouldn't take the drugs

Tim came, and we tried our best to apply what we learned in class. I couldn't sleep between contractions. There was a band around me to hold fetal monitor a fetal monitor on, but I felt better sitting up. The breathing helped, but not as much as it was supposed to. I held Tim's hand tight. I think I was crushing his fingers, but he didn't complain.

Finally, my doctor, who had been able to sleep in the on call room at the hospital, said my dilation was complete. Tim didn't have to tell me to push. It was all I wanted to do, but the doctor stopped me. The cord was around the baby's neck and had to be cleared. When I was allowed to push again, the baby came fast, and the nurses took him and worked on him. He was breathing, but his Apgar was low. Instead of giving him to me to hold, they took him upstairs to see a pediatrician.

That wasn't what I'd expected. I'd done everything right. I'd eaten what I was told. I took the vitamins the doctor gave me, even though they made me gag. I kept my weight where the doctor said it should be. I didn't take anything for the pain. However, something had still gone wrong. Tim held my hand as we waited to hear about our son.

A pediatrician came in. He was smiling. He told us that our baby was okay. He was breathing fine, and everything appeared to be normal except for a strange white blaze in his hair. The doctor asked if anyone in my family had one like it. I had pictured Mother before she had much gray and she'd started having it dyed. She did have a white streak. I told the doctor the blaze came from my mother and he accepted my answer.

Tim and I named our son James Shimon after my grandfather Levi. Most of Tim's family was still alive, and in my Jewish tradition, children were only named after the dead. We immediately nicknamed our son JS. I would have loved it if Mother's effect on JS had ended with the blaze and the family name, but she had insisted on coming to Saint Paul from New York. My first problem with that was that she was in my hospital room when Eric, the pastor at Tim's and my church came to visit. The two had met before, looking in on JS at the nursery. Eric commented that he liked the baby's name of two apostles, the second one being the Hebrew name for Simon who became Peter. As Mother started looking very hostile, I wished I could disappear, but I just had to let it happen.

Before I left the hospital, as a first-time mother, the nurses taught me about bathing and changing JS. They had also helped me make sure I could nurse without hurting my breasts. I got a bag of goodies, including the cream the hospital had used on JS's skin. Tim and I brought JS home in a brand new, highly rated, infant seat, despite Mother pleading that we should just let her hold him. We'd both studied statistics on babies and car accidents, and we weren't taking any chances.

Mother slept on the foldout couch in the living room. I did my best to follow the nurses' advice, but JS had cried a lot and was hard to comfort in the hospital. That didn't change when we took him home. I would sit for hours in the new rocking chair Tim and I had bought, nursing him when he'd take it, trying to get him to sleep. I got so frustrated that I even cried to Mother, who kept giving advice that contradicted what I'd read and what the nurses told me. Mother was even worse at getting JS to stop crying than I was, and after a few days, she decided to return to New York. I was glad to see her leave.

JS had a rash that kept getting bigger. I took him for his first baby check, hoping that the doctor would have something to take care of it. The pediatrician acted like I was doing something wrong. JS had gained almost no weight, and his rash was covering a lot of his body. The doctor said he suspected I was not putting out enough milk and that something I was putting on JS was causing his rash. He told me that JS could be washed with nothing but water, wear nothing but cotton clothes, and diapers washed in only the gentlest soap. He was to be covered by nothing but cotton blankets either, for a week. Then I was supposed to bring him back. If he hadn't gained enough weight, they would weigh him before and after I nursed him, the doctor would talk about what I'd have to do.

I felt like the building had fallen on me. I'd worked so hard to be the best mother I could, and the world was coming apart around me. JS would not be able to wear his cute stretchy sleepers. The only cotton clothes I had for him were t-shirts. The disposable diapers from the hospital were out too. I had cloth ones but had not counted on using them yet. I was also worried that there was something wrong with my milk.

I was very nervous through the next week. As I stopped using the cream the hospital had sent home with me, JS's rash started to go away. As it did, he cried less. I nursed him every minute he seemed to want it. He was getting bigger. I could feel it.

At the next check-up, JS had no rash. The doctor's scale showed he had gained at least as much weight as he should have. The doctor was surprised, but just told me to keep doing what I was doing. It was a lot easier for him to say, than for me to do.

A couple of weeks later, Sue Jensen gave birth to her baby, Ethan. It seemed so much easier for her. Ethan cried a lot less, drank from a bottle and easily wore anything Sue put on him. I knew that I was doing the right thing for JS, nursing him. Research had proved that. Still, I wished I had at least much quiet time in my life as Sue did. When Sue and I started going out together, I discovered how to get it. Tim and I had bought a front carrier, one with a zipper that would allow JS to nurse without anyone being able to tell. I found that whether he was nursing or not, if JS was in close contact with my body, he almost never cried. I began to wear the carrier all the time, and when JS grew too big for it, I got a baby backpack.

Up to that point, I'd kept my hair long, usually braided to keep it out of the way. The braids were too handy for JS to grab, so I got my hair cut short. I could tell that Tim didn't like it much, but he understood why I had to do it.

With JS in a backpack, I was also able to go shopping with Jane. She got to know JS well enough that she could babysit for me. Tim and I were excited that we were able to see a couple of movies together, especially since the movies were *Star Wars* and *Superman*. We both still loved science fiction.

We also had to think about real life. We had decided that it would be easier for us and JS if we raised him as a Christian, especially since we were both involved with a church. I wanted the JS's first Christmas to be perfect. I was afraid JS might be allergic to a live one, so we bought a small, artificial tree. I sewed unbreakable ornaments out of scraps of fabric and felt, just in case something fell off the tree while JS was on the carpet. With our budget being very tight, I sewed Tim's present too, a new winter jacket. Toward the end of my pregnancy, I'd already made a new warm coat for myself, because my old one couldn't fit around me anymore. I always found men's clothes harder to sew, and the jacket was a lot of work, but I was proud of it.

My life became even more complicated when Morty and Alice Scott announced that they were coming to visit Tim, me, and JS for Christmas. I was determined to be the best hostess I could be.

I planned meals, from a fancy cookbook Tim had bought me when I was competing with Jo Markey. Things didn't always work out as I planned. Alice like her meat much more well done than the book recommended, and when I made Steak Diane, I had to put hers back in the pan for her. Morty complimented my cooking a lot, which caused Tim to make a big mistake. He told Alice that she'd never be the cook I was. Alice was very upset. Tim's comment was not my fault, but Alice blamed me anyway. I liked the Scotts and felt much closer to Alice than I did to Mother, but I was relieved when they went back to California.

When the end of my leave of absence was coming up, I found out I had a problem I hadn't seen coming. One of the reasons Tim and I had chosen our apartment, besides low rent and the swimming pool was its association with a childcare center. I had assumed they would be able to care for JS when I went back to work. I'd assumed wrong. The center only took babies over two years old. I had no family to turn to, and Sue wasn't interested in dealing with another baby, especially one with JS's limitations. Jane had a job of her own and the private sitters I contacted charged as much or more than I'd make working. I would have to officially resign and stay home with JS. More than that, Tim and I would still need extra money.

The only solution was for Tim to look for a better paying job. He sent out resumes everywhere, but the only response he received was from Humford, in California. They paid for him to fly out for an interview, and hired him.

I didn't like the idea of having to move to California. I liked Saint Paul, especially since I had friends there. The move wouldn't cost us anything, Humford would be picking up the tab for it as well as for a hotel room, until Tim and I found a new place to live, but it would be a big change. The good thing was that Morty and Alice would be there. My grandparents had been willing to care for me when I was growing up. I hoped, despite what happened at Christmas that JS would have helpful grandparents as well. I convinced myself that everything would work out for the best, so Tim drove me and JS cross-country to California.

In Saint Paul, we'd only had to worry about the cold. The trip to California was the reverse. The car we'd bought in Saint Paul wasn't air-conditioned. There was no reason for it to be. When we crossed the Mojave Desert, I had to keep JS cool by constantly pouring water over the vinyl surfaces of his baby seat. Tim and I just coped with sweltering ourselves. Things were better when we made it to Los Angeles, and we gratefully checked into our hotel.

Chapter Thirteen

I liked living in a hotel. The only housework I had to worry about was laundry, and the facilities for that were at least as good as they had been at the apartment house in Saint Paul. I could take JS to sit by the pool, and he seemed to like the sunshine. At nine months, he wasn't walking yet, but he could crawl fast enough that I would have to run after him in a hallway. The staff was friendly, and the food was good.

Tim's job at Humford was only a few minutes away, so after his workday and on weekends, we took JS with us to look at apartments. I'd decided that I wanted to be near the ocean. I'd always found it calming when Grandma Levi took me as a kid, and I hoped it would have the same effect on JS. Apartments in California were more expensive than in Saint Paul, and our budget ruled out any place right on the water. We were able to locate an apartment in Redondo Beach, two miles inland. It wasn't fancy. With other apartments, it formed a square around a courtyard. It was within walking distance of a supermarket, a library, and a clinic so that I could take JS anywhere we needed to go. Like Saint Paul, there was also a daycare facility nearby, but also like Saint Paul, JS wouldn't be eligible until he was two years old. There was no air conditioning, but the ocean breeze kept things comfortable most of the time. I doubted we would need heat much. That would save us money.

One of the first things Tim and I did after settling into our apartment was to join the choir of a local church. It was a larger choir than I had ever belonged to before. There were two other couples who had babies about the same age as JS, and there was nursery care during rehearsals. JS got off to a bad start during the first rehearsal, He wouldn't stop crying until one of the teenagers volunteering in the nursery came to get me, but I was able to quiet him down enough to get a chance to sing. After that, things went more smoothly. The two other sets of parents, Rob and Jean Carson, and Dunn and Molly Bean, invited Tim and me along for after choir ice cream. After that outing, Tim and I became part of a small church-based group of parents. The other members were the Carsons, the Beans, and the Caldwells, whose children were older.

I had expected that Tim's parents would want to spend time regularly with JS, as most of the grandparents I knew seemed to do with their grandchildren, but the Scotts didn't seem to want to. They did come to dinner at our apartment once in a while. They also invited Tim and me to bridge games, where we could bring JS along. I didn't have to worry about snack competitions with Alice, who seemed to be more interested in sipping alcohol when she played, but I soon found out that winning bridge games against Alice was a very bad idea. It made her almost as upset as what Tim had said about her cooking. Throwing a game was not fun, and I began to dread the family visits. It was better to concentrate on hanging out with our friends at church, and I threw myself into that.

The churchwomen and I visited a fabric store as a unit, searching through remnants for bargains that could be sewn into clothes for our babies. All the couples in our group formed a singing ensemble to perform at church functions. We also kicked in together for sitters to cover all the babies, so we could do outings like Renaissance faires, for which Jean, Molly, and I sewed costumes. We also all had a dream of owning houses. Tim and I were still barely making it from paycheck to paycheck on Tim's salary, so I decided the only way they could ever save enough for a down payment on a house, would be if I went back to work. Molly offered that if I found a job, she could take care of JS for a few hours each day.

The only way the timing would work would be if I found a job on the night shift. When JS was eighteen months old, a position opened up at a local medical laboratory. I would be working from eleven p.m. until seven a.m. Tim would watch JS overnight, and Molly would do it while I slept for a few hours during the day. The schedule would still allow me to stay in the choir and go to all the church activities. It seemed like a great way to go.

Under the laws of California, my chemistry background didn't qualify me to be a medical technologist, so I was designated as a laboratory assistant. The position was not well paid, but it was more than I made as a teaching assistant or a file clerk. The job let me pay Molly and still put money in the bank towards a house. My schedule wasn't easy. Tim dropped JS with Molly on his way to work, but I had to take a bus to pick him up. The situation was so unwieldy that I decided that I would finally have to get a driver's license. I signed up for a night school driving class I could fit in before work.

For me, the memorization of motor vehicle regulations and the written aspects of the class were simple. Actually learning to drive a car wasn't any easier than it had been when I tried it with Les or Irv. However, I was determined. Every experience I'd had in California told me that without a driver's license, I wasn't a real person. Tim took me out for practice, and so did my friends. I realized that one of the reasons it was so hard for me, dated back to the lazy eye I had as a child. Despite patches and three eye surgeries, it had never been fixed. When I got older, my ophthalmologist told me that my brain was always blanking out one eye, so I didn't have any depth perception. He was upbeat about the diagnosis, saying the only thing I would never be able to do, would be to fly a plane. I'd never seen any other way, so I'd adjusted. My vision was a problem when I was trying to drive. My inability to judge distance made parking, as well spacing my car with other cars, difficult, especially at night. I worked hard to make my brain learn to do those things anyway. I failed my road test three times. I was lucky that a co-worker had agreed to pick me up for work and drop me at home. I also knew her generosity couldn't last forever.

A week before JS turned two he suddenly started to read. His first word was Sears, which he learned from seeing commercials on TV. After that was Montgomery Ward, which was obviously in the same category. The stores' names were followed by reading the makes of cars. JS would point to them when we were out. After that, I began taking him the children's section at the library to choose simple books. I was proud of him. He had been the slowest walker of the babies in my group of friends and barely qualified as potty-trained, as required by the daycare he went into when he turned two. Now he had a skill to set him apart and ahead of the other toddlers. I worked with him on it every spare minute I had, although I didn't have that many.

My schedule was getting hard on my health. The few hours of sleep I caught in the morning plus whatever I could manage when Tim was home, weren't enough to keep my immunity up. I caught a series of infections deep in my chest that not only made working harder but messed with my singing as well. When the doctor at the nearby clinic gave me antibiotics, he warned me that I would most likely keep getting sick until I was off the night shift. There was no way that could have worked with Molly. However, now that JS was two and enrolled in the daycare center, I applied for a change of hours. The best I could get was four A.M. to noon. It was still considered a day shift, so I lost the premium of a paid half hour for lunch I'd received for working nights. Worse than that, it meant I would lose my ride. I needed to pass my driving test.

Having Tim take me to be tested had just made me more nervous, so the day before my hours were scheduled to change, my lab friend took me. The change worked. For me to drive the car, meant that Tim would be taking a bike to work until we could afford a second car, but the commute for him was very short, and all during the day. With daycare within walking distance, Tim got JS up and ready, and dropped him off before he went to work. I picked him up in the afternoon. Tim and I saw each other less during waking hours, but with our determination to accumulate a house payment, we accepted the situation.

It was in the middle of stagflation, and interest rates were high. The price of houses had been rising ever since Tim and I had been in California. We could see that if we didn't buy a house soon, we'd lose our chance. We also watched as the Beans managed to buy a home because Dunn Bean's parents gave them a down payment. No one could give us that kind of money, or would have if they could. I worked as hard as I could, earning a raise. Tim and I loaded as much money into our bank account as we could, even if it meant cutting everything to the bone. There were no trips, movies, or anything we didn't absolutely need.

We began looking at houses, but the prices anywhere around Redondo Beach were too high. The nearest place we could afford was North Long Beach. It was not nearly as nice an area and nowhere as close to the water. We would be far away from our church and our friends there. We would also need a second car. There would be no way either of us could bike to work.

Even with all of that, we found a house that I loved. It was old, built in the 1930's, but seemed to be in good shape. The ceiling in the living room was high and arched, and I could picture a huge Christmas tree under it. There were three bedrooms, including one with an attached bathroom, in an addition. The backyard was big and fenced, with two storage buildings sitting on a wood deck. It would be a safe place for JS to play while I used what I'd learned from Grandma Levi to put in a garden so that I could grow some of our food. There were fruit trees too, including an apricot tree, Tim's favorite. In the front, there were rose bushes. The price was low because it was only two houses from the freeway, but it was the freeway both Tim and I would need to take to get to work. That seemed to make it more of a convenience, than a drawback.

The money Tim and I had saved would still only allow for one financing option, an FHA loan at three percent down and a ten percent interest rate. For the time, that wasn't bad. We put in an application and were very nervous until we got word back. When we got the loan, I couldn't believe it. Being able to buy a house meant that Tim, JS, and I would finally have what I'd pictured as a normal life, like on the old TV shows. It was the kind of life I'd dreamed of as a kid.

The fence around the house was chain link, not white picket, but everything else fit. I had a husband and a child and the kind of home I'd always wanted. I could picture a future with Tim, enjoying raising JS and maybe even another child. I would do a better job than Mother had, a much better job. My children would be loved and cared for. I would also be a better wife to Tim than Mother had ever been to my father.

I'd thought that Tim and I would still try to go to our old church for a while, at least until we could make some new friends, but getting JS ready and making the drive on Sunday mornings was too much. We gave up and looked for a church closer to our house. Not having the other women in my life to share what was happening with our kids, was lonely, but Tim and I did find a new place to join a choir. We didn't fit in as well as we had before. There was no group of parents our age. We liked singing, but that was all we could do there. I was also getting sick again. With work, keeping house, the garden, and taking what I hoped was perfect care of JS, my body just wasn't able to handle it all. I got the chief tech, who thought I was very smart, to agree that I would work six and a half hours a day as long as I covered as much work as the lab assistants who worked 8 hours did. I could do that, and my hourly wage was raised to compensate.

The shorter hours helped, but I still started looking for a job closer to our house. I was surprised when I found one, as a real chemist this time, with a chemist's salary. Tim and I had been keeping JS in his old daycare while I worked, adding to both of our commutes. I found a new one, right on my route to my new job. Everything seemed perfect.

Morty Scott had also switched jobs. He went to work at an aircraft company in San Diego. He and Alice bought a little house there, with a deck that extended into the backyard. It also had a large spare bedroom with a queen bed. They started inviting Tim and me to bring JS, who could still sleep in a portable crib in the den, for weekends.

As heavy as my schedule was, I couldn't cope with the migraines I'd found out were brought on by birth control pills. Tim and I had switched back to condoms or simply going by the time of the month, since I was still very regular. One weekend, before Easter, when we were at Tim's parent' house in San Diego, JS was asleep, and Tim's parents had gone to their church, Tim and I made love. We could never be away from our church on the actual holiday because as choir members we always had to sing, but having a day off was nice. After Tim's parents had come home, we all went to a small park where the adults could talk while JS played within easy reach, on toddler sized playground equipment. We hadn't even had a bridge game, and Tim and I were feeling pretty good about the weekend and each other. We had no condoms with us, and the calendar said we were just on the edge of a safe time. Tim had earned a raise, and I had managed to save more money with my better paying job. We decided that if I did get pregnant again, it would time out well, and the baby would be welcome.

A month later, I was pretty sure I was pregnant. I was even surer when I did one of the new pregnancy tests. I took a half vacation day and hired a retired nurse, Cybil, who lived down the block, to watch JS while I went to an ob/gyn to have it confirmed. There was no doubt.

My second pregnancy was nothing like it had been with JS. I felt fine. Instead of throwing up every morning, I only did it twice with the new baby, but I began to worry about my exposure to chemicals in the laboratory. None of the materials I worked with had been found to cause birth defects unless I ate them, but there were a few heavy metals I was concerned about. I only handled them gloved, and in a hood, so I wouldn't breathe any fumes, but the idea of being around them still made me nervous. Again, I looked around for another job. I never thought about a source of heavy metal, the lead from the freeway, just two houses away.

Having already been officially working as a chemist, it was easier to find another job as one. I found it at a water laboratory, where I would be dealing with tiny concentrations of things, mostly in drinking water. It seemed a good way to go, although I was warned by the director of my old lab, that the new boss was a hard taskmaster. I had also been told I wouldn't be working with him, just his partner whom I'd already met and liked.

The job was swing shift, starting in the late afternoon. Tim was able to adjust his schedule so he could come home and take care of JS when I left, a little bit like the way he had when I was working a night shift. We would all have early mornings together, and I would be with JS most of the day. That meant we wouldn't need to pay for daycare anymore. Things at the new lab seemed to be good at first. Then Dan, the nice partner at the lab, decided to retire and Art, the owner, took over.

It was just like I'd been warned. Art found fault with everything I did, but he also needed my help. The water control district had decided that he had to put in a quality assurance system. That was something I knew a lot about from my time in the medical lab, where the controls were very strict. They wouldn't have to be quite so stringent for a water lab, but setting up the system for Art was still a lot of work. When I finished it, he told me that he would be switching me to on call. That pretty much meant I'd be paid when he felt like it, but I hadn't officially been fired, so it would be difficult to apply for unemployment.

The loss of income quite that soon, had not been in my plans, but I was only a couple of months away from delivery, so I adjusted the budget as much as I could. I didn't buy anything that wasn't essential, and Tim and I didn't go out at all. We had given away our baby bath/ changing table when we moved from Saint Paul, but instead of buying a new one at a store, we found one at an estate auction. The new baby would inherit JS's crib. We found a new bed for JS at auction too. I got into the spirit of bargain hunting so much, especially at auctions, that it became fun. I even managed to resell a few things that I bought, at a profit.

Even with worrying about money, I enjoyed my time at home. Mother had sent me a gift of a book that was written with only ten words. The book was meant to be a joke because it was named after one of the foods that I obsessed about eating when I was a kid. JS loved the little volume, reading all of it right away. I begged Mother to use her discount at the publisher where she worked, to get the other nine in the series, as a gift for JS to read. Proud of her grandson, Mother did, and JS learned all of them. After that, JS and I went to the library every week, getting new primers for him to read. In a couple of months, he made it through books that should have taken him years to read in school.

I'd also turned back to writing, both poetry and stories. I'd hoped to make some money selling a story, but I didn't. Just writing felt good, though.

I was still in favor of natural childbirth as the best thing for a baby. In order to be in the natural birthing room, the local hospital made Tim and I take a refresher course in Lamaze and birth procedures. I didn't believe nearly as much of what I was told about labor this time around. I knew it was a lot harder and hurt a lot more than the instructor said it would. I worked much harder at my exercises to try to make things go as well as they could.

Without as much to do, I noticed that Tim would be gone for a couple of hours, every so often. He never told me was going out, and when he came back, he never explained where he had been, He didn't take a car, so I knew he wasn't going far, but his absences combined with pregnancy hormones, gave me all sorts of fears about another woman. It was like my nervousness about Meredith being in Saint Paul, only worse. This time, getting pregnant wouldn't help, because I was already pregnant, very pregnant. I couldn't imagine how I'd manage JS and a new baby if Tim decided to leave me. At least when my parents had broken up, Rachel and I had been old enough, more or less, to take care of ourselves. I knew many single women with small children worked, but it was usually with the support of family. I had none handy except for Tim's parents, and I doubted I could expect any help from them.

I was desperate. The next time Tim disappeared, I told JS we were going for a walk and did my best to follow him. He only went a few blocks, to an adult movie theater. I was both angry and relieved. The fact that Tim liked pornography had never been a secret. At times, I'd found it fun too; especially when we read it as a couple to turn on to have sex. When we were dating, we'd even seen a dirty funny movie together. At least watching porn wouldn't take him away from me for more than a couple of hours. It was the kind of competition I could handle. I just wished Tim had trusted me enough to tell me about it.

When he came back, I confessed that I had followed him. I wanted to talk to him about it. I knew there was a good chance JS would tell Daddy about his walk with Mommy, and Tim would figure it out anyway. Tim explained that sex had fallen off a lot since I was so close to having another baby. I told him I understood but asked him just to tell me if he was going to the movies again. It was a rare promise that he didn't always keep, but at least I was pretty sure where he was when he disappeared.

One nice thing was that I was in touch with Rachel, and we were getting along better than we had when we were kids. Rachel had moved to San Francisco and earned her high school equivalency diploma. I was proud of her for that. She was working for a cable TV news bureau. She'd started as a messenger, driving videotapes around, but she'd moved up and was now learning how things worked in the newsroom. She was very happy and dating a cameraman/tape editor named Richard. We talked on the phone, and she sounded happier to me than she had in a long time. We also shared memories of growing up with Mother. I had not been the only one who'd felt unwanted, ignored, and just being used for some sort of ego trip, or to take over the housework. Rachel had seen a therapist and he told her that she and I had been neglected and abused. In my mind, I had never put things in those terms, but I could understand how a therapist would think so. It gave me even more reason to give my children the best life I possibly could, do everything I could to keep Tim happy, and hold onto my marriage. Rachel and I were both living in California, but San Francisco was three hundred miles away. That made casual visits impossible, but I felt I had a friend at the other end of the phone. It was more than that, the memories I shared with Rachel were a bond I had with no one else.

As my due date got closer, the country was going crazy. Jimmy Carter had been beaten in the presidential election by Ronald Reagan, who would soon take office. More than that, Iran held many American hostages, and every night the news gave updates on their status. When I worked in a medical lab, I had some Iranian co-workers, who I thought were good people. We had discussed religion over meals, especially in the early hours of the morning. I felt that I shared a lot with them. I didn't hate Iranians, but the whole country, including me, was worried about the hostages. On the night before Reagan's inauguration, it was announced that the hostages would be freed, and I began having contractions. Tim was asleep, and I timed them myself for a while, wondering if they would stop when my excitement died down. They didn't become extreme, but they didn't go away either. Tim and I had one more

Lamaze class to go, but the class schedule had always made the chance that I wouldn't make it to the end a possibility. I was only one day from my due date. It looked like I would miss my last class. I woke my husband. Tim and I had made an agreement with Tim's parents to take JS when the time came, with Cybil watching him until they arrived. Tim called them, and I called Cybil. Tim drove me to the hospital.

The rules at the Long Beach hospital were stricter and more annoying than they'd been at the hospital in Saint Paul, even in the natural birthing room. In Saint Paul, after walking around to speed up my labor, I'd been able to wear a baby monitor that was attached to me by a band that circled my belly. I could sit up when I wanted to. In Long Beach, the attachment was internal, so I had to lie still. I'd had a much easier time when I was sitting up, and the pain was worse than it had been with JS.

Instead of picking up JS, Alice and Morty had decided to come to the hospital and demanded to see me. They wanted to take pictures, but I was in no mood to see anyone but Tim. I hated having my picture taken under any circumstances, and the idea of being caught on camera hooked up to a monitor and fighting the pain was something I couldn't accept. I refused to see them, and a nurse told me that Alice said I was a brat. I asked Tim if Alice gave birth to him naturally. He said that he didn't know for sure, but his mother had no labor stories, and he believed she had been anesthetized. Given Alice's tendency toward anesthetizing herself with alcohol, that made perfect sense. When Tim told the Scotts again, that I wouldn't see them, and then a nurse told them too, they finally left the hospital to pick up JS.

Unlike my experience with JS, my labor was slow, too slow to make my doctor happy. He gave me a hormone called Pitocin to speed things up. That made my contractions even more painful. When things still weren't moving fast enough for him, my obstetrician used a thing that looked like a crochet hook to break my water. After that, things went very fast, and I wasn't sure I'd be able to make it through. Besides squeezing Tim's fingers, I was screaming during transition, something I hadn't done with JS. The nurse said I was doing great, but I didn't think so.

When our new baby, another boy, was delivered, both Tim and I watched his examination anxiously, wondering if the problems JS had at birth would happen again. The team reported a high Apgar and the baby's cry was loud. Tim and I held hands in relief. After what we went through with JS, maybe our second baby would be the easy one. Tim and I had agreed that if the child were a boy, he would be named Lon Cates, after a Dutch uncle who Tim had loved very much. Lon was bigger than JS had been, and by every milestone continued to do very well.

I was not doing as well as I had with my first birth. My old school ob/gyn had performed a large episiotomy, and I was very sore. Despite that, Tim and I decided that we would report on the birth to our Lamaze class, which was meeting that evening. Starting out half an hour ahead of time and walking very slowly to the room in the hospital where the class was held, we told the most upbeat version we could, about Lon's birth.

My agreement with the Scotts had been that they would bring JS home as soon as I got out of the hospital. Getting back at me for what they considered my temper tantrum when I was in labor, they kept him for several days. He had never been away from home that long and I was worried about him. When they did bring him home, they had all kinds of complaints about his behavior. They blamed it on my being a lousy mother. I had no choice; I just put up with what they said. After they left, I was glad that since for Mother, coming for Lon's birth would have meant flying clear across the country, she had decided not to make the trip. At least I could take care of Lon and JS, in peace.

Lon seemed to be my hoped for easy baby, which was good since JS was still a handful. He was reaching the age when he could go to kindergarten. I'd read in the Long Beach newspaper about a new magnet school which would accept children with advanced reading skills. Tim and I left Lon with Cybil, and took JS to the magnet school to take the tests required for admission. We were both nervous, but JS wasn't. He found the reading fun and was accepted into the program.

Tim and I couldn't go long without something going wrong in our lives. Our second car was temperamental, and we often couldn't spare the funds to get it fixed. Tim needed the remaining car to get to work. That meant that a lot of the time, I had to walk everywhere. I didn't mind, since I'd never been comfortable driving anyway. Every morning I would load Lon into a stroller, walk JS to the pickup point, and wait for the bus to arrive to take him to kindergarten. JS never gave me trouble about getting on the bus. He seemed to like school.

His teacher, Miss Walters, was not enjoying him. He excelled at reading, as he had in testing, but didn't fit in in any other way. Although he wasn't defiant, he didn't follow her instructions. He was hopeless at the worksheets where the students had to draw lines to match things. He didn't play with the other children, and most of the time acted as if they weren't there.

Miss Walters began to send JS's unfinished, or not yet started, papers home by pinning them to his back. I discovered that, although I'd gone through matching of shapes and colors with JS, he hadn't understood what Miss Walters wanted on his worksheets. When I put my hand over his and guided him through the moves, he got the idea right away. I pinned his finished papers to his back again and sent them back to school.

Miss Walters was suspicious. I didn't have the money to blow to have Cybil stay with Lon, so I took him with me while I went to JS's classroom to demonstrate what I'd done with him. Miss Walters asked if I could come in occasionally and act as a volunteer in the classroom. I would need childcare for that, preferably free, and I could use some for an occasional outing with Tim, as well. Reading one of my favorite things to save money, the local *Pennysaver*, I found an ad for a mothers' babysitting co-op that was interviewing new members. As much as I hated making phone calls, I made that one right away.

The interview involved not only talking, but also checking our house for hazards. Tim and I had been very careful about babyproofing. Besides that, when Theresa, the mother who would be interviewing me rang the doorbell, I told her that I needed a second to button my blouse because I'd been nursing. Theresa was a member of the La Leche League, so she liked that immediately. Theresa and I talked, and I showed her around the house. It didn't take the co-op long to make up its mind. I was in. Babysitting would not cost me money, but I'd have to exchange hours with other mothers and sometimes work as the secretary, booking the babysitting and keeping track of everyone's hours. The mothers also met once a month. What was great was that I had a new source of friends.

When I was able to visit JS's classroom a few times, I could see for myself that although he was the top reader, he was different from the other children. He was in his own little world a lot of the time and didn't want to join the other kids when they were playing games. The school nurse tested his hearing and found nothing wrong. The school doctor told me, as nicely as she could, that she had observed some soft neurological signs like toe walking, and suggested that I take JS to a pediatric neurologist.

I asked JS's and Lon's grandfatherly pediatrician, Dr. Elliottson, for a referral. He thought that what the school doctor had said was nonsense because he couldn't find anything wrong with JS, but I insisted, so he gave me a name.

The neurologist, Dr. Kelley, was nothing like Dr. Elliottson. He was young and friendly, but intense. He examined JS for a long time. When he finished, he told me that he was going to issue a diagnosis of minimal brain dysfunction so that insurance would pay for the visit, but he agreed with Dr. Elliottson. He didn't believe there was anything actually wrong with the JS.

I was relieved at what he said, but I noticed that JS's behavior was not only different from his classmates but from the other kids his age in the co-op families. While his academic skills were getting better every day, he understood nothing about modesty. When he got new clothes as a gift, he would immediately take off his old ones in public if we didn't tell him to go somewhere private. He also almost never wanted to play outside. He just wanted to stay inside and make complicated things out of tinker toy and other building sets. He would also play the same record over and over again, listening to a particular spot while staring down at the spinning turntable. That part, I found helpful, because when the music was playing, I always knew where JS was. On the other hand, hearing "What's New Pussycat" twenty times in a row, could get annoying after a while.

JS also had a puppet of Animal, from *The Muppet Show*. When he wasn't at school, he would carry it around to speak for him. With Animal, he could talk all the time, using long words and phrases more like a professor than a five-year-old child. It was strange, but the doctor had said nothing was wrong, and I was proud of JS's vocabulary. It was a lot like my own had been, before I learned to use shorter words to keep from being teased as much by Rachel and the other kids.

Though he could manipulate small things easily and draw very well, when it came to running around and climbing, JS was clumsier than the other children. The school doctor suggested that I take him to the Sensory Motor Institute at Long Beach State University. The cost wouldn't be much, and by that time, Tim and I had traded in our second car for a former rental that seemed reliable. Tim was taking it to work and leaving the newer car with me to transport the boys.

JS liked Sensory Motor Institute. Guided around by students studying occupational therapy, he used therapeutic apparatus disguised as play equipment. He even played video games. While he was put through his routine, I shared a bench with other parents. It was a place where we could discuss problems with our children without being afraid or embarrassed. Usually, Lon sat in his stroller through all of it, his eyes taking in every detail. If he started to get cranky, I would walk him. He loved motion.

After JS had a session, he was ready for a snack at the Student Union. He always asked for a grilled cheese sandwich, cut on the diagonal. It couldn't be cut into rectangles, or he wouldn't eat it. That was strange, but at least it wasn't junk food, so I tried not to worry about it too much.

Tim got a raise, so I scraped the funds together to put JS in a private school for first grade. His reading talents were respected and encouraged there. The classes were small, and he could sit right in front of the teacher. When the principal told Tim and me that JS had gotten into trouble for standing up on a swing, we secretly loved it, because it was so normal. Life was getting better.

At eighteen months, Lon began to speak a few words. He was using a spoon and had graduated to toddler food. He also took off his shoes whenever he could. Tim and I decided that we might be able to manage a short vacation, as long as we didn't go too far or spend too much money. We waited until late fall when there weren't as many tourists and reserved a cheap cabin in Avalon, on Santa Catalina Island. Before we left, I sewed ribbons onto Lon's slip on canvas shoes so I could tie them on tightly enough to keep him from losing them while we traveled. For most people, cars were not allowed on in Avalon. Residents and tourists walked, rode bicycles, or drove electric carts. Our family arrived by ferry. The water had been smooth, and the trip was easy.

Avalon was pretty deserted, but some of the shops were open. It was pretty much the same with the restaurants. The fishermen caught fresh seafood every day and sold it to restaurant owners. I love both fish and shellfish, so for me, that was wonderful. I had the best fish I've ever eaten, at a reasonable price. Tim and JS were strictly into chicken and beef, which was the same as anywhere else, and we brought some toddler meals along for Lon. In the morning, the whole family, including Lon, managed with bowls of Cheerios in the kitchen of the cabin. After that, we played tourist, which included taking a ride in a glass-bottomed boat. Mostly, both kids were pretty well behaved, except that when Tim rented one of the electric carts, he had to keep stopping because despite my efforts, Lon kept pulling his shoes off and throwing them into the street.

Tim and I had planned to stay another day, but a storm was coming in and the ferry we had planned to take back would be canceled. There would be one last one. The seas were supposed to be rough, but we had no choice. Tim would have to be back for work.

The ocean was more than rough. The ferry was up and down more than a ride at Disneyland. The crew handed out seasickness bags, and almost everyone used them. Both JS and I threw up, but Tim managed to hold things down, even while holding onto Lon, who upchucked all over Tim's jacket. The voyage seemed endless, but when it finally finished, we all took a short bus ride to where our cars were parked, and Tim drove home as fast as he could through the rain, so we could all clean up. It was not the ending to a vacation that I'd wanted.

Not long after that, I noticed that I was hearing fewer words from Lon, and then he stopped talking entirely. He had also stopped using a spoon. He still did some things well, including playing with a shape sorter way above his age level, but I had to keep him in a crib or stroller or watch him every second. He climbed on everything. I noticed that other children his age in the co-op would stay with their mothers, even when not held or strapped in. Lon wouldn't. When he turned two and wasn't even saying "no." I took him to Doctor Elliottson to find out what was going on.

Elliottson admitted that there was cause for concern. Lon had suffered a series of ear infections, and Dr. Elliottson thought that his loss of speech might be due to a hearing problem. Because hearing tests on toddlers were hard to do, he referred me to the John Tracy Clinic in Los Angeles. They not only had means to test Lon, they would do it for free. The catch was that it would take a while to get an appointment.

The other parents on the bench at The Sensory Motor Institute were sympathetic because some of them had children with hearing problems, as well as with coordination. I poured my heart out to them and waited for Lon to be tested.

When I took Lon to the clinic, he grabbed everything he could get his hands on in the waiting room, and stuck it in his mouth, something the staff commented on. After the test had been performed, a supervisor talked to me. She explained that Lon had lost 20% of his hearing, something that could be most likely be treated, but the loss was not enough to explain either his loss of speech or his behavior. She referred me to the speech pathology department at Children's Hospital of Orange County. I took Lon there, and they took him on as a patient.

Between the drive to The Sensory Motor Institute and the much longer drive for Lon's appointments at Children's Hospital, it was as if I was spending my life on the road. I didn't like driving any more than I ever had, but there seemed to be no choice. My children needed help, and I was going to see that they got it, no matter what it took.

Lon wasn't making much progress, and one of the therapists suggested that some of his behaviors were autistic-like, and he should get a psychological evaluation. We had a couple of appointments with a psychiatrist and a psychologist. It seemed to me that they were evaluating me as much as they were Lon. They asked me if I ever resented getting pregnant, or was upset by the financial pressures Lon put on our family. Finally, Lon was tested by a doctor who had trained under an autism specialist at the Neuropsychiatric Institute at UCLA. She said that Lon was autistic. She referred me to UCLA and asked if I wanted her to call and tell Tim. I said no. I thought the person to tell Tim would have to be me. It was my responsibility.

On the way back from the hospital, on the Orange Freeway, I could barely see because of the tears running down my face. It had been a while since I'd thought about committing suicide, but I was thinking about it then. If I could drive hard enough into a concrete barrier, I could end things for Lon and myself. Tim could deal all right with JS, especially with an extended school day, and they'd be fine. I pushed those thoughts away. I had to pick JS up from school on my way home. That responsibility was mine too, and there was no way I would let my older son down. There was no way I would let either of my sons down. By the time I reached the school, my face and eyes were dry, and no one in the office even noticed I was upset.

When Tim came home from work, I couldn't think any easy way to tell him about Lon's diagnosis. I had no more tears. I had cried all there were. I just asked him to sit down in our bedroom and told him what the psychologist told me. We both knew a little bit about autism because Tim had a cousin who'd been diagnosed with it. There was no cure.

Chapter Fourteen

Tim and I decided that before we did anything else, we should take Lon to UCLA to have his diagnosis confirmed. I got an appointment with Dr. Terri Jo (T.J.) Denton. We took Lon to UCLA together, so we brought JS along. T.J. was friendly and cheerful, but she pulled no punches. She examined Lon and confirmed our worst fears. She told us that 95% of children like Lon ended up in institutions and gave me the number for my local Autism Association. She also got into a conversation with JS who told her about the three forms of symbols on Superman's costume and the difference between them. After that exchange, T.J. told Tim and me that she thought that JS should see Dr. Renberg, the head of the Neuropsychiatric Institute. Tim and I had no idea how to react, but we made the appointment.

Dr. Renberg was smiling and grandfatherly, with a habit of taking off his heavy framed glasses when he wanted to make a point. He gave Tim and me a questionnaire to fill out and had a long conversation with JS. In the end, he was no more reticent in his diagnosis than TJ, had been. He said JS was autistic too. In line with the diagnostic guidelines of the time, he called what JS had, autism in the residual state.

I didn't know what to do. I called Rachel, who by then was married to the film editor she had been dating. They sent us flowers. I appreciated that, but it did nothing to change the situation. Rachel and I also agreed not to tell Mother. After the talks we had about Mother's abuse and neglect, we couldn't see how she'd be useful, and I didn't want to have to cope with her reaction.

I did tell the members of my babysitting co-op about both boys. One of the women responded that she felt like she'd been punched in the stomach and asked if Lon would be sent away. Another one asked what I had done wrong. Tim told his parents, but even though the only other diagnosis of autism in the family was on Tim's side, Morty and Alice denied any chance of a genetic influence and blamed everything on me.

I had no idea how I was supposed to feel. I kept praying that the whole thing was just some big mistake. At my most hopeful times, I thought that if JS was autistic and Tim and I had managed do as well with him as we had, then maybe could manage with Lon too. We would sure as hell try.

I checked the library for books on autism. I found a thick one called *The Empty Fortress*, by Bruno Bettelheim. It was horrifying. Bettelheim wrote that autism was caused by "refrigerator mothers," and said that the best hope for a cure would be to take autistic children away from their parents. No one said anything like that at UCLA, but I remembered the questions I'd been asked at Children's Hospital. It was obvious that at least some psychiatrists believed Bettelheim's theory. Tim's parents seemed to believe it as well.

I felt alone and scared and ashamed. It took me two months to get up the courage to use the number T.J. gave me for the Autism Association in Long Beach, but I finally made the call. I expected to talk to a secretary or a switchboard. The person who answered was a grandmother named Mary Peoples, raising her autistic grandson. She didn't accuse me of anything; she just gave me phone numbers for resources that might be able to help and invited me to the next meeting, which would be held at her home.

When I arrived at Mary's house, I found women of all ages and backgrounds, with one thing in common; they were raising or helping to raise children with autism. No one cried. They told their stories, mostly about the general uselessness of most professionals in psychology profession. There were a few exceptions, T.J. among them. Most of the women had years of fighting the system to get what their kids needed. They were strong and stubborn but welcomed me. I paid attention to what they said.

I coped in a way that had worked for me before. I turned back to writing. I hoped I might even make some money at it, even if I hadn't been able to before. Tim was doubtful, but it cost me nothing but a few stamps to try, and it gave me something to concentrate on besides the therapy for Lon and JS.

Since Tim's parents rejected me, and Rachel lived three hundred miles away, Tim and I were completely without family support. One of Lon's speech therapists suggested to me that Tim and I might try some counseling to make our marriage stronger, to be able to cope better with the stress of dealing with our sons and their diagnoses. We were both hesitant, but we didn't see how it could make things any worse. We were referred to Reba Albert, a psychiatrist. In our sessions with her, she helped us see that we had been walking on eggshells around each other, afraid even to argue.

Tim was upset by what his parents had done, especially since they were still willing to talk to him, just not to me. He didn't blame me the way they had, but he was torn. He had always been more attached to his parents than I had ever been to mine. Unlike me, he had grown up trusting them, especially his father. He felt the loss more deeply than he had been able to tell me and was very upset by his parents' apparent abandonment of their grandchildren. I confessed that I was also upset by what I saw as his lack of faith in my writing ability and his total surprise when I finally sold something. Dr. Albert told Tim that he would have to make a choice: whether to stand with his wife or stand with his parents. All of my old fears came back. He had made a choice for me before, but it was during a much easier time.

Tim said he could see no choice at all. He'd made a promise, and he would keep it. He would stand with me. Knowing that helped a lot.

I contacted the local center providing services for developmental disabilities, for Lon, but they didn't offer anything that I wasn't already doing for him. T.J. Denton had suggested to Tim and me that services were better in Orange County than in Los Angeles County where we lived, so we decided to list our house for sale. Tim also looked for, and found a job in Orange County, with a longer commute but a higher salary. Unfortunately, the features of our house that had allowed us to buy it at a price we could afford, age and freeway noise, made it very hard to sell. I did the best that I could to keep it in perfect condition for potential buyers to look at, which wasn't easy with the boys constantly making a mess.

Even with the decision Tim had made to be on my side, between taking care of the house, driving both of my sons to therapy sessions, and trying to get some writing in during the short period Lon slept during the day, I felt like I was drowning. Between his commute and his new job, Tim was gone a lot of the time, leaving me to cope with JS and Lon mostly by myself. I needed the type of distraction from real life that *Star Trek* had been when I was growing up. I found it in a detective show called *Not Quite Real,* and Piers Brice, its handsome star. I never wanted to miss a show, and I checked the ratings listed for it in the newspaper each week, praying they would be high enough to keep it on the air. As I had with *Star Trek,* I made audio recordings I could listen to in-between live broadcasts, and I began to write my own *Not Quite Real* stories. I buried myself as much as I could in the slowly evolving on-screen love story, taking each small triumph of the hero as my own.

Tim and I were on our third real estate agency when our house finally sold. The sale price was not as much as we wanted, but the profit was enough to give us a small down payment on our next home. Interest rates were still high, but we had been very careful about money, and if we were able to give up JS's tuition payments by finding him a good public school, we could afford higher mortgage payments. An autism diagnosis would also help JS qualify for extra help in a public school, although he hadn't qualified for it before. When Lon turned three, he would be eligible to receive services through school too, simplifying our financial situation even further.

Tim and I spent our weekends house hunting. Since we'd be losing the friends I'd found in my babysitting the co-op, I was hoping to find a community that would provide some new ones. With Lon's behaviors, putting him in a church nursery was out of the question, so the impossibility of the companionship of a choir and a congregation made finding friends some other way even more important. It was a tall order. I fell in love with a condominium development in a beautiful city called Laguna Hills. It was a short drive from Tim's job in Irvine. The homes were built into hills overlooking strawberry fields. The air was clear, and there was both a playground and a swimming pool. There was also a clubhouse where, Tim and I were told, there were activities we could participate in, including a bridge group. The units were pre-wired for cable television, which I wanted. The school district was also well rated, and JS's new school would be within walking distance. The mortgage would stretch our budget almost to the limit, but the condo community seemed like a perfect place. Tim and I made the move at the end of the summer.

At first, I thought things in our new condo were going pretty well. Our next-door neighbor, with whom we shared a wall, was friendly, and had a son who could play with JS, but wasn't old enough for school yet.

When the school year started, I attended a meeting to work out JS's individual educational plan, known as an IEP. Orange

County was considered part of the covered area of the Long Beach chapter of the Autism Association, and I had continued to go to their meetings. The ladies had schooled me on what to expect at an IEP meeting, and I prepared myself for a fight. I didn't get one. JS would be in a class for normal children, as he had been in private school, but he would be receiving support for whatever difficulties he had, or at least that was the theory. The goals set were mostly academic, which had never been JS's problem. I'd had been told by the Sensory Motor Institute that they had accomplished what they could with JS. Physical education was supposed to help with the continued development of his coordination.

I had a more immediate problem. I had to teach JS to walk to school. The route had very little traffic and nothing dangerous that I could see, but JS wasn't used to functioning independently outside home or school. For three weeks, I had JS walk to the school building, while I trailed behind him with Lon in a stroller. That was a least a week longer than was probably necessary, but when I was finished, I was sure he could make the trip safely. I'd also been told the school would call me if he didn't show up on time, just in case.

I also went to work making our condo a draw to the other kids in the area. Among other things, I stocked up on popsicles. I also allowed myself to be fingerprinted and background checked to qualify as a block mom. Our condo was designated an official safety zone for all the kids in the neighborhood. The sheriff's department gave me a placard for the window, so that kids would know where they could come if they felt threatened.

With Lon's third birthday coming, I arranged for his evaluation by the school district for a special education program. They determined, and I agreed, that he would require a very high level of supervision, close to one on one. The nearest program that fit the bill was in Fountain Valley, a bus ride away. His class was only half a day long and I would have to get Lon up early to make sure he was ready on time to be picked up. Having him out of the house would give me the most freedom I'd had in years. The school would also be providing speech therapy to help him speak, and teaching him sign language.

I felt guilty about wanting some time for myself so much, even just a few hours in the morning. I was nervous about putting Lon on the little bus, even with specially trained drivers and aides, but I still couldn't wait. The first morning Lon was at school; I went to the mall. I didn't buy anything; I just walked around enjoying feeling normal. Lon seemed to like the bus, as he usually did any moving vehicle, and was not upset when he came home. That made me feel a bit better about being happy he was gone.

Since I'd stayed active in the Autism Association, I was elected Vice President for Orange County. I didn't think that I had any more qualifications than my address, but I decided to do the job as best as I could. Because I needed friends, I figured the other mothers must too. I decided to organize a support group, using the chapter list of addresses and phone numbers. The living room of our condo was large and would hold a lot of people. Every seat was full for the first meeting, and the group agreed to hold them monthly. Also, I would be the one to receive phone calls for referrals to services and supports. Mary Peoples assured me that all of the chapter leadership had to start somewhere, and that I would do fine.

The seats kept being filled for the support group. Unlike regular Autism Association meetings where we discussed conferences, speaking engagements, and fundraisers, parents at my group were just sharing their stories. Most of them had talked to me at one time or another on the phone, but many of them had never had a face-to-face conversation with another parent about their problems. I had no trouble keeping the discussion going. Mostly I just had to make sure the drinks and snacks didn't run out.

At the time, the mailing list of the Autism Association was managed by copying a typed list onto copier labels. I was sure there must be a better way. In that era, very few families had home computers. In our early years in California, Tim had occasionally brought home an old-style terminal, the kind where you inserted a telephone receiver and contacted a mainframe, but we'd never even had a simple game system. Computers were expensive, but I figured that if I was going to keep things organized for my support group, I was going to need one. That would mean taking on a chunk of debt, but Tim agreed to spend the money.

We bought a Tandy EX; a computer that people would laugh about years later. There was no hard drive. It booted from a five and a quarter inch floppy disc and had two floppy drives. There was some software available, ordered from other users through a magazine, at five dollars a disc. There was only one commercial game we could find. For most applications, it was necessary to write your own programs in a language called Basic.

I'd taken one computer class in graduate school, which I aced with Tim's help. I'd learned a little bit of FORTRAN. I transferred that knowledge to Basic, at least enough to cope with writing a mailing program. I also bought the one game, called Star Flight, which came on two discs. The graphics weren't much, but Tim and I enjoyed it.

The National Conference of the Autism Association was held in different cities every year. That July it would be held in L.A., and they promised childcare that could handle children with autism. Tim and I hadn't even tried to go anywhere together since the kids were diagnosed, so I suggested that we might both go to the conference. It would be an easy drive, and we could spend a couple of nights in the nice hotel where it was being held, at a discount. I also hoped I'd pick up some information that would help our kids and the support group. Tim agreed to go.

Things didn't go the way I'd planned. On the first day, Lon screamed until he was purple, in childcare. Tim and I were called to take him back to the plenary session with us. A few times, he got away from us and ran around the ballroom. The audience, mostly mothers, and fathers of children with autism, didn't seem to mind. The national president actually picked Lon up and held him for a few moments.

A babysitter we got for the evening did better, and for the first time in years, Tim and I were able to go to dinner together without JS and Lon. After that, Lon settled down, and I was able to pay attention to the presentations the next day. The best one was from a Nobel Prize winning physicist who had an autistic son who was completely non-verbal, even more so than Lon. He and his wife knew that the boy understood language and tried to use it. He had LP records, and when his parents came back from a trip, he would find just the spot on a record to put the needle, so that the singer could wail, "I miss you when you're gone." He just couldn't talk.

Due to both his prestige and his profession, the physicist had access to computers and had sat his son down in front of one. The results he talked about were incredible. Once his son began typing, his parents discovered that he had taught himself to read many years before. The words his mouth was incapable of forming flowed easily from his fingers. He and his parents were finally able to communicate. I couldn't think about much but that story. As simple as our little computer was, I wondered what would happen if we allowed Lon to use it. I decided to find out.

Unless he was strapped into a stroller or a high chair, or asleep, Lon was almost never still. He always wanted to climb on something or grab something, usually to put it in his mouth. He had never sat quietly with me for more than a minute or two. When Tim, I, and the boys got home, I put Lon next to me while I played Star Flight. He couldn't take his eyes off the screen and stayed with me for three hours. I was blown away. I wanted to order every piece of available software that Lon would find remotely interesting. With as few programs as there were, and at five dollars a disc, I could do it. I bought preschool learning programs and musical programs. He loved all of them. While Lon was at the keyboard, I could relax and breathe.

JS had also begun to do pretty well. He'd joined the neighborhood Cub Scout pack. There were only a few other boys, and the scoutmaster was the father of one of his classmates. The pack members walked back and forth to school together, and JS was invited to birthday parties, where because of his ability to assemble toys, he was a star. He had also begun to design toys of his own, making them out of cardboard. When transforming robots became popular as both cartoons and action figures, JS made those too, out of cardboard, building them to transform like the ones on TV. They worked. Neither Tim nor I could do anything like what JS was doing as adults, never mind at age eight. We thought that JS might be a natural mechanical engineer.

There was one problem with that view of the future. While JS's reading skills had continued to soar above his classmates, his proficiency in math had failed to keep pace. It was more than two years behind his reading level. It that way, at that point, he reminded me of me. As far as the rules of class placement were concerned, that gap had a silver lining. The discrepancy allowed JS to qualify for a learning disabilities class, which was much smaller and allowed the teacher to give more attention to his social deficiencies and the problems he was having with speech. One of the other students became a special friend for JS. He was large and friendly and thought JS's toys were cool. He also needed a lot of help with his reading. JS acted as a peer tutor and got to hang out with another child in return.

When the cat belonging to the family next door had kittens, we adopted one, both because JS wanted it and because the opinion of the more experienced moms in the Autism Association was that pets were good for the kids. The mother cat's name was Cinnamon, matching her orangey coat. JS named the kitten he picked out, "And Sugar," which seemed to him the only logical choice.

I was a little worried about Lon's behavior around the kitten. He would clumsily pick her up at random, but she tolerated it. He eventually learned to make a sound that approximated "cat," and I decided that the advice the other ladies given me had been good.

The Autism Association ran a free speakers' bureau of sorts, and Mary Peoples tagged me to be part of it. With the way I loved acting, I usually didn't have to worry about stage fright, but my first speaking assignment terrified me. It would be during the morning while Lon was at school, so I didn't have to worry about childcare. What did worry me was my audience at the University of California, Irvine. I had only lectured college students as a teaching assistant, and then only in freshman chemistry. This audience would be not only students but also professors. Even though knowledge of autism, even among professionals, was still sparse, I just didn't see myself as qualified to talk to them. I agonized over what to wear and made sure I carried a pouch with a puzzle child logo on it, for my notes and flyers. At least I'd look the part.

Before that, when I had heard the phrase about someone having their stomach in their throat or their mouth, I'd always thought it was silly, but that day I experienced it for myself. I could feel my stomach jumping upward, but I went to the podium and began to speak anyway. I started telling them about the history of autism, the ignorance about it, and my experience, as well as that of other parents. About halfway through, I realized I had their full attention. No one was squirming in their seats or looking at their watch. I could do that kind of thing, I really could. My knees didn't wobble anymore when I took questions at the end. The round of applause sounded real, not what you hear when people are just being polite.

The attendees passed a basket, and presented me with the cash they collected. I had no idea what to do with it. I was sure it wasn't mine to keep, although I could have used it. I was there on behalf of the Autism Association. I brought it to the next meeting at Mary's home and asked her. Mary was just as puzzled; she said it had never happened before. She handed the money over to the treasurer, to find some category to put it on the books. From then on, I knew I had some talent for public speaking.

Mary sent me out whenever she could, and I was also drafted to make announcements and introduce speakers at local meetings and conferences. It wasn't like being in play, but I'd found a niche. Still, even with all my autism connections, I still felt isolated from the real world. I rarely spoke to anyone outside the autism community. I wanted to have a conversation about something else, sometimes.

Chapter Fifteen

When I was home by myself and not taking support calls or doing housework, I was still attached to my favorite television detective. I continued to write stories using characters from the show. I joined, by mail, the Piers Brice fan club and kept aware of local events, but I didn't dream of going to any of them. For one thing, it seemed selfish. Something else was also holding me back. When we'd still lived in Long Beach, I had tried to take a full day away at an autism conference while Tim took care of the boys. It was a disaster. Lon had been screaming for hours by the time I got home. Then he'd regressed, losing months of progress. I hadn't dared to be away from him for more than a few hours at a time since. Then one day my fan club newsletter announced a write-a-thon. It was going to be held in a park in Arcadia, a little over an hour's drive away. I desperately wanted to go, to share not only my love of Piers Brise, but to write *Not Quite Real* with other fans. Tim urged me to do it. It had been a long time since my last try at leaving JS and Lon with him, and they had all learned a lot. I let him talk me into it.

The women I met in Arcadia were very welcoming. I immediately made myself useful. They couldn't figure out what to write signs on to guide people to the gathering, and I suggested paper plates. It was unusual for Southern California, but it looked like it would rain. Still, our little group settled at picnic tables with pens and notebooks and told to begin writing. Writers' block immediately hit everyone but me. I couldn't wait to write a story. As I wrote, the rain started to come down. No one wanted me to stop, and one of the other women held an umbrella over my head.

The other members of the group couldn't help gazing toward the parking area for a black Corvette, the car we all knew that Piers Brise drove at the time. There was never any sign of him. I had never expected there would be. Two women, Jane and Helen, who were not fans, did show up. They worked for Brise's publicist, Pete Groberg, and were the ones running the fan club and putting out the newsletter. Piers' fans, including me, were excited to be around someone, anyone, who actually knew him, but the rain became too heavy to stay in the park, even with umbrellas. A fan named Maria volunteered her home for the continuation of the meeting. We formed a caravan, and everyone, including Jane and Helen, followed Maria.

Maria's living room was small, and a lot of us scrunched close together on the floor while Jane and Helen told stories. Piers Brise was not Groberg's only client. Another one was a former member of the crew of *Star Trek's* Enterprise, an often-disliked member. He was fond of raising horses, and Jane and Helen talked about his requirement for the women who worked with him, to study up on his equine interests. They considered him obnoxious and actually borrowed some of the staff allocated to him, to work for Piers' fan club. They couldn't say enough about how sweet Piers and his wife both were. I felt warm just knowing that I had picked a celebrity to obsess over who not only looked wonderful, but actually was. I stayed to the very end of the get-together and hoped that I'd be able to come to the next one --- even if I was who'd managed to do any writing.

When I returned to Laguna Hills, I was overjoyed to find out that Lon had been just fine with Tim. His time in school had made him much less vulnerable to my absence. As tight as money was, I began to think about going back to work.

My first idea was to start with something part time and flexible. I'd not only taken care of the budget but had done our taxes, even though Tim was better at math. As tax season approached, I decided to take tax classes, thinking I might get least several months of work per year. I attended while both boys were at school. With my talent for memorization, especially of rules and regulations, I did very well. My math wasn't the fastest, but with almost everyone using calculators, it didn't matter. My teacher let me know that if I wanted to apply for a job as a tax preparer, I would have no trouble getting one. I kept looking at the want ads anyway. One caught my eye, a swing shift job at a medical lab. I was familiar enough with the job, and with working the hours mentioned in the ad. With some help from Tim, I would be able to manage with very little, if any, in the way of childcare expenses. The job would also be year-round and bring in more money than being a tax preparer. It would be a step down from being a full-fledged chemist. However, after almost four years away from the lab, it would be a way to get my feet wet again. I applied for the job and got it.

Tim shifted his working hours to start earlier in the morning. Our family could all have an early dinner together, after which I left for work, and Tim watched the boys for a few hours until they were in bed. In addition to ordinary medical tests, the lab where I worked did emergency testing for all the local trauma centers. They sent samples to us by messenger for STAT work ups. That included blood analysis of victims with presumed drug overdoses, to figure out what they took --- hopefully before it killed them. That part of the work was depressing, and the med techs and I did whatever we could to maintain a cheery atmosphere. The lab operated seven days a week, twenty-four hours a day, including every holiday. I was mostly working with men. Some of them were fathers who were doing the opposite of what Tim and I were doing. They were working at night and their wives worked during the day. We all became very close. In some ways, I was a work wife to the guys. I brought in food, with fancy dinners for holidays like Easter. The men liked my cooking, and telling me their problems, the way the boys had when I was a teenager. I even received a couple of not entirely joking proposals that if I ever decided to leave Tim, I could marry one of them.

I was closest to my supervisor, Vu, a refugee from Vietnam. Like me, he was married with children. We never actually touched each other, but sometimes we flirted, and we both knew there was an attraction between us. At one point, we even talked a little about doing something about it. We decided almost immediately that it could tear both of our families apart and would be an incredibly stupid thing to do. Still, knowing that I'd be seeing Vu, made me anxious to go to work, even if it meant putting up with a rush hour commute. The fun of that disappeared quickly.

Part of my job was to label test tubes. It was long before labs used bar coded computer-generated labels. Every night, I cut up pieces of masking tape and numbered them. Since I had written a mailing label program for my support group, I was sure there had to be a better way, and I suggested to Vu that the company computer might be used to make labels for the tubes. In his opinion, that would be a job for a word processor. He had no idea how to use the one at the lab, but decided that he would to learn it first, and then teach it to me. He spent several weeks making no progress producing a usable labeling system. Frustrated, I decided to do the work myself, on my own time, and using my own little Tandy EX. It didn't take too much effort on my part. I wrote a twenty-line program in Basic that did the job. When I put my program on the company computer, I was able to produce labels for all the test tubes. Vu said he liked what I'd done, but I didn't hear anything about it from the lab upper management. Since it made my work easier, I didn't pay much attention to the lack of praise from above. The Chief Tech did mention the cohesiveness of the staff on swing, and how it increased productivity. He never mentioned anything I did about that, either.

I noticed that the workload of our shift was higher than that of either of the other two. Much of the load was work I had to do, meaning that I worked overtime almost every night. The management didn't like paying for the extra hours, especially at time and a half. So, using my own computer and time again, I graphed when and how samples were being handled to determine how the workload could be better distributed. I presented my work to Vu, who took it to the Chief Tech and the Laboratory Director. Shortly after that, I found out that Vu had taken credit not only for my graphing but for my label program too, even though he had nothing to do with either one.

I was furious. First, I made Vu apologize, by taking me to the most expensive restaurant we could manage during a supper break at the lab. Even after that, working with him grated on me. Evenings that I'd looked forward to, I now dreaded. I decided to look for another job. After checking other medical labs, my new job came in a field I'd never heard of before.

There was a tiny little ad in the classifieds for a chemist to do quality control of the solutions used in a plating shop. I had no experience with plating, but I knew about quality control, and I'd be called a chemist again, instead of a technician. The job was also closer to our condo in Laguna Hills. The down side was that it was during the day, but it was part time and flexible, which meant I could make it fit into the hours the boys were at school. The hourly wage was a bit higher, which would help to compensate for the smaller number of hours.

Platology, the site of my new job, was a whole different world. Huge vats steamed with toxic chemicals. In a tiny little lab, just off the owner's office, I was expected to analyze samples from all the tanks, on a regular schedule, to make sure the makeup was correct and they were operating in the proper pH range. If something were wrong, I would have to give instructions to the line workers about what would need to be added to a tank to fix it. It was all wet chemistry, with primitive equipment like I had used in high school. I did my own sampling from the tanks occasionally with a little help from the men who did the plating.

The staff was mostly Hispanic, with very few speaking fluent English, or in some cases any English. However, they knew their jobs. Except for one supervisor and the two women in the front office, the place was almost entirely male, but that was fine with me. I was used to it.

I struggled through my first couple of weeks, learning all the new analyses, but after that, the testing went very quickly for me. At first, my work was compared to the results from an outside lab, but when the Quality Manager, who was also the owner's son, discovered that I was keeping all the tanks spot on, he gave up on spending the extra money for duplicate analyses. As in my first medical lab, I did my work faster than others chemists had, so I was given more to do, without costing Platology any more money. My first extra job was monitoring the pollution control system and filling out the paperwork required for the local water district. I hated the idea of releasing toxic chemicals into the sewer system, so I worked very hard to make sure it didn't happen.

The owner also asked me to do something outside of my lab. The state of California was giving grants for putting in new technology that would decrease pollution. He had been thinking about a system like that for a long time but had never had the money for it. He asked me if I would write the grant. I'd never written one before, but writing came so naturally to me that I agreed to try, especially since I'd be paid by the hour for something that didn't involve inhaling chemical fumes.

Not long after I got my new job, Tim found out that he would be losing his. The company he was working for in Irvine would be closing down. While working at the medical lab, I had started putting money away, like I did when we were saving for our first house. However, this time, I'd used the lab's plan to buy savings bonds and stock. They could be sold if necessary, but couldn't be drawn on like a bank account and wouldn't hold us long if Tim wasn't employed. He worked hard to find a new job. He did, but it was a long drive from our condo in Laguna Hills. With his new commute, he was gone a lot of the time. That meant that I was left to take care of the boys, pretty much on my own. Doing everything for them added to my paid work, as well as my volunteer responsibilities with my support group. Tim and I were both exhausted, with less chance to lean on each other for support. As much as we loved our beautiful condo, we decided we would have to move again.

As it turned out, selling a home this time was even more complicated than it had been the first time. Even though we'd bought the condo new, problems had developed with the some of the roofs in the development, although not ours. Those problems had resulted in a lawsuit, which raised our association fees and made potential buyers very nervous.

Also, Lon had done some real damage to the place. He had climbed the bookcase used to store his toys and puzzles in his room, over and over. He would pull it down every time. He didn't hurt himself, but every time the bookcase fell, it put a hole in the drywall. Finally, I just bolted it in place. Lon had also managed to destroy the doors to the closet in his room and crack the mirrors in the closet doors in the bedroom Tim and I used. JS had also spent some time as a bed wetter, and his room needed complete deodorization.

It took months to get a buyer. While we were waiting, Tim and I decided to scope out potential neighborhoods. We tried to turn our trips into cheap family entertainment. Every Saturday I would pack a picnic. We would find a park in the neighborhood we were exploring. Then we'd all eat what I packed, and the boys would play in a playground until they'd burned off enough energy to be reasonably quiet while Tim and I checked out potential homes. JS gave his opinion too, and we watched for Lon's reactions. We also asked questions about local school districts and the schools closest to the house. Tim and I saw several houses we would have loved to make an offer on, but there was nothing we could do without receiving one on our condo. Finally, it looked as if we had one. By that time, we had narrowed down the areas we were willing to live, and our realtor arranged for an associate to take us around to likely properties on a Sunday. She told us that the woman had given up a weekend in Las Vegas to do it.

That Saturday, Tim took a call for me from Maria while I was out doing the grocery shopping. Piers Brice was hosting the Golden Globes the next day. He was very nervous and wanted fans he could trust as shills in the audience. Without asking me, Tim said no. I wasn't sure whether to be mad at him or not. We were already scheduled for the next day, and someone had given up her own outing to help us. His answer made perfect sense. Still, I could picture getting a chance to see Piers up close. I fantasized about getting a chance to meet him. Tim could have told Maria that I would call her back and given me the chance to make my own decision. Maybe I would have made the unselfish choice, but now I would never have a chance to find out. I knew I was angry with Tim. I was pretty sure I shouldn't be, but I was.

Tim and I did find a beautiful house. It was walking distance from schools and a small shopping center that included a supermarket. The backyard was small because there was an addition, but there was an attractive front court. The landscaping was low maintenance, and best of all, it had a spa off the patio. It cost a lot, but our realtor was sure we could obtain financing. We made an offer.

As we began to plan our move, things started falling apart. I had filled out the paperwork to sell my stock, but the sale hadn't gone through when I had requested it. On Black Tuesday, the stock crash of the Reagan administration hit. My stock lost half its value.

It would take almost every cent Tim and I had to make our down payment, leaving us with no reserves, a very bad position to be in when moving into a new house.

Our buyer was also having difficulty being approved for a loan. He had a large monthly payment on his one indulgence, a Mercedes. The mortgage company was balking. Without any help from Tim, I worked with the realtor and another finance company to try to find solutions. I knew Tim couldn't help, not being around, but I still felt like everything had been dumped on my shoulders. I was still mad at Tim about the Golden Globes and Piers. A scenario kept intruding into my thoughts where we would have gone looking another day and found a cheaper house we would have liked as well. I made one decision that was entirely in my hands. Without saying a word to Tim, I had my hair, which was now past my waist, cut.

"Oh my God!" were the only words out of Tim's mouth when he came home and saw what I'd done. I saw the shock and sadness on his face. For a moment, I felt triumphant, then I felt sorry for inflicting that kind of loss on him without any good reason. I silently swore to myself that I'd never do anything like that again.

After pulling together a financing plan, our family faced one final obstacle to our move. There had been a snafu in the paperwork. The escrow company had used the wrong initial for me on an insurance policy. The closing had been scheduled for a Friday. Packing and the moving van had been arranged, fortunately, paid for by Tim's new company. It would have given

Tim and me the weekend to settle in. Now the closing would be on a Monday. The owners of the house we were buying refused to turn over the keys before all the paperwork was officially signed. For at least two days, our family would be homeless.

The moving company was willing to store our things over the weekend, but we would need a place to stay. It wasn't in the budget. I checked for the cheapest place I could find that could accommodate us, especially Lon. The motel was grubby and depressing. Lon insisted on climbing everywhere, including into the top of a closet, which he decided somehow was a place to go potty. He had chosen inconvenient and embarrassing places before, but that one was the worst. I did the best I could to clean up after him without my usual supplies. Gritting our teeth and with very little sleep, Tim and I made it through the weekend. The papers were ready on Monday. Tim had to take a day off from work to sign them and for the move, but our family was finally in our new home.

Besides unpacking, there was a lot to take care of. JS would have to be enrolled in the local junior high school, to begin the fall term, but before that, there were arrangements to be made for Lon. I had originally intended that he would be in a small, full day private school run by a non-profit out of a church. The program had been one of the attractions of the move. The school told me at the last minute that though afternoon care would be continue to be offered at the church, there would no longer be a school. That meant I'd have to do all the paperwork of getting Lon's IEP transferred so that he could attend public school. The best program for him, one I had learned about before the move, was operated by the county and was similar to the one he'd been bussed to every day, from Laguna Hills. I rushed to have him enrolled and set up his transportation, so he'd be taken to the church where I could pick him up later. It went more smoothly than I'd expected, and gave me a couple more hours to get things done during the day.

For JS, the move meant a complete change of program. He would no longer be in a learning-disabled class but fully integrated, with supports provided as necessary, through speech therapy and social skills training. Social skills training was unusual then, but JS had grown apart from his friends in Laguna Hills. They had gone from Cub Scouts to Boy Scouts. He tried to follow them, but as the other boys got older, they also got meaner. They had begun to use him as the butt of their pranks on the walk home from school, to the point where the school had to start letting JS go five minutes early to give him a head start to avoid the bullying. Still, some relationships had survived from his younger days. He would miss those, and if he was going to be able make new friends he would need the tools to do it. I had to dig up social skills curriculum myself, and fight to have it inserted in JS's plan, but ultimately, I was successful. I didn't enjoy butting heads with our new local district but felt I had no choice. Without being able to recognize the emotional responses of other junior high students, JS would have a hard time surviving in school, let alone be successful. It was my job to make sure he had what he needed to acquire essential skills.

When I'd taken care of the kids' problems, I still had my own. Tim was closer to work, but I wasn't. My new drive involved crossing all the lanes of freeway traffic, a move that terrified me. My route wore on my nerves more every day. I tried hard to find one that excluded the freeway, but all of the ones I found would have made my drive impossibly long. There were also parts of my job that had started to make me sick. One of those was the analysis of plating baths containing cyanide. The method involved adding acid, which released a poisonous gas. My lab didn't have a hood to protect me from the fumes. I would get headaches that I could feel at the roots of my hair, every time I ran the tests. Besides feeling sick, I was also getting bored running the same tests over and over again. I was doing everything in the shop that a chemist could do and I saw no chance of learning much that was new. The chances of finding another job that would fit my schedule didn't seem good, but I decided to try. I even prayed about it.

When I found a metal finishing shop, only a few minutes from our new house, that was offering a job; I was sure God had answered my prayers. I interviewed with the owner, Rand Deets, a short, bow legged, red headed man who reminded me of Yosemite Sam. He showed me around. The workforce was mostly Hispanic, as it had been at Platology, again with English speaking supervisors, one of whom was bilingual. There were a lot more women employed there. The shop, RD Enterprises, RDE for short, spray-painted as well as plated. The women did what was known as set-up, placing parts on special racks so they could be painted.

Some of the ladies even sat on couches, which seemed much nicer than what I had seen at Platology. The whole atmosphere was very friendly, and I liked it. Rand also agreed to pay me more than I was making at Platology, and I would still be working flexible hours.

I gave Eric Ekridge, the owner of Platology, two weeks' notice. I also got Lee, one of the women from my autism support group to replace me, going to Platology a couple of times to help train her. Though she'd stopped working because of her son's autism, as I had for years, Lee had a PhD. in biochemistry, and I expected her to pick up the job quickly. She didn't, at least not in my judgment, but I had done the best I could to avoid leaving Eric in the lurch.

Within a week of becoming a chemist at RDE, a large aircraft company did a survey that turned up deficiencies in their quality control system. To qualify for contracts from the new potential client, the system would have to be rewritten. With my previous experience, Rand asked me to do it, and made me quality control manager as well as chemist. He also built me a little lab to accommodate new equipment, a salt spray chamber. I would need to qualify RDE for the aerospace contract.

A few weeks later Eric Ekridge called me at RDE. Platology had won the grant I had written. Lee wasn't up to the job and was planning to leave. He wanted me back to administer the grant and offered me even more money.

I wasn't sure what to say. I'd made a promise to Rand, and he had built me a lab and given me an even bigger job. I didn't want to leave Eric with no one to deal with the grant I'd written either. I agreed to a meet him in the afternoon when I was finished with my work for SDE, before I had to pick up Lon.

When I met with Eric, I found out that he was in the process of finding a new chemist to analyze the tanks, but needed me for the grant. It was worth $250,000 to him, and he didn't want to lose it. I asked for $25.00 an hour, which to me seemed an impossibly high wage just to write grant reports, but he agreed. I had finally stumbled on a freeway route that didn't require the move across lanes that had driven me away from Platology in the first place. My new schedule would be hard, but doable.

The few hours of freedom in the afternoon that I'd had wanted so badly, would be disappearing. I would be working for RDE in the mornings and Platology in the afternoon, before picking up Lon at the church, but I'd also be making more money, which Tim and I could definitely use. Since RDE and Platology were competitors and I had no intention of trying to fool Rand, I told him what I would be doing. His first response was to ask what kind of a grant I could write for him. Unlike Eric, he didn't already have something in mind. I told him I'd think about it. I was running on close to empty, with working for two different employers and continuing running things for the Autism Association. Whenever I had a spare moment, I tried to take a little nap. Usually, a phone call, either from someone with an autistic child or from Tim checking up on me, woke me up.

With the move having wiped out our savings, the extra money was great, but I was so tired, I couldn't wait to finish Eric's grant. After six months, I'd written my last report and Eric had received all his money. Tim told me he could tell I'd stopped working two jobs because I'd stopped falling asleep at the dinner table. By then, I had also figured out what kind of a grant to write for Rand.

There were three more environmentally favorable technologies coming into metal finishing: water-based coatings, powder coatings, and radiation curable coatings. I'd checked out all three. The water-based coatings available at the time didn't pass my adhesion tests or survive in my salt spray cabinet. The powder coatings didn't come in enough colors and had problems in tight corners. There was no way I could test curing by ultra violet radiation in Rand's shop, but he arranged to take me to a demonstration, and the process looked good. The primary environmental advantages were energy savings and the absence of solvents to pollute the air. There weren't many radiation curable products available for metal, but one of Rand's regular paint suppliers promised that they had one. I started the paperwork to fund a system that cured by UV light. It didn't matter much in terms of the environment, but unlike the drying of paint, coatings solidified under the special lights almost instantaneously, allowing jobs to be performed very fast. That meant that Rand's labor costs would go down. The opportunity to improve his profit margin was his real interest.

The grant I wrote for Rand was approved. He ordered a small-scale curing system and it was delivered to the shop. It was up to me to make it work. I was disappointed when Rand's coatings supplier delivered the product they'd promised. Rand's workers used spray guns to apply coatings, but the coating the company sent was thick like toothpaste. It was impossible to use in any spray gun.

The salesman passed the problem off, saying I could mix it with seventy-five percent solvent. Unfortunately following his instructions would be a complete violation of the basis on which we got the grant. We would be back to putting solvent into the air, no favor to the environment. The product was useless. I looked for another supplier. I ordered samples from anyone who offered anything close. Those that would spray either had no adhesion to metal, failed my salt spray corrosion test, or both.

I had never formulated a product. That was organic chemistry, which I'd never been very good at or liked. I'd never meant to formulate anything, but we had the grant and Rand wasn't giving back the money. I had no choice. To make the UV curing system work, I would have to invent coatings myself. Instead of dealing with suppliers of finished products, I would have to work with suppliers of raw materials and use whatever starting formulations they could supply. Then I'd have to modify them to work for SDE.

Formulation was hard and frustrating, but I did my best. I tried formula after formula. There was no room in my little laboratory for both my quality control work and my formulation work, so Rand had his people build me a bigger one. Unfortunately, in the part of the building where they had to put it, it was impossible to hook it up to the air conditioning that cooled the offices. Southern California was warm anyway, but when I ran the curing system, the temperature in my lab went up to 120 degrees. I'd learned to use a spray gun myself, in my hood, but the hood wasn't as strong as the spray booths that were used in production. The chemicals I was using were all classed as non-toxic to inhale, but they didn't feel good at all in my lungs. I did my best to ignore all that. I was going to produce working formula.

Colored coatings were almost impossible to formulate. They were thick, and the UV light couldn't penetrate the pigments. After trying everything I could think of to make one work, I decided to concentrate on a clear that could replace solvent heavy lacquers. That wasn't what I'd hoped to do, but Rand had been presented with a potential job coating the brass plates for the backs of popular pairs of jeans. It would be the first chance to apply one of my coatings in production. The coating would have to keep looking shiny while standing up to tests that would simulate a number of runs through a washing machine. It would also need to be flexible enough to stay on if the plates were bent and beaten up in a dryer. I used everything I had discovered in my own tests, to make a successful formula, and Rand snagged the job using it. I was grinning as I called my supplier to request the raw materials in commercial quantities. Up to that point, I'd only been working with samples. I made the coating and Rand made a tidy profit. At that point, I had no way of knowing that as far as profits were concerned, the more ordinary work for RDE wasn't going too well

Rand acted like a showman and demonstrated the new curing system to every customer of RDE who came through the shop, bragging about the new formulations he'd discovered. That might have worked for him if I hadn't been out on the shop floor and overheard what he said. It was like Vu all over again. I did the work, and someone else was claiming it as their own. RDE had paid for some, but not a lot of it. I had also done a lot of the reading and studying required to make the formulations on my own time, as I had with the work for Vu.

Rand didn't have a clue how formulas were made. He hadn't sweated in the lab or breathed the droplets from a spray gun until it felt like an elephant was sitting on his chest. That was all my work. There was no reason for Rand to lie about it, but he did. In a way, I had understood Vu's lie. He was trying to impress his bosses. However, Rand had no boss. He owned RDE. I couldn't understand what he did at all, and I was as furious as I'd been with Vu. I did the only thing that I could think of; I started taking my formulation notebooks home with me for the night. If Rand wanted information about what I was doing, he would have to ask me. I didn't lie or make any secret of what I was doing. The company secretary, Rand's confidant, knew all about it.

Within a week I was called into Rand's office. Rand's lawyer was there, and I was offered a deal. Rand would be starting a new company, EC. I would own twenty-five percent of it, but I would have to agree to never take a formulation notebook home again. Any formulations I developed, whether on my own time or not, would belong to EC, and I would be the technical director.

I felt as if I was celebrating Hanukkah and Christmas. Other than a few shares of stock, I had never owned any part of a company before. I'd never expected to be a technical director either. Even though I'd always been the one in the family to handle the money, I talked the offer over with Tim that night. The deal sounded good to him. Within a couple of weeks, the official paperwork was ready for me to sign, and I did. There was officially an EC Inc.

Chapter Sixteen

Rand told me that he would be running some of the contracts RDE had through EC, just to provide some working capital, but since they weren't jobs stemming from my formulations, I wouldn't be eligible for any share of the profits. To me, that sounded fair. I was an idiot.

Rand had been renting space for RDE but decided to move the operation, along with EC, to a building he'd bought further inland, where it was cheaper to do business. I was upset that I would no longer be working so close to my house, but as an employee of RDE and a minor partner in EC, my vote didn't count. There was freeway almost all the way, so going the speed limit, the drive was only about twenty minutes long. That worked if there wasn't too much traffic. Still, I didn't like even a twenty-minute drive. I'd gone to work for RDE so I wouldn't have to drive as much.

Besides my regular work, I'd be stuck with everything it would take to close down the old location. Agencies that deal with environmental regulations are suspicious of finishing shops, often for a good reason. Even with treatment systems, chemicals are released into the water. In RDE's water district, they were monitored quite stringently. Vapors from cleaning solvents had to be controlled as well. I had worked on doing that and even won Rand an award from the EPA for decreased emissions. Chemicals put into the air from paint booths and ovens were permitted, but with strict reporting requirements. All environmental issues were part of my job, and everything concerned with them would need to be adapted to the new location. What worried the officials at the old location most was that finishing shops had moved, leaving contaminated ground and hazardous waste behind. I had to present them with plans and documentation to convince them that RDE wouldn't just pull up stakes to escape having to clean up a mess.

Most of the agencies' requirements for RDE's move involved writing. That was the easy part. The relocation also required me to research and learn about new pollution control systems. Rand's permits for releases of chemicals to the sewer, even with treatment to make them non-toxic, had been grandfathered in for his old location. He would not be allowed to release anything except water and waste from the bathrooms in the new one. I had to figure out an alternative. I did. I got Rand to install evaporators that wouldn't do anything but put clean water vapor in the air. The plating chemicals would be recycled back into the tanks. I didn't know it, but with the building in his name, EC would be paying rent to Rand and also paying for the new systems. He was spending some of my money for systems that were for RDE, not EC.

It took months to get everything for the move in order, a reprieve that was welcome to me, but we finally went. I had a nice office, which was air-conditioned. My lab was not, but the curing system had been connected to a paint booth and was well vented both by the booth and by fans on the shop floor. I didn't have to breathe any more fumes. My space for doing analyses was on the shop floor too, and not usually too uncomfortable. I still hated the drive. The distance was not usually a problem, but my exit from the freeway involved an uncontrolled left turn into heavy traffic. For me, that was every bit as scary as moving across the lanes to get to Platology had been. I arrived at work shaking every day, but there was nothing I could do about it. I was as completely trapped in a job as a person could get.

I worked hard for both RDE and EC. I finally found out that RDE was fighting for its life. When a new president was elected, a cut in military spending caused many of RDE's regular jobs to dry up. The contractors still willing to give RDE work had higher quality standards, meaning I had to redo the quality system, only this time, I did it in duplicate, to cover both EC and RDE.

I also kept developing new formulations. Rand went on with his UV demonstrations. He made them look almost magical, trying to pull in new customers, even if later he switched them to more conventional coatings so that the jobs could be run through RDE. One day, EC got an opportunity that seemed like a breakthrough. An upscale golf club manufacturer, Dalway, had a problem. Their golf clubs had a lifetime guarantee. The clubs were well made, and Dalway had never had to cope with many returns until golf courses installed automatic club washers. The new equipment caused the lacquer Dalway had been using on their club heads, to peel off. At the same time, the air quality district in the San Diego suburb where the clubs were made, had become aggressive in enforcing emissions standards. Dalway could no longer release the solvent from their lacquer into the air.

Dalway had researched the same solutions I explored before writing the grant for Rand, with the same result. None of the existing technologies would give them the finish they needed and achieve the close to zero emissions that their air quality district demanded. The coating they wanted would also have to stick to titanium the club heads, which was a very hard thing to do. I put everything I'd learned into the project, eventually making a coating that could stand up to Dalway's tests.

I was worried about a lot more than work. JS had finished junior high and moved up to high school. In some ways that was great, because the high school was right at the end of our block. The downside was that it meant going through the process of developing a program for him all over again. I was up against his guidance counselor, who simply did not believe that a child who was officially in special education could also be placed in the upper-level classes where I was sure that JS belonged. IEP meetings were a battle, but using what I'd learned as an advocate for all the kids I'd been serving in the Autism Association, I finally got the school to agree to what I thought would work best for JS.

At the same time, I had moved up in the Autism Association. Since I was already running a chapter of my own, as well as a support group, I was asked to run for the National Board. The leaders of the association were fighting, and I would be part of a group trying to come in to improve relations between groups of both parents and professionals advocating competing therapies. I had also become involved in planning a National Conference like the one my family had attended before I decided to try putting Lon on a computer. The conference meetings seemed endless, but the hotel we'd be using was not far from Lon's new school, so I was familiar with the neighborhood. I was drawn into every aspect of setting things up, even the seating at a luncheon, but the most important issue to me was the vetting of papers to be presented.

Since I was more familiar with scientific language than other people working on the conference, I read them all. I was disgusted to find that a large number of the presentations were thinly disguised efforts to sell programs designed to squeeze money out of desperate parents. There were true insights as well, on everything from gentle methods of controlling behaviors to brain structure. I absorbed everything I could. I was also the only member of the conference-planning group who had a computer. I used it as much as I could, to print out lists, schedules, and even introductions. I learned a lot as I went along.

I didn't believe it was possible, but I was elected to the National Board. I took office at the conference, and there were a lot of hostile members. Relations had become so bad that the national office had been sabotaged and the membership list on their computer was wiped. Somehow, the Board elected me national secretary, and it was my job, with the new president, who lived in Pittsburgh, to put the wreck back together again. The president hired someone to restore the membership list. Fortunately, whoever had deleted it had been too clueless to overwrite it. Tim could have recovered it, but that would have meant a trip to Bethesda, Maryland. The association needed someone who lived nearby, so that meant a local hire.

I was on a lot of conference calls. Normally I would have made out of town trips to go to Board meetings, but the association was so broke, it couldn't afford them. I made one quick trip to Bethesda, for which I prayed I'd be reimbursed somehow. Mostly, I did what I could over the newly developing internet. Slowly things began to straighten out.

One welcome change was that through my advocacy work, Tim and I had picked up some genuine friends, the Jensens. Since both our families had autism in them, weird speech and behaviors didn't bother anyone. We did cookouts on our patio and visited each other. Not long after JS had started high school, Sue Jensen told me that choir would be starting for the year at her church, and she would be going to the first meeting. Before the words were even out of Sue's mouth, I told her that Tim and I would like to go too. JS was old enough and smart enough to be able to watch Lon for the couple of hours it would take to attend a choir practice or a worship service. I wanted to get back to my music, and I knew Tim did too.

Chapter Seventeen

On our first Wednesday night rehearsal, the choir was glad to have me and even more happy to have Tim. He was the most resonant bass in the room. Tim and I had a scare on our way home. A police car was sitting outside our house, and we were afraid something had happened with JS and Lon. It turned out to be a false alarm. The presence of the unit had nothing to do with our family. It was there about a bogus gang activity complaint about one of our neighbors. Lon was in bed, and JS was doing his homework. I felt like I'd aged a couple of years within a couple of minutes, but Tim and I still thought of our night out as a success.

We hadn't expected to, but Tim and I performed with the choir the following Sunday. The Jensens were Baptists, a church Tim and I had never attended before. The hymns and praise songs were unfamiliar, but we read our way through them. Since I was still Jewish, I was a target of fascination to many members of the congregation, who were sure that they could save me from going to Hell. In the meantime, as I'd found before in other churches, my ability to hit the required high notes was enough to earn me a place.

Wednesday night rehearsals and Sunday morning church became part of our family routine. JS even seemed capable of handling Lon while Tim and I grabbed an after-church lunch with the Jensens. My schedule was stuffed full, but at least part of it had begun to resemble a social life.

Tim had gone through changes of his own. His job that our family had relocated to accommodate, had disappeared after a year, but he found another one. As it turned out, it was back in the Irvine area. Unlike me, Tim had no trouble shifting lanes on the freeway, so the commute wasn't disturbing for him. Like me, he had also become part of a second, start-up business, Ari Verma Technologies, known as AVT. Tim was writing software for a new device Ari, an electrical engineer, and former colleague, had developed. Unlike me, Tim had been required to invest some money. A number of his former co-workers had invested money as well, more than Tim and I could spare, but Tim's biggest contribution was his time, a lot of it. Tim spent hours at AVT headquarters, which was about twenty minutes from our newest home.

I decided we both needed a break. The next national conference would be in Seattle, Washington, which would mean a long and picturesque trip up the Pacific Coast Highway and Interstate 5. It would be the first time we attempted to travel any distance as a family since our short vacation on Avalon before our sons were diagnosed. Now we had a much better handle on the behaviors of both boys, especially Lon. I was sure that we could manage it.

Because of my nervousness on the road, Tim decided it would be better if he did all the driving. AVT was in the middle of working out quality control bugs, so Tim had to stay in constant touch with its potential customer. We made multiple stops along the way so he could make calls, which not only slowed the trip but put Tim in a bad mood. He was short with the boys, which made them jumpy.

One strategy I developed to keep Lon, and even JS, calm, was to give them gum to chew. That was no problem with JS, but Lon got it in his hair several times during our trip. It had happened before, and I'd made sure I had a bottle of orange oil to get it out without hurting Lon or having to cut any of his hair. Along with restroom trips, I used our stops for de-gumming.

Despite Tim's work problems, the trip was beautiful. Tim and I both loved the city of Grants Pass. We went so far as to pick up real estate flyers for the area, even though the idea of buying a house in the towering woods was a fantasy. When we reached Seattle, Tim had straightened out some of his software problems, and he was in better spirits. So were the boys. After having put on a conference myself, I was not easily impressed. Much of the information presented was repetitive and I found some of it laughable.

A professor from the University of Washington gave a presentation on a study, which she asserted showed evidence that children with autism actually loved their parents. I whispered to Tim that any parent or grandparent of a child with autism could have told her that, but she had made the announcement pretentiously, and even put out a press release. I had hoped for something more interesting, and I finally got it. Dr. Renberg, the psychiatrist who had diagnosed JS, presented a paper. He had conducted a study, enlisting almost every family with autism in the state of Utah. Using the extensive genealogical records maintained by the Church of Jesus Christ of Latter Day Saints, the ancestry of all of the autism families had been traced back to six ancestors. He had made the best statistical fit he could to patterns of inheritance known at the time, and had concluded that autism was a double recessive. According to his theory, each parent would have to contribute an autism gene to produce a child with autism. He felt that his findings provided strong evidence to set aside some of the still pervasive theories that bad parenting caused autism. The only way parents could cause it was by contributing their chromosomes, and the genes would have to be on both sides. What he proposed greatly over simplified what was discovered in later genetic research, but back then it was comforting to me.

Dr. Renberg's conclusions were welcomed by some parents in the autism community, but not by others. To the older parents, who had been dumped on by Bettelheim's disciples, they came as a relief. I had experienced enough blame from professionals when Lon was first being diagnosed, as well as from the attitude of Tim's family, to understand the feelings of parents who had been abused by the psychologists who believed Bettelheim. Some newer autism parents had never encountered accusations that they'd caused their children's autism, but did not want to believe they'd passed autism genes to their children.

Tim was somewhere in the middle. His family had stubbornly dismissed the fact that he had a cousin who'd been diagnosed with autism as having anything to do with Lon and JS.

Now it seemed obvious that it had a lot to do with it. He intended to present the evidence to his parents, in part in the defense of me, but he knew that they would not take it well, if they accepted it at all.

JS also had a positive experience in Seattle. He made a friend there. A mother had come from Canada, bringing her son Owen, who had a diagnosis similar to the one Dr. Renberg had given JS. The two boys immediately latched onto each other in a way neither I nor Owen's mother had ever seen either of them bond with anyone. They stayed together as much as they could during the entire conference and promised to write to each other when they returned home. It was the first hint I received, that people with autism, at least the ones like JS and Owen would enjoy each other's company. With all the talk about the necessity of social skills to build relationships, it was a revelation. When the conference ended, the two boys hated to say goodbye.

I returned home with new insight, and to a never-ending pile of work. My chapter and my support group were expanding, meaning I had a house full of visitors at least once a month. Enough money had been raised for at least quarterly national board meetings, which meant I'd have to manage to travel at least one weekend a quarter. I was also doing my jobs for both EC and RDE and singing with the church choir.

The choir became more engaging for me. David, the director, was conducting the usual Sunday morning warm up for the choir when he heard an optional high B flat hit and held for five measures. He asked who did it, and I had raised my hand. From that moment on, I was given more to do, and David expected me to lend strong support to the high lines, especially above the staff. That meant that I'd need a lot of practice if I was going to avoid embarrassing myself.

There was a passage in the cantata David had picked for Christmas Eve that was complex and very high. I worked at home with the sheet music and a tape to master it. Lon began to look over my shoulder at the music and listen intently while I practiced. He stayed quietly through my endless repetitions of the most difficult measures. He also started to want to sing *Sesame Street* songs he liked, with me, and to try to play my guitar. We sang, "Who Are the People in Your Neighborhood," while I fretted the notes and Lon strummed the strings. Lon didn't seem to mind being close enough to me to do it. He just wanted to make music. I loved that I'd found something that Lon and I could share.

Alongside the computer, music became Lon's teacher. He learned words and phrases from Disney musical video tapes. When I wanted him to pay attention to what I told him, I'd put it in a song. Sometimes he sang a request or answered one by singing. If the area of his brain that controlled speech didn't function well, the part that dealt with music worked just fine. I had found an effective way to communicate with my son.

As one piece of the puzzle of my life was fitted into the full picture, another one slipped loose. The coatings that I had been making for the Dalway project, with some help from Rand's staff, developed flaws. I tested all the materials as best I could, with almost no analytical equipment, and concluded that the solvents floating around from the SDE jobs were acting as contaminants. If I was going to continue working on the EC coatings, I needed a lab in a separate facility.

I decided to turn the setback into an opportunity. For me, that meant having a new lab that was close to my home. Even if I'd be working alone, I'd have more time, without the commute, and could avoid the left turn that still gave me the shakes. JS was reaching the age to hold a summer job, and I might even be able to give him one.

Rather than risk losing the Dalway business, Rand gave in to my lab request. I found a thousand square foot rental in a business center a mile and a half from my house. It had a tiny office up front with warehouse space I could convert to a lab. It also had the three-phase power I would need to run a curing light. The place was fully climate controlled so that I wouldn't be sweating over my experiments, and my chemicals would be more stable. I would also be able to set up a small hood for spraying parts. The business center even had a Deli where I could buy lunch if I didn't want to bring it from home. It even sold my favorite frozen yogurt. The location was perfect.

I found that most of the time, I was happiest by myself. Although I kept very regular hours, I still set my own schedule. I could start an experiment going or a formula mixing and sit at my desk and write, with no one to ask me what I was doing. I was getting my work done, but I was also filling up legal pads with stories. I wrote about whomever on television was in love, or about characters of my own. I could also take care of some Autism Association business if I wanted to, but I usually didn't. The lab was my own little private world, and I liked hiding there.

Tim had made yet another change as well. He had been offered work he could do as a contractor, programming for a banking organization. The money would be good, even if we'd lose a chunk of it paying extra taxes. He would be working from home, which meant he'd be able to pick up the load more easily when I had to travel for the National Board. It would also make it easier for him to combine his regular job with his work for AVT.

Chapter Eighteen

Things were becoming complicated again with the Autism Association. Dan, the president, was term limited, which to me was a good thing. In some ways I liked him, but I also thought he had no idea how to conduct a meeting. Small topics dragged on for hours. As secretary, I had ended up with reams of notes, but very little was accomplished. One meeting had even gone on for seventeen hours, causing one board member to resign. Those problems never occurred at my chapter meetings. I had an agenda, and I stuck to it. Everyone had a chance to speak on a motion if they wanted to, but chatter and small talk were limited to social times over snacks. My meetings were short and efficient, and I couldn't figure out why other people, especially the current national president, had problems conducting them that way. I decided it would be better for the organization if I ran for the job. Even though Dan and I had worked closely together, and he had even told me multiple times that he was closer to me than he was to his own daughter, I wasn't his pick as a candidate. He preferred Wayne, a Texas businessman with one high functioning son. Wayne knew a lot about money but knew almost nothing about autism. I didn't consider that acceptable. There were so many quacks trying to rip off desperate parents; I couldn't imagine anyone running the organization that had no experience uncovering frauds. I was sure I was the better candidate. With Tim working from home, I would be able to manage whatever extra travel the top position required. I went about the process of being nominated.

While mucking through the politics of the Autism Association, I ran up against another challenge at work. Up until that point, the air quality districts had been accepting a manufacturer's certification that a coating met the standards of being essentially solvent free, based on the formulation. In a new decision, Dalway's district decided that EC's word would not be enough. Certification would be based on an EPA test. There was not yet one designed specifically for radiation curable coatings, so one designed for coatings cured by heat would be used. The test involved was not even close to relevant to my formulas, so I had never performed it before, but to maintain EC's position with Dalway, I would have to. I would have to do it under the eye of an air quality district investigator.

On test day, I was so nervous that my hands shook, something that didn't usually happen to me. The inspector, Ross Thompkins, stood right next to me as I weighed a metal panel on a precise scale. I sprayed it with my coating under my hood and ran it through my curing light. I had no more than thirty seconds to weigh it again, something that wasn't easy with shaking hands. I got it done anyway. Next Thompkins made me put the panel in an oven. That would have made sense for a coating from which heat would evaporate a solvent. It made no sense for my coating, but I followed his instructions. The panel had to stay in the oven for an hour. I suggested we might spend some of it at the deli. Thompkins refused. I spent a very uncomfortable hour attending to other laboratory tasks while he just stood there. When Thompkins agreed the hour was over, I was allowed to move the panel to a desiccator, where it could cool off without picking up any moisture from the air. I had picked up both the oven and the desiccator as surplus, for almost nothing, when I was setting up my new lab. As far as I could tell, they worked fine. I prayed that I hadn't missed anything. When the panel was cool, I was allowed to weigh it several times, to show that no solvent, or anything else, would be evaporating from it. My hands shook more every time, but I had results for Thompkins. I was relieved when his quick calculations showed that any weight the panel lost was within the limits allowed by his test. My coating would be certified as effectively zero emissions, the first radiation curable to get that certification. The district would allow Dalway to continue using it.

Rand decided to get as much hype as he could from the district's decision. He had new brochures printed saying my lab was the global research headquarters of EC. He called his building the corporate headquarters. He also encouraged me to go to local industry seminars to present my work and my test results.

By then I was very comfortable making presentations for the Autism Association, but doing them for business was different. I was forty, but there was almost no gray in my hair. It would have helped if there was. My face didn't have any wrinkles, either. Since I was small, most strangers thought I was in my twenties or early thirties, at most. My audiences were often filled with white haired principal engineers, who were skeptical that someone who looked like me could know what she was talking about. Not only did my hands shake, but my monthly bleeding also increased, with cramps so bad they reminded me of labor. I'd bled a lot before when I was nervous, so I took pills to kill the pain as much as possible and went on with my job. I made a habit of wearing my hair down when I spoke about autism but put it up to lecture on what I'd done in the lab. My hair was like a costume that made me feel more secure.

As the National Autism Association election got closer, I was shocked to see that people were writing things about me that were untrue and nasty. I had seen that sort of thing pop up before about Dan, but he had a long history of personal conflicts, and people had been saying terrible things about him for years. He considered it the cost of trying to get things done.

It was different for me. I hadn't picked a fight with anyone. Some of the people writing about me had worked with me on projects and never said a mean word before. Suddenly, they were slamming me in newsletters and taking advantage of the internet to flame me. It hurt. Dan suggested that I might drop out of the race in favor of his candidate, who seemed to be receiving less criticism. His suggestion only made me more determined to keep up the fight. If I could face intimidation by an air quality investigator and rooms full of principal engineers, I could stand up to cowards who leveled their insults with poisoned pens.

Using everything I'd learned about writing, I sent answers to newsletters and made my points directly but politely on the web. I continued to lead meetings of my local chapter and my support group, bringing speakers with prestige in the autism world, into my living room. I also flew to National Board meetings in three different cities, including the hometown of my opponent. My work was visible to anyone in the autism community who was even slightly willing to pay attention.

On the day the votes were counted, I was out of the house and away from a phone. Through picking up equipment for both SDE and EC at auctions, I'd started to enjoy them. A local manufacturer had gone out of business, and I went the sale of their property, to try to get a good deal on computers, both for my lab and for Lon and JS. When I came home, the back of my station wagon was jammed with auction wins. While he helped me unload, Tim hummed "Hail to the Chief." I'd won the election, too.

I was going to be installed as president at the next annual conference, which took place in New Mexico. Installation was scheduled for the end of the week, but Dan's wife had suddenly become ill, so I filled in for him in presidential functions. I'd brought mostly casual clothes to sit through the seminars, but I had to wear dresses or something nice, on the proscenium. It wasn't the conference I'd planned on, but I got through it.

As an auction fan, I loved the auction benefitting the Autism Association. I'd been warned by the conference chair, who served with me on the board, to bring money --- and I had. There were two previously owned but spectacular gowns up for bid. They had been worn by the heir to a vitamin fortune and were completely beaded, one in black, one in white. They were estimated as being worth several thousand dollars but were a size six, too small for most of the women there. A size six was perfect for me. I bid three hundred dollars for both of them and won. To me, that was still a lot of money, but I was amazed that I could own something so beautiful. They were like the things I had seen on television most of my life but always considered out of reach. It made me feel special to know they would be going home with me.

I made my speech as incoming president at the plenary session that served as the annual meeting of the association. It was hard to write. At first, I thought about giving up on a speech altogether. With the division going on in the association, I'd considered just singing a slightly rewritten version of a church song about letting walls fall down. Besides fearing being heckled by the audience, I hadn't been able to find the accompaniment tape. Even if I had, I had no clue as to how it could have been tied into the sound system. So I stuck with a speech.

I told them a story about what we did in my chapter. That year, the county school district had decided that their special education summer programs would be cut by two hours a day, not to serve the students better, but to save money by giving the teachers a shorter day, that would cost the district less money. They had done it without a single IEP meeting, and without consulting the teachers or administrators.

We parents were furious. Losing hours a day would have meant much less education for our children. Many, like Lon, would not adapt well to the change, especially since it would be only for the summer. Also, many mothers and some fathers would have to change their work schedules or lose their jobs entirely, to cover the time their children were not in school. The teachers didn't like it either, both for the effect it would have on the students and because it was an attempt at an unscheduled pay cut. The district had also ignored that the teachers' contract would allow them to stay at school anyway and get paid for not teaching. The proposal was ludicrous, but it would have been a serious risk to their jobs for the teachers to try to fight the change openly. That didn't stop them from doing it under the table.

As president of the local chapter, I was the one they'd slipped information to, including a copy of the district budget. I found line items that could be cut to save money, without jeopardizing the education of the children, so I wrote everything up in a letter to the editor of the local paper and sent it off on Autism Association letterhead. The newspaper was heavily Libertarian and very opposed to wasting taxpayer money. I emphasized that paying the teachers for nothing while sabotaging the education of the children was cheating everyone.

It was like poking a bear with a stick. I got editorial attention. A reporter called me for an interview and wrote a story about what the district was doing. Opposition to the district snowballed from there. A federally funded advocacy group took on the case, helping fifty sets of parents, including Tim and me, to sue the school district simultaneously on behalf of our children. Lon's situation was one of the primary ones cited, especially his difficulty in adapting to change. We parents all pulled together to reach a settlement with the district. It was a compromise. The students would still be losing some time, but not as much, and they would all be in a better position than if we had done nothing.

In my speech, I tried to use the incident to illustrate my point: that when we all worked together, we could reach a solution. That solution might not be perfect, but it would be progress. My audience paid attention. I found out later that some of them paid attention because they were curious about how to get a summer program in the first place. However, I had caught their interest and earned some respect by sharing my in-the-trenches experience. After that, the meeting went much more smoothly, and with fewer conflicts, than the annual meetings usually did. Things still weren't perfect, but I thought I'd made a good start.

To celebrate, I wore one of my new dresses, the one shimmering with shiny black beads, to the awards banquet. I sat through the kind of small talk that always made me uncomfortable, and through speeches that were way too long. The banquet went on until late at night. I was up even later, packing for my early flight in the morning. My hands were warm and had started to shake. I felt spacey when I got on the plane in the morning, but I believed that going through what I had that week, had been worth it. I had real hopes for getting something useful done in the year ahead.

Right off the bat, I had a major job. I had requested that the board appoint Wayne, my opponent in the election, as treasurer. He accepted the job, on the condition that he would be in charge of the first international conference, which was to be held in Toronto, Canada. I would have preferred to supervise the conference myself, especially as far as the vetting of speakers was concerned, but I needed Wayne's financial expertise. He also had more time to make trips to Canada than I did. I made the bargain.

It turned out to be the right choice. Wayne examined all the records of Sam Gold, the executive director Dan had installed at the national office. He found serious problems. Sam had applied for an Autism Association credit card without proper authorization, even by the bank's own rules. He charged expenses, travel, and even late-night deliveries of pizza and nachos to it. The Executive Director had also been working to undermine the Board's credibility with chapters across the country. The Board and I fired him, and Wayne negotiated with the bank, getting the credit card charges forgiven. Then it was my job to interview new candidates for the job. Several of the office staff applied for it. That created a difficult situation for me. One candidate had facial burns acquired in a fire and was obsessed with insisting that any choice that I made not be based on appearance, something I would have never done anyway. Another was deaf. The position involved a great deal of telephone work, raising the question of whether she could function.

When I talked to them, I could tell that they had both been aware of Sam Gold's activities and had supported them. Conversations with the other officers on the Board made it clear that the Board would approve firing the women, as opposed to promoting one of them. That was something I didn't want to do. Sam Gold was a very persuasive man, and I was pretty sure that he had taken them in. They would keep their jobs, but couldn't be rewarded with a promotion. I chose an outside candidate. I felt a little guilty about not picking a candidate with a disability after I'd worked so hard as an advocate, but even without the mess concerning Sam Gold, the new candidate was more qualified for the position. It made my stomach twist, but I couldn't recommend a different choice. Tim noticed that I was starting to get my first gray hairs.

Despite my rocky start, I liked being national president. I memorized a lot of Roberts Rules of Order and always had the book with me at meetings, so we'd have something concrete to work from. My board meetings were of a decent length and followed an approved agenda, making all the board members happier. Reporters called me for my opinion on autism related issues, which was exciting. Dr. Renberg even asked me to write a blurb endorsing a book.

Chapter Nineteen

One afternoon, Dr. Renberg called me about something very different. He said he was collecting data about previously undiagnosed autism phenotypes. As the parents in a family with two autistic kids, Tim and I would be likely members of the cohort. Having our family act as research subjects was nothing new. JS and Lon had been included in several studies. In each case, they'd received free testing, free therapy, or both. It had been a win-win relationship. I answered all of Dr. Renberg's questions but didn't give the matter much thought once we finished our conversation --- until a few months later.

Dr. Renberg had written a letter to the premier autism journal, outlining ten autism phenotypes, including a married couple. The remark the wife had made about her sex life was a direct quote from me. The subjects in the letter were identified by number only, but the situation couldn't have been clearer. Dr. Renberg had diagnosed both Tim and me as, although quite functional, autistic. It made sense, given his previous paper about genetics, but it still came as a shock. It also explained a lot. Lon's jumping and flapping his arms was no different from what I'd done as a child, and what I still did sometimes as an adult. However, when I did it, it was just weird. When Lon did it, it was labeled as stimming. Tim and I both shared a strict adherence to rule and promises, no matter what the situation. We also shared social awkwardness, although in very different ways. I coped by taking charge of whatever group I was in. Tim coped by a retreat into the numbers and computers that were much easier for him to understand than people were. One grandfather also accounted for both Tim and his cousin.

Tim and I talked about what to do about Dr. Renberg's conclusions. We could see little upside to identifying ourselves as his subjects. There were practical considerations. Autism could be considered a pre-existing condition on our health insurance. We both required trust in our expertise, to pursue our work. I, in particular, was the face of EC. Neither one of us could afford to jeopardize our positions. Confessions could be made here and there within the confines of the autism community, especially if they would turn out to be helpful to others in the same situation, but we wouldn't say anything to the outside world. Tim and I had unknowingly been in the closet our entire lives; there was no reason to come out at that time, and a lot of reasons not to. Still, I was glad that we'd agreed that our diagnoses could be revealed inside the close confines of our society if it was appropriate.

Toward the end of my tenure as National President, Tim's contract with the bankers ran out and was not renewed. He found a short-term job with a company his client had been working with, but that disappeared too. My wages had risen, and I was trying to work as many hours as I could, but I still didn't earn nearly enough to compensate for the lack of a paycheck for Tim. Things began to fall apart in the house. The dishwasher broke, but we didn't want to spend the money to fix it. The dryer stopped functioning, and I put up a clothesline. I was working all day and running the Autism Association at night, as well as taking care of the house. I began to get angry with Tim.

One afternoon I just lost it. I came home from the lab to find a sink full of dishes and Tim lying on the bed reading a romance novel, a habit he'd picked up from me. I started to scream. Tim just looked at me, completely confused. Then he asked me what I wanted him to do. When I told him that he could at least do the damn dishes, he said fine and from then on started washing them. I realized I had never told him I wanted help, and he had no clue. When I asked, he was willing. Money was still a constant worry, but even though my hands continued to shake, I felt calmer.

After some wrangling with Wayne, I had arranged to vet some, but not all, of the papers for the international conference. There was one presentation by a twenties-something man with autism, named Tom McClane. Tom had also been elected to serve on the National Board. I didn't know what to expect from him.

The conference was coming, along with the end of my term as president, even though I would continue to be on the Board. Tim was up for a new job, and I was traveling with all fingers crossed that we'd be able to afford whatever I had to spend that wasn't picked up as a Board expense. When I arrived in Toronto, I found that Wayne had arranged a huge suite for himself and a smaller one for me. I considered both suites an extravagance, but I enjoyed having one anyway. I had multiple messages from Tom, who had been trying to meet up with me. When I met with him, I disliked him almost immediately, something that had never happened before when meeting other high functioning people with autism. Even though he had the capability to write a book, work with electronics, and play an instrument, he had no job. He lived off public funds and his parents. I found that hard to understand. The others I knew with autism at that high a functioning level tended to enjoy the independence of earning their way, even if they coped with complications like seizure disorders. Given the way Tim and I were struggling, I didn't appreciate that Tom was living off our tax money.

As I got to know Tom in a gathering of incoming board members, I didn't like him any better. He seemed to survive by beating his chest about his autism and living off the pity he aroused. With so many high functioning members of the autism community, including myself, working hard to contribute our fair share, I had no sympathy for him at all.

Most of the members of the Board liked to drink, and a great deal of business was informally conducted in bars. I attended those gatherings when I could, usually drinking a glass of club soda with a swizzle stick in it. I could take or leave alcohol, mostly leave it. I would have a glass of wine sometimes, especially when it was called for on religious occasions, or to keep Tim company. If I had to do anything the least bit important, I preferred to be sober. The whole Board was in the Banyan Tree, the bar attached to the hotel. I wasn't drinking, and neither was Wayne; we were discussing the logistics of the conference. A speaker had pulled out, leaving an empty session for the next morning. It might have been because I was totally fed up with the message Tom was sending about adults with autism, being out of the country may have had something to do with it too, but I whispered in Wayne's ear that I would like to do a fill-in presentation on an autism family: my own.

Wayne didn't have a better idea, so he agreed. I went back to my room to write up notes for what I would say. I finished after one in the morning, and I was due to present at ten A.M. the next day. Notices had been hurriedly printed up about the change in the program and I could hear whispers of interest in the halls. My room was packed. I began by telling my audience about Dr. Renberg's conclusions about my husband and myself. Then I explained how things were for me when I was growing up, concentrating on stimming and what it felt like. I told them that what ran through my head when I was jumping and flapping was a little like sex. It had a beginning, middle, and an end. Being interrupted before the end could be as infuriating as a knock on the bedroom door at the wrong time. I suggested that if an autistic person had ever tried to hit them when they were interrupted while stimming, now they knew why. I talked about JS and Lon, and how Tim and I coped with their two very different forms of autism.

I was a little surprised that at the end of my hastily thrown together talk, not only was there applause, but a stream of people who came up to thank me, some with tears in their eyes. Women also followed me to the ladies' room, where others who had listened to me, gave me their thanks as well. I was grateful for the praise, but I didn't expect much else to come from my presentation.

Talk about my revelations didn't end with my visit to the restroom. All of the presentations at the conference had been audiotaped, to be sold both to attendees who missed sessions and to those who missed the conference altogether. The keynote speaker at the plenary session at the end of the conference mentioned in his talk that he had bought and listened to my tape. At that point, it was the second best-selling tape from the conference, topped only by the one from Tom McClane's presentation. I would have liked it better the other way around, but given that I hadn't even been listed in the conference program, it was pretty good. My message that someone with autism could put their talents to work and be productive, even while raising children with autism, had gotten through. I'd also managed to communicate what it felt like, instead of just complaining.

When I returned to the United States, things were as I'd hoped. No one in the neurologically typical world knew about a word I'd said. There were still echoes in the autism community and from people connected to it. I began to receive speaking invitations all over the country. Tim was working again, outside the house, so I had to turn most of them down to make sure Lon and JS were properly cared for. I was able to accept a few, and in one case was even paid for speaking.

I found out about more fallout from my presentation when I got a call at work. I'd heard that people from thirty-eight countries had attended my session. One of those countries was the United Kingdom. I remembered a woman with a British accent as being one of the teary faces that came up to me afterward. My caller informed me that the face belonged to an author of a prominent book on children with disabilities, Mona Rothenstein, who was friends with the world-famous author/neurologist Manfred Sayers. I knew who Sayers was because I'd seen a movie based on his life. That was exciting. What was more exciting was that Dr. Sayers wanted to come to California to visit with our family and to gather material for a section in his next book. Meeting him would mean taking a day off work, but I thought it would be worth it to accept his visit. Dr. Sayers had come up with many insights that the rest of his profession completely failed to perceive.

Dr. Sayers managed to make his visit on a holiday. It was one on which I would normally have been working anyway, but Tim was off from work, and Lon and JS were off from school. He was a kind man with brilliant white hair and beard, and even brighter eyes twinkling behind wire-rimmed glasses. I liked him immediately, as did the rest of my family. He came with a stack of his books, which he signed and gave to me. Then he talked a bit, asking questions about our lives. Mostly he observed us. He was very careful not to intrude into Lon's space, and Lon was fine with having him around.

I made hamburgers for lunch, and he ate with us while continuing to comment on heeverything going on around him. During the afternoon, Lon spent a long time at one of the computers

I'd won at auction. He had taught himself to touch type, and his fingers flew over a keyboard he never even looked at, while he concentrated on the screen. Sayers watched him intensely, exclaiming, "What a strange creature!"

If anyone else had said anything like that, I would have immediately asked him to leave our home, but it was obvious that with Dr. Sayers, what he said wasn't a put down. He was just fascinated.

I decided to make my own version of lemon chicken for dinner. When I sent JS out to the backyard to pick a lemon for me, Sayers insisted on going with him. The dish was new to the doctor, and it was obvious he didn't expect to like it. When I put out the platter, he cut a small piece off what would be his serving and put it on his plate. I thought it was funny as he cut more and more pieces until he'd eaten his whole portion.

We were all sad to see Dr. Sayers go. Even Lon paid attention as the doctor hugged me goodbye before he left. Dr. Sayers had asked if our family's name could be used, but since his books were for the general public, both Tim and I asked that it not be. Dr. Sayers agreed and said he'd disguise us. I knew his next stop would be in Colorado to visit the most famous person with autism in the country, Seeley Grand. Seeley and I knew each other. She had not only served on the National Board; she was part of the panel of professional advisors for the Autism Association. She had written several books and was known worldwide. It was no surprise to me that Dr. Sayers would want to spend time with her.

After a couple of days went by, I received a call from Seeley, which was a first. During Dr. Sayers' visit with her, I had been a topic of conversation, and Seeley had several hours' worth of things she wanted to discuss. The two of us had occasionally shared a lunch table, but it was the first in-depth conversation I'd ever had with her, and I enjoyed it. The two of us had things in common we had never realized, including being respected in our professions. We also discussed how strange Dr. Sayers was. We'd both been watching him, as he watched us.

When Dr. Sayers' book came out, the chapter on autism was mostly about Seeley, but a couple of paragraphs were devoted to "Family S." Sayers sent me an autographed copy. Our house was described, including Lon's drawings, which Tim and I allowed him to put up on random spots on the walls. The rest of the world remained ignorant, but all the families who had passed through our house for support knew exactly whom Dr. Sayers had written about. I didn't mind; it was all in the autism family. I was beginning to have other worries.

Lon was getting increasingly harder to handle. For quite a while, his teachers and I had a system going that seemed to work. A communication book went back and forth to school each day in Lon's backpack. Every week, Lon was earning something, usually a trip to a restaurant he liked. If he behaved at school and at home, he got his reward. Chances of the loss of his treat were usually enough to curtail troubling behavior, but increasingly, they had not been enough. He was biting, pinching, and punching both at school and at home and the frustration of losing a treat, only made him more violent.

As he grew bigger and stronger, I was becoming afraid of him. So was JS. Almost no one on the National Board had their sons and daughters with autism at home with them, including some of the children much younger than Lon. In my weaker moments, I had visions of sending Lon away, too.

I was also having increasing physical problems. When I was stressed, which was more and more often, my heartbeat would speed to up to a point where I couldn't stand up. My heavy bleeding hadn't improved either. My migraines had come back, often preceded by scintillating auras that would obscure my vision for about twenty minutes. I pushed myself to function at home and as well as in my lab, but sometimes I just fell asleep at my desk.

I had tried to simplify my life in some ways. I'd always preferred scratch cooking, but I had started using commercial mixes for one-pan meals. Lon loved the meals, especially the ones with ground beef mixed with some form of rice or pasta. One night, a headache, not a migraine, but one I recognized as coming from the MSG that was often put in Chinese food, came on after I ate one of those boxed meals. Almost simultaneously, Lon exploded into violent behavior. Suddenly I had an epiphany. If MSG could give me a headache, it could be having a much worse effect on Lon.

I tested my theory. I got rid of all the prepared meals with any iota of MSG in them. That included microwave cups Lon had been taking to school for his lunches. It was almost as if a fairy godmother had waved her magic wand. Charting of Lon's behavior showed his violent episodes decreased by seventy percent and were continuing to fall off. I created a whole new set of recipes, imitating the mixes Lon liked, but without any MSG. I called them, "Scott Helpers." Lon accepted them without any problem, as did the rest of the family.

At the time, autism clinicians were concentrating on the neurotransmitters serotonin and dopamine as significant, treating many of the kids with serotonin reuptake inhibitors, similar to Prozac. Some of the patients made some improvements. Some didn't. The side effects of the drugs were sometimes serious. After a quick review of my old biochemistry books, and checking out updates online, I wondered if they were going down the wrong path. I realized glutamate is a major neurotransmitter, used in the body even more than the other two. If small amounts of it had such a huge effect on Lon, that had to be an important clue.

In addition to searching the literature, I wrote letters and emails to researchers I hoped would listen. Some of the responses I received were verbal pats on the head, but others took me seriously. I established a pen pal relationship with Dr. Sayers. He acknowledged that he was not expert enough in neurotransmitters to judge my theories as right or wrong, but called them ingenious. The autism researcher I admired most, and also had a little crush on because he was gorgeous, told me that my speculation was probably very wise. Just reading his email gave me a high. I began talking about glutamate so much that Tim began to tease me about it, but I was determined that I would someday find a way to use the information I was gathering, to do more than just change Lon's diet.

Despite my enthusiasm for my research, there was something that I had slowly come to accept. Barring a huge breakthrough or divine intervention, Lon was likely to need major supports for the rest of his life. I had attended seminars on estate planning for families with disabilities and knew that if I didn't make sure Lon was provided for, he could end up in conditions where unhappiness would be the least of his problems. Tim hated the idea of even talking about when we would be gone. He agreed that I was right, he just didn't like to think about either of us dying. To him, putting together a will and a special needs trust was very uncomfortable, but he agreed to do it anyway. We sat down with a sympathetic counselor, who had a disabled son of his own and knew the ropes, including where to get legal work done at a reasonable cost.

We decided that Lon's trust would be funded by an insurance policy that would pay off upon both of our deaths. A simple physical exam would be done for both of us, mostly weight, blood pressure, and drug testing. Tim passed fine, but my blood pressure, which for much of my life, including through both of my pregnancies, had been low, was high. To qualify for a policy, I was advised to have my pressure taken three times by a doctor.

I did it. The doctor found it high too, but had me lie down and stare at a poster of a waterfall for a while, which brought it down a bit. He wasn't sure if it was spiking because I was nervous, or because something was very wrong. In the pit of my stomach, I suspected something was wrong and allowed him to schedule what he considered a full workup. To my relief, he found nothing. He concluded that I had white coat syndrome, meaning that I got nervous when someone took my blood pressure. The insurance company agreed to a policy but underwrote it as if I was older. I could understand how what I'd been through could be aging, even if it still didn't show on my face, and accepted their conditions.

I was finishing my time on the National Board, and things were settling down for our family. JS was doing well at the local high school. Lon had been transferred to a local district school much closer to home. He seemed happy there. I was able to work around his schedule. I could put him on the bus in the morning, go to my lab, and get home in time to get him off the bus in the afternoon.

Rand told me that he had decided that EC should have a facility in Ohio, so it would be easier to serve customers in the eastern part of the country. A lot of his family lived there, including his brothers and two nephews. He claimed his brother Roger was the mixing supervisor at a tire company and could help with making coatings. He also said one of his nephews was a chemical engineer. I liked the idea that what now mostly took place in my thousand square-foot lab could be going national. I also looked forward to the recruitment of some muscle for producing my formulations in quantity. I had been mixing batches of coating mostly by myself, five gallons at a time with a laboratory mixer. The buckets weighed forty pounds each. So did the pails of chemicals that went into them. I might make as many as ten in a week. It was hard work, especially in addition to carrying on all the quality management work that was still my responsibility. I received progress reports from Rand's nephews in Ohio from time to time on how the construction of the building was going, until it was finally ready.

I took a trip to Ohio to help design an automated system to do what I had been doing by hand. Rand's family was welcoming and kind, but Rand had told them an entirely different story than he told me. As far as they knew, the Ohio facility was a separately incorporated finishing shop, Noro coatings. Rand owned the major part of it, as he did with EC, and the nephews were minor partners, even though they were expected to do all the work. Rand had also lied about the qualifications of his family. Roger worked for a tire company but knew almost no chemistry. One nephew, Joe, had a degree in engineering, but it was civil, not chemical. The other one, Cal, was a math major who had dropped out of college after two years when his girlfriend became pregnant.

Rand's nephews were not surprised that we'd been told different stories. Rand's endless capacity for lying was the family joke. They gleefully told me stories about Rand telling a builder that he owned all of the woods around the building, even though the leaves had begun to fall off the trees exposing the houses on the supposedly empty land. They told another story about Rand bragging about how rich he was to a supplier, then asking about financing in the next breath.

I was aware that Rand hadn't been straight with me, but I had never realized he was a pathological liar. I couldn't get my head around that much dishonesty. I hated the idea of not being able to trust a single word Rand said, but I had no alternative. Through all of Tim's job changes, my work at EC had kept us afloat. As JS neared high school graduation and college, it would provide him with summer and holiday work. The flexibility of my hours allowed me to care for my family and still run the local chapter of the Autism Association. As nauseating and confusing as Rand's behavior was, it would be foolish and irresponsible for me to give up on EC. I had real doubts about the ability of Rand's family to manufacture coating without my supervision, but I would be able to talk to them and take an occasional trip to Ohio.

When I came back to California, I was too busy to worry about Rand's family. A possible customer, a sporting goods company, called LS, needed a specialized coating to use on the equipment for professional athletes. LS was about a six-hour drive from Noro, but it would be my job to do the formulating in California. With my lack of depth perception, most sports were never a big interest to me, but the specifications were clear. The coating had to withstand high impact without cracking and endure changes in temperature and humidity. It also had to deform in certain ways that made the players more confident in making a shot. I was able to use some of what I'd learned in my work for Dalway and adapt it until I got a result that seemed ready for testing by the players.

Applying the coating was a whole different problem. Rand had planned for it to be done at Noro, or at least that was what he told his family and me, but LS wanted their own system. They wanted it built and demonstrated at Noro, then transferred to their plant. Unlike the human controlled applications at Noro, it would have to be automated, with very little margin for error. Joe and Cal brought in one of Cal's friends as engineering help. They also spent a lot of time on the phone with me, trying to figure out what spray equipment would work with my coating.

It was months before the equipment for LS was built and ready for demonstration. In the meantime, I unexpectedly started another project. A medical manufacturer, Medro, wanted an adhesive to stick metal to plastic. I had come up with coatings that would stick to both, but an adhesive was a slightly different problem. It was rare for me, but I got lucky. I came up with the formula not in weeks or months, but in a single afternoon. The engineer on the project was amazed, but not much more amazed than I was, especially when he told me that my formula would potentially be used to stick heart catheters together. That meant that a raft of tests would have to be run to assure at least temporary compatibility with the human body, but if the tests were successful, EC would have a major sale, and I'd be helping a lot of people.

Like the formulation of the adhesive, the tests went faster than I could have imagined, and my adhesive passed. Medro gave me machinery to fill small syringes with the coating. They would be buying each syringe for about a dollar apiece, a price fifty times higher than EC would charge for a coating like the one for LS. The equipment Medro provided could hold very few syringes at a time. If EC continued to sell them, I would be spending all my time on one project.

Rand decided that he would negotiate a license with Medro. I would disclose the formula and instruct Medro's staff how to produce it, in exchange for an upfront payment. As the developer, Rand promised me half of the money we'd get. Despite Rand running much of his business through EC, all I had been making was my hourly wage. The licensing deal sounded great to me. Everything Rand said always sounded terrific until I found out what was going on. However, I had made the contact with Medro, and pursued the project through their engineer. The engineer and I talked to each other, so in this case, I stood a good chance of hearing something resembling the truth.

While the Medro project was going on, JS graduated from high school. He was the first student in special education to be eligible for valedictorian, missing it by a few service points, because he was too modest to report the time he spent helping out with the Autism Association and the ministries at church. He had stubbornly refused to claim any advantage associated with his disability, including extra time for SAT's. Despite that, he qualified for a half tuition scholarship at a nearby Christian college, where our senior pastor was also a professor. As Tim and I had foreseen years before, he was interested in mechanical engineering. JS's college didn't offer engineering majors, but the state university across the street from it did. He enrolled in a joint program with both schools, with a double major in Christian Leadership and Mechanical Engineering. That was also a first.

JS went to college by bus. Both Tim and I took turns going out with him to practice his driving, but for some reason, he preferred me as a teacher. Maybe it was because I understood how hard driving could be. When he worked in my lab during the summer, I had him drive both of us there and back, so he'd get in a little practice every day. Tim and I also sprang for some professional lessons for him. It took him a couple of tries, but he finally passed his driving exam. Then he needed a car.

I was counting on the money from the licensing deal with Medro to buy him one. I almost threw up when I got a call from Kevin, the chief engineer on the project. The licensing deal was about to fall through. Rand was demanding too much money and refusing to compromise. If Rand didn't give in, Medro was going to scrap the project and develop its own formula.

As usual, Rand had been lying to me, telling me the negotiations were going just fine. I mentally kicked myself for not knowing better than to believe him and called Rand to tell him what Kevin had told me. I used every trick I'd developed as an advocate to get Rand to give in to what Medro wanted. He didn't want to, but he finally did. Of course, he always had something else up his sleeve.

He signed the agreement, and his attorney arranged to execute it. I would spend up to eight hours at the Medro plant, accompanied by EC's counsel, Jim Moglin, who would then take custody of Medro's payment. I would give Kevin the formula and teach his people how to make it. The Medro plant was in Temecula, which would be a hard drive for me, but Moglin cheerfully volunteered to take me. I fulfilled my obligation, showing Medro's staff how the adhesive should be mixed. Moglin drove me back to EC to pick up my own car, while he turned the check over to Rand.

Over a week passed, and I expected my share of the money as soon as Medro's check cleared. Rand gave me nothing. Finally, I had to go see him. He tried to pull out of the deal, offering me a few thousand dollars for a down payment on JS's car and then promising to pick up the payments. At that point, I knew what Rand's promises were worth. I demanded what he'd said I'd get, threatening him that the entire quality backup I provided for SDE and Noro would stop if he welched on his deal with me. Rand knew that without me to take care of the reams of quality assurance paperwork, he would lose most of his major contracts for both companies. I made it clear to him that I knew it too. He gave in but was very upset that I dared to threaten him. I didn't care. He'd lied to me too many times. It was one thing to try, and often succeed in ripping me off, but where my son was concerned, I couldn't allow it --- ever. Rand saw the look in my eyes that so many school officials had seen through the years I'd spent fighting for my kids, and knew he'd stepped too far over the line. I got my money.

The next Sunday afternoon, I took JS car shopping. With his typical modesty, JS wanted no part of a flashy car, nor did he want me to spend a great deal of money on him. We were both looking for new but cheap. We visited several dealerships, finally settling on a tiny white Korean compact with a minimum of features, but a decent warranty.

I put the car in both of our names, mostly because it was easier to get insurance coverage that way. I didn't know if I'd ever seen my son so happy as when I signed the final papers. He kept repeating, "No more buses," over and over. I could see a change in him in him, a confidence that I'd never seen before. I considered the investment worth every penny and more.

Lon was changing too. As he'd gone through puberty, he'd had a big growth spurt and was over six feet tall. He was now the largest member of the family. His body had become blocky, and the occupational therapist from school noted that he lacked flexibility. One morning, I'd put him on the bus to school and was about to leave for work, when the bus came back. The bus driver told me that Lon had a seizure. He was very drowsy and couldn't hold himself up. I tried my best to get him back into the house. We made it as far as the step in front of the door, and couldn't go any further, but JS, who had no classes that morning, came out of the house to help.

As soon as we got Lon to the couch, I called the new doctor we'd been assigned by our HMO, who told me to bring Lon into his office. Lon was too sleepy to want to go anywhere, but between us, JS and I managed to get him to the doctor's office. Lon slept in the waiting room until the doctor could see him. It only took one look for the doctor to get on his cell phone to ask for authorization for Lon to be seen at a hospital, although not the closest one. JS and I managed again, with me driving, following the directions I'd been given, and JS sitting with his barely conscious brother.

There was another long wait, first while Lon lay on the floor of another waiting room, because there was no couch, and then while he was in a bed in a room, while the neurologist on call was on his way in. I knew most of the neurologists in my county who had anything to do with autism. He one was not one of them. He began to lecture me about how most children with autism should be on seizure medications.

From my research and experience, I knew what he was saying simply wasn't true. The first drug he mentioned not only wasn't effective in autism but not for the type of fully involved seizure Lon had. About matters as medically established as that, I wasn't shy about putting up and argument. I knew most of the autism families in the county, what medications their kids were on, and what had worked, for seizures and otherwise. When the neurologist angrily demanded to know who I was and why I should have an opinion, I knew he wasn't plugged into autism at all, or he would have known my name. In our area, my number was the first one the doctors in the autism field gave their patients.

I explained about running both the local Autism Association and the autism support group. The doctor calmed down a little and gave into my suggestion of a seizure drug appropriate for Lon, whom he pronounced well enough to go home to rest until the aftermath of the seizure wore off. He gave me the prescription for Lon that I'd suggested, and Lon was discharged. I promised myself I'd get Lon on a different medical plan as soon as I could.

Lon slept again at home, and I left him with JS while I made a quick run to the drugstore. The medication I'd managed to get the neurologist to agree to was not only one I knew to be effective in other children with autism, but one of a very small list of drugs protective against glutamate. Of that very short list, it was in a small class used both for seizures, and occasionally to prevent migraines.

It took Lon a couple of days to be himself again and return to school. His tongue was sore where he'd bitten it during his seizure, and his teachers told me that he kept looking at it in the mirror. I kept him supplied with jello and pudding until he felt up to regular food again. There was an upside to what happened. Lon did very well on his new seizure medication. The few tics he'd had, disappeared. He was calmer, and most of his remaining violent behaviors disappeared. He also complained of headaches less often.

My belief in a glutamate involvement in autism, or least Lon's subgroup of it, was vindicated. Up to that point, Lon hadn't qualified for what appeared to be the proper intervention, but his seizure had made that possible. As far as I was concerned, the seizure had been a blessing in disguise.

Chapter Twenty

Our family made it through the next few years with JS in college and working summers in my lab. Lon gained more and more skill with computers. At one point, he had managed to lock the faculty out of a computer at his school. Without telling me, maybe because they were embarrassed, they had called in two district experts, neither of whom was able to fix the problem. When Tim and I attended a PTA meeting one night, Lon's teacher hesitantly asked Tim if he could help. It took Tim about five minutes to undue Lon's handiwork. When we got home, Tim and I had a laugh that it took the autistic father to undo the tampering of the autistic son. Lon's teacher was actually proud of him for being such a good hacker.

Lon was given a job in a workshop attached to the school, operating a computer driven etching machine. Lon liked doing it. It was the first vocational activity he had liked. It looked like he was on his way to some kind of useful employment, but the workshop closed down.

Lon wasn't the only one with work problems. The coating Rand's nephews in Ohio were making for LS, wasn't working right. It bubbled and cratered, causing piles of rejects. LS's quality manager was very upset, and I didn't blame him. I did my California work during the week and flew to Ohio over the weekend to check the coating coming out of Noro.

The available flights were not what I wanted. Changing planes meant that I had to spend several very early morning hours in an annex of the Detroit airport before picking up my flight into Akron. For most of that time, the food concessions weren't even open yet, and there was nowhere to try to sleep but the floor. I was used to traveling, from working for the Autism Association, so I did the best I could. I found an out-of-the-way place against a wall and rested my head on my carry-on so it wouldn't be stolen while I slept. Joe picked me up at the Akron Airport and took me directly to Noro.

I was horrified. I'd expected to see the equipment I'd helped design being used to make coating. It wasn't. To make room for metal finishing work, it had been moved to another room, where there wasn't the three-phase power needed to run it. When I asked how the coating was being made, I found out that instead of exact weights pumped from gently heated drums, the containers were lifted by a forklift and poured out as best as could be done, into small vats on a small scale. Nothing was close to precise. Cal had even been using the wrong equipment to add chemicals in small amounts. The nephews hadn't called in their father to check out the operation at all. I don't know if it would have helped. I had made the coating similarly in my own lab --- minus the forklift. However, my measurements were to hundredths of a pound, and I ran a full range of tests on it before I ever shipped it to the customer.

To make things worse, some of the chemicals didn't look right. One was a color it shouldn't have been, and Rand's nephews had ignored it. I couldn't confirm that any of the components were what they were supposed to be. Without decent test equipment, there was no way to determine exactly what had gone wrong except by exchanging the chemicals one by one in test mixes, to see if any of them had gone bad. On the weekend, it would be impossible for me to call my contacts at the chemical companies to get fresh samples. One thing I could do would be to mix up a test batch of my own and spray it on the small system at Noro, to see if it would work. It didn't. I had a lot of work ahead of me to track down the source of the problem.

I was working five days a week in California then flying to Ohio weekend after weekend to try to get my coating back to what it should have been. Joe and Cal took turns staying in the building with me while I worked twelve-hour days. Because Joe and Cal hadn't used the apparatus I'd specified, they'd put metal dispensers on the drums. The metal could react with the chemicals, spoiling them. To what extent, I could only determine if they had by trying them out. If I'd had the proper analytical equipment, it would have been a much easier way to go. I'd asked Rand for it, but he'd never wanted to spend the money.

The age of the chemical components was also uncertain. My investigation, calling my contacts, showed that some of the drums had sat in a warehouse in Europe for eighteen months before being shipped to the United States, but the supplier hadn't disclosed the delay on their paperwork. I stopped ordering anything from the company that had supplied the dubious chemicals, and tried other components that another supplier claimed were equivalent. To make things even more complicated, the nephews told me that air conditioning would be installed where the chemicals were stored, but they never had it done. That meant that any bad reactions taking place in drums during the warmer months would proceed much faster, leading to a possibly unusable product.

Weekend by weekend, I came closer to a solution until I was able to produce a product ready to run on the LS system. I was exhausted, but I still would have liked to be along on the test run. I couldn't because LS wasn't open on weekends and I needed to be back in California during the week. Joe would be making the test run, and I gave him every possible instruction and warning I could think of.

Joe told me, on a Monday a week later, that LS had found the coating good enough to put back into production, but wanted me to do further work on it. I was relieved. A few more trips to Ohio and I should have had things all straightened out.

The next day, an unimaginable disaster struck. Planes flew into the twin towers of the World Trade Center in New York. It collapsed, and thousands of people were killed. The government said terrorists had caused the tragedy and it was doing everything it could to prevent another one. U.S. airspace was closed, and I wasn't going anywhere. Neither was anyone else.

I tried to do the best I could to upgrade the coating from my lab in California. I gave instructions to Joe and Cal on the phone and sent faxes to them, but things weren't working. Finally, I received the call I'd been dreading, from the general manager at LS. They were discontinuing the project and looking for a new supplier. EC and I would be welcome to try to introduce a product again, but only if I was in Ohio to work on it.

I got another piece of news not much later, from Tim. The following summer the company he worked for in California would be shutting down their Irvine location. It might be possible for Tim to work for them in Silicon Valley, but that seemed like an impossible move. The cost of housing in that area was totally unaffordable. If we sold our house, there was no way it would bring enough to buy anything our family could live in if we relocated to the northern facility. Besides that, I would have to leave EC. As frustrating as it was to work with Rand, it was very doubtful that I could find another job that would give me the flexibility to take care of Lon. I did still own twenty-five percent of the company. I couldn't just let that go.

I could only figure out one solution that made sense. Tim and I would have to move to Ohio, where I could work out of Noro. Rand was fine with the idea because EC would no longer have the expense of maintaining my lab. Living and housing costs were lower in Ohio than they were in California. We could manage on my earnings, though just barely, until Tim found work. Of course, we would take Lon with us. JS was due to graduate from college in the spring. If he wanted to go to Ohio, we could take him too.

We'd lived in the house much longer than we had in our condo. We'd lived there longer than we'd lived anywhere. Lon had caused a lot of damage. The worst of it came from the most disgusting thing Lon had done, smearing his feces on the wall. That was not unusual with children with autism, but no one talked about it much. Putting what I knew about chemistry to work, I'd developed a mixture to that would clean up the mess. I used it myself and gave away bottles to any family that shared our problem. Even with my special cleaner, keeping up with Lon was a hard and nauseating job. Eventually, I just covered the walls of his room with burlap. It didn't look great, but he didn't like the feel of it against his hands and left it alone. Lon had also broken a lot of things. I'd always handled problems with the house. Tim's artistry at the keyboard did not extend in any way to home maintenance. I enjoyed working in the garden, what little there was of it, but with everything else I had to do, I'd had a hard time keeping up with the rest. There were also repairs we just couldn't afford. As a result, realtors would be pointing out the "potential," of the house, rather than how beautiful it was.

The amount of work involved in moving to Ohio would be huge. Aside from selling the house in California, I would have to evaluate new school districts to find the best one for Lon. I hoped I could find one near Noro. I had steadily been training people to lead the local Autism Association, but I would have to make sure they were ready to take over. We'd need real estate agents who could get the most money for the house. All the legal matters relating to taking Lon to another state would have to be resolved too. Almost all of that was on my shoulders. Then, still, another complication came up. Elliotta, a nurse and one of the most faithful members of the support group, was staring at me one day and asked about a swelling on my throat.

I had no idea what it was. Elliotta was very calm, but she suggested, in nurse-speak, that I should see my primary care physician.

I did as Elliotta had advised, and found that I had two problems, one was a mass on my thyroid, and the other was an extreme case of anemia, due to my heavy bleeding. Both required biopsies. I also needed another appointment for an ultrasound. I was going crazy waiting for the results. I didn't want to say anything to Tim until I knew the truth, one way, or another.

I wasn't afraid of dying. There had been so many times when I had viewed it as a welcome escape. I was upset by the idea that I might leave a mess behind me for Tim to handle. While I waited, I was grateful that Tim and I had done our estate planning, and wondered what else I could do to make sure he and the boys could manage if I weren't around.

One result arrived on a post card. The cells in the mass on my neck were not consistent with a malignancy. The other one required a visit to a gynecologist, who explained that I had several large fibroids causing the extreme loss of blood.

The surgeon who'd done the biopsy on my thyroid wanted to remove the whole gland to stop the flood of hormones pouring into my system. I hated that idea. I was sure I'd inherited the problem from Mother, who'd had a lump on her throat when I was little and had surgery to take care of it. Mother's singing voice was never the same again. She also had to take synthetic thyroid hormone for the rest of her life. The surgeon smugly quoted the odds against damage to my voice. Because of the boys, I had dealt with more than enough smug doctors in my life. I quoted the odds of giving birth to two children with autism to him. At the time, they were thought to be four in ten thousand, squared, yet I had the boys. I decided to research other options.

As usual, I dove into medical literature. I didn't have to dive deep. Not only was surgery not the only possible procedure, according to the College of Endocrinologists, it was not even the recommended one. The preferred solution was called radiation ablation. It would be more complicated than surgery for my family and me. I wouldn't be sick or lose my hair, but I would sweat radioactivity for a few days. It would be low level, but I would still have to protect the people around me, especially any young ones. That meant sleeping separately from Tim, with separate linens. My clothes would have to be washed separately as well. I'd also wear gloves whenever I touched anything that anyone else would eat or put in their mouths. I'd also keep my distance as much as possible from other people.

I had to visit a radiologist for the treatment, which turned out to be just swallowing a pill, and not even a big one. I made myself a place to sleep on the living room floor. I hated to admit it to Tim, but I actually enjoyed that part because it meant I didn't have to put up with his snoring, which had been getting louder, causing me to get even less sleep than usual. Gloves were no problem for me. I wore them every day at my lab anyway, and there wasn't much I couldn't manage to do with them on.

I had a couple of bad episodes. One was when a fellow soprano at church tried to show me her new baby. I screamed for her to get the baby away from me; then I had to explain why. The other was scarier. At a choir rehearsal, I had carefully set myself up, so no one would get too near me. I sat in a pew a couple of feet from the nearest person and put binders of music next to me to make sure that no one would accidentally come closer. It was all working fine until Debbie, an alto who had been fighting a brain tumor, had a seizure and fell at my feet. I forgot everything except helping her. I turned Deb's head to keep her from choking, then proceeded made sure she didn't hit herself against anything while she convulsed.

Someone called the paramedics. They knew Deb; it wasn't her first seizure. They took her to the hospital. Chris, the choir director, decided that it would just be better to pray and then send everyone home than to continue the rehearsal. A few days later, Deb died.

Deb's death came as no surprise. Most of the congregation knew she was fighting a losing battle, but I was afraid that by touching her, I might have hurried her passing in some way. I worried about it until I had a chance to check with my radiologist. He told me that whatever small amount of radiation I might have passed on could not possibly have made a difference. I still kicked myself for breaking my own rules.

Curing my fibroids, something both Mother and Rachel also had, turned out to be more complicated. The doctors refused to schedule surgery until my blood count rose, but the fibroids were causing my anemia in the first place. My gynecologist suggested a monthly hormone injection that would induce all the symptoms of menopause. I'd get it at a nurses' clinic. I asked the nurse who gave me the shot, about side effects. She just handed me the package insert. Even with my experience with deciphering medical terminology, it wasn't much help. She did tell me that it wasn't likely that I'd experience anything noticeable for at least a week.

The nurse was wrong. Two days later, our choir was singing a special anthem. Instead of singing from our usual spot on the steps of the altar, Chris, our director, had lined up the men against one wall of the sanctuary and the women against the other. We were singing the third service of the morning. I'd felt fine through the first two, but as I began to sing again, I felt hot. My knees were weak, and I could barely stand up. I wanted to finish the song like I had when I was pregnant with JS and got faint. I just couldn't. The best I could do was slip into one of the pews so that I wouldn't fall.

Most of the choir noticed that I sat down. When the song ended, the organist, Mary Eve, came and sat beside me and asked if I was all right. I admitted that I wasn't, and Mary Eve signaled across the church to Tim, who came to sit with me. He asked if I wanted to go to the hospital, but all I could think about was getting out in some fresh air for a while. He held on to me, and we went outside slowly. We sat on a concrete bench near the parking lot until I felt steady. Not long after that, I felt much better, so we just went home. I checked with my doctor the next day. She said I'd been hit with the side effects of the injection --- a week early. I was furious that the nurses hadn't warned me, especially since I'd made a point of asking. Then I felt stupid for trusting that much in the medical establishment. I'd had to research everything carefully for both my children and myself up to that point. I shouldn't have expected anything to change.

Despite the scary beginning, the injection did work. I got hot again a lot, but I didn't get faint again. My bleeding stopped, and after a couple of months, my blood count was high enough so I could have surgery. I had been warned that it would be better to take at least several weeks off work. I took nine days, until I was off pain pills so I could drive safely enough to get to my lab. Even with that short a break, things had fallen behind. I worked hard to catch up, and soon I had a solid timetable for our move to Ohio.

We received an offer on the house. Actually, we got three. Tim and I agreed not to take the highest one. We accepted one that would allow us to stay in the house until JS graduated from college. That also gave Lon as much time as he could have with a teacher he seemed to love. It also gave me time to turn over the reins of my chapter of the Autism Association to new leadership.

I'd picked a small city near Noro that I thought would be a good location for Lon, and made contact with its director of special education. She started the process to put things in place for Lon. Tim and I would still have to find a new house there.

Cal, Rand's younger nephew at Noro, came in handy. His fiancée worked in a real estate office. I asked her for a referral to their best agent, a man named Ron, who had lived in the area all his life. JS was able to care for Lon for the few days while Tim and I would be in Ohio, house hunting.

Tim and I had both spent time in Ohio before, but we were both still overwhelmed by the amount of green when compared to the water-starved foliage in Southern California. I had searched for the cheapest motel that had free internet access, a Motel 8. After my radiation therapy, I had a habit of leaving our bedroom whenever Tim's snoring became too loud for me to sleep, which was a lot of nights. At first, Tim was hurt and believed I was rejecting him. Then on a retreat with the men's group from church, the other men gave him the nickname, "Chainsaw." He realized that I hadn't been exaggerating about how loud he could be. Trying our best to keep our costs down, we'd only rented one room. The heating system was loud but the pitch didn't bother me, and I hoped that it would be enough to drown out Tim. It wasn't. I ended up using some chair cushions to make a place I could lie down under the sink in the bathroom, where I could close a door between us. It was cold, damp, and lonely, but at least I could sleep.

Ron picked Tim and me up at our motel early the next morning, to start showing us houses. I had my own list, assembled from what I'd seen on line. Some of my entries matched his. Tim and I resolved to see all of them before making our choice.

Ron found our requirements weird, but he went along with them. Most families liked open floor plans. I wanted doors that could be closed, giving Lon as much private space, as possible. We also needed a room with a ceiling high enough so that Lon could jump on the medium sized trampoline we'd been keeping in our family room, with Lon's computer and a television set. I didn't care too much about the size of the yard, although I thought it would be nice to have a garden. We needed at least three bedrooms plus an office. I also wanted a kitchen I could easily use for cooking.

We looked at a lot of houses I didn't think would work for us. We didn't have much time, and Tim and I realized we would have to make some compromises. We settled on a house from the list I had originally put together myself. There was no room that would accommodate the family room trampoline, but it would fit fine on a large outdoor deck. The ceilings in what would be Lon's room were high enough to allow him to jump on a smaller one without banging his head on the ceiling. A finished basement had a lot of extra space, but the determining factor for me was the kitchen. It wasn't large, but it had a beautiful stove and my dream refrigerator. There was also a screened in porch, called a Florida room, that looked out over the back yard. I could picture serving meals out there, surrounded by all the Ohio greenery. The location was great. The house was only two miles from Noro. I would be working full days, because I would also be the quality control manager for Noro, something for which Rand had promised me more money, in a letter that I would be giving to whatever company would be financing our new mortgage. The nearby location meant I'd have a very quick commute and be able to go home to make lunch for my family.

We moved to Ohio at the end of May. We'd wanted to stay long enough in California to sing one last Pentecost service with the choir, but the service had been rescheduled. Tim and I had to turn in our choir folders and our music, with our season incomplete. We both hated to leave work undone, but there was nothing we could do to change it.

There was no way Lon could sit still and be quiet enough to travel on an airplane, especially with everyone afraid of terrorists, so we drove across the country in my minivan. The drive from California took several days, and we stayed in motels. Tim and JS's cars were shipped ahead. Lon had spent so much time in cars and buses, that he was comfortable with the trip, except for one thing. He had always had a love hate relationship with electric hand dryers. He would always check bathrooms for to see if there was one there but refused to use a restroom that had one. On the trip, Tim and I found out that most stops along the road, especially fast food restaurants, used the dryers. Kentucky Fried Chicken was the exception, but they were usually not close to the interstate. They also put MSG in a lot of their food, putting most of it out of bounds for Lon. As a result, Lon was sometimes wet when we arrived at our rooms for the night, running for the shower the minute the door to the room he would share with JS was unlocked.

I had offered to drive part of the way, especially since we were all in my car. Tim gave me one chance but was upset enough by my technique that he decided to drive the rest of the way himself. As usual, I didn't want to be behind the wheel anyway, but that meant very tiring days for Tim. Still, he preferred that to having me drive. JS didn't even try to offer his services. He'd never done a long freeway trip.

When we drove through Missouri and into Ohio, Tim and I were still amazed at the amount of green. Since he didn't remember any home but Southern California, JS was taken with it as well, and it seemed to calm to Lon. We made it to Ohio in good shape.

I had heard that interstate moves were full of glitches, but hadn't known what kind of problems we might have. We took up temporary residence in the motel where I had stayed on my previous work trips to Ohio, not the one where I'd stayed with Tim. I still had a snoring problem with him, and on several nights when I kept waking him up to get him to stop, he left and slept in the car. He dropped me at work every morning and picked me up in the late afternoon. He arranged for some part time consulting for a new company, AVC, Ari Varma had started. Tim accepted the job despite the fact that Tim's return on Ari's last venture was far less than Tim should have earned for the amount of work he'd done. I thought Ari had cheated Tim, but Tim would never say anything to Ari about it. Tim's silence turned out to be a good thing. He and Ari were still on good terms, and he could do his work from his laptop, anywhere.

Rand had promised me an office at Noro, but I didn't get one. That was just another one of his lies. Joe set up a card table for me in the small laboratory I'd worked in before. The raise in pay Rand had assured me of in his letter didn't materialize either. Rand's behavior was consistent, if awful. In spite of the fact that Tim and I had both been lied to in business, neither one of us could understand how people could continually make promises they didn't keep. It was bewildering and frustrating.

The purchase of our Ohio home closed on time, but our furniture was still on the way. So was the truck that was supposed to deliver JS's and Tim's cars. The lack of furniture meant another week in the motel, but we did have a picnic on the floor of the new house and let Lon explore it. When the furniture was close, the moving company informed me that even though I was allowed to use a credit card when I paid fifty percent down for the first part of the move, the people on the truck would only take cash. Tim and I had some money left from selling our house in California, but the movers wanted $4000, way too large an amount for an ATM. We had to make arrangements with the bank.

When the truck arrived, and it was unloaded, boxes were piled everywhere. It was hard to move around in some of the rooms. Tim thought priority should be given to the kitchen. After the stretch of food on the road and in a motel, he wanted me to cook. That was fine with me. At least we wouldn't have to worry about Lon and MSG.

Tim joked that our vehicles must be coming by mule train. They still hadn't made it to Ohio. He still dropped me off in the morning and picked me up in the late afternoon. He also brought me back and forth at lunchtime. Joe teased me every day, asking me where my vehicle was. I called the trucking company twice a day from Noro, but couldn't get a firm delivery date.

When the cars finally did arrive, Tim's car had a dead battery, and JS's windshield was cracked. Our move had gone way over budget. Even with paying off the movers, we still had some money in the bank, but between Rand's broken promise and Tim only working part time, it would go too fast.

JS was worrying about finding a job as well. As a college graduate, Rand had declared that my son was overqualified to work at Noro. A delay of the paperwork certifying his graduation in California caused by the move became another snag. He couldn't apply for engineering work without it. His other degree in Christian leadership would make him welcome at church, but not serve as more than a curiosity on a job application. He tried his hand at factory temp jobs, at or a little above minimum wage, but he wasn't good at them and never became a permanent hire. He was often at home with Tim and Lon, who, without a summer program, was waiting for the new school year to start.

Lon didn't seem to mind. As far as we could tell, he liked our new home. A field belonging to neighbors stretched beyond our backyard making a wide-open space. The summer temperatures were warm like California. He would sit in just his shorts in the center of his trampoline on the deck, and gaze peacefully out over the grass. For him at least, life was good.

I worked on some new formulations for LS, but they had taken their manufacturing in another direction and weren't enthusiastic about coming back to EC. Before my arrival, on Rand's orders, Joe and Cal had employed an outside salesperson who was supposed to drum up business for both Noro and EC. Mostly he'd drummed up entries on his expense account and Rand fired him. Business was falling off. Rand decided that this time, building sales would be aimed mostly at EC and let me have a hand in the hiring of the new salesperson. As a quality manager, I had hired inspectors, but never anyone in sales.

For the last few years in California, Rand had hired large breasted women to do sales, claiming that it got them in the door. While they had been able to meet with men in many companies, their ability to close sales hadn't been great. Rand finally changed his list of qualifications and hired an older, church oriented, experienced woman. I had loved her. We were friends and sometimes prayer partners. She was the one person from Rand's operations that I truly regretted having to leave behind in California. I had no idea how to find someone else like her.

Joe, Cal, and I put out an ad on an industry job board, and I interviewed the people who answered it. None of them seemed to know much about EC's area of the coatings industry or impressed me much, but I had to pick one. His name was Bob Roberts. He had at some point worked with an equipment company that I'd had dealings with for EC. That wasn't much of a qualification, but it was something. Bob was a tall, aging, balding man, who insisted that I would hardly ever see him because he'd be out on the road every morning. He also claimed to have a lot of contacts in the industry.

His first claim was completely false. In fact, he was at Noro most mornings, and when he wasn't, it was not because he was out on the road, but because he called in sick. His second assertion was a little more accurate, but his contacts weren't of much help. He did manage to bring in some projects that sounded promising but he never checked on the financial stability of the companies that offered them to him.

That meant I spent weeks or longer developing coatings acceptable to the customers Bob brought in. We'd be on the verge of signing a deal, then the company involved would declare bankruptcy, leaving me with nothing to show for my efforts.

I didn't have the time to spare on worthless projects. I was also still doing all the paperwork as Quality Manager for SDE, as well as for EC and Noro. Before I left, I'd finished the getting SDE certified under an international quality standard that would allow Rand to qualify for more jobs. I'd had to complete more and different paperwork than in our previous quality systems. Rand's foreman complained about the extra documentation, but I put the new system in place. My name was still on all the manuals and procedures. That meant I had to fly back to California for quality audits.

In some ways, that was a nice break. Rand put me up in nicer hotels than I would have picked myself, and I didn't have to think about cooking meals or mixing pails of chemicals. I just sat with a professional auditor, answering whatever questions he had.

While I was in Ohio, Rand had complicated my job by getting away from the approved procedures, usually so parts could be shipped faster. That had resulted in rejects, for which I had to figure out corrective actions. Rand completely misunderstood how advanced quality systems were supposed to work. He saw claiming he'd fired whomever he blamed for a mistake as a fix. No matter how many times I told him that quality systems were supposed to prevent mistakes no matter who was doing the work, he didn't get it. My obsession to tell the truth came up against his tendency to use any story, usually made up on the spot, to excuse failures. As owner, Rand was officially in charge, but other than having him answer the questions for which an answer from the owner was mandatory, I kept him away from the auditor. That process and Rand's continued disregard for anything resembling truth drove me crazy, and I was always glad to go back to Ohio, regardless of the problems I faced there.

Chapter Twenty-One

As part of trying to settle into Ohio, Tim and I looked for a church. Our choices were limited. In California, JS had attended services on Saturday nights, so he could watch Lon while Tim and I sang through three services on Sunday mornings. Our family was hoping to find some combination of services that would allow JS to go to one, and still be home to watch Lon for Tim and me. Tim and I visited church after church. The ones that had workable schedules weren't a good fit, and the ones that were a good fit didn't seem to have workable schedules. Finally, while I was out shopping, I spotted one we hadn't tried yet. Murray Avenue Church was small, like the church we'd attended in California was. That was a start. The services listed included one early on Sunday morning, followed by a break for Sunday school, and another one after that. That would allow JS to attend the first one and Tim and me to go later.

Tim and I decided to try a service there. The choir was on a break for the summer, as was the case with many church choirs. The music was filled in by other performances. On the Sunday we chose, the special music was a duet between Scott, the musical director, on trumpet, and his teenage son, Dan, on clarinet. To me, it was painful to hear. The instruments were out of tune with each other. I could barely stand the dissonance. It was hard to suppress the urge to cover my ears or run out of the sanctuary. The sermon wasn't bad, just too long, and Jeff the pastor had a beautiful baritone voice and led the hymns very well. After the early music, things were much more bearable. I had an easy time talking with Nancy, the woman sitting next to me, who turned out to be a church secretary. She also had two adult children with disabilities. There was an instant understanding between us.

Tim and I filled out visitors' cards and decided to go back the next week. The following Sunday, the duet had been replaced by a soloist who was not only perfectly on pitch, but wonderful to listen to. The congregation was welcoming as well. During the week, two elders visited our house and didn't seem upset by the sight of Lon running around in shorts --- only shorts. We had found a new church home.

When September came, choir started again, and Tim and I showed up for the first rehearsal. We were greeted by Scott, who asked us if we were there to join up. Tim explained that we were, that he was a bass, and I was a soprano and we could both read music if that made a difference. Scott said that it did, and looked up toward the ceiling, murmuring "Thank you, Lord."

I thought Scott was kidding, but I found out he wasn't. There were six altos, four tenors, and Tim was one of four basses. I was alone in the soprano pew of the choir loft. Two sopranos were having surgery, and another had left the church. I wanted to run out of there, but made myself do the best that I could, alone in my section.

I looked through my pile of music. The songs were repeats for the choir, but I had never seen any of the pieces before. I managed to sight read through them. I got a lot more praise from

Scott and from the altos who could hear me than I thought I deserved, but decided I could stick it out until my section had more sopranos again.

In late August, Tim and I went to court to replace the conservatorship for Lon that we'd left behind in California, with an Ohio guardianship. Since Lon was over eighteen, it was the only way we'd have any legal control over his school program, or any of the services Ohio offered for him. I was amazed at how easy the process was.

In California, we'd had to go before a judge, Lon had a public defender, and Tim and I needed a lawyer of our own. Each of eight rights we would be overseeing for Lon had to be justified. Besides that, the agency that oversaw Lon's benefits, as limited as they'd been, gave their own report. Because of my advocacy work, my relationship with them was not the friendliest, and neither was their report. However, the lawyer we'd had hired had a disabled son and understood how to work the system. He'd gotten us through.

Ohio was completely different. Tim, Lon, and I sat together in comfortable chairs in a magistrate's office. She even thanked us for volunteering to do the work of being guardians and explained how the system worked in Ohio. Our guardianship was granted immediately. I hoped it was a good omen.

When Tim and I used our new authority to enroll Lon in school, the district seemed equally cooperative. Lon would be assigned his own aide, something that hadn't been possible in

California. He would be in a special class, but in a regular high school, about three long blocks from our house. At least something in Ohio was going right.

Tim and I had grown up with seasons, but JS and Lon hadn't. As the temperature dropped and Lon couldn't spend his peaceful hours on the deck anymore, his behavior began to go downhill. He was also craving much hardier food than he'd wanted in California. He was eating chili almost every day for lunch at school. The pinching, biting, and hitting that had been reduced to almost nothing for years, came back, both in school and at home. Lon was suspended a couple of times for hitting another student, but that was not the worst of it.

I was his major target. He would look for me, grab my arm, and sink his teeth into it, or bite my shoulder. He had always enjoyed going out to restaurants and fast food, but he was so agitated that Tim and I could barely control him. Our outings were nerve wracking. We tried to get some help from the doctor we'd found to write the prescription he needed for his anti-seizure meds. He prescribed a fast-acting tranquilizer we could give Lon if we thought he was about to get violent. The pills helped a bit but still took twenty minutes to take effect. Those minutes were scary.

As usual, I turned to research. I knew that part of Lon's reaction was fear. He was experiencing situations he'd never coped with before, and adrenaline was flooding into his system. I found a blood pressure medicine that acted against the fright and flight response and convinced the doctor to prescribe it. That helped a little too. Then came the revelation, the chili Lon was eating at school was full of MSG. He was also getting into snacks belonging to the other students that were loaded with it. I took care of that, and his violence decreased but didn't go away completely. He was also showing tics so the doctor raised the dosage of his seizure medication. The tics disappeared, and the violence dropped off more, but still came back whenever Lon was stressed.

The law in Ohio only provided that Lon be allowed to attend school through the end of the first year we were there. When school ended, he was in the house with Tim all day. I would see him in the morning, when I came home to fix lunch, and after work. I actually liked being away from home because I was always afraid Lon would attack me.

A recession had hit, and any jobs, even low paying ones, were very hard to get. JS decided his best course of action would be to go to graduate school. At first, he wanted to follow in his father's footsteps, aiming more toward computers than engineering. He applied to nearby Kent State University. When they dragged their feet on a financial aid package, he applied for admission in a future semester to the University of Akron.

The Akron school had more immediate ideas. Their policy had been to romance overseas engineering students, especially from China, because their backgrounds in mathematics were strong and they paid full out of state tuition. Unfortunately, many of them didn't speak fluent enough English to be teaching assistants. The university was desperate for TA's and offered JS admission in engineering a semester early, free tuition, and a stipend, to work as a TA. He decided it was the best opportunity he was likely to get, and jumped at the chance. Most of the time that put Tim and Lon in the house together during the day, while I worked and JS was at school.

The economic downturn had different effects on Noro and EC. For Noro, business held steady, as hesitation about buying new equipment caused companies to ship their finishing work to outside contractors like Noro, rather than set up their own lines to do the work themselves.

Unfortunately, adopting EC's technology required investment in new curing equipment. Bob Roberts' efforts were going nowhere fast. Rand wanted to fire him, but I saw that move as completely destroying any chance for success that EC still had. Even though I owned only twenty-five percent of the EC and was also working for Rand's other two companies in which I had no stake, he told me that if I didn't pick up half of Bob's salary, Bob was gone. The money came from what was left of Tim's and my profit on the house in California, and that was disappearing too fast. Even though I was paying for Bob, Rand continued to threaten me with the complete shutdown of EC, at which point I would be working for just Noro and SDE. If that happened, my salary would be lowered, and our family wouldn't be able to pay our bills.

Tim and I talked about what to do. We also prayed a lot. I began looking for jobs outside Rand's companies. Tim was looking too. We agreed that if one of us found something decent, they would take it and the other one would stay with Lon.

Life had something else in mind. One of Bob's contacts told him that he had a friend, Burt Backstrom, who loved new technologies. Burt had recently sold a company he'd developed, at a large profit, and wanted to try something new. Burt would be coming to see me to evaluate what I'd developed. If he liked it, he'd buy out Rand's holdings in EC. I wouldn't have to worry about working for SDE or Noro anymore, or paying Bob, and Burt would be picking up the costs of developing new formulas. I checked Burt out on the web. I could only find one article, but it was an interview with Burt about what it was like to be rich. In the article, it said Burt owned a fleet of cars and was worth millions. Buying struggling little EC would be a fun challenge for him. It seemed like God had heard our prayers and was sending me an angel, as investors like Burt were called.

When Burt came to visit, I tried to figure him out. I noticed that he dressed down like executives in California did when they were making the point that they could do whatever they wanted. He sat in my chair at my small desk while I sat on a crate on the floor in my tiny laboratory. To me, his behavior was as much an act of asserting dominance, as the displays of turkeys I'd been forced to observe at college, who raised their heads and flapped their wings to force birds lower in the pecking order, away from their mates. Even with acting that way, Burt seemed to like my work. He also talked about building a billion-dollar company. With my history of hand-me-downs and lifelong financial struggles, the thought of being rich was unreal. I wanted Burt to be telling the truth. I wanted him to buy Rand out. I hoped I could leave working for a pathological liar behind.

The sale went quickly, almost too quickly. There was no time to look for a new building. Burt made a deal with Rand that Bob and I could stay put for a while and use Noro facilities, while he picked up all the costs. Burt lived three hours away in Michigan but made regular trips to Ohio to look for a new site for EC with me. He drove a Cadillac Escalade, and I occupied the passenger seat. If Bob was along, he had to sit in the back.

I had never been completely comfortable in a car seat. They'd always seemed to be built for someone bigger and never completely adjusted to my size. That all changed in Burt's car. I loved the comfort, imagining owning a luxury car of my own someday. He was pulling me deeper and deeper into a dream.

Burt had talked about buying a building but decided to rent one instead. We found one that I thought would be perfect. It was fully climate controlled and had a built-in air compression system to power our spray guns and mixers. There was space for laboratory equipment and offices. There was even more than one restroom. It was further away than Noro, but it was still a short drive from my house.

I prepared for the move from Noro. That meant contacting the best local equipment moving company and getting a quote. My research indicated their price was well within industry boundaries, but Burt didn't like it. He sent a short and insulting letter to the moving company. They didn't like what he said either and immediately pulled out. I was confused, I'd heard about millionaires being skinflints, but Burt had never shown behavior like that before. In a way, it reminded me of Rand's behavior when he'd almost blown the deal with Medro. I began to get uncomfortable feelings in my stomach, but there was no going back. I could just do my best to make things right. I'd never thought of myself as a schmoozer. Mostly I left that to salespeople, but I called Burt and convinced him to change his mind, then smoothed things over with the moving company.

Unfortunately, by that time, Burt had started another battle. He had agreed to rent my dream building, but at the last minute, he had insisted on improvements. The landlord refused. EC had an agreement with Rand on our departure date from Noro, and the move was already scheduled. I suddenly had to find another place. I did. It was a cheaper rent, but not nearly as good a building. It was only partially air conditioned, which meant that the heat of the summer could still affect the chemicals. The neighborhood was not as savory. It was full of strip joints, and there was a dirty video store across the street from where we would be. It was also a longer drive for me. I wouldn't be able to make it home for lunch, but I still had no choice. We made the move.

The largest office had been set aside for Burt, and I expected him to occupy it, at least once in a while. He didn't. We spoke on the phone occasionally and emailed, but the administrative chores were all mine. I was, among other things, Bob Roberts' boss, but the salesman's salary had been raised, and mine had not. I found the salary situation confusing and frustrating, but at least I wasn't paying Bob anymore. It was just as well. Tim and I were almost out of reserve money. Besides my lab work, I was also in charge of keeping the books and taking care of health insurance and any other personnel matters. I was doing a lot more at EC for the same money, and getting paid less than the employee I supervised.

I set up two labs for myself, a small one, in the air-conditioned office portion of the building, and a larger one in the more warehouse-like portion, where my curing equipment was installed. For my small one, I'd picked the only room with outlets on all four walls. I put my office right next to it, so I could hear timers go off and mixers spinning. That put me in the smallest office in the complex. I would have liked to have room in my office for a small trampoline. I'd had one in my lab in California, to help me think. There had been no place for one at Noro. I'd paced instead, which wasn't as good. The trampoline went in another room, which made it harder for me to get on when I needed to. I was also afraid I'd look weird to Bob, so I stayed away from it when he was in the building.

Once we settled in, things seemed to be going pretty well. Burt leaned on Bob to look for business as much as he could, so he finally spent more time on the road. That left me alone in the building, which I liked. I played the music I wanted to hear, worked on developing products, and found time to write, while my formulas mixed and experiments ran. I had expected Burt to invest in more analytical equipment, but he didn't, so I used what little I had.

To compensate for the lost facilities at Noro, Burt had promised me a spray booth system. He didn't buy one of those, either. Bob and I jerry-rigged one out of cardboard boxes, a furnace filter, and a ten-dollar fan. When we prepared samples and test parts, we opened the roll up doors to the warehouse area, for ventilation.

Slowly I had to accept that Burt was as much of a liar as Rand. I could tell that he didn't have the money he'd claimed he had, or if he did, he wasn't willing to spend it. The mental picture he'd painted for me of a modern development facility wasn't going to happen, but Burt still talked about a big company and big profits. He hired a PR company in California to help make that happen. He also found a California law firm that specialized in going after venture capital and handled patents.

Up until that point, my formulas had always been treated as trade secrets, even the one licensed to Medro. Burt had other ideas. Whatever new I came up with, would be patented. He told me to start the process myself, using a few hundred dollars' worth of software to generate provisional patents. They were cheap to register and only served as placeholders since they were never actually examined. I knew nothing about patents. It was one more thing that I had to research. I'd taken the mechanical drawing course that was a requirement in my high school, but I wasn't up to the drafting required for a patent. JS was a good drafter, and Burt allowed me to pay him for doing the work.

The PR firm was doing its work too. Magazines and newspapers began to churn out stories about the leading-edge technology being produced at EC. I was asked to write articles as well. While I worked in the lab, Burt went to see the top venture capital firms in California. He seemed to be getting somewhere. A representative of the second largest firm in the country came to spend a day in the lab with me and said that he thought we could do business. One day, I even got a call from the man known in Silicon Valley as "Midas," because everything he touched turned to gold. He was looking for Burt, who of course wasn't there. I promised I'd have Burt call him back and called Burt immediately. He never returned the call, and I couldn't understand why.

The PR firm continued to work their magic. Burt got an offer to take EC public on the Toronto stock exchange. I would have jumped at it in a heartbeat. It wouldn't have made me rich, but Tim and I would have been comfortable and able to provide for Lon and JS, if necessary, for life. Burt turned it down. Another offer came, to be acquired by a company in Reno. I would have received a lot of saleable stock. Burt turned that one down too.

Finally, Burt asked me what I thought of a "PPM." To me, that meant parts per million, but to Burt, it was what he called a financial instrument. He wanted to get a lot of investors to chip in so EC could go public on its own by a process called a reverse merger. I looked up reverse mergers, and what I found wasn't good.

Most of them resulted in unsuccessful companies. I tried to suggest to Burt that the process might be a risky way to go, but he wouldn't change his mind.

While Burt's financial dealings were going on, Bob had become more of a problem. His smoking made him keep getting sick all the time. I could cope with that. Even when he was working, he couldn't close a deal. He got vendors involved whose spray equipment wouldn't work for our coatings. He couldn't even make a sale when I produced a product that met with a customer's approval. Burt told me that Bob would have to be "transitioned." I wasn't sure what Burt meant by that, but I found out that Burt wanted to make things at EC so bad for Bob, that he'd want to leave.

The first thing Burt did was to say that Bob and I would have to pay for forty percent of our health insurance. That would be expensive. As part of my personnel responsibilities, I had picked a plan that would cover Bob's illnesses and various doctors, which was harder than finding one to fit my own family, even with Lon. It was a top of the line offering. Bob protested Burt's decision, but there wasn't anything he could do. Since I was paid less than Bob, it would have been even harder on me, but Burt raised my salary just enough to compensate.

After a few months with that change, Burt told me to inform Bob that his hours were being cut back. Bob looked straight at me and asked when he was going to be terminated. I wasn't about to lie. I told him I didn't know when or if, but it might not be a bad idea to start looking for a new job. After a while, Bob found one. I was relieved I hadn't had to fire him, but now I had no one to help me. I took all the calls about sales that would have come to Bob. Trying to talk like a salesperson made me very uncomfortable, but I treated it like playing a part and hoped that Burt would agree to hire a replacement.

Burt had other ideas. He was proceeding with his financial dealings, which involved keeping expenses to a minimum, at least until he'd corralled enough investors. When he did, he went on a spending bender on everything except my salary and equipment for the lab.

To make the company look more prestigious, Burt hired a high profile CEO. It wasn't who he had originally wanted. That would have required a salary too high for Burt to consider, even with the way he was throwing money around. I had met Frank Klavan before. He had come to see me, looking for help for a client of his consulting business. Frank had been more impressed with me than I had been with him, but I did my best to make him feel welcome. I cleaned out the office Bob had been using, so Frank could have it, and sent him a welcoming email.

What I hadn't counted on was having a boss besides Burt, and one who knew almost nothing about what I was doing. Frank had a PhD. It looked good on the header of company presentations, but it had been decades since he'd done any lab work. He'd had a long history with coatings companies, and at points in his career, had been a big shot executive. He had no experience with the kind of products I formulated, and not even the most basic understanding of how they worked. A high school student would have understood my explanations as well, maybe better, because a high schooler would have had fewer preconceptions and a better memory.

To make matters worse, I was still handling some of the administrative chores, because my name was on them and they had been set up that way. One of those was payroll. From doing it, I found out that Frank was earning four times what I was, but I couldn't see any reason why he deserved it. The company was based entirely on my work. I thought Frank could have just stayed home, made a few phone calls, and let Burt use his name, but my opinion didn't matter.

Using the funds he raised, Burt set up an office in Michigan. He hired a chief financial officer, a corporate attorney, and a fund-raising consultant. What he didn't do was raise my salary, but his plans started moving along to complete the reverse merger. A Board of Directors was appointed and paperwork put together. I asked Burt to put me on the Board of Directors, so that I could present my ideas directly. After years on The Board of the Autism Association, and as the only who actually understood EC's technology, I felt qualified. Burt put me off, telling me that Board members were big investors. The one upside was that now most of the administrative matters were being handled in Michigan. With Frank still doing some fundraising, marketing, and schmoozing, in

Ohio, I was free to concentrate on the lab, as under-equipped as it still was.

A potential client with a new technology presented me with a project that involved printing circuits on paper. Before that, I had developed a coating that would waterproof paper. The publicity blitz had been huge, but we didn't get any buyers. I didn't think that Burt even wanted to look that hard for buyers, as long as his picture was in industry magazines.

For the new project, the waterproofing formula that I had developed would be adapted for a new purpose. I was working with a scientist, Bill Bentley, who was both a professor and a principal in a company in Michigan. He and I spent a lot of hours on the phone and developed a friendship. Bill didn't like Burt's pursuit of a reverse merger and warned me against it. More than that, he asked me to work for him in Michigan.

I liked working with Bill, but after all the complications our family had moving to Ohio, I never wanted to deal with moving again, so I didn't consider the offer seriously. One morning I got a call from Bill. He told me that he'd heard from his associates, that EC was involved with some very bad people who could take the company down. He explained that there were plans to use EC for what he called "pump and dump," raising the price of the stock through the hype and then selling it off at a profit before the company tanked. I took what Bill had said to Frank, who had no idea what to do about it. I couldn't think of anything else to do, so I called Burt, who said he'd check it out.

When Burt got back to me, he told me that there were some bad rumors about their fundraiser, Andy, but there was nothing to worry about. He also questioned Bill's motives in bringing the whole thing to me in the first place. I had wondered about that myself. It could have been a trick to get me to go work for him. Burt assured me that when the merger closed, I'd know that I was exactly where I should be. I'd be the best-paid person in the company.

When the merger did close, my ownership in the company had been reduced by outside investment. I had less than ten percent of the stock. On paper, that still made me a multi-millionaire, but it was money I couldn't actually spend. Under SEC rules, I was considered an insider. I had intimate information of the technology development within the company, so I couldn't sell my stock. I kept reminding Burt of his promise that I would get more money as salary.

After months, the company attorney drew up a contract for me, for two hundred thousand dollars a year for five years, a total of a million dollars. I knew that any contract that important should be looked at by a lawyer on my side, but it had been sent to me late on a Friday to be executed by Monday. I guessed that Burt would never expect me to be able to find a lawyer over the weekend.

I had a resource Burt didn't know about. For years, the graduates of my high school had maintained a private email list, and I was part of it. A surprising number of the members were lawyers. Our discussions over the years had been about trivia, politics, personal crises, and the occasional research oddity, but legal matters came up as well. I put out an emergency call for help from what we called a legal eagle and offered to pay for the hour or two it would take to evaluate my contract. I had a lawyer, Jared Lightner, within an hour. I'd never met him. He was largely a lurker, not posting his own emails, but he was willing to help. I scanned my copy of the contract and emailed it to him.

Late that evening, Jared called me back. He had noticed a couple of details that were less than optimal but posed no danger to me. There was even a penalty involved for EC if they didn't keep to the terms of the agreement. What concerned him was enforceability. If EC reneged, I would have to sue, which could be an expensive process. The fact that I worked in Ohio, EC corporate headquarters was in Michigan, but the company was incorporated in Nevada because of the merger, further complicated things. Still, all in all, Jared thought it was a good deal for me, so I decided I had nothing to lose by signing it. I did and forwarded it to Michigan.

Not long after that, I found out that Burt had lied to me again. I wasn't the best-paid person in the company. As far as I could tell, that was Burt. He was making more than three hundred thousand dollars a year plus his expenses for world travel. The CFO was making more than I was, too. At least I was now making a bit more than Frank. Maintaining the headquarters in Michigan was eating up company funds for no good purpose I could see, except for Burt pushing the company's hype to make the stock rise --- for all the good that did me.

I continued to ask for more and better equipment and maybe another chemist or at least a tech, to help me with developing the actual technology at EC. I didn't get anything I asked for. I still had a one-woman lab, with an occasional assist from Frank when I had to lift or move something. I continued to do the best I could with what I had, coming up with new ideas. EC continued to apply for patents as fast as I could develop my ideas and disclose them to our patent attorney. Burt had the company pay for a study that valued our patents at fifty million dollars. He used the report to sell more stock and raise more money.

While I was getting famous on EC publicity, JS was completing a master's degree. Part of the funding for the research of his group at the university was from the defense department. Since he was the only American citizen in the group, the funds were attached to him, making him popular with school officials. To finish his thesis, he required some specialized equipment that, as he'd done most of his life, he was building himself. I brought him into my lab on a Sunday to use the drill press, a tool I'd managed to buy cheaply online, with the tiny amount of funds Burt allowed me to spend on my lab. JS also needed a way to attach sensors in a way that they'd be insulated enough to avoid false signals.

He'd tried to find a commercial adhesive, but none of them had worked. As part of my project with Bill Bentley, I had been working on the insulating properties of nanoparticles in my formulations. I handed JS a beaker from my bench. His apparatus barely fit on the conveyor, but he used my formula and curing equipment to attach his sensors. His tests went perfectly, and he gave EC an acknowledgment in his thesis. His success also gave me another direction for my work. I could make insulating adhesives unlike any on the market.

JS decided to stay at the university. As he was about to start working on his doctorate, he was approached by a professor with a suggestion for a special scholarship. The Army would pay for the rest of JS's education, including a healthy stipend. JS would intern with them during the summers, earning even more. While he did this, the flow of research funds would continue to the university, specifically based on JS's native-born citizenship. In return, JS would have to work for the defense department for a number of years as a civilian employee, once his PhD. was granted. JS took the deal.

Like most government payments, JS's were delayed. He started his first summer internship with very few funds. I was worried about him and made sure that he had an account into which I could transfer funds in a hurry if he needed them. He also asked my advice on keeping himself going on a tiny budget. I suggested beans and rice. He combined them with some vegetables and developed a taste for them. He was living on his own and enjoying it. I suspected the absence of his brother might have been a chief attraction. I couldn't have blamed him if it was.

Tim and I weren't doing too badly with JS out of the house. I was finally making enough money to afford the services of a disabilities trained sitter now and then, especially for choir practice and church services, but Lon was still a lot for us to handle.

Ideally, there were support services available for Lon, and federal funds had even been allocated to the governor of Ohio to use them. Unfortunately, the governor had yet to sign the paperwork to get the money. I wrote letters urging him to pick up his pen. In the meantime, our family was on a waiting list, a long waiting list. I was relieved when JS returned in the fall and was around to lend an extra pair of hands.

Things fell apart again. Despite continual fund-raising efforts, Burt's spending sprees had depleted EC's bank account way past the danger line. Payroll was no longer being made, at least not for Frank and me. I had no idea what was going on in Michigan. Burt came up with a plan to enlist a private equity company. While he engineered a deal, Tim and I lived on money I'd stowed in the bank while finally being well paid. Frank had his own money too. We both worked on faith for four months. EC was offered several good deals, but Burt vetoed all of them but one.

Vermillion Skies took over the running of EC. Its principal owner, JD Jones, I would later discover, had been Burt's friend since boyhood. The deal was strict. Frank would no longer be CEO. JD would get to pick one of his own. The company headquarters would be moved to Vermillion's offices in Michigan. The provision that most affected me, at least at first, was the cutting of my equity in the company even further. I was still a major stockholder, but I was at the bottom of the list. The price of the stock also went down.

Frank and I were summoned to Michigan for a sit down with JD. I couldn't believe the opulence of Vermillion's offices, which had big flat screen TVs on the walls and even a tiny putting green. One thing I was curious about was JD's suit. With most of the high-powered executives I'd met, their clothes were tailored to fit. JD's vest fit him so badly, that if we'd been friends, I would have offered to take it in for him,

Despite his bad suit, JD bragged that he could write a check for twenty million at that moment, but he expected everyone to pitch in to save the company. As luxurious as his office was, I expected that didn't involve much of a sacrifice on his part. Frank's contract as CEO had expired. The back-salary Frank and I were owed would be paid, but Frank was offered a position as general manager at an 80% cut. I expected him to turn down the offer on the spot, but he didn't. He had pulled a couple of friends in as investors on the original PPM, and he was one himself. He wanted to see the project through. My contract would still run for years, and as far as I knew, there was nothing JD or anyone else could do to change it. At that point, he didn't ask me if I'd be willing to cut my salary. I did bring up the matter of upgrading the lab facilities, but JD didn't want to talk about it. The new CEO, Dave Crockman, was in the midst of signing on and would be coming down to Ohio to survey the lab and plan the next steps, with Frank and me.

Dave Crockman was part of an exclusive golf club to which JD, and the other investors also belonged. He was tall, bald, and claimed to be an expert golfer. He was also the stereotype of a salesman. He had been a Vice President at a company that sold auto parts until the company went under. Somehow, JD seemed to feel that implied Dave knew something about coatings. It didn't take me long to find out that he didn't. Frank was optimistic about Dave. He said that a good CEO was a good CEO and if Dave was good at sales, it could help the company.

When Dave came to Ohio, he said all kinds of nice things to me, but I could tell he was buttering me up. I'd found before, that people who praised me that much, usually wanted something. I wondered what Dave had in mind. He drank a lot of alcohol. He liked to wine and dine customers. He also drank a lot when he, Frank, and I went to lunch. Even though Frank had a beer to join Dave, I was glad he was the one doing the driving, instead of Dave. He was the less intoxicated of the two.

Dave's interests centered on the automotive industry. One of my projects had been a program involving coatings for aluminum wheels. Helicon, the company I'd been working with, had always been on shaky ground financially, and I'd never been satisfied with the test results they'd achieved. I didn't think much of anything would come out of the work. Ignoring my opinion, Dave looked at it as a golden opportunity. He was sure that he could use his automotive contacts to push it through, regardless of what I tried to tell him about the lab results. He immediately set it as a priority for EC.

A project that was looming even sooner, involved the production of labels. After all my work with paper, labels made more sense than the wheels. Dave knew nothing anything to do with coating paper, but he insisted on taking over the project anyway. The target company, Wisconsin Label, was headquartered in a small town near Green Bay. Frank and I had been working very well with them by telephone and email, but Dave insisted that Frank set up a face-to-face meeting for the three of us.

When we arrived at the airport in Wisconsin and went to pick up our rental car, we were offered a four-wheel drive, due to an approaching storm, which was expected to dump enough snow to make the roads dangerous. Under the circumstances, Frank was nervous about making the trip at all, but even though the rental had been in Frank's name, Dave offered to drive to the meeting at Wisconsin Label the next morning. We would be leaving early enough so Dave wouldn't be drinking yet, so at least I didn't have to worry about that.

There was a Native American run casino attached to the hotel where the three of us would be spending the night. Dave wanted to go, and I liked the idea. Since my first trip to Las Vegas with Tim and his family, I enjoyed playing slot machines. I'd spent some time in Las Vegas at Board meetings and working on conferences. It was also a layover on some flights to California, and the airport had machines like a casino. I'd gotten pretty good with poker machines. I played strictly based on the odds, which were never with the player. I made the best choices I could, and usually came out a little ahead or at worst broke even. I was still earning more money with EC than either Tim or I had ever made in our lives. I felt I could try my luck without any damage to our family budget. It didn't take me long to see that the machines at the Wisconsin casino were set at a return much lower than those I'd played on in Las Vegas, so I decided to make it an early night.

It was just as well that I'd had decided to get in some sleep. The storm had come in as predicted, and Frank, Dave, and I left early in the morning to make it to our meeting on time. Driving in the snow turned out to be the one thing I'd observed up to that point that Dave did well. He wasn't humble about it either, and as we passed cars that had plunged off the road, bragged about what a good driver he was. He also bragged about how good he was at sales, especially as a closer. I hoped he was telling the truth about that too.

If he was, there was no sign of it at the meeting. It was run by the engineer Frank and I had been working with. While we discussed moving forward on various potential projects, Dave had almost nothing to contribute. He was completely silent during the discussion of competing types of chemical reactions used to cure the coatings. The two main curing systems normally used in the business, plus a third I had developed myself, were something I'd had to explain to Frank. They had been outlined in some of the materials I'd given Dave to study, but it was clear he'd either never read what I gave him, or hadn't understood it. He'd never asked me any chemistry questions. On our trip to Green Bay, Dave had said that he was going to get the label company to sign some kind of development agreement with EC. He didn't even get close. Other than his driving, as far as I could tell, he was useless.

A week later, he turned out to be worse than useless. I was attending a meeting at Helicon and received a call on my cell phone from Dave. I left the conference room and sat on a nearby staircase to take the call. I had expected that he would be checking up on the meeting, but he usually called Frank to talk about things like that. He had something entirely different in mind. He told me that since my visit with JD in Michigan, JD had wanted me to take a salary cut of fifty percent. I thought it was strange that JD hadn't said so at the time. It was even stranger that since Dave had known all about it during our trip to Wisconsin, he'd said nothing then either. Even though I hadn't lost much, I might have thought twice about a trip to a casino. I pointed out that although Frank's contract had expired, mine was in full force and would be for years. Dave said he'd have to check on that. He repeated JD's words that everyone had to make sacrifices, although they were different, and his was working without a contract. I told him I'd think about it. Jared had warned me about how difficult it would be to put up a fight if the company reneged on my contract, and with my work and family responsibilities, I doubted I'd be able to do it. JD also had the ability to pull the plug on the company entirely.

I did give the matter a lot of thought. Even fifty percent of what I was making would still be a lot of money. It wouldn't provide the future I'd been planning on, but it was a lot of money. I would also still be making a lot more than Frank. Still, I wasn't ready to give in. Every bit of the fifty million dollars of value EC claimed to have, had been produced by my efforts, not by the executives in Michigan or by Frank or Burt, and now I owned very little of it. I was also angry with Dave for keeping what JD wanted to do, a secret. He hadn't exactly lied, but he hadn't told the truth either. He was just one more person I couldn't trust.

I didn't hear anything else about my salary for a week. Then Dave didn't call, but Burt did. He told me that both he and JD were disappointed that I wasn't on board with the company. He said JD was thinking about what to do. He never threatened me directly, but he when I asked what would happen if I refused, he implied I might end up with nothing. I was scared. Everything I'd worked for over during two decades to build, was on the line. I gave in and told Burt I'd take the fifty percent cut. Then he dropped the other shoe. JD wanted a seventy percent cut. I would still be doing better than I had been when Burt bought the company, but not by much. I could feel the tears in my eyes, and I knew Burt could hear them in my voice. He promised me that it would only be temporary, until a couple of deals closed. I gave in again.

Chapter Twenty-Two

The loss of the money was not my only problem. Lon's behavior had been disintegrating since JS had been away for a summer. The pinches, bites, and hits had come back and were happening more often. I often had to go back to wearing long sleeves, even when the weather was too hot for them. I was afraid again in my own house, and our family was still on the waiting list for help. Since I had no safe place, at home or at work, I used the escape that had always worked for me. I retreated into the worlds I could put on paper. I was never far from one of the yellow legal pads on which I wrote my stories. I wrote at my desk, sitting on the lab floor while watching chemicals mix, and any other place or time I could. At home, my characters were in my mind; ready to pull me from reality when Lon's violence sent me into hiding.

My pen was not my only defense. In every journal I read to keep up with my profession, I was always alert for some idea about what could calm Lon down again. One thing I liked about one weekly chemistry magazine, was the back page. It was usually filled with little bits and pieces of news from other professions, as well as a couple of jokes. What I discovered was no joke. I found some research on the use of an amino acid as an intervention for anxiety and behaviors. Autism was never mentioned, but a mechanism involving glutamate was. It was as if an old friend had come in and tapped me on the shoulder.

I dug up all the other information I could find. There were studies from both Yale and Stanford. There was no mention of autism in those either, but the biochemistry made perfect sense. Even better, the chemical involved was already in use as both a pharmaceutical and a supplement, and no serious side effects had been seen. I could buy a bottle for ten dollars at a health food store in the same shopping center as the supermarket where I bought groceries. Without a documented connection to autism, I still wasn't sure about giving it to Lon, so I decided to try it on myself.

I found it hard to believe what happened, just within a couple of days. I could push away the fear that came at me out of the night, and in my worst moments in the daytime. I wasn't tense all the time anymore either. I wondered if this was how normal people felt, able to move through the day, afraid if they had a real reason to be, but not engulfed by constant fear. I couldn't wait to try my newly found release on Lon. He was always so much more afraid than I was. I gave him his first pill.

Someone who didn't know Lon would not have observed an obvious change. His autism still ruled his life. The limits on his language were still there, and his choice of activities was still narrow, but to Tim, JS, and me the universe had shifted. Lon's violent episodes decreased a lot. There was still one now and then, especially when he was frustrated, but they were manageable. The maniacal glint in his eyes that had driven me to huddle in my hole beneath the stairs had disappeared. For the first time in years, I could sit or stand next to my younger son without fear. A cure would have been incredible, but the change in Lon that occurred, was the closest thing to a miracle I'd ever seen. The future finally seemed manageable.

Lon's amino acid was not the only place where I had made a leap. Back as far as my laboratory in California, I had been thinking about using natural, even edible, materials in my coatings. I'd gotten the idea after reading a paper on changes taking place in foodstuffs after they'd been irradiated to kill bacteria. By the wildest coincidence, the same amino acid that had brought about the change in Lon was involved. Dealing with it, had brought the old project to mind. A conference dealing with the concern for safety in coatings used in contact with food pushed the idea even more to the fore of my thoughts. Frank, who had not attended the conference, thought my idea a waste of time, but I pursued it anyway, ignoring his orders.

My new project became important when I was asked to speak at an innovation conference in New York. It would be a huge affair in a theater holding five hundred people from large companies all around the country. I had been instructed to try and get a DVD Burt had commissioned shown. I also played up my technology for waterproofing newspaper, demonstrating it like a magic trick. I would be the only one from EC going to New York, so I could say anything I wanted, without anyone to stop me.

I was looking forward to the trip, not so much for business reasons, but because it would be a chance to meet up with old classmates from the email list where I'd found my lawyer. Normally a group of them had dinner at a restaurant in Manhattan every month, and when I let them know I would be coming to town, the date was moved back a week to accommodate me. I was excited to see my old girlfriend, Sharon, who had also been my lab partner in advanced chemistry. We'd shared a lot of fun as teenage girls and written to each other occasionally over the years.

The conference hosts had been afraid I would be intimidated by the venue. The huge auditorium even had its own green room, where I was wired for sound. There were facilities for taping presentations and a huge countdown clock with warning lights. Like doing theater in college, I found the set-up fun, rather than scary. I did my presentation, throwing in a few lines at the end about seeing non-toxic, generally regarded as safe (GRAS) materials, as the future. The show's management was impressed enough to take me upstairs to a TV studio to tape an interview. I loved the whole adventure.

The conference location was only two blocks from the hotel where I was staying, and I had agreed to meet up with my email friends in the lobby before we chose a restaurant. I had a hard time finding them. We'd all aged a lot. I was in the middle of saying hello to everyone when several conference attendees showed up looking for me. They worked for a large paper company and had been impressed by my waterproofing demonstration. I didn't appreciate that they had followed me to the hotel, but I took their cards and promised to get in touch. My friends thought that having people work that hard to find me was impressive.

It took a lot of discussion, but we chose a restaurant. I sat at the end of a long table with Sharon, and list mates moved around to talk to me during the evening. I had a great time. It had been too many years since I had been with a group of people whose thinking was as quick as my own and were interested in as much nerdy stuff as I was. Though I hated the dirt and the noise in the city, leaving that part of my trip to New York behind was hard.

When I returned to Ohio, I contacted the paper company as I'd promised. I didn't think too much about what else happened while I was away from the lab. I was surprised not long afterward, when the staff at the EC corporate headquarters in Michigan was contacted by other conference attendees, from a tobacco company called Renco.

I didn't want to have anything to do with them. I saw smoking as a dirty and dangerous habit. Since Mother's boyfriend Sam had been a chain smoker, being around cigarettes brought back frightening memories. The upside was that the project they proposed involved the production of a safer cigarette, one less likely to cause fires. I couldn't turn down an opportunity to do something that might actually save lives. I agreed to make a trip with Frank for a face-to-face meeting at Renco's headquarters in North Carolina. Renco even sent a limousine to the airport to pick us up.

The conference room at Renco was like a throwback in time --- and not in a good way. Smoking was prohibited in most workplaces and public spaces across the country, but at Renco it appeared to be regarded as an act of loyalty. There was an ashtray at each place in the conference room, and everyone but Frank and I lit up. I breathed as shallowly as I could.

The first thing on the Renco agenda was a PowerPoint presentation on Renco's safety program. I couldn't believe what I was watching. A company responsible for so many preventable deaths was portraying itself as a good guy. Almost choking in the smoke, I couldn't even find the show funny, just nauseating.

Renco moved on to a display of their products, including some intended to be attractive to young, first-time tobacco users, whom they targeted as new addicts. They regarded new ways to sell tobacco as creative. If that was what Renco thought of as being creative, I wanted no part of it. I would have liked nothing better than to get on a plane back to Ohio, but there was no way I could get away. Renco hadn't even reached the main order of business yet, and they controlled my transportation.

Federal law already required safer cigarettes. Cigarettes that weren't being smoked were supposed to go out by themselves. The idea was to prevent deaths from smoking in bed. That was the first reasonable thing I'd heard since I'd arrived. Renco was already making the product, but the specially engineered paper was coming from an outside vendor and cutting into their profits more than they liked. They wanted a coating they could use in house to make the paper themselves.

The concept wasn't difficult. Renco just needed something that would block airflow. The complication would be that burning it would not add anything toxic to the cigarette. With all the toxic chemicals I knew were already formed by burning tobacco, I didn't know whether to laugh or cry. I knew that the waterproofing coating Renco had seen me demonstrate in New York wouldn't work for them. The GRAS product I'd been developing against Frank's orders just might. I explained it to the Renco executives the best I could without giving crucial information away. They were happy with what I told them, but it was clear there was a lot of paperwork to be done before we could discuss anything else. Frank and I were taken on a VIP tour of the Renco plant before a limousine took us to the hotel where we'd spend the night, before flying back to Ohio.

I'd expected Frank to be angry with me for disobeying him, but if he was, he didn't say so. Over dinner, he did comment about being afraid that I would blow my cool during the hypocrisy of the safety presentation, but otherwise, he seemed grateful that I had managed to get a promising project underway. It was something he couldn't wait to report to Dave Crockman. I had as little contact as possible with the new CEO, but Frank felt he had to give the man regular updates about what was going on in the lab. I still hadn't seen anything useful from Dave outside of his ability to drive on snow. I didn't feel obliged to tell him a thing.

There were now two things at the top of my priority list. One was continuing development for Wisconsin Label. The other was figuring out how to make my GRAS project work for Renco. When Wisconsin Label started long term testing on our coating, Renco took top billing. I formulated a product and tested it as well as I could with the cigarette paper they had provided. I decided we were ready for the next step. Frank and I would be returning to North Carolina to make my coating in the Renco lab and supervise applying it to cigarette paper on their pilot equipment.

Dave Crockman had negotiated a secrecy agreement that hadn't made any friends with the Renco staff. This time there was no limousine, and the reception was not as gung ho. The upside, at least to me, was that without another conference with the big executives, I wouldn't be trying to breathe in a room full of cigarette smoke. Even Renco didn't allow smoking in their laboratories.

The visit went almost smoothly. As a holdover from his big company CEO days, Frank had an obsession with spreadsheets. I couldn't understand it. In the time it took him to put one together, I usually had the calculations done on a calculator, with a lot of time to spare. He didn't care and insisted on using his technique. Frank had put together a spreadsheet outlining the proportions of the few components I would be using. Unfortunately, he had made a mistake in the base formula he'd entered. I realized that things were not looking right and the mixture would have to be redone before Renco ran any actual tests. Frank's error meant that we were short of materials, so we took a trip to a large supermarket to get more.

Not having received the memo about materials that were not only safe but edible, the supervising technical manager was dumbfounded that a chemical supplier was not involved, but our ability to just go out and get what we needed, saved the test run. Renco was able to produce their own samples, and Frank and I returned to Ohio to await the results of their tests. I was relieved that things had worked out, but from that point on, decided to double check all of Frank's spreadsheets.

A huge event in the label industry was coming up, and Dave Crockman was determined to go. He also decided that Frank and I would go with him. The show would feature exhibits and presentations in a big hall. Frank and I would be expected to visit those, while Dave made the rounds of the hospitability suites to meet, greet, and drink with whomever he thought could be useful to EC.

I got a message from Atherton, the largest vendor at the event. The contacted me instead of Dave because I was on record as a founder of the company. Dave, Frank, and I were invited to a brunch with some of Atherton's big shots. Dave was upset that the invitation hadn't come to him instead of me, but he was not about to turn down the meeting. Atherton was the largest supplier of coatings and ink not only to Wisconsin Label but many printers in the industry, a position that made Dave jealous. He couldn't ignore them.

I loved the brunch. The menu had smoked salmon, which I hadn't eaten since my trip to New York. With Atherton picking up the tab, I dug into it. The offer Atherton made was even better, at least to me, than the fish. Atherton had somehow managed to get their hands on a label I had coated and given to Wisconsin Label for testing. It had survived their testing better than labels with any of their own coatings. They'd had it underwater for six months with no deterioration, something they'd never before seen. Atherton wanted to partner with EC to distribute the coating I had used, and maybe some others as well.

I loved the idea. Aside from Frank and Dave, EC had no real sales force of its own. JD hadn't wanted to hire any. The one Atherton had was massive. With the stroke of a pen, EC's products would be pushed to label makers all over the country and appear at all the trade shows and expos. I expected Dave to be enthusiastic too, but he was cool to the idea and told the representatives from Atherton he'd have to think about their offer. I was confused. Atherton's presence in the market and huge sales force had been an obstacle to EC. A partnership with them was just what we needed to put EC's products everywhere. Dave should have jumped at the chance. When I discussed the proposal with Dave and Frank later, Dave was sure that he could lead EC to huge sales on his own. It looked like his decision would also be slowing any chance at getting my salary raised again. As far as I was concerned, Atherton's testing showed that I deserved it. If anything, I was the only one at EC who'd actually done anything to make the company successful. As usual, Frank backed Dave's decision. I was outvoted and disgusted.

When I got back to my lab, I had one reason to be hopeful. The preliminary test results had come back from Renco, and they were good. They wanted some changes made, but it seemed like another chance had popped up for EC to make some good money. I still hated the idea of working with a cigarette maker, but at least my work would be more for saving lives, than taking them.

Dave, who up to that point had been uninvolved in the project other than in negotiating the secrecy agreement, jumped all over it. He wanted to go down to North Carolina to make a deal. His plan was to demand money for any further time and money spent developing a product for them. I didn't like the idea. EC had never worked that way on any project before, and as far as I knew, neither had our competitors, but Dave had made up his mind, and Frank was on his side again.

The next thing I knew, Renco ended the project. Their official excuse was that the curing equipment would pump too much heat into their plant, but that was something they'd always known. Their mechanical designers had solved much more difficult problems. I was sure that Dave had ruined the deal with Renco, just as he had with Atherton.

I had even more reason to be angry. The financial statement that was a requirement for a public company showed that the salary that had been taken away from me was being paid to Dave. Burt and the CFO were huge drains as well, as were JD's fancy facilities, which EC was now paying for. It looked like the Board in Michigan had either lost their minds, or they were deliberately trying to bankrupt the company. Even though I could remember every word of Bill Bentley's warning, I didn't want either of those things to be true. It didn't matter what I wanted. EC's capital was disappearing, with not nearly enough coming in to replace it. Soon it would be all gone.

I'd stopped believing in white knights or saviors; I'd had even begun to develop doubts about the one I sang to in church. Everywhere I'd looked, for most of my life, was full of liars, thieves, or just plain idiots. Of the three, I preferred the idiots; at least they weren't trying to cheat anyone.

While the mess was going on at EC, JS had finished and defended his dissertation. He was now Dr. Scott and waiting for a government job, to fulfill the obligations of his scholarship. He continued to receive a government stipend, which would further add to his debt, but he was still at home. He was discouraged that he hadn't launched, especially since he was now in his thirties. Because of his agreement with the defense department, he couldn't look for a job anywhere else, so he was at loose ends. I appreciated having him around to help deal with Lon, but I also understood his frustration. During his years as a student, he'd never seen himself as an adult, but now he did. With all the qualifications to earn a good living, rather than working at the menial jobs he'd had through the years, he was anxious to get out on his own. He was also looking forward to not having to take care of his brother any longer. Both Tim and I knew JS loved Lon, but he still wanted some freedom from his brother's constant demands. It was something we understood perfectly.

After months, JS's call came. Part of the delay had been the background check required for him to obtain a security clearance. When it was finally completed, JS was given a position at an Army laboratory in Maryland. He would be a six-hour drive away, but in many ways, he would be in another universe. He took a preliminary trip to find an apartment. Through his summers as an intern, he was familiar with the area and had an idea where to look, but as an intern he had always just found a temporary room to rent in someone else's home. For the first time, he would have a place of his own. He was as usual, careful, choosing the cheapest apartment with the shortest drive to the laboratory. He didn't care if it was fancy. The only thing he worried about besides having a roof over his head was being able to get good internet. In the area around a government laboratory, that was no problem. When he'd signed a lease, he came back to Ohio to pack up what little he'd be taking with him. It reminded me of when Tim and I had moved from Iowa to Minnesota.

JS and I figured out what he'd need for his apartment. He had all the furniture that had been in his room, as well as his computers. I helped him put together the other basics to get along. I donated some items from our kitchen and linen closet, but JS mostly wanted to get his own.

Tim helped JS move. They rented a small truck for a one-way trip, which Tim drove, while JS drove his car. It was the second car I had financed for him, and I'd signed over my portion of the ownership of it to him before he left. Tim would be flying back after he turned the truck in to the rental agency in Maryland.

The period while Tim was gone with JS, was the longest stretch I had been alone with Lon in a long time. Lon kept repeating that JS would be home in August, as he'd always been with his internships. I had to keep telling him that Daddy would be home, but JS was moving to Maryland and wouldn't live with us anymore. Lon didn't like it. As proud as I was of JS's success, I wasn't sure I liked it either. I knew it was past time for him to leave the nest, but I was going to miss him.

With JS gone there were complications for Tim and me. When I was earning big money, I'd hired a special sitter to watch Lon when Tim and I had to go places together, and JS wasn't around to watch Lon. After my salary was cut, we had to become more careful about expenses. The choir didn't sing in the summer, so my presence at church was not necessary. I'd stayed home with Lon during services, while Tim attended because he was serving as an elder.

Now we'd have to figure out how to manage things that were simple for all the other members of the church. Their children went to the nursery, toddler room, or Sunday school. During service, there was children's church. Almost none of the members of the choir had children young enough to worry about during rehearsal, and if they did, they had family to take care of them. Now Tim and I had no one to help with Lon. I posted notices at church. Church members were usually willing to help other members in almost any situation, but no one stepped forward to spend even an hour with Lon. Tim and I were on our own.

We figured out a way to take Lon to rehearsals. The pitch of the choir was too imperfect for him to tolerate, but he could sit outside the glass doors of the sanctuary where practice was going on, using a portable player to watch and listen to DVD's, especially Woody Woodpecker. Lon could see us, we could see him, and for an hour and a half a week, it worked. Tim and I decided to shell out for a sitter on Sunday mornings. It was expensive, but we agreed that we could handle it. Eating out, except for Lon's Saturday trips, was off the table. We could go out separately for quick errands, but except for me going to work, we usually stayed at home.

Lon asked a lot about his brother. Tim or I told him each time, that JS was in Maryland and lived there now. Lon didn't like that answer. The violence in his behavior escalated again. When Lon got his yearly evaluation from his social worker, Tim and I found out that the services we had been waiting six years to get for Lon were finally available. They included having someone come into our home for a set number of hours a week, to work with him. Under the rules, the worker couldn't just be watching Lon, he would have to learn skills such as housekeeping or hygiene, but the effect would be to give Tim and me a little time off.

Tim and I felt guilty about how excited we were. Lon's social worker put out a call on the official portal, for service providers. The best candidate, Nick, looked unlikely, at best. He was tall, with big muscles, and had a Frank Zappa beard. He was also covered in tattoos. He knew his job. Not only did Lon like him, but he also respected him, and didn't try hitting, biting, or any aggressive behaviors when Nick was around. It was too good to last. After a couple of months, Nick told us that he wasn't getting enough hours with Lon to earn enough to live on, and took a job with a company providing transportation for the disabled.

After that, Lon's social worker suggested a day employment program. Tim and I looked at a sheltered workshop where there were several jobs Lon might like to do, like painting crockery, and even possible computer work. There was a woman with Down Syndrome, whom we knew from church, working there. After a tour, Lon told us that he might like to work there too, but the workshop didn't accept him.

It looked like he might be headed for success at the next job we tried for him. In the official plan, he would be sitting in front of a computer all day, an idea he loved. For the first couple of weeks, things went fine, but after that, the staff decided to change his assignment, and gave him janitorial work, cleaning tables. Worse, he had to do it around young children who got in his space. Lon had been promised a computer, and from what I could tell, felt the betrayal every bit as strongly as I'd felt the ones I'd faced at work. Unfortunately, his response was more direct. He struck out at the supervisor who took him away from his computer station. His behavior also scared the kids, although he didn't touch any of them. At the end of three weeks, he was fired. To add insult to injury, he earned less than a hundred dollars, but it was enough so that I had to fill out a bunch of paperwork about his financial condition and earning power and file his tax return.

In the fallout from the debacle, Lon was assigned a new social worker. Maureen had an autistic child herself, and she also had a clue. She knew of a more recreationally based program, but one where Lon might still be able to work on computers. The rules didn't allow her to make a choice for Lon, but she gave the Tim and me a very strong suggestion. We took a tour of the place, Connections, with Lon. The atmosphere was laid back, with plenty of room for Lon to keep his personal space. The drawback was that the only computer was in the office. Tim and I decided to donate one. We held a meeting, and the Tim and I were honest about why Lon had been kicked out of his last program, but the director at Connections was sure they could handle any aggressive behaviors. Lon's whole team decided that he could attend the program, and we arranged transportation. It would be a short ride. Connections was only five minutes from our house. That wasn't necessarily a good thing. The Connections program only ran from ten in the morning to three in the afternoon. Even with transportation time added in, Lon would still be home a lot of the day, and Tim and I would still be covering Lon every night and weekends. We needed at least a little time together without Lon when I wasn't working.

We tried home services again, this time, with a new agency. Miracle sent a man named Vince, who couldn't have been more different from Nick. He was slight and quiet, and much of his experience had been in working in halfway houses for recovering addicts, but he and Lon clicked. Tim and I could manage to go to choir and church together without Lon, again. We even managed an occasional trip to a restaurant. Even with the new services, Lon still had times of frightening violence, and I was still his main target. I didn't have to wear long sleeves all the time to cover the bruises anymore, but sometimes Lon would punch me in the chest hard enough to knock the air out of me, and I was still always a little afraid.

Lon's sensitivity to the sound of the heating and cooling systems also meant constantly negotiating with him to keep any kind of a comfortable temperature in the house, winter or summer. The event that convinced Tim and me that it was no longer safe for us to have Lon in the house with us was when Lon insisted that all lights be out at night, and I fell backward down a flight of stairs and broke my wrist in two places. The bones were so out of line that a surgeon had to operate to set them. Frank had to be my hands in the laboratory for a couple of months --- and he wasn't good at it.

Another thing that bothered Tim, and most of the men in our church, was that my knee length hair had to be cut. With my cast, I just couldn't brush and braid it properly. Tim tried his best to help, but he was never meant to be a hairdresser. I chose a short style I didn't have to do much of anything to maintain.

Tim and I hated to do it, but we started looking at homes for Lon. We thought we found what might be a nice one. It was owned by the same organization that ran Connections. Tim and I toured it while Lon was at his day program, and interviewed the house manager. It looked clean and welcoming with a room big enough to accommodate Lon's furniture, computer, and TV. There was also a basement where he could have at least his smaller trampoline. The director seemed understanding and knowledgeable. What we thought was a plus, was that one of the men Lon attended Connections with was also a resident of the house, so Lon would at least see a familiar face. We agreed to bring Lon to the house to eat a supper of his favorite hamburgers with the other residents, and see how he reacted.

From the time Tim, Lon, and I came to the door, the visit was a disaster. The resident, whom Lon knew, started attacking him. He was much more violent than Lon had ever been. He didn't want just a single bite, pinch, or punch. He charged and kept coming. I pulled Lon away, and the director was attacked instead. Lon was scared and wanted nothing to do with the place. Neither did Tim or I. After that, I checked carefully to make sure Lon was safe at Connections, but apparently, the violent behavior only occurred at the house.

For weeks, Lon keep repeating the address of the house with an emphatic, "No!" Tim and I would have to figure something else out.

Maureen had an idea. A mother of another one of her clients was trying to put together a living situation for her son, Jon, and would be using Miracle to provide the house and staff it. If Lon was included in the plan, Vince could go with him, and he'd have someone he knew and trusted. The trick would be to find a house or apartment that would fit the needs of both Lon and Jon. Accompanied by Charlie, a representative from Miracle, Tim and I trudged through one house after another; never finding what we thought would work. After weeks, Charlie was frustrated and his mother Linda, the owner of Miracle, started going out, primarily with just me, instead.

Finally, Linda and I found an apartment that seemed right. Like the first house Tim and I had liked, it was only five minutes from our home, so Tim and I could get there quickly in an emergency. It was also close to Jon's mother's house. There was a lot of space, and the two men would be at opposite ends of a hall, with separate bathrooms. Linda and I signed papers with the rental agent.

Now it was real , and Lon would be leaving. I was terrified for him. Tim and I had taken him to see the new apartment, and he'd even agreed that he wanted a place of his own, but I wasn't sure he understood that he would be there without Tim and me.

On the day of the move, Lon was transported to Connections as usual, while his things were loaded into a van and Tim and I helped to set up at the new apartment. I made sure that the stuffed doll he'd had since he was born, but still slept with even though it was in pieces, was in the center of his bed where he could see it. I provided Linda and Charlie with a book of all of Lon's likes and dislikes, the foods he'd eat, and even all the recipes I developed for him. He'd have his favorite drinking cup, and Tim made sure Lon's computer was up and running.

Tim and I went home to meet Lon when he was brought back from Connections, and take him to his new apartment. I had expected Lon to object to being left, or even to lash out in fear. He didn't. I thought I'd cry, but I had no tears. Tim did. He had always been the least expressive about his attachment to Lon, but when the time came, it hit him. Still, the cord was cut or at least stretched.

Tim and I didn't know how to handle our new freedom. Just being able to turn the furnace up when we were cold was a new experience. Eating what we wanted to, without taking Lon's restrictions into account, or even deciding to go to a movie, were all strange experiences. We also felt guilty.

Lon stayed close, in his own way. As part of his safety skills, he'd learned our phone number. He called me every day, always at five-thirty in the afternoon. He was only able to say a few words, but it was clear he was reassuring himself I was still there. I always made a point of being around to receive his call. If Tim and I were gone, it was never at five-thirty.

We kept taking Lon out on Saturdays. He would pick a restaurant for a few months, always ordering, "Juicy hamburger, French fries, and a soda." If it was a full-service restaurant, there was no problem. Lon would sit wherever the host or hostess led. When he chose fast food, we ran into trouble. He still insisted on always sitting at one and only one table and would wait restlessly until the table was free. Sometimes he'd get loud and point. Tim and I did our best to keep him calm and quiet. Usually, we were pretty good at it. Wherever Tim and I took him, the servers got to know Lon well enough to know what he would have without asking. All three of us had settled into a routine, at least in our home lives.

For me, with JD's and Dave's machinations going on, work was still a daily strain. One bright spot was that Frank and I turned out to like a couple of the same TV shows, neither of which Tim watched. It gave us some common ground that I'd never expected to have. Unfortunately, his understanding of my work or what was going on behind the scenes in Michigan, hadn't increased.

I continued to puzzle over Michigan myself, until one night while trying to lose myself in an old movie, I had an epiphany. What was going on at EC was worse than pump and dump; it was a con straight out of "The Producers." JD had never intended success for EC, and neither had Burt. They had raised funds, spent whatever they wanted, and then worked to send the company into failure so the investors' money would never have to be returned. Whether he knew it or not, Dave was their partner in crime.

I shared my idea with Frank, who shrugged it off, but I had no reason to trust his judgment. He had been wrong too many times. I was not about to let things slide. I'd been taken in and fooled too many times, and I'd had enough. There was no way I was about to see all my work come to nothing. I wondered about where to take my theory and settled on Jerry Ciolino. Jerry was a member of the board of directors and a large investor, but unlike other principles, had never blindly believed the words of JD, Burt, or Dave. He had been brought on board by a fellow investor who was also a lifelong friend, but he still asked the hard questions. His money to the company had been a loan, not a purchase of stock. EC's intellectual property was the collateral. Not being a member of the Board, I didn't have a vote, but Jerry did, and he was often the only dissenter.

I didn't have to do much convincing. Jerry had also read the financial statements and was very willing to partner with me to find the truth. Better, he had more than suspicions; he had the resources to launch an investigation.

After talking to Jerry, I breathed better than I had in weeks. High notes that had been sticking in my throat hit their pitch again, and even my writing took a more romantic turn. Still, as Jerry turned over more rocks, more of JD's slime seeped out.

Chapter Twenty-Three

Jerry talked to every member of his golf club. Slowly he got the picture. JD had gone to almost of all them for money, using the patent portfolio of EC as evidence of his own worth. They invested in various companies JD incorporated as equity contributors to EC. This gave JD more than three times the money that had actually been put into the company. Of what JD did invest, almost none had made it across the border from Michigan to Ohio. It was obvious that JD either expected me to fall on my face in an under-equipped, unstaffed facility, or leave to go somewhere I could earn a higher salary. Either way, he could take in a lot of money, with his investors never getting anything back.

I found out that the SEC had already expressed some doubts about the way EC was doing business, and Jerry encouraged those concerns. Eventually, the FBI was called in too, but JD had disappeared. He had not only stolen the money of investors but run up huge debts in the name of EC. In the condition he had left the company, there was no way we could repay them. EC had no choice but to file for bankruptcy. As part of the process, as the only one holding a secured loan, Jerry would be foreclosing on all of the patents and formulations I had developed. Despite Jerry's promise that everything would be fine, I was unemployed for the first time in twenty-five years, and Jerry owned all my work.

Money was not a huge problem, or at least wouldn't be for a while. I had stowed as much as I could in the bank, afraid that very bad times would come. I'd also been a high enough earner to qualify for the maximum in unemployment benefits. I just had to decide what my next steps would be. Even though I was waiting for something to happen with Jerry, applying for at least a couple of jobs per week was a requirement. I was glad to do it, but my work over the years was in a weird enough corner of the business, that I wasn't a very good fit for any position available. I kept trying, anyway.

At one point, I thought everything was going to be fine. Both Frank and I were invited to lunch by Mel Richards, the CEO of a company we'd tried to do some development work with before. As EC was going into bankruptcy, Mel had tried to buy it, and do a reverse merger of his own. I had been all for the idea, but the deal had been blocked by one of EC's creditors who was sure he could get a better deal, or even raise the money to buy EC himself. He hadn't been able to do either of those things and had ended up with nothing when EC went down the tubes. Mel was still interested in me, and maybe eventually even in Frank, and he gave me a written job offer. Mel's company, Melco, would be a long drive; something he knew would be hard for me. Because of that, the position would be three days a week for sixty thousand dollars a year. I was fine with that, and Tim was too when I showed him the offer. He even agreed to drive me until I could get used to the route. The job was supposed to start ninety days later after Mel got some other business out of the way.

I thought I could relax, with some time to kill. I binged on eight seasons of a TV show I had never seen and watched a lot of fan made videos of my favorite show, Keep. I also started writing fan fiction for Keep. I shared it on fanfic website, something I'd never done before. I was amazed and flattered by the reaction to my work. I got reviews every day. It started to seem like my writing was a mission. Other fans started writing to me, telling me that they were going through illnesses, hospital vigils, and all kinds of other hard times. They were using daily doses of my stories as something to hold onto to help them cope. I decided that turning out those stories was what I was supposed to be doing, and gave the effort everything I could. I had my own group of fans saying that I was getting better with every story. I was even worried about how I could keep up with all my writing when I started working for Melco. Then Mel pulled the rug out from under me. He told me that the legal complications of hiring me while the court was still handling EC's bankruptcy would too much for Melco. He withdrew his job offer.

I soon discovered that Mel wasn't the only one to whom I was poison. The technology I had developed, aside from the small amount of equipment I'd been permitted to have in the lab, was the only asset of the company. Until the bankruptcy was discharged, which could take the better part of a year, anyone who hired me could end up in a lawsuit.

I continued to apply for jobs; I had no choice, but I didn't expect to be hired.

The hours of work Tim was getting increased, and our savings weren't disappearing too fast, but I needed something besides writing fan fiction to do. I decided to write a mystery novel, using my experience with autism to create my hero. I had tried writing books before, for fun, but they had been romance novels and I'd always fallen out of love with my hero before I could finish writing them. This time I had a lot of motivation. To give myself even more of a push, I made myself write at least a thousand words of my novel before I wrote my fanfic every day. It didn't take long for the story to shape up. It was quirky and different, and I adored my hero. When it was finished, I let it sit for a while before writing my second and third drafts, but eventually, I posted it on a new website that purported to serialize stories and pay royalties to the authors.

Unfortunately, I discovered that as a writer, as with corporate business, I was an innocent. The website was not dishonest, it just wasn't very well thought out. Several of my contacts from my mailing list and some of my fanfic readers had tried to download my work, but couldn't. They had to read my story online, and most people didn't want to do that. They couldn't get it anywhere where there wasn't an internet connection. I received some good reviews and was even earning tiny royalties, but they would never add up to more than the price of a meal or two at a fast food joint. I would have liked to withdraw my book, and try to get it published elsewhere, but I had signed a contract and breaking it would make me no better than all the cheaters who had lied to me. I decided to try again with another book. By that time, I was so committed to writing, that I couldn't have stopped the outpouring of words every day, even if I had wanted to.

While I was beginning my new book, and pumping out more fan fiction every day, the court discharged EC's bankruptcy. I had fantasies that I might be paid my back wages, or even part of the hundred thousand dollars EC owed me for breaking my contract. That wasn't going to happen. The only one who received any benefit from the bankruptcy was Jerry. Every reasonable asset of EC now belonged to him, but he kept his promise that things would work out. He called Frank and me and told us that he wanted to form a new company to exploit EC's intellectual property. For that, he felt he needed both of us; Frank to handle the administration and me to take care of all the technical matters, and possibly even continue to develop formulas.

The business model for the new company, FSJ, would be something I had never dealt with before. FSJ would have no real facility. We would try to convince other companies to make use of EC's former intellectual property by acting as consultants and advisors. I had my doubts. I didn't know how I could function without a lab, but Jerry was willing to throw enough money into FSJ to pay both Frank and me. My stipend would be the same amount of money I would have earned working for Mel. I could work mostly from home, and if any long drives were involved, Frank could take me. More than that, I would have some ownership of my work again. For that, I was very willing to give FSJ a shot.

There were more trips than I had thought there would be. Frank, Jerry, and I went to see a company in Michigan to which EC had sold tiny quantities of coatings, while I was developing formulas for it. We were greeted with open arms, especially on the news we'd have absolutely nothing to do with Dave Crockman. The owner wanted us to help them launch some new business. After that visit, we offered my formulas to a former competitor, also in Michigan, who had the facilities to make them. Frank wanted to partner with them, to sell to companies that had been interested in EC's products before. Frank also wanted to hire a sales associate, George, who had been with EC for a little while before it closed down. Frank had hired George to work for EC against my better judgment, but as usual, since it was a sales decision, I had been overruled. George had previously worked for Atherton and was in fact, the one who had managed to steal my label from Wisconsin Label. Since I already knew he was willing to perform a dishonest act for business purposes, I had never trusted him. Frank disagreed. He considered a certain amount of dirty dealing part of doing business. His opinion made me nauseous.

Things were still moving very slowly for FSJ. The problem was that following Frank's lead, we were going over old ground and getting nothing from it. Too much time had passed, and other, bigger, companies had picked up on some of EC's innovations and run with them. Whatever successes EC had, always came when I had come up with something no bigger company had succeeded with or sometimes even thought of. I decided to try to do that again.

Frank didn't like changing FSJ's strategy, but since Frank was not delivering, Jerry decided that I was the one who would take the lead.

With no lab, I worked in my kitchen and on my porch. I completely avoided using anything toxic, or even any ingredients that couldn't be bought at a supermarket or baking supply company. I had done that before, even in my lab. What I hadn't done was to get away from my twenty plus years of radiation curing and use heat, air, or the combination of the two. It was much slower, but one thing that had always been one of my favorite tools in my kitchen was a convection oven. I mixed my formulas, put them on paper with rollers from an art store, and timed them in the oven with a stopwatch. Running what tests I could, I started to believe I'd discovered something that would work; using a food based chemical reaction no one else in my industry had tried.

In the meantime, Jerry, who was a genius at using personal contacts, had found an in with a company in Canada, who might be a customer for what I developed. Jerry had his own way of doing things, including traveling. I'm small enough to fit anywhere, even cheap airline seats, so I would have been fine flying coach. Jerry preferred private planes. He regularly went on junkets with his golfing buddies.

Except for the brief flight I had with Irv, in college, traveling on a private plane was a new experience for me. I'd never flown into another country in one. There was no line at the airport. No one searched my luggage or me. The pilot even filled out the customs documents for me. All I had to do was get on the plane and go, and the plane was beautiful. The seats were large enough to provide legroom even for tall men, not that I needed it. Instead of tray tables, full sized ones folded down from the bulkhead. There was no waiting for a flight attendant to wheel a cart down the aisle, there was a cooler of drinks and snacks available for the taking.

For me, there was one thing that wouldn't change. I wrote wherever I went, and for that, a private plane to Canada was no different from a commercial flight. Both Frank and Jerry thought that was funny, and when Jerry wanted to get my attention, he dangled his hand in front of the screen of my laptop.

The luxury of the plane made me feel like a fish out of water, and I didn't expect the trip to be a success. FSJ was the tiniest of companies and the one we were going to see, Cruge, was worth billions. It had survived a downturn in the industry that sent all their competitors into reorganization. I couldn't see them paying any attention to us. I was wrong. The web of Jerry's contacts had worked its magic. Roi, the head of research, picked us up at the tiny airport near Cruge's giant manufacturing plant and ushered us through the security check, which was conducted primarily in French. Having suffered through three years of French in high school and another one in college, I could at least follow what was going on. I didn't say much except *"Bonjour,"* and *"merci,"* but I didn't have to. Everyone at the main meeting spoke English, with varying French-Canadian accents. That was fortunate for Jerry since he didn't speak a word of French. Frank knew a little, but had trouble remembering it.

I sent rough samples produced in my kitchen before we arrived and they had already been tested in ways I couldn't have even tried to attempt. There were enough positive results for Roi to start looking at new markets for the company. The production of the next round of samples would have to be done in an environment much more like real world production facilities. We negotiated a non-disclosure agreement, so that I could send materials to Roi, for use by a contractor Cruge regularly hired. I agreed that once the paperwork was signed, I would send the components, formulas, and instructions. Roi took Jerry, Frank and me out to an upscale fish restaurant. After a quick ride back to the airfield, we boarded our plane to fly back to the United States.

When we flew back, I discovered another perk of going private. Instead of having to stand in line at customs, customs came to us. The customs officer got on our plane to ask the required questions and inspect our passports. I had made a complete round trip to Canada in less than a day and was home in time to make dinner for Tim. I was still uncomfortable with the privileged treatment, but I was willing to get used to it. I had also managed to finish my writing for the day.

Back home, there were some things about my formula that I had to fix. I started work on them every day in my kitchen, usually at the same time I was making breakfast. The coating had to be less sticky. It had to cure more quickly. The water content had to be in range Roi had specified. It also had to be applied on paper that Roi had provided.

I would do the first stage of mixing a formula, shower and dress, then do the next stage, and write, while it finished mixing. I would go through several formulas a day, sometimes even letting them mix at night. I worked longer hours than I had even on my emergency trips to Ohio for EC, but I didn't mind. I got in enough writing to enjoy my days.

In a few weeks, I had made the changes that I felt would produce coatings that would stand a chance of passing muster with Cruge. One of the hardest requirements of the project was putting together the paperwork. Everything shipped for industrial use, especially across borders, had to come with Manufacturer's Safety Data Sheets. The weird thing was you could buy the same exact things at the supermarket without any paperwork at all. I had to either find or write everything, especially step-by-step instructions that anyone could follow, then package it all up for shipment over the border. The actual shipping was easy. The documents required for customs were available online, and for a small extra charge, UPS could pick up the boxes at my house. After I shipped everything out, there was nothing to do but wait until Cruge's contractor reproduced my formulations and conducted their own testing.

In my head, working on a project was always easier than not working on a project. To fill my days, I wrote even more. I also became involved in the fan community for *Keep*. Since Tim didn't watch the show, about the only person I had ever discussed it with was Frank. Those discussions never touched the depth of passion I had developed for the show. I felt like I had about *Star Trek*. I also liked the lead actor, Terence, something I would never have mentioned to Frank. At first, I found people to talk to about *Keep*, on blogs. Posters were as into it as I was, and I poured my heart out. I found out quickly that things could get mean. People said nasty things about Terence and the other actors, which I couldn't stand reading.

For years, I had been resisting going on social media, but I decided to give it a try, for two reasons. The first was it would give me a tool to help me sell my writing. The second reason took me a while to admit to myself. Terence was considered a star on Twitter. His tweets and photographs were funny and intriguing. I wanted to reach out to him in some little way, and I wanted to get in touch with both his fans and the ones of the show.

Getting any kind of a Twitter following was a lot harder than I'd thought. I started out by begging on my email list for any of my old classmates with a Twitter account to follow me. That got me four. Then I put out an author's note to readers of my fanfic. That worked better. I started following other Keep and Terence fans, some of whom seemed very obsessed, even to me. There was nastiness on Twitter too, but I didn't have to follow anyone who spouted it. Slowly my list of contacts grew. There was also interplay between my fanfic followers and my Twitter followers, with each list picking up from the other. Along the way, I found people to help me with my non-fanfic writing as well.

I finished writing another novel, this time with a hero whose creation drew even more on everything I knew about autism. The book had a funny and paranormal twist and absolutely no resemblance to fanfic. I started looking for an agent. None of the responses I received said anything bad about my book, but no one signed me up, either. I decided to start submitting my book to publishers who would take on unrepresented authors. I'd given some thought to a vanity publisher where I'd pay to get my book published, but I decided I wasn't that desperate, at least not at that point. I also had other things on my mind.

The test results had come back from Roi, and they were good enough for a full-scale trial. That would mean making my product in a vat instead of a flask and applying it on a massive machine. I would be going back to Canada. Only two visitors from a company would be allowed into the test facility, so I'd be going with George, supposedly due to his expertise with equipment. I had never bought into his claims about that. I'd never seen them demonstrated, but Frank and Jerry wanted him to go with me, so once again I was outvoted. At least George would be doing the driving. He'd said that he'd be bringing his GPS navigation device with him.

George had a problem scheduling the trip. He had longstanding plans to be on a vacation with his wife and friends during the time the testing in Canada was slotted. He wouldn't cancel his vacation, but he was willing to leave it for a few days. Without Jerry, George and I would be flying commercially. Since

George would be coming from an area with limited flights, I would end up spending eight hours in the Montreal airport waiting to meet up with him. We'd searched all possible flights, but that was the only way that things would work. George's schedule also meant that we would be driving from Montreal to the small city where the testing facility was, after dark in a rental car. George had never studied a moment's worth of French. If there were street signs or anything else in French, I would have to translate them for him. George had also forgotten his navigator. There was one available from the car rental agency, but it took half an hour to reset its output to English. Unfortunately, while the navigator gave the directions in English, many of the signs were only in French and George seemed to prefer ignoring them, to paying attention to my translations. He ended up having to make several U-turns and backtracking, but we finally reached our hotel.

Thankfully, the clerk spoke English, but by the time we were checked in, the restaurant was closed, and there was nothing to eat but the junk from the vending machines. I was tired, hungry, and frustrated, but made do with very overpriced crackers, giant, but slightly stale cookies, and bottled water. It was not a great start.

The test facility was supposed to be ready to get started at seven in the morning. It was a short distance from the hotel, so George and I had arranged to meet in the lobby at six so that we could find a quick breakfast on the way. George pulled into a McDonald's, which looked the same as any other McDonalds in North America, except for the menu being in French. None of the staff spoke English, which ticked off George. I tried to explain that the servers had low paying jobs in a French speaking area and he had no right to expect anything else, but it didn't sit well with him. They wouldn't take George's credit card either. I managed to get the order in and because I'd had to buy things while I spent a day at the Montreal airport, I'd obtained more than enough Canadian cash to pay for both of our breakfasts. I supposed that if George bought anything the night before, he must have stuck a credit card in the machines.

We still arrived at the test facility on time, but we would have been fine being hours late. Unknown to KRS, Roi had taken our idea to coat paper for the fast food industry and run with it. He had invited all of Cruge's regular vendors to submit products. Those products included easier to use, but less environmentally favorable materials, than what I had worked used. FSJ's test wasn't happening until close to lunchtime and possibly even later. There wasn't a vat available yet for the mixing of my formula either. That would limit the time allowed for the process to below a safe level. The facility supervisor gave me a sheet with my formula and the instructions I'd sent ahead, to double check. It was correct. That seemed like one good break. As always, I had my laptop with me, so I found a place in the break room to wait and spent my time writing. As far as I could tell, George was out on the production floor monitoring the equipment, but I suspected that true to his past behavior, he was trying to gather as much intelligence as he could on our competitors' products. That kind of activity would sit well with Frank and possibly with Jerry, but it didn't with me.

Roi announced that lunch had arrived for visitors, with the crew engaged in cleaning a mixing vat for my formula. I discovered that French Canadians like French fries with their pizza. They also eat pizza with knives and forks. Both of those things were a new experience for me, but I was willing to go with it. Both the fries and the pizza were very good.

After lunch, I found out that the mixing process had started without my supervision. My instructions had been for the full amount of water to be added first thing. The experience of the supervisor, with materials he had used in the past, was to hold some water back, then add enough to make the coating thin enough to run on the machinery. I suppose that might have worked with other formulations, but I'd never tried it with mine. The knot in my stomach told me we were in trouble. My stomach was accurate.

As the mixer blades spun, the mixture heated up past the safety point I had specified and thickened like custard. I was going crazy. Charles, the mixing captain, offered to try to thin it out and told me I could wait in the break room while he did his best. I didn't know where George was and I didn't care. I had finished writing my chapter that morning and didn't have any more writing to do, so I had a conversation about screw-ups with a sympathetic colleague from another company. Unlike George or many of the other company representatives on site, Lou Finelli was a formulator himself and had run a pilot plant for twenty-five years. I felt a little better as he described a long list of failures. We swapped stories about the cluelessness of marketers and ended up exchanging cards. Lou told me that if Cruge wasn't interested in my formulations, his company just might be.

I was just finishing up my conversation with Lou when Charles came in and invited me to look at my product. It was hopeless. It was too thick even to try to feed into the machinery. We didn't have enough materials to make another batch, so there was nothing left to do but call it a day.

I sent off an email to Jerry and Frank with the bad news. By that time, George had turned up. We decided to head to Montreal, where hotel rooms that we would stay in until the next day when George would turn in the car, were, and we could take our flights back to the US.

George and I had gone from being in a mad rush to having more than enough time to fill. We stopped at a mall where we wandered around for a while then tried out the food court, where George could just point to what he wanted. After checking into our hotel, we found a nice restaurant where to George's relief, the menu was in both English and French. The food was delicious. Under other circumstances, I would have enjoyed the break, but I couldn't help obsessing about how wrong the trip had gone. The most comfort I had was watching an episode of Keep in my room that night, and exchanging comments with my friends over Twitter.

On an FSJ conference call when I was back in Ohio, I could hear that Jerry was very upset. In fact, he was almost ready to give up. FSJ would remain a company, but he had decided to add no further funds. Frank's and my stipends would be cut back until the money ran out entirely. He wanted to dump George right away. That was fine with me. I'd never wanted to hire him in the first place. I'd always thought he was useless, and the trip to Canada had just confirmed my conclusions. He was supposed to be the salesperson, but I was the one who'd had made the one contact that might still save us.

Frank wanted to arrange a call with Roi, to try and schedule a repeat test. I was game, but not too hopeful. I had no reason to be. Roi had other options to pursue, with much more longstanding vendors. Unless all the competing products crashed and burned, he had no reason to continue with FSJ, even if we were environmentally superior. It was obvious to me that Roi had never cared about being green. In addition, some of the other companies had sent their products premixed by their own manufacturing facilities. There was no opportunity for the test facility crew to mess them up.

I turned out to be right. Roi agreed to the call, but he was short with us and a little nasty. He informed Jerry, Frank, and me that three other companies had managed what at least appeared to be successful test runs. If the extended testing by Cruge proved them to be inadequate, he would be contacting FSJ again. Otherwise, we were out of the running.

We still had a small hope that other products would fail their tests, but none of us believed it would happen. Jerry encouraged me to contact Lou Finelli, the only thing left that I could do. Lou agreed to a conference call with Jerry, Frank, and me. He wanted to send samples of his own products to me, to explore how they might work with what I made. I was afraid that Lou was just thinking about making a sale of his own, but at that point, I had nothing to lose. Lou's company, Vaysol, was worth billions and based in Europe, where environmental restrictions were stricter and becoming more so by the minute.

Chapter Twenty-Four

It took weeks for Lou to get his request through the Vaysol bureaucracy, but samples arrived at my house. Although the paperwork said they were non-toxic, they weren't food products, so I worked with them on my porch rather than in my kitchen. They also contained solvents I didn't dare put in an oven I used for cooking. I tried a number of combinations of my products with Vaysol's. Putting them together produced better performance than Vaysol's alone and in some cases more than my own, alone. I sent samples of everything I did off to Lou, including some with just my products on them.

Again, there was a long wait. It was hard for me to understand how with the all the resources Lou had, he could move at such a slow pace. It was hard for Jerry to accept as well, But Frank told us that in his experience, that the larger the company, the greater its inertia. For once, he was right about something.

Months later, I received an email from Lou, with spreadsheets of test results, many of which looked promising for FSJ. We had another conference call, and Lou confirmed that many of the results were impressive, in fact, something Vaysol had never seen before. Since I had produced all the samples, my formulas would have to be reproduced in the Vaysol lab, and the results confirmed. That would mean quite a bit of legal work to maintain secrecy, which would take even more time.

FSJ was almost out of money. We could maintain our email address, our P.O. Box and afford to have the company taxes done, but that was all. Even though Frank had cut what he and I were getting from the company way down, we would be receiving no more stipends and would have to continue on faith. It wouldn't be the first time.

We went through the process of dealing with the paperwork. I was happy to let Frank take the lead on that. Weeks later, when it was complete, and the legal staff at Vaysol had signed off on it, I sent my formulations and instructions for obtaining materials to Lou. It hadn't been hard for me to buy anything. I used my local supermarket or bought things online. It took a few days at most. For Lou, things were more complicated. Vaysol, like many large companies, had a complicated system for their supply chain. It was another couple of months before Lou could even get his process underway, and even then, I had to send one of the ingredients, under the radar, to his house.

I expected that when the materials finally arrived at Vaysol, the work would be straightforward. All the techs at Lou's lab had to do was follow my instructions. Unfortunately, since the materials in their experience were so different, they had problems with that. Lou was so frustrated that he helped them make up the formulations himself.

After almost six months, the testing was a hit. Not only was Vaysol's lab able to duplicate my results, but they also added a few tests that hadn't been run before. The final conclusion was that they had a product to sell that not only showed superior performance but also met the rising ecological demands, especially in Europe. The last step was for Lou to try to sell it to Vaysol's business unit and then to the customers themselves. That was the beginning of another year's wait.

By that time, my life had changed in many ways. I'd had a book published and well reviewed, and was almost finished with a sequel. With my fanfic, writing of one kind or another filled up most of my days, and I'd started to think of myself as more of a writer than a chemist. I found out I liked it that way. I was happier at the keyboard than I had ever been at the lab bench. There were no Franks or Georges, and I got along fine with my editor and her publisher. I managed to place a couple of short stories with another publisher as well. Tim and I didn't have a lot of money coming in, but it was enough to get by. I began to realize that I didn't really care if Vaysol succeeded in selling my formulations or not.

After six decades, my life was finally starting to make sense. Lou kept me updated, but I wasn't bombarded by a stream of lies and manipulations anymore. What information I got, was straightforward and to the point, bench chemist to bench chemist.

For the most part, Lon was happy in his new home. He called me when something was wrong, like his internet being down, or when he disagreed with a staff member about turning on the heat, but his restaurant trips with Tim and me were mostly cheerful, and he hardly ever tried to pinch or bite.

JS was doing well too. He stayed in touch with Tim and me by email. He always remembered occasions when presents were appropriate and came home for Christmas. He'd also found a casual social group and even told me he was interested in meeting a woman for something more than playing a board game.

I'd never expected it to happen, but I had a group of close friends I'd never even met face to face. For a long time, I'd heard social media dismissed as isolating, but for me, it was just the opposite. I'd become part of a small tight Twitter group, scattered across time zones. I knew them, and they knew me better, with the exception of Tim, than anyone I'd ever known as a friend or at work. After so many years with no close confidant except Tim, I now had five. They were there for me at any hour, and I was there for them. We'd come together just as fans of Keep, but we discovered that out of six families, four had autism somewhere, and two of the group were on the spectrum with me. A couple of them used writing to cope with the world too, although they weren't as prolific as I was. Our group also discovered we had similar political beliefs, and worked in whatever way we could, for the same causes. We held on to each other electronically through family emergencies, problems with work, and even unwanted plot twists. I had never felt so unconditionally accepted before.

What was most important to me was that for the first time in my life, I could accept myself as I was. I didn't have to be the best chemist or the person who could memorize the most facts. I knew there would always be someone faster with an equation or who'd read more papers. I didn't have to be the world's greatest writer, just someone who could give my readers a better day. My real talent, and what I enjoyed doing the most, was creating something useful. Whether it was with low-allergy recipes in the kitchen, greener formulations in the lab, or words on the page, if I could make the world less stressful in some little corner, I was happy. After minimizing its worth for most of my life, I realized that just the act of writing was as essential to my life as breathing. My path to that conclusion had been painful, but somehow, I ended up at the right destination. No liar could convince me again, to be anyone but my quirky, autistic, self.